SOUVENIR

SOUVENIR

JAMES R. BENN

OPEN ROAD

INTEGRATED MEDIA

NEW YORK

Copyright © 2012 by James R. Benn

ISBN 978-1-4976-3755-9

This edition published in 2014 by Open Road Integrated Media, Inc.
345 Hudson Street
New York, NY 10014
www.openroadmedia.com

For Debbie.
Always.

The moments of the past do not remain still;
they retain in our memory the motion which
    drew them towards the future,
towards a future which has itself become the
past,
and draw us on in their train.

—Marcel Proust.

CHAPTER ONE

1945

"Burnett." The name drifted across the snow—an urgent, choked, clipped summons. Wind took the sound and scattered it on blowing pellets of snow. The wind was ice stabbing the men's cheeks, stinging their eyes. It was also their salvation, casting away the crunch of boots on snow, hurried whispers, the subtle sounds of fabric and gear as each man swiveled his body, moving head and eyes front and back, side to side. It blew their frosted breath behind them, instead of letting it drift up, or even worse, out in front of their faces. Even so, Jake Burnett heard his name.

"Yeah," he said, barely mouthing the word. He twisted his head to the right and felt the frozen snow tapping incessantly at the back of his helmet. The wind danced loose granules over the foot-deep snow pack, sending clouds of white over the surface so it looked almost like fog. Good cover for crawling on your belly, but hell on the eyes. Jake was glad to turn away, to rest his stinging face. Ice weighed on his eyelashes, creating a hazy white glow. He shivered, from deep inside, the spasms radiating out, rippling through his lungs and shaking his limbs. He tightened his grip on his M1, afraid it might leap from his quivering hands. He let the shiver run through him, keeping his eyes fixed on the lieutenant, a puppet pulled on strings of frost.

Hand signals shot out at him. Index finger stabbing at him, pointing at Clay Brock, five yards to his left. Hand down, keep low. Scout forward. Jake took it all in, nodded, and turned away. Cradling his rifle in his arms, he heaved a deep breath, and pulled himself forward by his elbows. He felt the cold on his thighs the most. His feet weren't too bad, encased in a couple of pairs of wool socks, combat boots, and four-buckle overshoes. He had lost count of the layers under his field jacket, sweaters and shirts compressed into one sweat-encrusted stinking second skin. Even with long johns and the heavy wool pants, crawling in the snow left his thighs numb with the cold. No, numb would have been good. They were bruised with cold, prickly and raw, razor blades slicing them each time he propelled himself, elbows and knees pushing his body forward. Towards Clay, with the bad news. Clay had crawled to the base of a thick pine, and raised himself up on one knee. The edge of his helmet and one eye peered out from behind the tree, just under where the first branches, heavy with iced snow, hung down and disappeared beneath a drift. He was still, except for his eyes. Jake couldn't see his eyes, but he knew. He knew all about Clay. Knew his smell, what his cough in the night sounded like, how he moved through cover, and what he'd say next. He knew Clay had chosen exactly what tree and which side of that tree to crawl to for a better look ahead. Right behind where Clay stuck out his head was a jumble of thick brush, brown branches with lines of white snow on them weaving patterns in every direction. Patterns that wouldn't betray a helmet edge. Stick your head out with a nice clear background of white behind it and Western Union would be knocking at the door.

Clay slowly pulled his head all the way behind the tree trunk. No sharp moves, nothing to draw the eye. He slumped down, leaning his back against the tree, and looked at Jake. Jake rolled behind the tree and got up on his knees. Snow clung to his jacket, and worked its way down the olive drab scarf knotted around his neck. He brushed himself and hugged his legs, willing warmth into his thighs. He looked like he was bowing to Clay, who waited patiently. Clay was never in a hurry. Nothing the Army wanted him to do was ever good enough to be in a hurry for. But that was Clay's nature anyway. Slow and calm, deliberate and predictable.

"Red wants us to scout down to the tree line," Jake whispered.

"Fuck," Clay said. Jake knew that would be his first response. If he had told Clay that they were to head back to Company HQ for hot chow, it would have been the same. Anything the Army wanted Clay to do was greeted with the same contempt, and carried out with the same determined resignation. It was one of the things Jake really liked about being buddies with Clay. That, and his being a good shot.

"Observe across that field, then report back," said Jake. "Look like about a hundred yards?"

"Yep. Fuck," said Clay. He leaned his head forward and tapped the front sight of his M1 on his helmet, a little habit he had started about a week ago. Jake didn't ask about it. He had his own superstitions, his own fears, secrets and rituals. "Let's go."

"Fuck, yeah," said Jake, trying to imitate Clay's flat Tennessee drawl. He tried to smile, to make a joke of it, but couldn't tell if it showed under the frost-encrusted stubble on his face and the scarf drawn up over his chin. Clay caught himself as he began to roll over to begin the hundred-yard crawl. He looked at Jake, raised an eyebrow like he did whenever he noticed something interesting. With a guy like Clay, that was nearly a standing ovation.

"When'd you start being funny, Jake?"

He smiled, and it was easy to see. A big, broad grin lit up his narrow face. There wasn't a lot of stubble, more like strands of thin, faint brown hair that sprouted here and there on his chin and upper lip. Razor once a week did the trick on this boy. His face was dirty. Grimy really, and it looked like the kind of face that when you gave it a good scrubbing, it would uncover a sweet country boy, more Tom Sawyer than Huck Finn. But this wasn't dirt from playing down by the stream. It wasn't the dirt of mischief and mumbley-peg. It was fox-hole dirt, muddy earth overlaid with black cordite smudges, white crows-feet showing at the edges of his left eye where it squeezed shut when he aimed with his right up against the rear sight, easing his finger against the trigger, lining everything up, spinning a straight line from his eyeball through the rear sight, along the barrel, over the front sights, across the gulf separating him from the target, the enemy, the quick from the dead, or so he hoped each time. Final pressure on the trigger and the slam of the shot, M1 jarring his shoulder, smoking cartridge ejecting into the air, and direct line between brain, eye, weapon and enemy soldier disconnected as a gray uniform slumps to the ground, gone. Another dead German, and the tension releases as if a thin line was cut, like a kite on a windy day when the string you're holding snaps and falls from the sky.

Jake smiled, or tried to again, and it felt like his cheeks would crack from the effort. Clay could smile with ease, as if a grin were the natural set of his jaw. Jake had seen him walking a muddy road, weighed down with combat gear and sucking his boots out of the ooze with every step, all the while a half smile playing around the corners of his mouth, as if it was all so funny. Look at us. Ain't we something?

Smiling wasn't something Jake was known for. Shorter and stockier than Clay, his dark, wavy hair and thick beard surrounded deep brown eyes set under heavy eyebrows that looked permanently knitted. Jake's home was Pennsylvania coal country, where the towns lay in cramped valleys, steep hills cutting sunsets short and letting in the morning light a full hour after dawn. Side streets ended in one or two blocks, dead ends hitting granite looming like a giant wall over skinny brick houses. Outside of town, mineshafts descended underground, carrying men in and bucketfuls of black shiny coal out. The men came out the same color as the coal. Some of it washed off, some didn't. It was the kind of landscape that got you worried just waking up in the morning.

But that was nothing compared to this country. There was so much to worry about here you couldn't afford to, not enough time or energy for that. You just tapped your helmet, made your little joke, did whatever you could do to convince yourself you'd get through this day, and maybe the night.

Clay went left, Jake right, around the tree. They were flat, as low to the ground as they could get, keeping their heads down like swimmers doing the crawl. Elbows out, pull. Push with the knees. Butt down. Head down, but eyes up, into the wind. They kept apart, but within sight of each other as the land sloped down, the pine woods thinning out into a field. They could see it clearly now, a wide strip of cleared land, probably a farmer's field. Maybe three hundred yards wide. It curved to the right, rising up as it did so they couldn't see beyond that small hill. To the left, it went on, widening before it disappeared into the pines again. Winds drifted the snow, and in some places only a thin covering remained. Stubble stuck up through the white cover. Sugar beets maybe, they grew a lot of that around here. But the field didn't matter, unless it was mined, of course. What the Lieutenant really wanted to know was about the tree line on the other side of the field. Was that the German MLR?

Main Line of Resistance. Go find it. That was their job today, a simple one, really. It wasn't hard, just sneak around a few outposts and keep going until lots and lots of people started shooting at you. Not a few rifle shots, there had to be more, and heavy stuff too. Machine guns? Mortar fire? Good, you found it. If you didn't get hit right away, or pinned down, you had a chance to hustle back, keeping an eye out for patrols, outposts, minefields, and your own trigger-happy buddies in their foxholes. Good luck, men.

Clay signaled to Jake. They were behind the biggest pine trees they could find, their branches screening them. They'd stopped short of the scrawny trunks, the smallest growth at the edge of the field, going to cover behind thick green branches coated with snow, hung down to the ground, frozen to it by snow and ice. Good visual cover, but that was it. Clay pointed to a rock outcropping about twenty yards away. A jumble of boulders, five feet tall. Perfect cover, good angles between jutting rocks to observe through. Jake nodded, and they both crawled around the pine trees, giving the branches a wide berth. A slight touch and the snow could slide right off, sending the green fir flying up like a penalty flag to betray them. It happened all the time when the sun warmed the snow. You heard it sliding off, hitting the ground with a soft crunch, then the whoosh of the branch springing up out of the snow. Only there was no sun now, nothing but grayness and wind and a white swirl along the hard ground.

Instinctively they moved in front of the trees, trying to keep them to their backs. Jake stopped to look across the field, as much as he could without lifting up his head. He saw white, the ground in front of him blending into the open ground ahead. The field dipped down on the far side, and he couldn't see the beginning of the tree line. Tops of trees stood out along the horizon, under the rim of his helmet. A mix of pines and bare branches, standing out against the sky like latticework. What were they? Lots of oak around here, old growth, thick-trunked trees in forests where you could walk with your arms out-stretched, no new growth in the way. Schu mines were another thing, anti-personnel mines that would blow a leg off but not have the decency to kill you outright. Generations of clearing and grazing left clean woodlands, nothing like the overgrown, spindly, vine-choked thickets back home. German immigrants had broken their backs clearing land for farming, cutting the ancient trees and hauling rock to coax what they could from flatland plots. When Jake was first old enough to wander off by himself, those untended fields were already reverting back, saplings and brush growing faster than corn ever had.

Clay was at the rocks. Jake scuttled sideways until he was behind them, rolled over, shifted up and laid on the rock, helmet tilted back, mouth hung open gasping frigid air. Clay propped his rifle against the stone and tried to pull himself up, giving up halfway and collapsing on his side, his shoulder grinding against the sharp edge of a crevice. He didn't move, except to push his scarf up over his mouth so he could create a little pocket of false hope as he exhaled the air warmed by his lungs.

"Fuck," he finally said. Jake knew what he meant. He could feel the sweat dripping down his back, matting his damp hair, gathering on his stomach. The exertion had warmed him, but in a minute the sweat would soak into his clothes, chilling his skin as he lay, exposed to the wind and cold.

Clay took off his helmet and his wool cap, pulled off his right hand mitten and glove, scratched his scalp, shook the damp cap, and then jammed it back on his head. He pulled the glove back on and looked at Jake, who raised a finger as he brushed snow from his face with the other hand. Gimmie a sec. Clay nodded, minutely, a slight dip of the head as he closed his eyes, then opened them as he looked away. Okay, no problem, take your time buddy. Neither man knew it consciously, or thought about it, but they shared a secret language. Looks, gestures, nods, a raised eyebrow, everything had a meaning that was bound up in who they were, unintelligible to anyone outside their foxhole, outside of their experience of each other. Days and nights together, on marches or waiting by the side of the road, or in some nameless French village, sleeping in a hastily dug hole, huddled for warmth, or in a bombed out house or maybe a barn with clean hay if they were really lucky, had given them time to decipher each other, taking in moods, reading between the lines, learning from silences, until it was second nature to read the other man, know his thoughts from the set of his shoulders, the look in his eyes, a catch in the voice. The shorthand of men.

All this took time, of course, and ability, and the willingness to observe and listen. Infantrymen who came ashore in the spring and summer of 1944 without the skill of observation and a keen ear for listening, whether to their buddies or to the sounds coming across the fields and woods of northern France, didn't need to worry about time. By the winter of 1945, in Belgium or

Germany, maybe Luxembourg—nobody was really sure where the hell they were—they were already dead.

Clay took his other mitten off. Except for the extra trigger finger, they always made him think of being dressed for school and how he had hated wearing those mittens. It was a nice memory though, standing next to the woodpile in the kitchen, the stove radiating heat and cooking smells as his mother forced pale blue knit mittens over clenched fists, stubborn little fingers jammed into fuzzy warmth. He stuffed the olive drab mittens into his pockets, as he always had done with the blue mittens right after he turned the first corner down the dirt road and the farmhouse with the collapsed front porch disappeared from view.

Clay pushed himself up, one hand on Jake's shoulder, the other steadying himself against the cold stone. Two large rocks, about five feet tall, leaned against each other and left a small cleft at the top. Clay flattened his face on the rock and peered sideways through the cleft. He looked down the edge of the tree line, waited, and watched. Nothing. Not a sound, no movement to catch the eye. He crouched and slowly moved his face to the bottom of the cleft, looking straight out across the field. He could feel the wind blowing on his face, could hear it swishing the pines and drifting up snow in front of the rocks. The wind lessened and he heard another sound. Scratching? What was that? The wind rose up and he heard it again, his ear tuned to it now and picking it up clearly.

Scritch. Scritttttttch.

He tapped Jake, a slow deliberate two-finger tap to the shoulder. Jake took off his helmet; neither man wanted to risk the telltale clunk of metal helmet against rock. He moved slowly, coming up to just below where Clay's head was. Clay motioned with his hand, and Jake moved his head up as Clay leaned to the left. Their heads joined, one right eye and one left eye each with a clear view.

Scritch.

An oak leaf. A big one, from one of the giant oaks across the field. Brown and curled, its sharp lobes turned downward so it looked like a prehistoric insect, teetering on its pointed tips, stem straight out like a tail. The wind pushed it along the top of the crusted snow, its protesting sound unnaturally loud in the silence.

Then it was gone. Jake blinked, thinking he had lost sight of it. Clay raised his head just an inch, tilting it back to get a better angle on the field. Jake looked at him, saw his eyes widen. Then he saw it too. A line of footprints, almost obscured by the drifting snow, but still deep enough to capture the oak leaves blown across the field. They both raised their heads as high as they safely could, and from this added vantage they saw little clusters of brown leaves, partially covered in snow, caught in a clear trail of footprints that led along their edge of the woods, right in front of them, and curved right, heading across the field, to a spot where the woods jutted out onto a small rise. Perfect spot for a machine gun. Both men eased their heads back behind the cover of the rock. Jake shivered.

"Fuck," whispered Clay as he drew out binoculars from his field jacket. They were German, taken off an SS officer Clay had dropped with a single shot from two hundred yards. The binoculars were the main reason Red had chosen them for this job, and now Clay blessed them with his curse. First chance he got, he'd sell them to some rear area slob who wouldn't have to worry about taking them on a walk in the woods.

Observing the rise was going to be a problem. It was on their right, and slightly above them. So if he went to the right of the rock, he'd have a good view and so would any alert Jerry, or even a half-awake one with his own binoculars. If he went left, he'd have good cover from the rise, but be exposed to the rest of the tree line to his left. Fuck.

Clay wished he had his helmet on, and was sitting so he could hold his M1, butt to the ground, and tap it on his helmet two or three times. Three times would be good. But the helmet was on the ground, there was no reason to pick up the rifle, and nowhere to go but up. Fuck fuck fuck. Clay could hear his daddy say it clear as day. Fuck this tractor, ain't worth shit. Fuck this engine, and fuck Henry Ford, too. Fuck that banker man.

Clay felt his stomach in a knot, like he always had when his daddy swore like that, at least when he was a little kid. Then there was a brief period of confusion when he learned what the word actually meant, and he wondered how a tractor could have that done to it, and who was supposed to do it to Mr. Blasdale down at the bank? But then he understood his daddy never, ever used it in that way. When he said it, it was to mean, I ain't got nothing left but this awful, terrible swear word, and by god you ain't taking that from me. And that's just how Clay used it, never to mean something dirty, but to show his daddy, wherever he was, that he too still had something left when he stood at the end of the road.

Clay turned his wool cap around so the visor wouldn't get in the way of the binoculars, pulling it down to his eyebrows so his skin wouldn't show. He gave a curt nod to Jake, who gave it back. No expression. That meant, if I get my head blown off, it was good to know you, buddy. Didn't want to leave without saying goodbye. He didn't put the binoculars right on top of the rock, but below the top, so the bottom half of what he saw was a blur. The top half was enough. In the tree line, past where the sugar beet field turned to brush and pine seedlings, he could see logs, stacked up about three feet, with cut pine branches strewn around them to soften the straight lines, German helmets, bobbing up and down, rifle snouts sticking out, and two heavy machine guns, one oriented in the other direction, one straight towards him. The woods curved away to the right, beyond the rise. The Germans had a good spot there, good fields of fire in either direction. He scanned left. No more log emplacements. Maybe they were dug in, camouflaged? The rise was either a strong point on the MLR, or an outpost in front of it. He knew what that meant. Fuck. He slid down, head low.

"MG-42s, two of them, with plenty of Krauts, in that hunk of woods, on the right, up on the rise," Clay said in a low voice.

"See anything else?" Jake asked.

"Nope. Can't see a thing anywhere else."

"Shit. I'll go tell Red."

Jake went flat, crawling back and staying in the tracks he had made coming out. No nods, winks or other gestures were necessary. Clay was safe behind a big rock, and Jake was headed the same way he had gone before. Such things were left for the obvious dangers, not the everyday routine of patrolling. A guy would be one big, constant, twitching nod if it were.

Red and the rest of the squad had moved up about twenty yards to the edge of the tree line. A sergeant should have been leading the patrol, but Marty Dorsch got his right leg ripped open in a mortar barrage when they advanced on Hoffelt a couple of weeks ago. Marty was probably in England right now, maybe with his leg, maybe not. It was a favorite debate in the squad as to whether that was a good trade. The optimists didn't think so, but there weren't many of them. Jake missed Marty, one-legged or whole. He had been with them since Basic, made corporal in

Normandy and buck sergeant when the leaves were still on the trees. He watched out for his men and was a good sergeant, but not so great that his squad got all the dirty details, the perfect combination in his opinion. There was no corporal to take over since a sniper got Hartman outside of Dinant. No one missed him. Replacements were slim, and everyone worried about who they'd end up with. Meanwhile, Red—Lieutenant Christopher Monahan—except no one ever called him anything but Red, led them on patrols when he needed something done, like today. Red wasn't a bad officer, and the men liked that his foxhole was right up with theirs, not as far back as he could get and still say he was at the front. Like some.

Jake scrambled around the base of the pine Red was behind. He put his arm over Red's shoulder and pointed to the rise on the other side of the field.

"There, two MG-42s, camouflaged behind logs, buncha Krauts around 'em." Jake kept his fingers pointed until Red got out his binoculars, not as nice as Clay's German pair, but that's the kind of officer Red was. Their first lieutenant might've confiscated them as a military necessity, but Red knew that a two-hundred yard shot was something, and that the man who made it was due whatever loot he got off of it.

"Yeah," Red said, "Got 'em. Any more?"

"Can't see on the right, and Clay couldn't make out anything along the left side there. Could be dug in."

Jake couldn't put much certainty into that last statement. They could be, or not. He knew he might be back here with the whole Company, waiting out an artillery barrage on that line. If it wasn't there, if this was nothing but a single machine-gun nest, then they'd have to do this all over again until they found the MLR. Or it found them.

"Let's find out," Red said. He looked at Jake and the others gathered around him. He wasn't asking, not at all, but Red liked everybody on board. He liked everyone to understand, that it was important, not some chicken-shit order he didn't like any more than they did. So he waited.

"OK," said Jake. Five other heads bobbed up and down.

"Big Ned, Little Ned," the lieutenant said. "Get the BAR set up over there, under that fallen pine. Here, check out the Kraut position first." Red handed Big Ned the binoculars. Ned Warren and Ned Kelleher were a team, and it was obvious which was Big

Ned and which was Little Ned. Big Ned handled the Browning Automatic Rifle, a 16 pound monster that looked like a BB gun in his big, beefy hands. Big Ned was the strongest guy in the platoon, a Michigan lumberjack who almost split the shoulder seams of his field jacket. A jagged scar ran from his left ear across his cheek, the result of either a faulty chainsaw or a knife fight with an Indian from Mackinac Island, depending on how much Big Ned had had to drink. When he drank too much he could be a mean drunk, and no one dared ask if the knife fight story was true or not. Little Ned was the ammo carrier for Big Ned. In addition to all his own gear, he had to carry an extra ammo pouch for the BAR, which could eat up rounds in no time flat. Little Ned was a small guy, but appearances weren't everything. There was wiry muscle on every bone, and Little Ned could walk lighter than any man in the squad. His union card said he was a structural steel worker, used to climbing up I and H columns floating far above city streets and bolting steel beams with a spud wrench. Little Ned was great with tools, and could fix a jam in the BAR faster than Big Ned could get his trigger finger mitten off.

"OK," Big Ned said.

"That fallen pine is a little exposed, Red," said Little Ned, not arguing, just pointing out a fact.

"Yeah, but you can crawl down to it, dig out a little snow, and fire from underneath it. It's good cover, don't worry."

"I ain't worried about getting there, Red," said Little Ned, looking out at the field and not bothering to say the obvious. He saw Red was right. They could crawl through some brush easy enough. The pine had toppled over from the edge of the tree line, and lay at an angle, facing away from the machine-gun nest. Broken branches held the tree up just off the ground, and they'd be able to fire through a narrow slit between the frozen ground and the trunk. But if all hell broke loose...

"I got two smoke grenades," Red said, willing himself to speak slowly and calmly, as if explaining to a kid that a shot at the doctors wasn't going to hurt. "When I throw them in front of you, haul ass out. Everybody gives covering fire. Understood?"

"Yessir," said Miller, the newest replacement.

"Shut the fuck up, asshole," said Hank Tucker. He had been in the line three weeks now, and considered himself a veteran, since

Marty had told him he'd be a combat vet if he lasted three days. "What if some goddamn Kraut heard you call Red that? Jesus!"

"OK, Tuck, simmer down. You and Shorty take Miller here and set up just above Big Ned and Little Ned. Jake, get Clay back up to the tree line and watch our left flank. No surprises, OK? When I fire, we open up on that position, find out what they've got out there. Smoke is the signal for you guys to clear out, plenty of covering fire. Got it?"

"Sure, Red, OK," said Tuck. "C'mon, Shorty." Shorty was six foot barefoot, and walked with a permanent stoop, the result of his intense desire not to get shot in the head simply because he was the tallest guy in the squad. It might happen anyway, but he hated the idea of some Kraut seeing his helmet bobbing along over a hedge or stonewall somewhere and sending a slug through it, while the other guys, who had it easy at five foot eight and less, walked on without a scratch. Miller followed, miserable. Everyone else was paired up, he was odd man out. All he could do is hope for another replacement to come along, so he could call him a dumb sonovabitch, and take him under his wing, dig foxholes together, complain about the chow and the Army like the other guys. Give each other nicknames, too. Failing that, maybe one of these guys would get killed. Or maybe he would. He was so cold, and lonely, he didn't even care that much. If it were quick, anyway.

Jake made sure he kept Red in sight as he chose his position at the tree line. He didn't want him opening up too soon, leaving Clay hanging out there. Clay was prone, a bit of his head to the side of the rock, scanning slowly with the binoculars. Jake moved in the snow, just enough for Clay to hear. He looked up, shook his head. Nothing else out there, nothing he could see. Jake motioned him to come back up to the tree line, and Clay slithered back the way he had come. When he got close enough, Jake reached out and pulled him in, the darkness of the pine forest a welcome contrast to the stark white of the field below.

"OK, see that dead pine?" Jake whispered. "BAR down there, the other guys above them. Red fires, we all open up. We watch the left flank. Smoke is the signal for Big Ned and Little Ned to pull out, once we know what's up."

"Sounds easy," said Clay, trying to catch his breath. It did. Plans always sounded good. They were soothing, giving you the illusion of something to count on. Red was good at that. He trusted Red, trusted him with his life, he knew. Red, and the guys in the squad, the ones that had been around, at least. It was the rest of the world, the world across the field, he wasn't so sure of.

Clay settled in, resting his M1 in the snow, twisting the sling around his forearm to steady his aim. At this distance, aimed fire didn't mean much, but it was how Clay did things. The right way, even when it didn't matter, the way he was taught, whether it made much sense at all. He was as much behind the pine tree as he could be and still see the target. Like deer hunting, the way his big brother taught him. If you can see them and they can't see you, why then, you got the drop on them and its venison steaks on the griddle tonight.

Jake was above him, up on one knee. He gave the high sign to Red. All set. He'd watch the flank in case any fire came from that way, or even worse, Krauts in these woods. But right now they both watched Big Ned and Little Ned snake their way down the slope from the tree line towards the fallen pine.

Jake had his M1 up, elbow on his knee. He knew Clay was drawing a bead, working his rear sight and filling the front with the target. It was just a smudge in the woods from here, but once you saw it you knew. Jake's frosted breath blew out his nose, obscured his view, and he dropped the rifle to his knee. At this distance, he didn't have a rat's ass chance of hitting anything he aimed at. When Red fired, he'd empty his clip at the clump in the woods and then turn, reload, and watch the flanks. You never know, he might hit something if a Kraut was dumb enough to stick his head up and run into one of his rounds. The geometry of death. He suddenly couldn't get Miss Peabody out of his mind, her white lace collar burned into his memory. High school math. Intersecting lines and angles. It wasn't too hard, once you worked it out. The path of the bullet was one line, the path of a Kraut, or G.I., was another. Intersecting lines. You could draw a straight line from where the bullet started, and where the poor slob who got it began, and you'd have a nice triangle. Somewhere, maybe from deep inside a factory in Germany, a bullet was moving towards him, in a shipping crate, on a train to the front. Could he draw a line from Minersville to that factory?

Big Ned moved easily for such a large guy. He dragged the BAR by the barrel, too big to cradle in your arms like a rifle. Big Ned was strong and heavy, and he moved over the snow like a plow, flattening it as he went. Little Ned was to his right. He scuttled like a crab, too light to weigh down the snow. He didn't have the best technique, too much elbow and butt above his head. But he'd stop often, freeze himself motionless so if his movement caught a Kraut's eye, maybe he'd blink and look again before he shot, and think, damn, I'm too jumpy out here, it's nothing.

Little Ned moved from one of his frozen positions and crawled forward. He glanced at Big Ned, who had stopped behind a small pine tree to wait for him. They had about twelve yards to go. He got to the pine, the last bit of cover before the fallen tree. He looked at the path Big Ned had made crawling down and decided at the first sign of smoke, he'd run his ass up that path into the woods. It'd be easier than running through the soft snow. Good plan.

Big Ned saw him and nodded. Damn right that's the way home.

Big Ned and Little Ned didn't really like each other. Big Ned was an outdoorsman, a backwoods boy. Little Ned had a few years on him, and at twenty-five thought he knew all there was to know about the world. He had worked in Philadelphia, D.C., Richmond, and Baltimore, seen more people from up on those beams than they had in all of Michigan. Some guys, with different backgrounds like that, would pepper each other with questions about their home, eager to learn about a part of the country they had never seen, never would have known about, except for the war. Then they'd write their Mom and Dad about this swell fellow from Idaho, or a great pal from Georgia, and little stories about distant states would be scattered around the nation like fireflies on a summer night.

But Big Ned and Little Ned's parents would not read much of their son's foxhole partner, except maybe the names, the names were funny, the kind of thing you could write your folks about and distract them for a minute from the constant worry and dread that hung over the homes of G.I. parents in the cold winter of 1945. You won't believe it, Mom, but my ammo carrier is named Ned, and they call him Little Ned. Funny, huh?

They tolerated each other, didn't hate each other or get into fights, except for that time in Paris and that had been the liquor talking, they both knew that. They never took a liking to each other, that was all. Each knew the other guy pretty damn well, and could count on him. But they grated on each other in a way that let them know, if they lived through this, they'd shake hands at the end, turn away, and that'd be enough.

But this wasn't about being pals. This was serious, a job to be done like so many others done before. They both moved to the side, to skirt the small pine on the final approach to the fallen tree. Big Ned moved off, going wide to be sure his trailing BAR didn't snag on a half-buried branch.

Jake could see Little Ned move right, and stop, like he always did. Big Ned was almost to the tree now, and Little Ned scurried forward, flailing his arms too much like he always did, then stopped again. Jake could feel his heart begin to thump louder in his chest. Jesus Christ, Big Ned is about ready, he's got the BAR under the tree. Sweat broke out on his forehead, feeling like it might freeze before it dripped off. He shivered, trying to still himself. He looked at Red, saw him aiming, waiting for Little Ned to get in position. Any second now.

Little Ned moved. He stuck his elbow in the snow and pushed off with his left leg, aching to get behind that big pine tree, aching even more to be running up that packed snowpath with clouds of smoke between them and the Kraut gunners. His foot hit something.

Clump.

Jake saw it, a tremor at first, then the achingly slow slide as heavy snow slid down a thick pine branch. He saw Little Ned turn his head as the snow hit him and buried his feet.

Whoosh.

The green fir arced up in the air, freed of its snowy burden. The tip of the branch had been buried, but Little Ned had pushed off on it, dislodged it, kicked off the terrible chain of events that left a clear signal, green against white and G.I. brown half buried in snow.

Jake knew light traveled faster than sound. But he didn't think it possible ever to see it, or some of the things he saw in combat. It didn't happen often, but at a time like this, when everything slowed down, and you had a clear view of the Krauts firing at you, it was true. Waiting those last seconds, with the green fir flying up, Little Ned twisting in the snow, Jake couldn't feel anything, not the cold, not the weight of his M1 as he raised it, couldn't hear either, not even Red's first shots, then his. Everything in sight was crystal clear, intense, as if it were suddenly blue skies and sun, all color and clarity. In that moment he saw the twinkling, before he heard it. Bright exploding whiteness from machine-guns, but also sparkling lights all along the woods, hundreds of them. They were everywhere, silent, incandescent, and it was beautiful.

Clay heard the snow fall from the branches. He didn't wait for Red to fire, he squeezed off his first shot, then the second, breathing in and out, not wanting to be some trigger-happy fool firing into the air. Take aim, fire at the enemy. He knew it was useless.

"Jesus Christ," Red said as he fired, over and over. He pulled the first smoke grenade and threw it. "Jesus Christ."

Big Ned turned in time to see Little Ned try to pull himself out from under the snow. The MG-42 chopped up the top of the dead pine, and he had to duck and cover his head. He knew. He didn't look back, he fired the BAR and tried not to think about it.

The German machine-gunner aimed his bursts at Little Ned and so did every other German dug in under camouflaged trenches and foxholes along the MLR. Little Ned and the tree were the only things moving, and they drew fire. Little Ned was hit, hit, hit and hit again, killed twenty times over as swarms of bullets chopped the branches and brush all around him. He never had a chance to say a thing, to curse the branch, think about home, never even took in exactly what was happening, or saw the bright bursts of gunfire that Jake saw as a strange thing of distant beauty.

Red pulled the pin on the second smoke grenade and flung it out in front of Big Ned as a round caught his left arm, passing through it, spraying blood on the snow. He saw the blood, didn't feel a thing, but couldn't get his arm to work.

"Pull back!" he yelled to Big Ned.

Tuck and Shorty were blasting away at the machine-gun, each on their third clip. Bullets made a thrumming sound around them, steel wasps buzzing their ears. Snow flew up in clumps and pine bark rained on their heads. Miller fired a few shots, then dove behind a tree when the return fire grew ferocious.

"Pull back," said Miller, first to himself. It was like an incantation, magic words that would save his life. "Pull back!"

"Not you, shithead!" Tuck yelled, "that's for Big Ned."

"No, pull back, the lieutenant ordered it!" Miller ran.

After Big Ned saw the first smoke grenade hit the ground in front of him, he rammed a fresh clip into the BAR and figured he'd wait until the second one, then go. More smoke, more cover, good plan. He fired, amazed at still being alive, wondering how many of those fuckers they had over there.

The second smoke grenade hit, bouncing and rolling as smoke spewed out. He let the BAR hang from his neck and ran over to Little Ned, grabbed him by the collar and pulled him up the slope into the tree line, not even thinking about the path. A trail of glistening red marked their leaving.

They finally grouped together about five hundred yards back, deep in the darkening woods. They had found Miller, sitting on a tree stump, shivering. They ignored him. Jake was bandaging Red's arm, Tuck was pulling wood splinters out of Shorty's hand where a bullet had shattered his M1.

Clay watched their rear. Big Ned had dragged Little Ned through the woods, and was frantically looking for branches to make a litter.

"I ain't leaving him here," said Big Ned, to himself as much as the others.

"He's dead, buddy," said Red, as if that settled everything.

"I know he's dead, I ain't leaving him here. You guys go on if you want."

It wasn't easy. They found pine branches to make a sled, instead of a litter. Clay had a length of rope and cut it into pieces to tie the branches together. Little Ned was shot up bad, and if it wasn't for his clothing and web belt cinched tight, it would have been a lot harder. Miller looked away for most of it, then threw up. When they were done, Big Ned handed him the rope.

"You pull."

"I can't—"

Red looked away as three M1s rose up, pointing at Miller's gut and motioning him to move. He took the rope.

"Tuck, take point," said Red.

They set off, trudging through the woods, hoping to get back to their lines before dark. Clay took the rear, and Jake followed Big Ned behind Little Ned. After an hour, Jake heard Big Ned talking to himself, whispering, the words rising and falling on currents of quiet anger. Straining to hear, he realized Big Ned wasn't talking to himself, he was talking to Little Ned.

Shit...what am I supposed to do...you stupid fuck...put up with you for five long months and what do I get? What a fucking stupid thing...almost got me killed too. I always told you...you crawled like a fucking recruit. Now I'm going to have some asshole like Miller here carry ammo for me and he'll finish the job...point me out to some Kraut sniper...I'm fucking dead... thanks for nothing, shithead.

The cursing continued into the night, after they made it through their lines. Clay and Jake brought Red to the Aid Station. Big Ned made Miller drag Little Ned back to Company HQ so Graves Registration could get him in the morning. Big Ned covered him with a tarp, pulled up an ammo crate, sat down and lit a cigarette. It started to snow. As the whiteness graced them both he started all over again.

You fucking bastard.

CHAPTER TWO

1964

THE WOOD FRAME OF THE SCREEN DOOR WAS warped, so as the delivery guy knocked, it clattered back and forth against the opening, twice as loud as it needed to be. The rattling hook added a metallic urgency as the knock came a second time.

"Clay Brock?"

"Hold your horses, I'm trying to open up in here."

Walking through the storeroom and unlatching the hook, his forehead furrowed in irritation. He opened the door for the delivery guy to wheel in his hand truck, top-heavy and wobbly, loaded with cases of cigarettes. Cartons of Raleighs, Luckies, Kools, Winstons, Chesterfields, and Old Golds. The delivery guy let the hand truck go and it fell forward with a clank as it hit the old wooden floorboards. The cases tottered like they might topple over, finally settling down, towering over the delivery guy as he watched them for signs of collapse. He pulled a pen from the front pocket of his blue jacket. Tri-State Brands was embroidered over the pocket, same thing on his cap.

"You Clay Brock?" he asked again, handing over the pen and a clipboard.

"That's what it says over the door. Clayton Brock, Permitee. Why are you so late? Where's Petey?"

"Dunno. Heard he had an accident. I'm new, don't know the route too well."

He said all this while working a hunk of chewing gum, snapping it with every other bite, mouth wide open, displaying the gnawed white ball as it rolled around on his tongue. He spoke with disinterest, nonchalant about Petey, the late delivery, everything but his wad of gum.

"Well, get to know it," Clay said, signing and thrusting the clipboard back at him. "I needed to make my run in the morning to be back here for the lunch crowd. Now I'm screwed. What's your name, anyway?"

The delivery guy didn't take the clipboard right away. He snapped, waited a beat, then took it, grabbing it forcefully, the sudden movement sharp in the small room. He clipped the pen, slowly and carefully, in his jacket pocket. He was young, twenty, maybe a couple of years older. Thin, wiry with some muscles, it was hard to tell with the jacket and work shirt. Thick dark hair showed beneath the baseball cap with the red Tri-State logo. A good looking Italian kid who thought a whole lot of himself. Not quite arrogant, but wishing for arrogance, making do with surly and bored for now.

"Al" he said. "You got something else for me?"

"Yeah, hang on." Walking to his desk, Clay opened a bottom drawer, and took out a large, thick, worn manila envelope. He gave it to Al. Al took it from the bottom, held it in the palm of his hand as if weighing it. He raised his eyebrows and nodded his head, as if giving Clay his approval, letting him know he was a little impressed.

"So who's Jake?" Al asked.

"Just the name of the place when I bought it. No sense paying for a new sign when everyone knows it as Jake's Tavern."

"Yeah, makes sense." Again, the appraising nod. "See you later." Al turned and walked out, throwing open the screen door and letting it slam back and bounce noisily on his hand truck as he pulled it out behind him. Clay watched him unlock the back of the delivery truck, put the hand cart away, then lock up tight. He started up the truck, revved the engine, and backed down the driveway from the small parking area at the rear of the tavern. Barely room enough for Clay and Brick, who closed up most evenings, and for Cheryl, who worked lunches until her kids got out of school.

If you went to Jake's you parked on the street, or walked from your place. It was a neighborhood joint, on Mill Street, between the train tracks and Broad Street, the main road that cut across the top of the hill overlooking Meriden. Broad Street went places, to Wallingford or Middletown, aloof from the rest of the city with its churches, big houses and the tall World War One monument that stood at the middle of the intersection, doughboy at attention night and day. Down from Broad Street ran East Main, the library and city hall a few blocks away from Jake's Tavern on Mill Street, a cramped, bent little street that didn't even last a quarter mile before it ran out of room at the edge of the train tracks. Jake's anchored the street on the north end. A few stores, big houses long ago subdivided into apartments, and narrow duplexes tumbled down the hill toward the train tracks. The closer you got, the dingier and grimier the homes became, and the walk up to Jake's was a better way to spend the evening than listening to the rumble of freight cars. For Connecticut, Meriden was a big town or a very small city, depending on your perspective. They called it the Silver City, for something not done here in decades, a richness long gone before Clay had stepped off the train, not a ten-minute walk from where he was right now.

Clay locked the door, and sat down heavily on the ancient wooden banker's chair by his desk. This really screwed him up. He gazed at the cases of cigarettes, knowing he should jump up and get started, but instead he sat and stared at them. He could do part of his route now, come back for the lunch crowd, then back out again and finish up. It meant a late night here, paying bills, checking the inventory, making orders. Keeping the place afloat.

He laughed, almost out loud. The storeroom looked like a closet no one had cleaned out in a generation. His desk was an old roll top so warped and beat that it was permanently stuck in mid-roll. It looked like a mouth disgorging carbon paper, receipts, mail, tax forms, and other paperwork too depressing to think about. Empty kegs were stacked at the far end of the room, and dusty wooden shelves held cardboard boxes of glasses, cleaning supplies, snacks, and unknown things on the top shelf, their contents now long forgotten. Yeah, keep all this afloat. Who the hell would notice if it sank, remember it had even been here?

Jake's Tavern. He had first seen it sometime after he started at New Departure, a ball bearing plant just a few blocks up on Pratt Street. He'd kept to himself mostly, no close friends at the plant, so it was a while before anyone invited him along for a beer after work. Then Jimmy Doyle did, and with a few of his buddies they walked down to Mill Street. An easy walk after a hard day on the factory floor, downhill, lunch pails swinging, their time their own. When they turned the corner, Clay knew he wouldn't be getting a gold watch one day from New Departure. The sign said two things. Jake's Tavern, and For Sale.

He hadn't blown his back pay when he got out of the army, like a lot of guys. He got a job the first day he was in town, and opened a bank account on the second, so the down payment wasn't a problem. He always told the story about the sign like it was a smart business move, but he knew. He knew in a place deep inside him, almost lost to him, that this was Jake's Tavern, and that sign was never coming down.

He got up, pushing back on the chair so it moved on its wheels, hitting the wall behind him with a clatter. Little things like getting out of a chair were starting not to be hard, exactly, but not easy, either. Clay looked down at himself and wondered when he had gotten thicker, lower to the ground. He shook his head as he dialed the telephone on his desk and got Cheryl at home. He asked her to come in early and finish opening up for him. He hated calling her, since he knew she didn't want to come in and would be sure to let him know what a burden it was. Since she made her real money in tips, and tipping customers were rare before lunch, all it meant to her was a lot of extra work for a little dough.

"Clay, can't you get someone else? I ain't ready yet."

"C'mon, Cheryl, you know there isn't anyone else. I'm real backed up here. Please?"

He could hear the TV on in the background as the announcer intoned, "The Edge...of Night". He knew he was in trouble. Cheryl loved her soaps, and if she started watching this one, he'd never get her in.

"There's a five-spot in it for you. I'll leave it on the bar."

"Okay, Clay. I'll be right over." Cheryl knew the difference between business and pleasure. Pleasure didn't pay the bills. It was one of the things Clay admired about her. He put down the phone and walked into the barroom, slapped a five-dollar bill on the bar and set an ashtray on top of it.

Loading his station wagon, Clay felt something nag at his mind. Petey? Wonder if he was okay or not. Petey was a regular guy, an okay guy, someone you could shoot the breeze with for a while, and then he was gone, until the next time. Dependable, like a good alarm clock. But this Al character. A punk. The more

Clay thought about him holding the envelope and looking at him, the less he liked it. Something wasn't quite right with that one.

He sorted the cartons into the order he needed, then shut the rear door. He checked the lock on the back door, got in the car and turned the key. It turned, turned, trying to start. He switched off. Easy, don't flood it. It's only a '58, for chrissakes, it shouldn't be conking out this way. Clay slammed his hand against the steering wheel, feeling himself bounce on the bench seat, anger vibrating his body. He blew out air from his lungs and shook his head, like a swimmer breaking the surface of the water. He wanted to wrench the key forward and slam his foot on the gas, will the damn thing to start.

He didn't. He smoothed his hair, arched his head back, twisted his neck so it cracked. He reached up to the steering wheel, gently this time, to coax the car into starting. The Chevy Belair wagon was a good car for his job, lots of room for cigarettes and his tools. It was two-toned blue, and he kept it washed and waxed, nice and clean, the way he liked it. He ran his second business out of it, so it had to look good. It was his calling card.

He turned the key again, and the engine started right away, no hesitation. One of life's little pleasures, a car starting up when you need it to. The kind of thing you take for granted until it doesn't happen. He backed down the narrow driveway, pulled out and headed for his first stop. City Hall, a couple of blocks away. He didn't worry about parking tickets. He kept a delivery sign on his visor, which he always turned down when he double-parked. Besides, when you kept folks supplied with smokes, they generally cut you some slack. It wasn't like you were coming to read their meters or bother them somehow. You made sure that they had a good supply of their favorite butts. All they had to do was dig down into the loose change, drop a few coins in, pull out the knob under their brand, and listen for the satisfying clump as the pack dropped down, and there they were, ready for another day, maybe more, maybe less.

Clay parked on a side street by City Hall. Plenty of spaces today. He picked one in the sun. It was a chilly autumn day, and it felt good to sit in the car for a minute and feel the warmth. As he relaxed, that vague unease crept back into his thoughts. Something wasn't right. It stayed out at the far edge of his waking mind, the kind of warning that you usually didn't recognize until it was too late. Clay remembered that feeling, remembered cultivating it, listening for it even when it wasn't there. A long time ago, listening to that little voice meant life or death. Be careful. Watch that cellar window. Stay behind that tree. The signs that were too slight to be seen fully, the noises that were out there, beyond his range of hearing, gathering together and nagging at the border of his mind, calling out to him in a faint, tiny, faraway voice. Listen to me, listen to me. He had been careful, he had listened. He had watched the barn door, seen the snout of that Mauser. He did stay behind that tree, he could still feel the bark against his cheek, the thud of bullets.

Jesus fucking Christ on the cross! Clay opened his eyes, found his hands gripping the steering wheel, white around the knuckles. He let his hands relax, dropping them to his lap and resisting the desire to bring them up to his face and bury it in them. Breathe. Look around, it's Meriden, not anywhere else. He pulled the keys out of the ignition, stuffed them in his jacket pocket. He held out his right hand. It shook a little. Too much coffee, maybe.

He got out, opened the rear door and grabbed the first box, arranged with an assortment of brands, extra Raleighs and Luckies. The Police Department was on the lower level, heavy smokers among that bunch. He crossed the street, whistling softly, a tune long ago forgotten but now in the forefront of his mind, pushing everything else out, demanding to be heard. He walked down a long hallway, his whistling echoing off the painted cinderblock walls and linoleum floors. The cigarette vending machine stood at the end of hall, a municipal worker bending down to grab his pack. He gave Clay a wave. Glad to see ya.

Clay set down the box, took out his keys and opened the front of the machine, revealing rows for each brand, Camels already sold out. He broke open a carton, and dropped a handful of them down the slot.

"Aw shit," he said out loud, surprising himself. He looked around, feeling foolish and guilty. They had done it again. This carton had Virginia tax stamps, not Connecticut. No accident there, Virginia had the lowest cigarette tax in the country. A big distributor could shave off a bundle in taxes by bringing a truckload up from the south. He'd bet some of the cartons had no tax stamp at all.

Tri-State my ass. Not unless it was Virginia, North Carolina and Connecticut. There was nothing left to do, nothing he could do. He had hours of work to go, and he couldn't worry about tax regulations. He filled every brand, not looking at the stacks of packs as he slid them down each row. If anyone said anything, he'd plead ignorance. Let 'em talk to Al. He locked the machine and squatted to cover the single packs at the bottom of the box with empty cartons.

"What's new, Clay?"

The voice came out of nowhere as Clay was starting to stand up with the cardboard box. A sharp jolt went through him like he had touched a frayed electrical cord. Dropping the box he turned, jerking his hands up to protect himself, or fight, or plead, he didn't know which. He saw a uniform, and his eyes widened, a gasp escaping his lips, his hands nearly formed around the shape of a weapon he hadn't held in almost twenty years. All in a second, a slowed-down second in which the blur of the uniform resolved into blue and the smile on the face peered out from the veil of panic that Clay's brain had sent rushing through him.

"Jesus, Bob, don't sneak up on me like that, willya?" Clay dropped his hands, then brought one up to his heart. He smiled, willing the sweat to soak into his skin before it streamed down his temple. Make a joke. "You almost gave me a heart attack."

"Cripes, Clay, you look like you saw a ghost. You okay?" Bob put his hand on Clay's shoulder, as if to steady him, like he might topple over any second. Was he swaying a little, or was that the room moving? Bob looked him in the eye, gave him the kind of look a cop couldn't help giving. Penetrating, studying him.

"Yeah, yeah, you just startled the hell out of me, that's all, and then I got up too fast. I'm okay." Clay gave a little embarrassed laugh, shook his head. I'm such a klutz.

"Good. I called you when I came in, but you didn't hear me. Deep in thought, huh?" Bob moved back half a step as he let Clay's shoulder go. He stood a couple of inches taller than Clay, clear blue eyes and a crew cut giving his face a chiseled, steely look. The look matched his deep blue uniform, pressed and creased like it was new, badge gleaming, leather holster shined as well as his black shoes.

"Not too deep. How are you doing? Back on duty?" Officer Robert Quinn had been shot about a month ago, after pulling over a black Chrysler for speeding through a red light. He couldn't have known it had been stolen a half hour before, by two guys from the Latin Kings who were going to use it as their getaway car for a hit on a rival gang president. Instead of license and registration Bob got six bullets fired at him, one of which hit. The driver was a lousy shot. Bob wasn't. Down with a bullet through one leg, he squeezed off two rounds and watched the car swerve off the road and hit a telephone pole. The passenger hoofed it and was never found. The driver was slumped over the wheel, one bullet in the neck, another in his shoulder.

Bob had been a good customer. Came in most nights for a beer or two before he went home. Taking it down a notch, he called it. Clay had visited him in the hospital, complimented him on his shooting. There was something icily calm about how he had fired those two shots, closely grouped, and at a moving target at that. Not to mention having taken a .38 slug in the leg besides. Something recognizable.

"You in the war?" Clay had asked, as he stared down at the floor, counting the alternating blue linoleum squares. He was nervous in hospitals, the closeness of disease and death causing him to focus on the details of the room or the hallways to keep his mind off of the misery within.

"Yeah."

"Figured. Where?"

"Army. Infantryman. New Guinea. Didn't like it much."

"Which?" Clay asked, smiling because he knew the answer, remembered the familiar complaints, the chickenshit, the officers, the chow.

"Neither," Bob had laughed, then winced a little. "You?"

"Infantry, too. Europe. Can't say I liked either much myself. But still..."

Clay had looked at the floor, then his hands, and then out the window. It was late morning, no one else was around, and the sunlight filtered into the room between the open blinds, scarring each man with lines of light and shade.

"Yeah," Bob had said. "Yeah."

They sat for half an hour, the noisy clanking of carts and nurse's chatter passing them by. Everything that needed to be said out loud had been, and they sat in graceful silence in a clean room with white sheets, far from the fetid greenery of New Guinea or the cold white woods of Belgium, each knowing nothing else needed explanation, each knowing theirs was an unfathomable mystery that stretched from horror to love in that half whispered phrase, but still....

"Nah, desk duty for a coupla more weeks," Bob said. "Everything okay with you?"

"Yeah, except there ain't enough hours in the day. I'm running late, Bob, gotta go. Stop by one night soon, we'll have a toast." Clay picked up the box, looked to Bob for a response.

"Well, Joanne took all this kinda hard. I dunno. I think I need to stick around the house with her until she's alright, know what I mean?" Bob looked down at his feet, a little embarrassed, as if his wife's reaction reflected on him.

"Hell, Bob, you were shot. That's gotta take some getting used to. Tell you what, bring her with you, after supper one night."

Bob nodded, gave a wave, went back down the hall. He didn't say no, didn't say yes. Clay walked as fast as he could out the main door, back to his car. He hated the thought of Bob finding out about the cigarettes, about the stammered explanations and excuses. Bob was a stand-up guy, so how would he feel to be buddies with a cheat and a...what? What was he exactly? He started the engine, listened to it rumble as he tried to finish the sentence. He couldn't, he wouldn't.

Clay shifted into first and pulled out into the road. He didn't like the direction his thoughts were going, so he changed them. He rubbed his forehead, felt the headache forming behind his eyes. Think of something else, move on. Would Addy come with him to Jake's one night, if Bob and Joanne dropped by? The four of them could sit in a booth and just talk, like they were all out on a date. If he promised not to get caught up in any work, then she might come along. You never knew, did you? She might change her mind, come down to the Tavern like she used to, back when they were busy fixing it up every morning, hoping the paint would dry before the first customers showed up. Back when— what? What were they then that they weren't now? Too many missing words this morning, too many blanks in the conversation he carried on with himself.

He pulled out onto East Main, heading down the hill to the train station and the vending machine in the waiting room. More empty spaces to fill up.

CHAPTER THREE

2000

THE PEW WAS SMOOTH, HARD WOOD, POLISHED to a bright sheen by generations of backsides. Oak of a deep-varnished hue, it curved to create a place for the ass-end to deposit itself while the soul lifted itself up in prayer, or simply tried to stay awake, depending upon the person and maybe the preacher.

...reading today...Book of Job...

Clay tried to sit up straight. The pew played with him, its surface gliding him forward every time he relaxed his posture. He'd push himself up, pressing his hand down on the seat to brace himself, and in a minute he'd ease up and feel the slow slide begin again as his suit pants, worn to a glean almost as shiny as the pew, rode the curve of the oak and drove him into a slouch.

...I go forward, but he is not there; and backward, but I cannot perceive him; on the left hand I seek him, but I cannot behold him...

Addy reached over with her right hand and patted his, giving him a wan half smile. Clay felt his face redden as he realized she was comforting him, thinking he was distraught, upset, when he was just uncomfortable. Fidgety. He closed his other hand over hers, giving it a squeeze. Her skin felt like paper over wood, like the kites he used to make from newspaper and whittled down branches. Kites strewn with stories of Abyssinia and Nanking, book burnings and the Katzenjammer Kids, sailing over their heads, into the wind. He saw the kite, felt the breeze vibrate it and whip it out of his hands, heard himself laughing...

I turn to the right hand, but I cannot see him. But he knows the way that I take; when he has tried me, I shall come forth as gold.

Silence. No laughter, only the quiet of St. John's Lutheran Church, a flag-draped casket in front of the altar, mourners sniffling, coughing, shushing the few children, hardly making enough noise to fill the big church. Clay uncupped his hands, releasing Addy's. He rubbed his fingers against his own palm. Paper, yes. And not supple branches beneath, either. Not the bendable green wood of his youth, no.

...why do those who know him never see his days?

Come forth as gold...is that what the preacher said? Is that what this is all about? He tries us, and then we come out golden. Some of us ought to be 24-karat, then. Clay let his eyes set on the coffin. Bob would be one of the golden boys. The Depression, the war, the cops, his family. It all added up to something. Why did he feel like he was so much less? Had he traded away his gold before he earned it?

Men remove landmarks; they seize flocks and pasture them.

Clay felt irritated with himself as he tried to focus on the service. He sat up straight for the hundredth time, taking Addy's hand again, wanting to feel connected to her, not wanting his thoughts to wander, visiting the distant past that was growing more vivid and alive as he aged and his own life moved more slowly, winding down to a weary grayness. He looked at the coffin again, then at Addy, wondering, wondering.

They thrust the poor off the road; the poor of the earth all hide themselves.

What is this guy talking about, anyway? The Book of Job, was that Old Testament or New? Sounded dark and gloomy, why is he reading this at Bob's funeral?

They lie all night naked, without clothing, and have no covering in the cold.

Clay shivered. He was wearing a topcoat, but he shivered like a man out in the cold, alone. He hunched his shoulders and rubbed his hands on his thighs, trying to stir some warmth into his thin frame. He didn't realize he had closed his eyes until he saw gloved hands rubbing green pants, saw his breath frost and felt the cold, cold earth at his back. He opened them, afraid of crying out. He looked around, at Addy, the preacher, the coffin.

They are wet with the rain of the mountains, and cling to the rock for want of shelter.

Who? Why was he saying this? Clay felt his face flush, as if he had been slapped. Shame? What did he have to feel ashamed for? Or was it the rain, the near frozen rain, pelting them in the foxhole, stinging their faces and puddling up, drawing their sleeping bags into the wet, brown ooze. Open your eyes, dammit!

He was moving his feet, trying to get them above the water, slamming them against the riser. He stopped, calmed himself down. Addy looked at him, strangely, concern and fear flashing over her face. He smiled.

From out of the city the dying groan, and the soul of the wounded cries for help; yet God pays no attention to their prayer.

Oh no, oh no no no, don't go on, end it here, now. Clay balled his fists up in his topcoat, fighting the urge to get up, leave, scream, beg, plead. But he had done that all before, just like this character Job. And still, the hurt came, in waves, fresh and new each time, not even familiarity deadening the impact. He felt his eyes water and his lips tremble. He bit the inside of his mouth, incisors snapping down, drawing blood, warm, soothing, the tiny bit of pain well worth it, his own tranquilizer.

Bob, you are one lucky sonovabitch.

The preacher finished up the reading, gave his sermon. Clay tried to follow it, to keep his mind occupied. He listened, but couldn't keep from straying into the past again. Not his own, but the past of the Bible, as Job's pain spilled out from the pulpit and washed over the mourners. Did things make any more sense back then? Or do they today? He went over the story, trying to find some comfort, solace, or even holiness.

So this Job is a good man, and God makes him suffer. A lot. Job's pals say it must be because he's done something wrong. He says no, he's a stand-up guy. He's pissed at God and wants his day in court, wants to know what the deal is with all the suffering. God shows up, says what's your beef? I'm running the show, where were you when I created the world and everything in it? Job's rocked back on his heels, eats humble pie, and it's all supposed to mean we should be glad God is in our lives, no matter how much we suffer. Or something like that, the kind of answer that shows these guys don't really have any answers at all. Holy roller bullshit. But it all worked out for Job, didn't it? Lots of sheep, camels, sons and she-asses. Lived to be a hundred and forty.

And Job died, an old man, and full of days.

The family led the casket out, Joanne supported on either side by her daughter and granddaughter, each of them towering over her. Joanne disappearing beneath their arms as they encased her, her bent and thin frame bowed under the weight of her grief and their youth. As Clay watched, he saw her face from forty years ago. Full, fleshy, smiling, dark hair framing her clear white skin. He looked at Addy, conjuring up her face from the same time. The light brown hair, bright hazel green eyes, thin nose, full lips, the long graceful neck she always showed off with her treasured strand of pearls. As he looked at her, she turned and smiled at him. Only the right side of her mouth moved. She pulled her left hand onto her lap with her right as she turned to watch the procession.

Clay looked at his hands again. They used to be beefy, a strong grip bred of a lifetime of work, hoisting boxes, stacking cartons of liquor, carrying a rifle. Now they were husks, aching, thin, spotted with age. Whatever happened to his strength, his ease of movement, his will to act?

"C'mon, Dad," Chris said, standing up. He took his mother under her arm, supporting her by the elbow and helping her stand. Clay grabbed at the pew in front of him, pulling himself up, and fumbling, trying to help his son. Addy was already on her feet, steadying herself with her good arm as Chris stood behind her, holding her under her left arm.

"Ahm okay," Addy said, slowly and deliberately, like they taught her in rehab. She nodded her head forward, telling Clay to get a move on. Addy didn't waste words these days, they were too hard to get out. In the aisle, she took Clay's arm as Chris stood by her left side, his arm under hers and enfolding her hand in his. Addy moved slowly, but she moved, mostly under her own power. Step, drag, step, drag. It took all of her concentration, but she could do it. She had to remember to use her whole body to move that leg forward. Her steps had a rhythm to them, and if she remembered the tune she could do it. Some days the tune was jumbled, and she couldn't trust herself going from one room to another. Those days were awful, humiliating. Today everything was clear, the tune played throughout her body, step, drag, step, drag, and she moved down the aisle, past the empty pews, husband and son on either side of her, proud of her accomplishment. Proud she was still here. She squeezed Chris' hand, then realized it was only the memory of a squeeze that she felt. That hand was heavy, a weight at the end of an arm that had some feeling, but it only went so far. Her hand seemed too distant, the journey too far for her will to reach. Oh well, there are worse things. Worse things indeed.

Chris drove, his unmarked State Police cruiser leading the procession with lights flashing, along with the motorcycles from the Meriden police. Chris had come up from the Meriden force, one of the first classes to graduate from the new State Police Academy built on the outskirts of the city. As a patrolman, Chris had worked under Bob, and that made for complications. It was easier when Chris joined the Staties, fewer occasions for Bob to come between them. There had been a time when Clay wondered if Chris would have preferred Bob as his father. He had naturally spent more time with him, gravitated to his circle of police pals, away from Clay and his work at the Tavern. Reason enough for that, Clay thought.

The ground at the cemetery was damp, wet with the spring thaw. Chris wore only his suit jacket, enjoying the warmth of the sun and the promise of release from the cold and dark. Crocuses were popping up in front of tombstones where the sun warmed the stone, bright dots of color scattered among the gray markers. Clay and Addy were bundled against the lingering chill, thick wool coats and gloves aiming to do what their bodies no longer could. Clay looked at his son, saw the light breeze blowing his jacket open, and shivered, feeling the wind on his own ribs.

Chris stepped in to help his mother to one of the folding chairs as Clay walked behind them, too old to lead, but not feeble enough to need help. Not the graveside front row, but the second. They weren't front row candidates, the odd shifts in relationships, the secrets, the collisions of honor and duty with the bonds of friendship and family thrusting them into an honorable but secondary position here, behind the cousins from out of town, but in front of the police chief. Their intimacies, though troubled, trumped simple rank.

Addy looked up to Clay, then down to the empty seat next to her. Chris stood aside from his sentinel position to let his father through. Clay signaled no with his hand, and Addy nodded her understanding. It wouldn't do to sit as Bob was lowered into the ground, his friend, the twenty-two year gap in their relationship notwithstanding. Bob was a comrade, one of the lucky ones, who came home to live a life and be buried in a satin-lined coffin, surrounded by friends and family, and in his best suit. Clay would stand, all right. Stand as he did so often, from Belgium to Meriden, from pits hacked out of frozen earth and marked with a helmet and an up-ended M1, to the precisely cut graves in manicured cemeteries, under sunny springtime skies.

A plane droned overhead, a Piper Cub, probably from Markham Municipal Airport, some guy out for a joyride, or maybe a lesson. Clay craned his neck back, watching it climb and level out. He couldn't hear a plane without looking up, following it, tracking it, judging altitude and distance. He shook his head, still angry, still not able to understand after all the years gone by. How come those fucking Me-109s could get up with all that cloud cover, but our planes couldn't? Still fearing that next snarl of engines coming over the treetops. Jesus H. Christ on a crutch.

Prayers floated out of the preacher's mouth, blown away on the breeze that flapped the pages of the little white book he held in his hand. Clay felt the wind on his face as he turned to look for the bugler, standing apart, away from the firing party, separate from the mourners. He had been to funerals where it was only a recording, and he was glad today wasn't a busy day for the Army graveside teams. His pal deserved the real thing.

Mournful, haunting notes sang to him. Taps. Squeezing his eyes shut, trying to keep the sound at bay, Clay felt his body tremble. He ran thoughts through his mind, busying it with everyday details, trying to remember what they needed at the store, when his next doctor's appointment was, how much money he had in his wallet, anything to fill it up, outlast the song, drown out the emotion, drain it away, leave nothing, nothing, nothing.

Silence, broken by a curt command, the sound of heels turning, palms slapping wood and the metallic snap of seven bolts.

Fire.

Clay kept his eyes on the casket as the seven shots rang out. Are you hearing this, Bob? Did you ever think you'd make it this far, having the Army give you a song and a salute, or were you certain some Jap bullet had your name on it?

Fire.

Knowing it was coming again, Clay still flinched. Can't help it, Bob, you know that. Were you surprised to find yourself home, alive, the victor? Did you wonder about that, about living? If making it out alive wasn't maybe the most terrible loss of all?

Fire.

Jesus Christ!

"You okay, Dad?" Chris whispered as the smoke drifted over the tombstones and the firing party returned to their positions. Clay looked at him, wide-eyed, his mouth hanging open.

"I—it caught me off guard, that's all."

He shook off Chris's hand on his arm. Who the hell did he think he was anyway, his nursemaid? The sudden movement left him unbalanced and he wobbled, slipping in the damp grass, regaining his footing after a brief flail with both arms. He felt his face flush, his mouth turned down in a grim frown. He wanted to go home, fed up with this foolishness. Bob was dead days now, put his body in the ground and be done with it. He didn't look at Chris, or Addy. He watched as the folded flag was handed to Joanne, who cradled it in her hands.

"Let's go," Clay said, and stalked off to the car. Chris could take care of Addy, he'd only be in the way.

Bob and Joanne's house was filled with people. Joanne's house now, Clay corrected himself. Wonder if she'll move. Florida? In with her daughter? Or will she stay here, with the memories embedded in the walls along with the family photographs and pictures of Bob in uniform? A small snapshot in a standup frame stood on the mantle. A black and white, nearly faded, of Bob in khaki, standing in front of a tent, a big grin spread across his face.

Clay sat next to Addy on the couch in the living room. Folding chairs were everywhere and people scurried busily between rooms, trays of food, bottles of liquor, cakes on platters, all being transported to the kitchen and then dispersed throughout the house.

"Clay, ah could eat somethin'" Addy said. When she said his name, she had to roll it around so it would come out right. It sounded like two words, Cla – ay. Clay smiled, hiding his secret wish that Addy might recover, speak clearly, walk easily with him. He felt ashamed, but couldn't stop himself from wishing it. He patted her knee, pushed himself up and off the couch with a grunt, and walked through the narrow archway into the kitchen.

Nodding at people he knew he should know the names of, Clay shuffled along in line, paper plate in hand, scanning the mounds of food set out on the kitchen table. Addy liked little bites, things that were easy to chew on one side of her mouth. Especially in public. He chose chicken salad for her, a small roll with roast beef for himself. He wasn't hungry, but it gave him something to do.

In the living room, Joanne was in his seat and Addy was holding her hand.

"...blessin'. Coulda been so much wor...wor...been so bad," Addy said to her. Some words defeated her entirely. Clay was never certain if she couldn't say them or couldn't remember how they ended. Either way, she was right. Bob was too young to go, but who was to say a sudden stroke now was worse than a lingering disease five years from now? It had been quick, out on the sidewalk on Colony Street, right after a cup of coffee at his favorite diner.

"I know, dear," Joanne said, "I know. Like Marcy Stevens, her husband had brain cancer. He wasn't the same man after the operation, and she cared for him day and night. I don't know if I could—" Joanne stopped, suddenly aware of Clay standing in front of them, holding two plates of food. She hesitated, not knowing what to say next. It wasn't her place to comment on the ability of people to take care of each other, not with Clay and Addy.

"Here, Clay, sit down," she said, halfway up before he put a hand on her shoulder.

"You stay, Joanne," he said, as he handed Addy her plate. "I can eat a sandwich standing up. I'm not that decrepit."

"Yet," said Addy. She smiled her odd half smile, as if she wore that theater mask, half comedy, half tragedy.

"Sweetie," Joanne said, leaning her shoulder against Addy's, "I'm glad you're here. I can use all the laughs I can get."

"You an' me both," Addy said, raising a forkful of chicken salad to her mouth. That cracked them both up, it was so funny in a sad and unintended kind of way. Clay smiled, felt good for the first time that day. The grieving widow and the stroke victim, yukking it up. Good for them. He grabbed an empty folding chair and pulled it over, put his plate down on it.

"Can I get either of you a drink?" he asked.

"What are you, a bartender?" Joanne asked. For some reason, this was even funnier than the last crack, and they hooted. People turned their heads, wondering who was disrupting the solemn occasion. Joanne cupped her hand over her mouth and buried her head on her knees. Clay, worried she was sobbing, put his hand on her shoulder. She popped up, looked around the room, looked at Addy, and they started all over again.

Sometimes you just gotta let them laugh at you. Like that time they took over some K Company foxholes outside of—where was that—Durier, maybe. Kraut artillery was dropping all around them, and everyone raced for the foxholes. Clay jumped in the nearest one, landing right in a pile of shit. The foxholes were about five yards apart, but everyone heard him yelling and cussing. The previous occupant had taken a crap into an empty D-Ration box, common enough when getting out of your foxhole for any reason meant a sniper's bullet or an artillery barrage. Usual practice was to toss the box out, but this guy must've done his duty right before pulling out, and left it, maybe because he forgot or maybe he was a real bastard.

The whole squad laughed at him for two days. All they had to do was look at him and they'd burst out laughing. He was mad at first, then irritated, then he gave up. If it was good for a laugh, so what? He came back with a scotch and soda for them both. A good bartender knows.

He sipped his own drink, good bourbon from a bottle he had given Bob for a birthday present last year. It stinks when your whisky outlives you. He looked at the empty glass and was about to get another when Joanne leaned forward from the couch. She was laughed out now, eyes red with tears, spent. She rubbed her hands together, massaging aching knuckles and trying to bring back any of the warmth they had once held.

"Clay, I want you to know how much it meant to Bob that you two patched things up, or whatever happened. Maybe you just put it aside, I don't know, and I don't care. You were there when he needed you. You both were." She turned and grasped Addy's good hand. "You were a good friend to him, Clay."

He couldn't speak. He took her other hand and the three of them sat there, faces set in grim smiles, connected to each other through death in more ways than Clay dared count. After twenty-two years of not speaking, of not acknowledging each other on the street, at ball games, restaurants, anywhere their paths might cross, Clay had heard the news. Bob and Joanne's boy Gary, their oldest, had been killed in a car accident. Clay drove over to their house, this house, with Addy nervously standing behind him. She and Joanne had not been party to what had driven the men apart, but had drifted apart themselves, the gulf between their husbands too great for them to bridge alone. The house had been full then too, cops and casseroles wall to wall. Clay found Bob and said, "I'm sorry, Bob," and it was all over. Clay and Addy entered their grief and stayed on, as if the intervening decades were just a blip, a little misunderstanding that no one even remembered.

Clay let her hand go, sat back in his chair, contented. Thank God I did something right.

Chris drifted into the room, trailed by two young boys, somebody's nephews, Clay couldn't remember whose. Chris was holding a bottle of beer and answering their excited questions about the State Police.

"Auntie," the older boy said to Joanne, "did you know Mr. Brock is a detective? A real State Police detective?"

"Yes, Matthew, I think I did know that," Joanne said. These are Mr. Brock's parents. Say hello, boys."

They managed a nod towards Clay and Addy, too excited to complete their manners.

"Uncle Bob got a twenty-one gun salute, didn't he?" Matthew said. He and his brother had managed to pick up a handful of shell casings after the funeral, which had turned out to be much more interesting than they had ever hoped when they realized the soldiers were going to fire their guns.

"No, not exactly," said Chris. He squatted down, so he could look at them directly. "A twenty-one gun salute is fired all at once, and it's only for presidents. Today the seven soldiers fired three times, but it's not the same thing."

"Why not?"

"It's an old custom from the Civil War. Back then, they used to stop battles to pick up the wounded and the dead from the battlefield."

"Wow," said Michael, the younger of the two. "Dead army men?"

"Yep," said Chris, "and when they were all done, and the dead were all carried away and safe, each side would fire a volley of seven shots, three times."

"Why?" asked Michael.

"It meant that they had taken care of their dead, and could start up the battle again."

"You mean they weren't done, even if they had dead army men?" Michael screwed up his face, as if he were trying to see all his plastic army men in their greens and browns and camouflage colors, spread out on the ground, killed.

A chair scraped back on the floor, and Michael jumped, startled by the sudden noise.

"Sorry, kid," Clay said, standing up. "Didn't mean to scare you."

He retreated to the kitchen, clutching his empty plastic cup in his hand, making his way back to the bourbon. Scared? All the stories, shocks, surprises in the world couldn't scare you as much as one day, no, one hour out there.

Dead fucking army men, all right. They had no idea.

CHAPTER FOUR

1945

JAKE AWOKE, HEAD JAMMED UP AGAINST JAGGED clods of cold earth, the rear rim of his helmet pressing into his neck. His feet scraped the other end of the foxhole, inches from Clay's head. There wasn't room enough for the two men to lay down any other way in the cramped coffin-shaped hole. It was deep though, and Jake liked deep, appreciated the ground when it didn't offer up boulders or tree roots the size of his leg. This was fine ground to dig in. Lying down, he had a good sixteen inches up to the parapet and open air. He twisted, feeling the pine boughs beneath him, catching their sharp odor as he crushed the needles with his weight.

Above him were three thick logs, covered on top with layers of soft piney branches. Digging it out, they had built up the sides with the dirt and laid logs across the top, leaving enough room to slide in at the rear, and enough at the front to aim and fire. It was a good hole, as holes went. Not much snow got in, and it was too cold for mud. Way too fucking cold.

Jake checked his candle. Set inside a hole carved into the side of the foxhole, it nestled at the bottom, large enough for him to stick his hands in. He dug into his jacket pocket, pulled out his Zippo, removed his mitten, and flicked the lighter. Once, twice, it lit on the third try. No one had lighter fluid anymore, and Jake had filled the lighter with Calvados in Normandy, cognac in Trois Ponts, and schnapps in some farmhouse last week. Clay had made a joke about the lighter getting lit more than they did, or something like that, but Jake couldn't remember what was funny about it. He lit the wick and snapped the Zippo shut. Clink.

"Toss it over." Clay was awake too. He tossed it, and Clay reached over Jake's boots into his own hole in the wall, lighting his candle stub. Frosted breath flowed from Clay's face, like a steam engine at rest.

Jake took off his other mitten, then both gloves. He blew on his bare hands, and stared at the candlelight, encased in the little hole. He watched the spark at the tip of the wick, concentrating on the thin blue light that shown down from it, and the supple yellow flame that seemed to float above it, incredibly bright at its center, a spear point of hope. He slowly edged his hands into the hole, on either side of the candle, until his fingertips touched.

He felt warmth. Not the absence of cold, but real warmth, the feel of hot sun on his palms, reaching between his fingers, easing the pain, thawing his hopelessness, caressing him. The warmth settled into the base of his fingers, gathering in the swirls of flesh until it was almost unbearable. Not the heat, but everything else. Knowing he'd have to leave here, first his hands back out into the frigid air, then his body. Exposed to cold, steel, shrapnel, fear, loss. He rested his helmeted head on the wall of the foxhole, feeling as if he were at prayer, afraid of tears.

You weren't supposed to have a light in a foxhole. Any little pinprick of light, even a faint glow, and Kraut gunners somewhere would get an order from an observation post for a fire mission. They'd probably curse and stumble out of their foxholes, saying Fuck it's cold out here in German, load up their 88s or 75s or mortars, drop a half dozen rounds on you, then go back and try to sleep if they could, maybe have a smoke and curse you for being so stupid, getting spotted and making them go out into the cold and kill you.

So no warmth, no fires. But everyone had their candles. If you were dumb enough to let it be seen, by the Krauts or an officer, well then you wouldn't be around too long, so enjoy it while you got it. Jake and Clay were smart though, plenty smart. Brains enough to know they needed these tiny flames, needed to draw warmth from somewhere, and brains enough to keep it well hid, burrowed deep, their bright shining secret.

"Hey, you guys," Tuck whispered hoarsely. He was ten yards behind them, squatting down, not daring the slight rise in the forest floor that would expose half of his head to the unknown.

"Yeah," said Clay, squirming around to face the rear opening.

"Company cooks are bringing joe up, 'bout a hundred yards back. Ammo truck too."

"Fuck," said Clay.

"Shit," said Jake, blowing out his candle. Hot coffee, extra ammo and they had found the MLR yesterday. He rolled up his blanket, grabbed his pack and his M1, and followed Clay out of the foxhole. A couple of inches of new snow had fallen last night, covering the log-reinforced foxholes around them. It looked peaceful, soft, white and gentle. They stumbled out into it, running low, dirty and brown, a collection of rags bound by webbing, belts, canvas ammo pouches tied over their shoulders, field packs worn high on the back, knives, canteens and more ammo hung from belts, softly clinking and clunking as they ran.

Strands of sunlight broke through clouds, forcing them apart like a pry bar lifting granite. Clay squinted up at the unfamiliar sun as he walked alongside Jake, his belly full of lukewarm coffee and oatmeal, his pockets stuffed with grenades and extra clips of .30 caliber ammo. He looked around and saw the whole company on the move, on the road that led into the woods, and out on the flanks too. Probably other companies moving up with them, headed for the MLR. He shook his head, driving that thought out, no reason to worry about it right now.

He went back to thinking about food. Guys groused about the coffee not being hot, but Clay knew it was impossible to keep it hot after it was brewed at the Company kitchen a mile back. He was grateful to have it, happy that somebody went to the trouble of cooking for him. Clay knew about going without, knew what an bare table looked like, knew the feel of an empty stomach, and the loneliness of an empty kitchen. He knew enough that he never complained about something not being quite right. It was there, and he was glad. He might bitch if there was nothing, which he had every right to do. But when the cooks poured coffee with the last few pitiful remnants of steam swirling above the surface, and plopped oatmeal almost ready to congeal into the consistency of cement into his mess tin, he smiled and said thanks, buddy, and moved on.

There was a lot about the Army Clay didn't like, but it always fed him, and that was something he took with a seriousness that only someone who had gone without could muster.

Gone without. Funny when you thought about it. Gone. He hadn't gone anywhere, just stayed at home. Stayed after they'd buried his Mama, dead of consumption in the winter of 1936. Stayed with his older brother when his Dad told them there was enough food in the larder for two weeks, then walked down the road to get to Nashville somehow, where his cousin had promised him a job. He'd write, send for them. Teddy would have to get a job, whatever he could find, to keep them in beans until then. Dad never made it. The railroad police found him dead in an empty freight car on a sideline in Topeka. Rolled for two bits and his shoes, hit a little harder than the bindlestiff meant to, but that was that. Cops came to the door one day with the news, the bank came the next. Teddy couldn't earn enough in a year to pay what they owed, even if he had found work. That was a bad winter, but then again, so was this one.

Well, no mama, no poppa, no home, not even a big brother no more, with Teddy lost deep in the Pacific, off the Solomons, since his cruiser went down in '43. Clay felt the losses rip through him, as he shook a couple of cigarettes loose, giving one to Jake, who lit his, then Clay's, with his Zippo. The pain was fresh and new, as if right now he were standing over his Mama's open grave, reading the telegram from the War Department as the Sheriff brought him the news from Topeka. The sudden realization. He was the last of them.

"Fuck," said Clay.

"You said it, brother."

Jake inhaled and blew out blue smoke mixed with frosted breath. The trucks hadn't brought only chow and ammo. They brought replacements, and Jake stared at the three who had been assigned to their squad. They looked the same, they all looked the same when they climbed down off the truck. Twenty of them, clean, scared, wide eyed, huddled together, their shiny new helmets impossibly huge on thin, freshly-shaven faces.

Jake looked at Clay, Shorty, Tuck, Big Ned. They looked like hell, like something out of a monster movie. Filthy, unshaven, bristling with death. A dull, sullen stare, unfocused, the kind of stare you hoped didn't land on you if you didn't know the guy. Even Miller, a few paces behind Big Ned, burdened with ammo pouches bulging with BAR clips, was starting to look worn and mean. No wonder they looked so scared. They'd probably shit their pants when they saw the Krauts.

"You guys," Jake said, pointing at the three replacements, feeling like he was talking to children. "Don't bunch up."

He watched as they split apart, and in a minute were back together, whispering, looking around at the men spread out on the road on either side of them, the thick fir trees towering above their heads. Jake felt pity for the poor bastards. They had been dumped off trucks after a night on the road and parceled off to squads in twos and threes, finding themselves in the company of wraiths; men festooned with grenades, knives, belts of machine gun ammo, caked in dirt, week-old beards obscuring faces, eyes darting out to the horizon, not lingering on human company. They looked like they came from a different army, a horde from the forest, acclimated to the terrain of death. Their helmets were battered, painted olive-drab with sawdust grit mixed in the take off that shiny glare. They smelled.

Sharp thuds echoed from the rear and one of the replacements dove flat, his hands over his helmet. The other two stood silently, looking around at everyone else walking on, calmly. More thuds and a shrieking sound overhead, and the replacement on the ground looked up sheepishly.

"That's ours," Shorty said as he walked by him.

"Better to duck and live to tell, than not duck and die, kid," said Tuck, laughing as he lit a cigarette.

His pals helped him up. Dull crumps sounded ahead of them as the shells hit their target. The firing continued, thuds and crumps blending into a thunder of sound, surrounding them, echoing off the hills and rolling back at them.

"Where are we going?" Having been acknowledged, the replacement who hit the ground felt he could ask a general question. No one answered him. Jake shook his head, feeling sorry that the kid didn't understand how meaningless the question was. New to the front, he wanted an answer in a geographical sense, a specific location. Where are we going – what town, what hill, what terrain feature are we walking towards? No one knew. They were following the company, which was following the battalion, which was…well, they all hoped there was more than their battalion involved, but who knew?

Jake knew the real answer, but it wasn't something he could readily explain, couldn't even tell the kid how off his curiosity was. It was that the names of things didn't matter. What difference did it make if you got yours on a road you knew the name of? Or if your legs got blown off in a town you could point to on a map? Or were blinded on a hill you could pronounce the

name of? What the fuck did that matter? They were going to
attack the MLR, which is the only place there ever was. It might
be a village, or a ridge, or a road intersection, or a farmhouse.
Advance. Attack. Dig in. Defend. That's where you're going kid,
and you're going to freeze your balls off on the way there.

Today he knew even less than usual. No sergeant, and now
the platoon didn't even have a lieutenant, what with Red back at
Battalion Aide, a nice clean hole in his arm. Not that it mattered,
they knew enough.

Jake thought about the possibilities. This wasn't the route they
had taken yesterday. They were following a logging road out of
the forest, down into cleared land in a broad valley to their east.
Probably trying to flank the MLR, or avoid nasty spots like that
machine gun nest they found yesterday. Bombardment or no,
the Krauts made themselves some good bunkers when they had
the time, and they might be in position and waiting for them.
The artillery had to let up once they got close, or at least walk
the shelling back. Either way, it gave the Krauts the time they
needed to get out of their holes. He put that worry away, no sense
stewing about it until he had to. Maybe they were going after a
village on the other side of the MLR. That would be good, since
it meant they could sleep inside tonight. If they held it that is, and
if the Krauts didn't have every building already zeroed in.

Jake tried to remember the last full night of sleep he'd had. He
couldn't. Not on the line anyway. They had two nights in a rear
area about twenty days ago, showers, new uniforms, hot chow.
Guard duty one night, an hour of shelling the next, and then back
in a cold hole in the ground. Sleep. It sounded like a luxury, like
something in a store window you knew you could never afford,
but couldn't stop staring at either. Unobtainable. Like the ring he
had wanted to buy Mary Lou, to show her he was serious, that
he had some class. It wasn't an engagement ring, he'd have to
work up to that, but it had a real amethyst and some cut crystal
that looked like diamonds. Mary Lou's father was a doctor, not a
rich man, but somehow above the rest of the folks in Minersville.
Not a snob, but he read a lot, he knew a lot of things, and was
always telling Mary Lou to remember there was a world beyond
the ridges that sliced their part of Pennsylvania into thin strips
of road and river. Mary Lou always said she wanted to marry a
boy who'd show her that world. Jake had no idea how he could
manage to do that, but he saved and saved for that ring, feeling

it would set him apart from everyone else, put him up there with Mary Lou and her father, a young man who was industrious and thrifty, but also knew his way around things like rings and fancy jewelry. He'd had great plans, but that was before things fell apart.

Jake felt the weight in his pants pocket as the grenades banged against his leg with every step. Too many in there. He pulled two out and hung them on his web harness, something he did only when he had to. It was dangerous to go around like that, except in the movies. Hanging grenades off your gear was an invitation to get them stuck on something and pull the pin—while you were wearing it. But if they were going into a village he'd need grenades, plenty of grenades. You had to toss grenades into a house to be sure, unless you wanted to risk your neck busting down the door.

He knew civilians too dumb to see what was coming sometimes hid in the cellars. He had tried not to grenade cellars, until Samuelson, that kid from Brooklyn, said he heard voices in a cellar on a street in Eperany that sounded like children. A small casement window was open an inch or so. It would have been easy to shoot out the glass and toss in a grenade, send any surviving Germans stumbling dazed up the stairs into their sights as they covered each other going in. But Samuelson was sure it was children. They tossed one grenade in the first floor window, went in, checked the first and second floors out, found nothing. Samuelson lifted up the door in the floor of the kitchen that led to the basement, called out for them to come up, it was safe. No one knew any French, but he said it slow and calm so the kids wouldn't be scared. The darkness in the cellar lit up with fire as a burst from a Schmeisser submachine gun hit Samuelson in the chest. A Kraut came up, boots loud on the wooden steps, spraying bullets around the kitchen, the noise piercingly loud, bullets cracking wooden cabinets open and ricocheting off hanging cast iron skillets. Jake spun around the corner into the hallway, and waited until he heard the Schmeisser stop. He turned and caught the Kraut, an officer, putting in a fresh clip. The German froze, his mouth open in surprise. Jake dropped him with one aimed shot to the head, taking his time, letting the bastard see what was coming. The shot thundered inside the hallway. Jake saw a blur of red as the Kraut's head exploded, the back of his skull splattering against the wall. He stepped over the dead officer to check Samuelson, but it was no good. He was a mess, his neck ripped open, holes in his chest, blood everywhere. Jake turned around, and fired his M1 into the officer's body again, again, again, until his empty clip ejected and bounced on the linoleum floor with faint metallic sound. Jake didn't feel anything except the pounding in his head, his own blood vessels pumping away, keeping him alive. He couldn't hear anything, except that damn pounding in his ears. Then a shuffle. Sounds from the basement, more of them. Panic grabbed him by the throat, he fumbled for another clip, hand shaking, feeling like he was dreaming, stuck in slow motion while everything around him sped up. The next thing he knew a grenade was in his hand, he was pulling the pin, tossing it into the blackness and hearing it bounce down the wooden stairs.

A screech, a thin shrilling voice, a girl's voice, a child. It carried up the stairs and stabbed him in the gut, forcing him back until he fell against the kitchen table, went down on the floor and felt the force of the explosion against the floorboards from the small basement below.

Clay found him there, lying on the floor next to the two dead bodies, his hands pressed over his ears. Clay got him up and out of there, sat him outside with Tuck and Shorty watching him. He went back in, found a candle, and went down the steps to the basement. He hadn't even made it down halfway before he turned, ran up the stairs, stumbling and falling, propelling himself out of the house to vomit on the street.

Tuck and Shorty never asked him what was down there. Clay never said a thing about the little girl and the baby in the cellar. Jake never asked either. In Jake's dreams, the girl was alone, and she felt the grenade as it struck her, bouncing off a stair and onto her shin, knew what it was, knew who he was, and screamed a curse for him to listen to for the rest of his life.

He remembered the scream. He also remembered the Schmeisser and that if he hadn't listened to Samuelson, had shot out the window and tossed in a grenade, the girl would still be dead, same result, and the Kraut would be dead, same thing there, but Samuelson would be alive. He'd be having bad dreams too, but he'd be alive, or maybe she wouldn't have screamed if it happened that way and they wouldn't bother checking out the cellar after clearing the house, so who knew what was best anyway? He'd stopped worrying about all the possibilities in all the cellars since then, imagining a street full of houses with sturdy stone cellars reaching all the way to Berlin. He tossed grenades, remembering the scream, remembering Samuelson, remembering everything.

Jake reached up and felt the grenade hanging on the canvas webbing over his heart. Hearing engines, he turned. Three halftracks came down the road, grinding gears and churning up snow. The big .50 caliber machine gun mounted above the driver gave the armored vehicles a menacing look, and Jake could see each carried a heavy mortar crew in the open rear compartment. With all the artillery fire blazing overhead, and the halftracks and their added firepower, maybe this wouldn't be so bad. The halftracks passed Jake, and he heard the three replacements cheer as they went by. Okay, he almost felt like cheering himself, but fuck it, he'd save his cheers, he wasn't sure how many he had left.

The head of the column was clearing the forest, coming out on a wide slope of land, pastures maybe, that rolled down to the valley floor. Lines of trees and rocks divided the fields, little bits of cover and concealment but not a lot, not enough. The road curved left, into the clearing, as Jake followed the halftracks. Sunlight hit his face, and he saw the biggest patch of blue sky he'd seen in weeks. The glare off the snow was blinding, and he shaded his eyes, holding his hand up to the rim of his helmet. He scanned the hills in front of them, searching the dips and rises of the land for traces of the enemy, glancing back and forth between Clay and the others, marking where they were in relation to him. His eyes scouted the nearest cover, a barely perceptible gulley, a depression in the snow, alongside the road. Everyone was walking in the tread marks from the halftracks now. They had flattened the snow, compressed it along two parallel paths, perfect for easier walking.

Jake felt something wrong, in the air, in his mind, over his skin as it tingled a warning. Everything looked okay, but he felt like someone had him in his sights. His body tensed, a flush of sweat drenched his back, and the bottom dropped out of his stomach. What, where? He swiveled his head, searching for some sign from anyone else. Nothing. He looked off to either side, unsure, wondering if Krauts were on their flanks. Nothing. He unslung his rifle, gripping it tightly and holding it across his chest, ready.

A buzzing, faint, like a mosquito at the screen door. He cocked his head, trying to catch the direction.

"Hey!" It was one of the replacements, a kid whose eardrums

hadn't been battered by constant rifle fire yet. "We got planes too, here's the Air Force!"

"There, fighters!" Someone pointed to the right. Jake picked them up, four dots racing towards them along the length of the valley. Or away? He didn't know, the glare of the sun on the snow was too blinding to tell. They were low, lower than the crests of the hills that uncoiled above the cleared land. The buzzing became louder, a constant drone increasing each second, until he could see the wings grow larger and waggle slightly. More cheers from the men around him, the replacements most excited of all, being treated to a big show their first day at the front.

Jake knew what was wrong, knew in an instant that he must've heard an echo of the engines somehow, or seen the dots flit against a cloud without actually registering it. The planes were too far off to waggle their wings in greeting, unless they had just passed over the German lines, and they were giving the common flyer's salute to ground troops, those poor fuckers beneath their wings. The artillery bombardment had been going on for quite a while now, long enough for the Germans up ahead to know they were going to be attacked, know that the Amis had to cross this open land to get into position. Plenty of time to call for air support, Luftwaffe fields in Germany were only minutes away—

"Take cover!" Jake yelled from deep inside his lungs, pushing Clay off the road with him and burrowing into the snow-filled gulley. His cry spread and men were moving in every direction, scattering away from the road and praying they weren't in the fighter's sights. Not me, not me, not me, not me.

Jake rolled into the gulley and saw the yellow noses of the Me-109s, heard the chatter of machine guns and cannon, saw the sparkling lights along the wing and from the nose of the low-flying planes. Tracer bullets, bright glowing lines of phosphorescence reaching out from the planes, guiding their aim, seeking out their victims.

"Get down!" he yelled at the replacements. Caught in mid-wave, thinking they were greeting their own air cover, they stood in the road, three of them next to each other, shoulders touching, rifles raised over their heads, whoops of joy stuck in their throats, a sudden flash of fear and terror rooting them to the spot. Jake heard a roar, one explosion followed by another as three of the Me-109s focused on the halftracks, lighting up two of them, turning steel and flesh into pillars of fire.

The fourth was strafing G.I.s in the field, kicking up tremendous geysers of snow and frozen dirt, lines of fire stitching the field with death as the pilot fought for control, trying to stay low and slow without plowing into the ground, trying not to get so caught up in targets that he forgot his altitude. He saw one last quarry below, a clump of Amis in the road, waiting, not scattering like all the others. He eased his stick a touch, kept his finger on the trigger and arced his fire into them, pulling up at the last possible second, barely clearing the tops of the pine trees, sending them swaying into his prop wash as he flew over the woods and climbed away from the sudden carnage.

Jake saw it coming. They saw it coming. The Me-109 turned slightly and came straight at them, going right for them, singling them out for destruction. They didn't believe it, weren't able to handle the shifts from joy to terror to flight, couldn't fathom how such a lethal machine appeared from nowhere and then darted towards them, deliberately, like a wronged and vengeful wasp.

The fire was on them before they could blink an eye, raise a hand, do any of the useless things men did when hot steel was about to find them. One replacement was ripped in half, 20mm cannon shells severing him at the hips, his torso tumbling backwards, bright geysers of blood and strands of darker red spewing out from it. His legs, barely still connected, skidded down the snow-packed road, skewed in impossible directions. They came to rest twenty yards away, toes pointing to the sky, the tightly pulled, neatly tied laces a poignant, futile final preparation, a girding for battle that would outlast the girder. A second replacement was thrown backwards violently, as if a giant had him on a string and yanked him with all his might. One arm was shot off between shoulder and elbow and a tracer round burned in his chest, his clothing smoking as he convulsed on the snow. Clay ran over to him, heard Shorty yelling for a medic, but knew it was useless. No sound came from his mouth. It was wide open, bubbles of red froth bursting out as he worked his jaw. Clay knelt and saw the kid's eyes dart around, saw the jaw working, trying to say something, maybe ask what was wrong, not understanding, beyond comprehension. The phosphorous still burning away on the bullet inside him as Clay smelled the flesh cooking. He pulled out his medical kit, scattering morphine syrettes at his knees.

"You're going to be fine, kid, you did swell, hang on," Clay said, chanting the lies into his ear. He jammed a syrette into the kid's thigh and then cut open his pants so he could get at the skin for a second dose, holding down the quivering leg as he did it.

"Medics are coming, kid, hang on, you'll be okay, medics are coming." The second syrette was done and the leg stopped shaking so hard. Clay watched his eyes, saw the morphine work, wondered if he should give him another, put him under good and let him die with his eyes closed. The eyes locked onto Clay's, stayed with him, and Clay couldn't look away, didn't look away until the last movements ceased and the replacement stared, straight up, through him, beyond him.

Jake was up as soon as the plane cleared the trees, watching Clay, seeing the other replacement in pieces at the side of the road. The third kid, who had been standing in the middle, was untouched. His rifle was on the ground, but other than that he hadn't moved, still standing in the same spot as he had with his buddies. Their boot prints in the snow were on either side of him. He was covered in blood, and Jake checked him, looking for a wound, waiting for him to collapse into the road. He didn't, didn't say anything, he just stood there, one side of him flecked with blood like a fine spray, the other soaked in deepening red. Jake stood in front of him, looked him straight in the eye.

"What's your name?"

The replacement said nothing.

"What's your name? Tell me your name."

The replacement squinted, as if Jake were a mile off. He looked at his arms like he just discovered them, just noticed the blood all around him.

"Oh—" He fell to his knees. "Oh." It wasn't much, not even a real word, but he seemed to be out of his trance. Jake took the replacement's helmet off, tossed it to Tuck.

"Clean this off."

"Huh?" The replacement looked at Jake, trying to form a question. Jake saw him lose his thought, start to drift away, fear and shock pulling him under to some deep safe place.

"Get up," Jake said with as much harshness as he could muster. "Get up!"

He slapped him, trying to shock him back to here, now, to the reality of what had just happened. It was terrible, but it was the real world, the only one Jake knew, the place they all had to be right now. It was either here or maybe so deep inside the kid would never find his way back. He pulled him up and dragged him by the collar off the road, away from the blood, into fresh white snow. He thrust the replacement down to his knees, pushed his face into the snow, working it back and forth, cleaning the blood away, praying for the cold to shock the kid's brain into letting go, letting him come back to now. He pulled him out of the snow, grasping him by his hair. Snow slid off his face, pink riveluts running down his temple. He gasped, spitting out snow, choking and spitting. Good.

"What's your name?" Jake asked again, yelling into the kid's face.

"Cooper, sir."

"Do I look like a fucking officer to you?" Jake studied the face in front of him, looked into the brown eyes and saw the freckles dotting his cheeks. The kid didn't think Jake was an officer, he was just a kid who had been brought up to say sir and ma'am. Jake was twenty-two but probably looked like a real grown up man to this kid.

"No, no." He was afraid. Everything had gone wrong and now he was covered in blood and this guy was yelling at him.

"Okay, Coop. Relax. I'm Jake. C'mon, we gotta get outta here." He took him by the elbow and helped him up. Big Ned and Miller were behind him. Miller had Cooper's M1 and had snow cleaned it too. Tuck trotted up, Cooper's helmet in hand, clean and glistening wet. Shorty had an overcoat slung over his arm, taken off a G.I. who got hit in the back of the skull as he lay in the snow. There was not a mark on it. They all gathered around Cooper, undid his web belt and took off his pack. Miller unbuttoned the overcoat and Big Ned grabbed it by the shoulders and pulled it off, throwing it into the snow. Cooper's mittens came off too, replaced by a dead man's pair. They dressed him, like five mothers sending a first grader out in a snowstorm, even buttoning his coat back up and buckling the web belt. Cooper let them do everything, relief at being alive showing on his face, a stunned half-smile leaving him looking delirious. Jake watched Cooper's eyes dart about as he tried to take in what was happening, to enjoy this attention that had seemed improbable when he first got down off the truck. Everyone heard stories of guys up on the line ignoring replacements, not learning their names, sending them out on point, giving them all the dirty jobs, using them to save their own lives. This wasn't anything like that. Cooper had been transformed before their eyes, from hapless replacement to impervious survivor. When they were done, Tuck stood in front of Cooper with his helmet, put it on his head, and patted it. Then Shorty stepped in front of him and gave it a pat, then Big Ned, Jake, Miller last. They all wanted a touch of Cooper's luck, the guy who stood there, men on either side of him mangled and killed, and stayed on his feet.

"Where's Clay?" Jake looked around. Except for medics tending the wounded and a few G.I.s helping the less seriously hurt down the road, they were almost alone. Up ahead, two halftracks burned, mortar rounds exploding as they heated up. The trail end of the column disappeared as the road descended into another patch of woods. Jake saw Clay, unmoving, kneeling over the dead replacement. His head was bowed, and he held his rifle by the stock, butt on the ground, and was slowly hitting it against his helmet. Tap, tap, tap. Tap, tap, tap....

Tuck and Shorty led Cooper down the road, and Big Ned stood behind him to block the view in case he turned around. Jake wasn't sure if he had seen his buddies up close, but there was no need to, no need to lose your cherry over guys you knew. They had all seen bodies ripped open, the mysterious workings of the inner sanctum laid bare, organs, intestines, bones, flesh, thick veins and arteries, all steaming in the cold, the last bits of human warmth drifting off into cold air. Jake and the rest of them knew too that if Cooper was indeed a lucky charm, and managed to live for weeks or just a couple of days, he'd see his share, puke his guts out the first time he saw a man, G.I. or Kraut, alive enough to beg to be shot as he watched his intestines slide out of his gut, a shrapnel wound dissecting him like a scalpel, opening him up for inspection without inflicting a mortal wound, or at least an immediate one. If he were really lucky, he'd live long enough not to puke the next time, and get to decide if it was a crime or a mortal sin or a good deed to kill a guy like that. Then, if Cooper really were pure gold, a walking rabbit's foot, he'd still be around one day when he'd walk by a wounded guy and not give a shit. Shoot him in the head, or ignore him, let his pleading and crying bounce off his back, it wouldn't matter, not one fucking bit. Killing and indifference, one and the same.

If he were really lucky.

CHAPTER FIVE

1964

WIND BLEW RAIN AGAINST THE WINDOW AS CLAY pressed his hand to it, feeling the coolness bleed into his palm. He wiped the condensation from the glass, rubbing his fingers over the red reversed letters that spelled out the Jake in Jake's Tavern. It was after three o'clock and Chris should have been here by now.

"Where the hell is he?" Clay said, low and quiet. He turned away from the window and straightened the chairs around the two round tables pushed up next to it. Some folks liked to sit there, watch the cars drive by, wave to people on the sidewalk, be seen drinking their Schlitz or Seven and Seven. Others liked to take up position at the bar, right behind the two tables, where they could hook their heels around the wooden stool legs and study their drinks.

"Give the kid a break, Clay," said Brick, wiping down the bar, dumping ashtrays as he went. "Maybe he's got a girl."

Clay moved to the half dozen booths lining the opposite wall. Coat racks rose like flagpoles between the varnished oak backrests. Folks liked the booths too, a good place for conversation or serious drinking not on display for the neighborhood to see. Off duty cops from up the street liked the rear booths best, where they had a view of the whole room and an exit at their backs. So did Clay.

He picked up the ashtrays from the tables, empting them as he went, knocking them on the inside of the metal trashcan he carried in one hand. Then he changed course, wiping down the heavy glass ashtrays with a damp rag and setting them back in the center of each table, until he reached the front of the room. He viewed his work, liking the neat cleanness of the ashtrays set dead center, exactly the same on each empty table. A rainy mid-afternoon was the best time to clean up, no customers to get in the way of a clean sweep. He stepped up to the window again, looking up and down the street and shaking his head.

"Not girls I'm worried about." He spoke to the glass. Brick had already moved off to the kitchen in back of the bar, a galley space really, hardly wide enough for two people not to get in each other's way. Clay could hear him scraping grease from the small grill where they cooked up hamburgers for the lunch crowd. The grease trap would have to be cleaned out soon, not a job Clay wanted to do himself, or would give to Brick. It was just the job for a teenage kid earning a few bucks under the table working after school. But lately he couldn't get Chris to do anything he wanted him to do. Everything was a struggle and a fight, and an overdue grease trap was going to be no exception. Now Chris was late, and Clay didn't know if he should react like a boss or a father, or both, or exactly what the difference was supposed to be. What if Chris turned up his nose at cleaning out the trap, what was he supposed to do, fire him and then say see you later at the house?

He shook his head, wondering how things had gotten so complicated. Last week, he'd blown up at Chris when he found him going through his cigar box. The one he kept in the small drawer in his dresser, crammed with tie clips and a few old cuff links. Chris had said he was looking for a tie clip, but he'd never put on a tie after that. It was the memories he was after. He had the small cigar box open, flicking the dried out Zippo, little sparks flying from the flint. A photograph, folded and creased, worn at the edges, had fallen to the floor. Clay winced inwardly as he remembered his reaction. He yelled, pointed at Chris to get out, stop pawing through his stuff.

"But who are these guys, Dad? Is one of them you?" Chris scooped up the photo from the floor, holding it close to his face, squinting. It was faded colors of white and gray, snow and seven men, cradling M1s and wearing their helmets like crowns.

Clay had grabbed it away so quickly he'd been afraid it would rip.

"It doesn't matter," he'd said to his son, and pushed him out of the bedroom, leaving the door open while he put everything back where it had been, carefully sliding the little drawer shut.

A car came down the street, too fast, braking to a stop in front of the tavern, the sound jolting Clay from his thoughts. Chris got out of the back seat and sprinted to the door, his open jacket flapping behind him. Clay felt the irritation rise up, filling his mind, driving everything else out. That was a good fall waterproof jacket Addy had picked out for Chris at the start of school. Didn't the kid have enough sense to zip it up in the rain?

"Dad!" Chris said, before he was halfway through the door. "Brick! Take a look at Tony's new car!"

"What is it, kid?" Brick said, drying his hands as he walked around the bar.

"A '56 Dodge Coronet, two-tone. V-8. Look at those fins!"

The car was black on the roof, hood and tail fenders. The rest was yellow, the colors demarcated by shining chrome. A thread of rust ran along the bottom by the rear wheel, and the exhaust showed blue smoke as the car sat in the road, jammed with teenagers. Tony rolled down the driver's window, lifted his head hello to Chris' father, and took off with enough acceleration to show the power under the hood but not enough to leave rubber. That would have been too blatant, insulting to the parent of a friend. Instead, Clay heard the squealing of tires on wet pavement after the car vanished from sight, up the hill, closer to the police station, which showed daring as well as consideration, not to mention deniability.

"Where were you?" Clay said, pronouncing each word hard, stressing the importance of location, time, and relation, willing Chris to understand why each of them, or even only one of them, was important.

"Out with Tony and the guys. He bought the car from a guy in Wallingford, we had to go get it."

"You," said Clay, "were supposed to be here, at three. To work."

"Jeez, Dad, it's only twenty after, don't blow a gasket."

Chris turned away from his father, taking his jacket off and walking towards the back room.

"Where're your books?" Clay said to his back.

"No homework tonight." Chris kept walking.

"Wouldn't kill you to study some," Clay said, raising his voice, going for the last word even as he knew it wouldn't be. Talking with Chris was like boxing with a tar baby, every time you thought you landed a good one you only got more stuck, unable to make a clean break.

"For what?" Chris opened the door to the back room, got rid of his jacket, and took a wooden push broom from against the wall. He started sweeping up in the bar, pushing dust, matches, cellophane from the tops of cigarette packs, crumpled bits of paper and the other debris of drinkers into a central pile.

Brick was back behind the bar, counting out the change in the cash register, not wanting to be in the middle. He avoided both of them, trying to get things ready while there was time before the first of the day shifts got out and business picked up.

"For your future, Chris. So you can make something of yourself. Do something more than make ball bearings at New Departure for the next forty years. No offense, Brick." Clay glanced at Brick, who had done his forty with a two- year break when his Guard unit got called up for Korea.

"Forty years?" Chris said, stopping and holding the broom handle up with one hand. "I'm not going to do the same thing for forty years, what're you crazy?"

"Don't talk to me like that," Clay said, advancing and raising his hand. Chris flinched and Clay tried to calm down, not make a fool of himself, or hurt Chris before he got things under control. He felt his hand hanging in the air and brought it down in an arc, grabbing the broom away from him, thankful there was something to latch onto. They both stood looking at each other, Chris surprised, his eyes wide open, ready to step back but not wanting to, not wanting to give ground. Clay, strangling the broom handle with one hand, trying to stop his forward movement, wishing his son was ten, or eight maybe, not fifteen and talking like such a punk, asking for trouble.

"I'll sweep up. You clean out the grease trap."

Chris swiveled on his heel, giving his father a clear berth as he walked to the kitchen. He stopped at the bar. "Sorry, Brick, I didn't mean you."

"Don't worry, kid, I know what you meant. No offense taken, either of you." Brick closed the register and kept his head down, setting up beer glasses, giving them a final rub with a clean cloth to get the water marks off.

Two customers came in, locals from the neighborhood. Clay watched as they ordered beers. Brick served them, money changed hands, and two little slips of paper went into a cigar box under the counter. Couple of five dollar bets, big spenders. Nice and low key, like Clay liked it. Nobody made a fuss about it or made a big show of putting down their numbers. It went on when off-duty cops were in, but it was done so casually that it was part of the scenery, like the picture of the old Silver City Brewery on South Colony Street, hung up over the bar. The place was long shut down, but it was famous around town since Legs Diamond owned it during Prohibition, and had kept producing bootleg beer along with the soda pop that was supposedly keeping the brewery in business. This was a lot like Prohibition. Nobody wanted to embarrass their buddies on the force by breaking the law right out in the open, but everybody knew what was going on. What people didn't know was how much of it was going on. Even with the share he gave Brick and Cheryl out of his cut, Clay ended up with a fistful of cash every week, plus, it brought customers into the bar. The number slips he collected on his rounds filling cigarette machines were all his. He didn't have to divvy up that cut with anyone.

Clay looked away from the customers, leaving them to their small beers and big dreams of hitting the numbers as he swept the floor, keeping his eyes down, piling up dirt from corners, under the booths, along the bar. He swept everything up he could, then turning the dustpan at a right angle to the thin line of dust left on the floor, swept it up again. He repeated the process one more time. Any job worth doing was worth doing right, that's what he'd learned growing up. That was when jobs were hard to come by, and you were damn glad to get any work. Now there were plenty of jobs, but not enough good hard workers to fill them. How was that kid ever going to make it? All he wanted was a car when he turned sixteen, something with big fins and lots of chrome. Chris couldn't see beyond the next hood ornament, while Clay worried what would happen once he got what he wanted. What would it be then? Drag races, drinking, an arrest, maybe an accident, maybe worse.

The door opened and Clay went to put the broom away. Business, about to pick up, demanded his attention. Chris' job was to get the place cleaned up for the after work crowd, then do whatever chores were needed. It was only for two hours, but Clay had talked Addy into letting Chris have the job. He'd get to spend time with his son, Chris would earn his spending money, and they'd know he wasn't out getting in trouble with his pal Tony. A year older than Chris, Tony already had been in juvenile detention for a fistfight last summer that sparked a near riot at the A&W drive in. That convinced Addy, and she agreed, as long as Clay promised to keep Chris clear of any of his arrangements with Tri-State Brands.

Clay leaned the broom against the wall, chuckling to himself. Yeah, I'm worried about Chris turning into a juvenile delinquent, but maybe I should be worried about my own problems with the law. He picked up Chris' jacket, thrown in a wet heap on a folding chair. He hung it on the back of the chair, shaking his head at the carelessness of his son. Seeing a bulge in the pocket, Clay reached in, pulling out a half-empty pack of Winstons.

"Damn!" he said, picking the folding chair up and slamming it on the floor. He stared at the chair for a minute, seething, and then walked into the kitchen, gripping the red and white pack in his hand.

Chris had an apron on, and was scraping out the open grease trap, filling a metal can with the fatty yellow and brown sludge. It smelled like bad meat and burnt rancid butter, which wasn't far off. The smell rose up into Clay's nostrils and he felt like gagging. He took a deep breath but it was worse, more of the same awful odor crawling into his mouth and lungs. Clay was thrown off stride for a second, surprised at Chris already hard at work on the trap. He half expected to find him goofing off.

Chris' face wore a look of disgust as he grimaced at the sight of another hunk of aged grease dumped into the can. He looked at his father, not noticing the pack of cigarettes he held.

"Yeah?"

Clay fought to keep his stomach in control. The smell overpowered him, tried to open him up and spill him out. He felt his eyes water and his skin go clammy. He wanted to turn and run, but he had come in here for a reason. He had something to say. He was confused. What was happening? The cigarettes, he was going to tell Chris—what? That he was doing a good job, doing what he was told? Or was he?

"Dad?" Caution edged into Chris' voice. "What's wrong?"

"I...I told you..."

The putrid smell rose up again, like a wave rolling over him. He didn't understand what was happening, why everything was so off kilter, why he couldn't make sense of anything.

"Dad?"

Then he knew. Knew what the smell was. Knew the difference between this smell, here and now in this kitchen, with his son kneeling on the floor, and that other smell, the one switching on the memory like pulling a light cord, filling the room with blinding white brightness.

Bright light like the white phosphorus shells that rained down over them in that little village, the one they took right after Hartman got killed. WP. Willie Peter. The Germans must have wanted to burn them out, or maybe that's all they had left. Incendiary shells exploding into white-hot flame. Clay saw them bursting all around, in the street, on walls, houses, vehicles, setting everything on fire. Not the bright yellow and cherry red of regular fire, but a furious stark white incandescence. He had crawled under a tank out in the main square. One shell fell through the roof of a small thatched stone house opposite the tank. It exploded inside the house, and the screams told him a full squad had taken refuge inside. The screams didn't last long, but the fire did, burning everything away except the stone. Clay stayed under the tank all night, and in the morning when he dared to look inside the stone house, nothing was left but the stone floor and walls. Inside were burned bones, blackened metal and a thick, gooey layer of grease. The stone house had been well built, and acted like a cauldron as the phosphorus burned itself out, igniting flesh and fat, the commonest of common graves, eight men melted into a single substance. He had gagged then, the stench worse than anything he had ever smelled, ever imagined, ever wanted to think about. He felt it coming back, but determined to stay here, to deliver the message to his son, not to be drawn back into ancient history. Clenching his teeth, to keep the odor from reaching farther down his throat, he brought up his hand.

"I told you, you're too young to smoke."

"You sell 'em, why do you care who smokes 'em?"

Chris turned away, working the compacted grease loose inside the trap. Clay watched him, angry at the comment and unable to argue with the logic. Chris scraped a corner of the trap and lifted out the oldest, bottom-most layer of grease, soft and gray, dripping thickly off the large metal spatula. He ladled it into the can, tapping the spatula on the edge to get it all off. The liquid squish of the grease falling into the bucket released a cloying, dense odor that seeped into your skin, eyes, mouth and nostrils. Chris drew up his tee shirt, holding the thin cotton fabric to the ridge of his nose.

The Graves Registration unit had used shovels, and it had made that same sound as they dumped it into a big steel drum. Clay turned, walked out of the room, out the back entrance, and fell to his knees, as he had that day in the village, and vomited. The odor of the grease ran through his body, forcing everything out, doubling him up on the gravel next to the garbage cans. He felt the acidic bile at the back of his throat, the smell of the grease twisting through him, leaving him gasping for air as he sat up and cleaned his lips with his handkerchief.

There wasn't a day that went by that Clay didn't think about the war. There was always some fragment of memory, a thought that brought him back, once in a while it was even something funny. But this hadn't happened in years. Right after the war, it was every night, in his dreams. He'd scared Addy half to death, digging a foxhole in the bed with his hands, screaming as the nightmare shells burst all around him. Some nights, when he could feel it coming, feel the memories pressing against the inside of his skull, ready to burst out, he'd sleep in the big chair in the living room, feet up on the hassock, and he'd feel safe. Alone. Unable to frighten anyone, unable to do sleeping harm.

When Chris came along, the nightmares seemed to fade away. He had a family. A tavern to run. Money to earn. Ashtrays to clean. Cigarette machines to fill. Numbers slips to pack in a bag. There was an order to everything, and it calmed him. If the ashtrays got dirty, it meant he'd be cleaning them tomorrow. When people bought cigarettes, he'd be there tomorrow with a new supply. Sometimes he felt giddy with the joy of an endless string of known tomorrows.

The pack of Winstons was still in his hand. He got up, spat, and lifted the lid of the garbage can to throw away the soiled handkerchief and the cigarettes. As he was about to drop them, he noticed the tax stamp. Virginia. One of his own.

Addy was there at five, like always. Pulled over alongside the bright yellow paint on the curb, the no parking zone by the corner perfect for her. A spot always waiting when she came to pick up Chris, and one that required her to stay in the car, motor running. A tentative, apologetic honk on the horn to announce herself, and she'd sit patiently, waiting for her son.

"Mom's here," Chris announced as he came out of the back room, throwing on his jacket. Clay was coming up from the basement with a case of Narragansett Ale. Chris didn't meet his eyes. He could've been talking to Brick, one of the customers, or the walls. Clay set the case down on the floor and followed Chris outside. They hadn't spoken a word since Clay had fled the kitchen. Chris had finished cleaning up, left the grill sparkling, emptied the trash, smiled at the customers he knew. This left Clay without resentment, but wide open to the shame and embarrassment he felt as he ran away from his own kid, felled by a random twenty year old memory. He couldn't leave it like that, but he had no idea what to do, no concept of what he could possibly say to explain himself. He followed his son out the door, suffering with the small contentment of sharing the same space, breathing the same air, even if the connection went no farther than that.

Chris opened the car door and got in. Clay leaned on the open door, keeping the connection open, three of them now together, the front seat of the Nash Rambler and the open door encompassing them, clarifying their relationship, defining Chris. Their boy, who they fed, clothed, employed, transported. Addy and Clay smiled across the gulf of their son, fidgeting in the front seat, his hand on the door handle.

"My God," said Addy, "what is that smell?" Her nose wrinkled as Chris leaned forward to turn on the radio and tune into his favorite station. The Beatles sang Twist and Shout through the static and Chris lowered the volume, hoping that would keep his mother from turning it off.

"Me. I had to clean out the grease trap," Chris said. His eyes stayed on the radio.

"Well, those clothes will have to go in the wash, young man, and you scrub yourself when we get home. You smell like a greasy spoon."

"What's for dinner?" Clay asked, not caring about food, but wanting to talk about something else, anything else.

"Meat loaf. Clay, you look pale as a ghost. Are you all right?"

Clay rubbed his face with his hand, trying to bring some life back into it. He was surprised it still showed, not happy that his face betrayed him so readily. Chris glanced up at him, then back to the radio. C'mon c'mon, c'mon, baby, now, come on and work it on out—

"Yeah, fine. Tired and hungry is all. Chris did a great job today."

"Well, good," Addy said. She moved her eyes from Clay to Chris, then back again, trying to signal Clay to tell Chris, not her. Clay understood what she meant, but what the hell was he supposed to do, repeat himself?

A long black car drove past them, a Cadillac Deville, polished and gleaming in the late afternoon sun. Clay knew the car.

"You'd better go," he said. "I've got business coming. I'll be home at seven." He shut the door, patted the hood, and stepped back. He watched the Nash drive off, heard the rumbling noise that told him it would need a new muffler before long. It was a '59, bought used last year, and it was going to start costing money. It was just for around town, but he wanted it to be in good shape for Addy. She deserved better. Clay looked to the Cadillac idling double-parked. The polish job looked a mile deep as it reflected the overhead sky. Last year's model, it was sleek and lean, clean lines, classy. Addy would look good in that car, maybe a white convertible. He imagined them driving, top down, heading to the beach, sunglasses on, wind swirling over the windshield, cooling them in the summer sun and asphalt heat.

A car door opened and slammed shut. The driver was out, a big fella in a green sharkskin suit. He opened the rear door for his passenger, a smaller man dressed in a black suit. Except for a stark white shirt, everything was black. Pointed toe shoes, tie, cufflinks, hair, mustache, even his eyes looked like black dots on white. He walked towards Clay, looking into his eyes, searching for something. He stopped when he was nearly toe-to-toe. He was a couple of inches taller and tilted his head slightly. Clay smelled cologne, cigarette smoke, and sour wine.

"Inside," he said.

"Sure, Mr. Fiorenza," Clay said, and followed.

Clay wasn't surprised when they went inside and another well-built guy in a dark suit was standing by the back booth. Like the last time, the only time, Pasquale Fiorenza had come to Jake's Tavern, he sent one of his men around the back first, to check out the place. Then he made his entrance. Mr. Fiorenza hadn't made it to where he was today by walking into rooms without knowing what was on the other side of the door. Mr. Fiorenza sat in the last booth, facing the room. The dark suited guy sat on a bar stool facing the rear door. He didn't order a drink.

Clay slid into the booth, glancing at Brick, who shrugged, raised his eyebrows, and pulled a draft. Clay turned to Mr. Fiorenza, who sat with his hands up to his face. He looked tired. Clay was wary, uncertain of what the visit meant.

"Can I get you anything, Mr. Fiorenza? Coffee?"

Mr. Fiorenza pulled his hands down his cheeks, stretching his lower eyelids until the wet, red inner lid showed. His eyeballs were bloodshot, not the crystal clear white they had seemed outside. His hands finally left his face, which returned to its normal hardness. The hands went flat on the table.

"How long have we known each other, Mr. Brock?" Mr. Fiorenza was always businesslike and proper, an Old World formality draped over his shoulders like a black topcoat. He was Clay's age, a few years younger maybe, but he was from another world. A world of Cadillacs and cufflinks, a world far away from the worn wooden floorboards of Jake's Tavern.

"More than fifteen years," Clay said. Since that first visit fifteen years ago, he had seen Mr. Fiorenza a dozen times or so, mostly at Tri-State Brands, sometimes at baseball games at West Side Field, and once at City Hall, whispering with a councilman.

"Seventeen years, this December," he said. "Seventeen years ago I came to you and we made a deal, yes?"

The answer was so obvious all Clay could do was nod his head. Sure, they had a deal. Clay ran numbers for him, used his tavern and his cigarette route to bring in business, and in return he got a piece of the action.

"And this arrangement has been good for both of us, yes?"

Another nod. Clay was sure it worked out well for Mr. Fiorenza. Everything did, or else he wouldn't have made the deal. It worked out for Clay too, even though he felt the pressure with the cigarettes. He was in no position to complain, given how deep he was in. Playing the numbers was no big deal, everyone looked the other way. Running numbers, that was different. Serious, like tax evasion.

"So, Mr. Brock, if that is true, what happened to my receipts yesterday?" Mr. Fiorenza leaned forward, whispering, getting his face close to Clay. Clay saw the jaw clench, the eyes widen, the signs of physical anger uncoiling beneath the expensive suit. He wanted to back up, get away from the smell of the man, but his back was against the booth, nowhere to go.

"I gave them to Al," Clay said, feeling thick and stupid. He knew something hadn't been right about that guy. He shouldn't have handed the receipts over to somebody he didn't know. So obvious now, with this angry man poised across from him, looking like he wanted to leap over the table and strangle him. Mr. Fiorenza eased back and folded his hands in front of him, as if praying.

"Al. Whenever have I sent a stranger to you?"

"He was driving a Tri-State truck, had the uniform, said Petey had been in an accident—

how is Petey? Is he okay?"

"He was beaten, my truck was stolen, and this scum," Mr. Fiorenza waved his hand in the air, dismissing the lowlife Al, "this scum, works his route, and takes the receipts. Finally, someone with an ounce of brains calls me to check. Someone who can think, lifts up the telephone, and ends this, but not before I have lost thousands."

"I should have..."

"How much did they give you?"

"What?"

"How much!" Mr. Fiorenza's right hand slammed down on the table, the sharp snap of flesh on wood rattling the glass ashtray, still clean and clear in the middle of the table. Clay took a deep breath, trying to figure out how to calm the man, figure out what he needed to say.

"I didn't know anything, it was just another delivery, another pickup. The guy was a little strange, he was late, but everything seemed normal."

"A little strange, and you think that normal? Mr. Brock, you are one of my most successful associates. The bar, the cigarettes, how you do business, very quietly, nothing to draw attention. This is very good. Someone as smart as you, you are fooled by this man? I am not sure."

"Why would I—"

"Has anyone contacted you," Mr. Fiorenza interrupted, "about our business?"

"No, nobody," said Clay. "Was anyone else?"

"Never mind who. Several weeks ago I was made an offer on my business."

"Tri-State?"

"Yes, and all the associated business that goes with it. The price was very low, and I have no desire to sell. But these people, they have a great desire."

"So, Al was one of them?"

"See, Mr. Brock, you are very smart. Yes, Alphonse DePaoli, he is a ladro giovane, a boy who steals from his elders, who has no respect." Mr. Fiorenza took a pack of cigarettes from his pocket, shook one loose from the pack so it stuck out an inch or so, and pulled it out with his lips. Old Golds, Clay noted absently as Mr. Fiorenza lit up with a gold cigarette lighter.

"This act was a message to me, a message that caused me to think how I would proceed if I were in their shoes," Mr. Fironeza went on. "I would contact associates like you, explain to you how it would be in your best interests to do business with me. Get information, learn about how we conduct our business. Then, pull something like this, intercept revenues, cause a disruption." He blew out a stream of smoke right at Clay.

"No one has done that." Clay felt calm now that the cards were on the table. It was bad news, but at least he understood where he was, what was going on around him. He was in the middle of a war, something he could grasp, maybe even manage. They both sat silently for a minute, watching each other. Clay had passed a test, he knew that much.

"All right, then," Mr. Fiorenza said as he unfolded his hands and spread them open. "If anyone does, call me immediately. We will deal with them. One of the two men with me today will accompany the new driver. You will remember their faces?"

"Yes," said Clay, glancing at the man at the bar.

"If one of them is not with the driver, give him nothing."

"What if he insists?"

"That is your problem, Mr. Brock. And, for the rest of this week, there will be no percentage for you. We have to make up losses. I still have to pay the winning numbers."

"That's not—"

"Do not dare tell me what is fair," said Mr. Fiorenza, holding up a finger, as if stilling a rowdy child. "Nothing is fair. Nothing."

He slid out of the booth and walked out, the cleats on the heels of his black shoes sharp on the floorboards as he passed. The guy at the bar followed him, nodding to Clay as he went.

Clay couldn't argue with the logic. Fair was a fairy tale.

Chapter Six

2000

CLAY POURED COFFEE FROM THE POT, ENJOYING the aroma and the look of the hot steam swirling up as the liquid filled his cup. He set the pot back down on the burner, stirred in a touch of sugar and carried his coffee cup to the kitchen table.

Addy didn't drink coffee anymore, so one day Clay had put away the Mr. Coffee and dug out their old aluminum coffee pot. It was with the camping gear, covered by a canvas tarp in the garage. It was beat up, dented, and scorched black on the bottom, but it had cleaned up pretty good, and it wasn't some piece of plastic crap. It was real metal, something you didn't plug in, it worked indoors and out, and you could watch the coffee cooking up, water bouncing up against the little glass top over and over again until it turned dark black and smelled like heaven.

He sipped the coffee. It was hot and strong, really hot, not like the lukewarm stuff that came out of those drip pots. He had to slurp in air with it to cool it down. It always brought back the memory of drinking coffee brewed up in mess kits. Nescafe, instant coffee in little plastic packs. You'd dig a small trench in the ground, and stick in one of those heating tabs that came in C Ration packs. Burned hot and bright, no smoke. Put your mess kit over that, and heat up your chow or water for coffee. Once in a while, he'd get some real coffee from the Company kitchen and throw it in with the water and let it boil up. But that was rare good luck, or from bartering souvenirs when they had them. Most times though, it was instant coffee, the water poured burning hot into an aluminum canteen cup and the Nescafe and sugar cubes stirred in. You'd burn your lip on the hot rim, because the coffee cooled down sooner than the metal. But it tasted good, hunkered down in a hole with your buddy, the warmth filling your stomach, while you waited for the sun to come up. The days were short that winter of '44-'45, the nights long, cold and dark in the hills and forests of who-the-hell-knows-where.

This past winter, as the last year of his century wound down, Clay would lie awake at night, listening to the hard wind outside, wondering how he had ever lived in that weather, with nothing but what he could carry and his buddy to sustain him. Once, he had gotten up early, before dawn, and quietly dressed in his winter coat, warm boots, gloves, scarf, and wool cap, then went outside. He'd stood in the driveway for a minute, wind blowing gusts of snow over the plowed blacktop. It hadn't felt right. He walked past the garage, into the backyard. That felt better. Hard ground. He went to a thin strip of trees separating his back yard from the back yard that came up behind him, where the land sloped down toward the other house. He moved branches aside and ducked into the trees. Another time, another place, this is where he would have dug in. In the cover of the trees, with a clear view to his front, the row of houses behind his house the enemy lines. This is what it felt like, he reminded himself as he knelt in the snow, fifty-five long years ago. He had to stop himself from getting a shovel and chipping away at the frozen ground. He couldn't really do it, the sound would wake Addy, and she'd think he was crazy, and probably be right on the money. He'd grunted as he got up. Made his way back to the house, inside, carefully hung everything up so Addy wouldn't notice.

He set the cup down on the table and looked out the kitchen window, out at the line of trees, now sprouting springtime leaves. They lived on Buckwheat Hill, a small knoll above the city. When they had built the house, they had a clear view over to the Polish Cemetery, but now there were houses in the way on roads with silly names like Jimmy Lane and Louis Drive. From this window though, looking towards the northeast, they still had a clear view of Lamentation Mountain. Dark brown shale spilling down the sides, a covering of green clinging to the top. Perfect name for a mountain that was falling apart, chunks of rock falling off and choking the trees below as it piled up all around them. Clay thought about how long the mountain had been there, shedding its outer surface, laying itself bare to the world. What would be left when it had all fallen away?

A shudder of sadness swept through Clay. Looking at his hands, cupped around the coffee mug, the warmth bleeding into his aching knuckles, he tried to nail down where the feeling came from. Surprises scared him. He could handle it if he were prepared, like he was prepared for the volleys at Bob's funeral yesterday. It still got to him, but if he knew it was coming, he could steel himself, like a G.I. digging in. Give me ten minutes and I'll bury my ass. Getting caught out in the open was the last thing he wanted.

Death? How far off could it be? Was that what slid its knife into his gut? No, not that. He felt a calmness about death. Not about dying, exactly, but the whole idea of being dead, after being alive so long, didn't chill him like it did when he was young. It had once seemed terrifying, the complete absence of himself. Now, it was the next logical step, and he had to admit to himself, the years had built up to a weariness he had never conceived of. Some day, it would be enough.

He looked out of the window again. The houses. He smelled the coffee. He turned to look at the calendar on the wall, next to the refrigerator. That was it. He closed his eyes, leaned forward and rested his elbows on the table. He missed his old world. A world without plastic Mr. Coffee machines, streets named after some contractor's kids, houses jammed up against each other, computers, cheap telephones, passwords, log in codes, everything that was supposed to make life easier but really confused him, left him wishing he could step back in time, walk into the bank, hand over his bankbook and chat with a teller for a minute. He wanted to be back in a century with real years and decades, not some zeroed out year that no one even knew how to say. Home alive in '45, they used to say in December 1944, before all hell broke loose, and the less popular Out of the Sticks in '46 started making the rounds. What would guys even rhyme with today? Two-thousand? O-O? Aught-aught?

Clay wanted coffee perked on a wood stove, a clear view out his window, Addy whole again, a second chance at so many things. But that was impossible. Here he was, washed up on the shores of the future, a relic, like a character from an old black and white movie thrown into a special effects blockbuster. Sam Spade in Star Wars, shades of gray tones stunted against computer generated color images of aliens and space ships. It was almost funny.

Eyes still closed, hands around the coffee mug, he felt the warmth on his palms and remembered. The candle. When everything else was too much, the cold, death, stupidity, and chickenshit piling up all around him, he had the warmth from his candle. Such a simple thing. He couldn't recall the last time he'd even lit a candle. Now the desire brewed up inside him, like a coffee pot on the boil, and the only thing in the world he wanted was to flick that Zippo, light a wick, and stare into the candlelight. His mind surveyed the house, wondering where Addy kept candles. Surely she kept candles somewhere, for a power outage, at least. He calculated the chances of waking her, of being found out, trying to explain himself, but he didn't really care, all he wanted was a candle, to touch his fingertips behind it and study the flame.

A sob choked him and he clapped a hand over his mouth, gritting his teeth, trying to swallow it, to not let the desire out into the silence of the kitchen. He felt the sob form a bubble in his throat and the pressure pained him but he didn't let go. Tears spilled from his eyes, catching him off guard, lessening his concentration. He choked, coughing, burying his face in his hands, trying to stem the flow of tears as he gasped, choking some more, trying to regain control, to keep his body from betraying him.

"Are you all right, Dad?"

"Jesus Christ—" Clay coughed again and rubbed the sleeve of his robe over his face. He took a deep breath, and let it out without coughing. "Don't sneak up on me like that. Coffee went down the wrong pipe, then you scared the daylights out of me."

Chris had slept in the guest room last night, instead of going back to his empty apartment. His parent's old bedroom, actually. After the stroke, Clay and Chris had moved the bedroom down to the first floor, so Addy wouldn't have to climb stairs. The room had been repainted and a new double bed set up, but it still felt odd to Clay to have Chris sleep there. As if he was trespassing.

"Sorry," Chris said. "You sure you're okay?"

"Yep, sure." Clay got up and went to the sink. He splashed water on his face, filled a glass, swirled some around in his mouth, and spit. "Went down the wrong pipe, that's all."

"Whatever you say," said Chris. He was dressed for work, his suit jacket slung over one arm, blue tie knotted tight on a crisp white shirt. He kept one of the bureau drawers in the guest room filled with spare clothes for the times he stayed with his parents. Since his divorce, and his mother's stroke, it was something he did frequently. His office, part of the State Police Criminal Investigations Bureau, was on Broad Street in Meriden. He could walk to work from their house. He had no wife, no kids, no pets, hobbies or friends to draw him back to the apartment complex. Clay figured he lived there because he was too old to move back in with his parents, but not for any other real reason.

"Want some coffee?" Clay asked.

"Sure." Chris hung his jacket on the back of a kitchen chair. In his hand he held his holstered automatic and State Police badge in its leather holder, both of which clipped to his belt. He set them down on the table, and sat in the chair. It was more comfortable to sit without them on his belt, the badge in front, visible, and the holster to the side, hiding the Glock 19 from view.

Clay poured a cup of coffee and set it in front of Chris, along with the sugar bowl. He topped off his own cup and sat down. The emotions had gone underground, tamped down by effort and fear, fear that they would betray him, reveal him for who he really was. Clay blew on his coffee and sipped, looking at the gun on the table. It was a dull black beneath the heavy-duty nylon holster, an even duller dark gray that seemed to absorb light into its thick stitching.

Chris caught his father's eyes on the gun, and moved the holster and badge to the side, as if to make room for his arm on the table. Clay looked away, back out the window, willing himself to look away from the hypnotic dark sheen of the handgun, wondering at the irony of Chris going into law enforcement. He was good at it, no doubt. Sometimes it worked out that way for hell raisers. If they didn't get in too deep as kids, or get caught, they had a fine eye for judging people and understanding the law. Skirting it during your teenage years had a way of building a familiarity with its boundaries, and learning how it should be applied fairly.

"Mom still sleeping?" Chris asked in a low voice.

"Yep." Addy never used to sleep in. She always had been up before Clay, padding around the house in her slippers, getting the coffee going, organizing things, doing all the little jobs Clay never took notice of, until she stopped doing them. After her stroke, magazines stopped appearing in neat piles in the morning, dishes stacked up in the rack, and there weren't always fresh color-coordinated towel sets in the bathroom. Things still got done, but slowly, so he could see the progression, understanding now how she did things, how much work it had been for her to make it all seem simple, invisible, as if clean towels all the same shade of mauve or plum or peach simply appeared on the rack.

Truth was, Clay knew Addy was probably awake by now. It was hard for her to get up, get going in the morning. Clay used to hover over her, trying to help, getting her bathrobe, lending an arm to walk her to the bathroom. She had hated it, and one day told him to get out. Not an affectionate get out from underfoot kind of thing, but a curt, angry, clipped, get out. He did, and now he was the early riser, brewing up coffee and memories, waiting for Addy to get herself ready for the day, appearing to him as fit and cheerful as she could be, the struggle of preparing for the day left behind in the empty bedroom.

"She seems better," Chris said. He stirred a teaspoon of sugar into his coffee. "Don't you think?"

"Yep," said Clay, sipping some more of his coffee. He wished he could say more, confess his deepest wish for Addy to recover, but it was too close to his heart, a dream of his heart, and he couldn't let go and risk it breaking completely. The memory of the candle was too recent for him to risk anything at all. But he knew Chris was concerned, worried, scared, and needed reassurance, more words than the single affirmative he had managed to squeeze out.

"Yep, I do." Smile, he could smile.

He looked at Chris and smiled, trying to communicate confidence. Chris set down his cup and turned in his chair, facing his father.

"You're a man of damn few words, Dad."

"True," Clay said.

"Why? Why so stingy with something that's free and easy to give?"

"What do you mean?"

"I don't know. A story about when you were a kid. What it was like in Tennessee, who your buddies were in the war. Who you really are."

"I'm your father." He set his coffee cup down and folded his hands on the table.

"Who are the guys in that photo? And why do you have that other guy's dogtag?"

Clay picked up his coffee, blowing on it although it had already cooled down. He set it down without taking a drink.

"You ask me that question about once a decade. The answer is the same. They were guys I knew, and I don't want you pawing through my souvenirs."

"That was over thirty years ago."

"It still stands."

"A couple of dogtags, a beat-up Zippo, and a creased photograph in that cigar box, along with a bunch of junk. Why do you have your own dogtags and one from this guy Burnett?"

"I ought to have mine, shouldn't I? And the other is a guy, that's all."

"And?"

"And that's it."

"What's the big deal, Dad?"

"That's for me to know."

"That's the real problem between us, Dad. It's for you and no one else, right?"

"A man's got a right."

"Maybe. But what about you and me?"

"What about us?"

"Maybe it's me, I don't know," Chris said. "You and mom always got along, always held each other close. I couldn't hold onto Kathy, but maybe that was our fault, maybe we were wrong for each other. But you and me—"

"What?"

Chris slapped the table with his left hand and turned away from his father. He rubbed his chin with his hand, grimacing as he tried to get the words out.

"You and me—do you remember when I was a little kid, and you used to take me down to the train station? We'd watch the trains come in, they were so big and loud they scared me. I remember you holding my hand, I can even remember the coat you had on. It was long, gray, with a fur collar and a belt around the waist, like a trench coat. I don't think I was any higher than that belt, I had to stretch my neck back to see your face. But as long as you were there, I knew I was safe. I can still see the wheels of the engine start to turn. Do you remember?"

"Yep," said Clay, "I do." He knew it was important that he remember, but for the life of him he couldn't. Funny how little things you do with a child assume an importance far greater than you ever thought it would. It sounded right, so he knew he must've done it, and saw no reason to admit otherwise.

"Christ, Dad, I'm older now than you were then. I've got no family other than the one I started with, Mom's had a stroke, and we barely talk. If you took out the yeps and nopes there wouldn't be a whole lot left."

They both looked out the window, hands on their coffee mugs, one man not knowing what to say, the other wishing he could take back what he'd said, the honesty too sharp for this quiet kitchen morning. Clay's mind raced, trying to hit upon the right thing to say, to string words together in such a way that they would satisfy Chris without undoing himself.

"You're half right about your mother and me," he finally said. "It wasn't always easy between us. But we ended up okay. She's the best thing that ever happened to me."

"So I'm, what, second best?" Chris said. He smiled as he sipped his coffee, but Clay knew it was half a joke, at best.

"It's different. You're with your wife longer than you are with a child, if you play your cards right. Sorry, I didn't mean it that way."

"No, that's okay, I know what you mean."

"You're important to me, Chris. Now that you're grown up, I figure you know that. It was different when you were a kid. You needed me."

"It's not about needing, Dad. It's about what I want for both of us."

"What's that?" Clay felt stupid having to ask, but he was wary, afraid of what Chris might demand, or what he might misunderstand. Better to get things straight.

"Understanding," he said, with a shrug. "What did you want from your father?"

"My father's got nothing to do with this," Clay said. "Leave him out of it."

"Sorry. I forgot about the forbidden topics."

"Don't get wise."

"Dad, let's not do this."

"Okay," Clay said, holding up one hand in truce.

"Look, I'm good at catching bad guys. I'm lousy at having a relationship. Is it me? Outside of work, I spend more time with you than anyone else, and we argue most of the time, or don't speak at all."

"We get along okay, and your mother—"

"Everyone's mother loves them, Dad. And we coast along, but I still don't know a lot about you, not really."

"You should know me fine by now. I'm the guy who raised you, provided for you, sent you to college, remember?" Clay tried to say this with a smile, to soften it, but he was good and pissed off. What did Chris know about mothers? He had the best there was, and probably thought the Addys of the world were standard issue.

"Tell me about your mother, Dad."

"I'm not going over all that again. The past is the past."

"Someone once said those who forget the past are condemned to repeat it," Chris said.

"Yeah? Well, he probably was a rich kid whose folks never got their hands dirty. Put him to work on a farm sunup to sundown, seven days a week, year-round, kill off the only people who love him, then send him to war, and I'll bet you dollars to doughnuts he'll want to forget the past in no time flat!"

"Point taken," Chris said. He sipped his coffee, waiting for Clay to calm down. "But I still want to know about all that. It's part of you, and you're part of me. Everything I do, Dad, is about looking into people's lives. I know more about most of my suspects than I do about you."

Clay wrung his hands, massaging his arthritic knuckles. He knew Chris was good at his job, and a big part of that was being an interrogator. Chris could keep at him, advancing and retreating, but always coming back to the question until he found a way to ask it that Clay couldn't deny. He needed to steer the conversation away from mothers and fathers and the world before the war. After the war, that was his world. Why did Chris need to push him back, back into the past, where the killing and the dead lived? Why couldn't he live out his years here, up on Buckwheat Hill, have a cup of coffee with his son, talk about baseball, maybe?

"What else do you remember, besides the train station? How about the airport?"

"Yeah," said Chris, accepting this bit of offered memory. "Markham Municipal Airport. We used to drive out there and watch the planes. You'd let me sit in your lap and help you drive out on those back roads."

"I forgot that part. We had an old Studebaker back then." Clay could see the bright red finish, the chrome steering wheel, and could feel Chris on his lap, tiny legs dangling over his, small hands gripping the wheel. The window was down, he had one arm resting on it, and the warm breeze swept over them. He smiled, glad to have the memory back.

"Did you ever drive on your father's lap?" Chris asked.

Clay got up. Goddamn it! Things were so much easier when Chris was a child. He could tell him stories, put him on his lap, watch Piper Cubs land and take off, it was all wonderful. If he wanted more, it was always more of what Clay had to give, which was fine with him. But Chris turned some sort of corner when he was fourteen or so. He started wanting more of what Clay didn't have. Money, new cars, cool clothes, whatever was beyond reach, more than Chris should reasonably expect out of life, that's what he wanted. Clay had no concept of that desire. He was alive, made a living, had a good wife. Period. It was enough.

He was Chris' father, had done everything he knew how to do to raise him, but still that wasn't enough. More, more, more. A grown man now, and Chris was still following after him, wanting to claim his birthright. If he only knew.

Clay turned away, faced the stove. He had to put that thought away. He took a deep breath. Calm down, speak naturally, remember who you are.

"Nope. Too damn busy on the farm for that." Clay poured himself more coffee. He didn't offer any to Chris. He leaned against the counter and raised the cup to his lips. It was the dregs of the pot, gritty and acidic on his tongue.

"You've never wanted to go back?"

"No reason to. Everyone's dead by now, the place is probably a development, worse than this place. We used to be able to see clear down to the Polish Cemetery."

"What was it like?"

"Looking at the Polish Cemetery?"

"Jesus Christ! Talking to you is a waste of time."

"Chris, be reasonable, will you?"

"I know more about Bob and what he did in the war from working with him than I do about you. I saw how you reacted at the funeral yesterday, it had to have an effect on you. What was that like, how did you feel?"

Clay felt his stomach drop out. The funeral was a blur except for the volleys and the airplane. That march across the open field and the Me-109s were more vivid, more real in his mind. He wanted to scream at Chris, tell him about the bodies cut in half, arms flying through the air, dead men, screaming men, still in his head, clearer every day. Six decades of self-discipline took over, and he said nothing. Nothing was best, since one thing would lead to another and then everything he ever did would be open to inspection, judgment, penalty. Nothing is best.

Seconds passed. Chris watched his father, waiting. Clay stared out the window.

"Forget it. It's almost seven, I gotta get up to Hartford." Chris took his cup to the sink and dumped the coffee. He clipped on his holster and badge, put on his jacket, and stood in front of his father. They were eye to eye now, no more looking up to see his face at a great height. Clay could see the muscles along Chris' jaw clench and unclench, and the raw power of an angry armed man flowed over him.

"We have our own secrets, Dad, but at least they're between us, something we have in common. Didn't Mom ever ask you about your childhood, the farm, the war? All those forbidden things you won't talk about, doesn't it drive her crazy? How can you cut that part of yourself off from everyone else?"

It wasn't the first time he had heard this from Chris, but his son had never asked him about Addy that way before. What was he supposed to say, that she was a good woman, accepted him as who he was, didn't ask useless questions, so why do you? Addy's acceptance of him was a cocoon. Chris' questions came like wasp stings.

"It wasn't pretty. But what's done is done. Far as I'm concerned, my life started when I moved here, met your mother. You're part of that, why isn't that enough for you?" Clay spoke in a whisper, his voice nearly quivering, every effort expended to keep a lid on it, not let anything else out.

"Ever since I was old enough to put things together, I've felt there was a missing piece you kept from me. Don't I deserve to know everything about my father? Is it something terrible? Do you think I'll be ashamed of you?"

"You've known me all your life, Chris, what more do you want? Do you think I'm a terrible person?"

Clay felt his voice break, tried to keep the challenge in his tone, but afraid the question had come out wrong, as if he really wanted an answer. But Chris wasn't picking up on nuances now.

Even a trained police interrogator misses things arguing with his father.

"People don't start their lives at twenty-two, a lot goes on before that. And you're capable of terrible things. Believe me, I know."

"Yep, that you do."

Chris started to say something. Clay saw the anger flash in his face, the same anger that he wore as a younger man but now kept in check, fastened away, clipped down like his gun and badge. Then the flash was gone, and Chris turned away, resting his hands on the sink.

"Good-bye," Clay said as he left the room.

Chris took a deep breath, and exhaled, shaking his head. So many missing pieces to his father's life. He grew up hard, nearly alone, and went off to fight a war, but hardly spoke of either. The war, he could understand. But what happened before that? What else happened after that he didn't know about? What he did know hinted at dark possibilities.

He stared at the countertop. The glass his father had left stood alone. It had come out of the cupboard clean. There would be no other prints on it, only his father's.

Why not?

No, he couldn't. It wouldn't be right. A violation of state regulations, for one thing. But, that could be finessed. What wasn't right was a son investigating his father. Then again, it wasn't right for a father to withhold himself as much as his did.

He took a small plastic bag from a drawer, stuck two fingers inside the glass, lifting it up and dropping it into the bag. He walked out the back door.

Clay heard Chris pull the unmarked Crown Vic cruiser out of the driveway, and down Dexter Avenue toward the highway. He thought he heard the chirp of tires peeling out, anger and frustration pressing down on the accelerator, the last word in the argument. My son the state police detective, and he's just aching to solve the mystery of his old man. Good luck with that one, kid.

Clay stood in the kitchen, alone. Alone. It was best this way. What else could he do? Terror and shame knocked at the door every day of his life, and he had held off this long. A little while longer, and he could rest.

He waited in the kitchen, listening for the bedroom door to open. The ticking of the clock filled the empty room, and the rest of the house was in silence. He felt his skin prickle, and he strained to hear the muffled sounds of Addy preparing for the day.

Tick tock, tick tock.

Clay knew, before the next second passed, that he was utterly alone. Knew it as a man knows when he steps on a mine, the hard feel of steel under his foot, and everything around him takes on an otherworldly cast, mocking him with what he once took for granted. You will never again have this, this normalcy, the reliability of love and companionship.

He stood and stepped away from the table, advancing to the bedroom, his hand on the wall, steadying him. He opened the door. The curtains were still drawn, and Addy's head rested on the pillow, eyes closed, one hand out of the covers, as if she were about to throw them off and get up.

Clay took her hand, felt the coldness.

"Oh, Addy, oh Addy."

He fell to the side of the bed, clutching her hand, willing warmth back into it.

CHAPTER SEVEN

1945

"MOMMA! MOMMA!"

Shut the fuck up, shut the fuck up was all Jake could think as he ducked below the window to put a fresh clip in his M1, holding the bolt back and slipping it in, bright brass and steel gleaming as wisps of smoke drifted up from the over-heated receiver.

"Momma—ahhh!" Cooper cried as he writhed on the floor. Everyone was firing as fast as they could, but Jake could still hear him. Shut the fuck up, goddamn you sonuvabitch!

Jake gritted his teeth, squeezed his eyes shut for a second as bullets struck the wall behind him, scattering plaster and dust across his back. Noise surrounded him, the heavy, steady stammer of the BAR's automatic fire from upstairs, where Big Ned and Miller had a good field of fire. Jake was downstairs with Shorty, Tuck and Clay, each of them firing through the three windows and smashed door of the farmhouse. Cooper, through it all, screaming for his mother, legs thrashing on the floor, holding his belly as dark red blood seeped between his fingers, his head arched back as if he were trying to get as far away from the pain as he could.

Jake swung his arms, hoisting the M1 up onto the shattered window frame and saw blurs of white moving out of the woods, darting between small folds of ground between the fir trees and the village. If you could even call it that. He focused on one, squeezed the trigger twice, hoping as much for the sound to drown out Cooper as for a hit. The German went down, Cooper kept on, momma, momma, momma.

Fuck you, fuck you, fuck you. Jake chanced a glance at the

barn, off to their right. It was burning, but he still heard rifle fire. Two squads had hunkered down in there last night. Two other squads had taken over the two small, single story houses that straddled the one road in this tiny village. Jake could hear shooting, the clear fast crack of M1s coming from those houses, but he couldn't see anyone, couldn't tell how many.

He ducked down and popped up on the other side of the window, two more shots, then down again. Don't give them a target. His breath came faster and faster. Up again, this time four Krauts running right at the house, rifles in one hand and grenades in the other. They were yelling as they came, strange words shrill in the clear air. Everyone fired at them in the same second, screaming their heads off too, as fear tore roars from their throats, as loud and hot as their gun barrels. Jake thought he heard Cooper join in, lending his awful shrieks to the struggle.

The four Germans were cut down, tumbling forward on their own momentum, arms and legs flailing wildly, bodies spinning, their screamed oaths reduced to silence, replaced by the grunted, exhaled acknowledgement of pain and death. Grenades slipped from limp hands, two exploding among the downed men, shrapnel ripping into lifeless flesh, decorating their white camouflage winter smocks with holes of charred black and red. Two other grenades bounced forward, exploding in front of the house, yards short of their target.

Jake heard Clay drop his rifle, saw him reach his hand up to his cheek. As fast as he dropped it, Clay had the weapon in his hand again and turned his face toward Jake. He held his eyes wide open, making sure he could still see, presenting his face like a child hurt on the playground. Am I okay? He felt blood but not pain. Clay knew that in the frenzy of firing and killing, fear could numb a wound, and maybe his face was shot through, ripped open, teeth and jaw visible and naked.

Jake rubbed a dirty thumb over Clay's bloody cheek, felt a tiny sliver of metal, pulled it out and flicked it away. Nothing, just a piece of spent shrapnel. They both went back to their work. Clay could feel the sticky blood from his cheek as he rested it against the stock of the M1, sought a target in the tree line, and fired, once, twice, take a chance, three times, then down.

Fucking Krauts were everywhere. No warning, no bombardment, not even mortars. A dawn charge from the tree line, a horde of white-clad demons whooping and yelling, firing from the hip, going for the sudden shock, hoping to overrun the platoon that held the village. Jake had seen one of those first wild shots hit Cooper, as he walked by the window, in one side and out the other. Before Cooper hit the floor everyone else was at a window, trying to stem the tide of Germans with a wall of rifle fire. Not a moment to spare for mercy or morphine, so it was momma, momma, momma, over and over and over. Each man knew how much time it would take to crawl to Cooper, get out a morphine syrette, hold him down, jam it in. He'd probably grab at you, ask you if he was going to be okay. Two, three, maybe four minutes, and there wasn't a second to spare, not with beaucoup Krauts swarming down the hill.

Jake couldn't believe it. They kept coming, out over the two hundred yards of clear ground, no good cover between the houses and the forest. He swore they were drunk, the way they yelled and ran straight at them. He could smell the schnapps on the breeze, the odor released as they screamed unknowable things into the cold morning air. Curses, slogans, prayers, Jake had no idea. It wouldn't be the first time the Germans got their men good and plastered for an attack. Jake didn't like fighting drunks. They didn't have enough sense to take cover or turn and run, they just kept coming at you, as likely to smash your head in with a rifle butt as shoot you.

Duck down, new clip in, watch out for Cooper thrashing around, get up, shoot, shoot, move, shoot, duck. Momma momma momma, Cooper begged. Jake had heard that cry before. He'd heard mother, mommy, mama, mom, and momma, he'd even once heard a guy cry out for his auntie, but it was all the same, and it was the one thing Jake hoped he didn't scream for if he was hit, down on the ground, crying like a new born babe and just as bloody.

Another clip in. Jake lost count of how much ammo he used. Bullets from a heavy machine gun raced across the front of the house, blowing away the stucco finish and sending chips of granite flying, the sharp flinty odor of the split rocks mingling with the coppery smell in the air, the odor of a welling pool of blood. Chalky plasterboard exploding in the room as rapid fire went through the windows and doorway. Everyone was down now, curled up, face to the floor, hugging their rifle and waiting for the fire to lessen. It didn't. This wasn't random fire from drunken riflemen. This was a MG-42, set up in the woods, pouring over

1200 rounds per minute into the house, sounding like a chainsaw revved up high it fired so damn fast.

Jake looked over to Clay. They both knew they had to get out. They were pinned down, and that meant there were probably Germans working their way around either side. The MG would keep up firing until they were close enough to throw grenades in the windows. As soon as the MG went silent, they'd move in for a close throw and then there'd be less than a minute to live. Clay glanced over to the windows, then to the back door. Quick nod of agreement, and Jake crawled backwards to Cooper. Maybe there was time.

Clay crawled, flat as he could, to the narrow stairs. Shorty and Tuck had taken all this in and Tuck gave a hand signal to Clay, pointing towards the kitchen and the back door. They'd head for the rear of the house to check for Krauts on their flanks. Clay got to the base of the stairs and was about to yell for Big Ned and Miller, but he didn't have to. Big Ned looked down from the top of the stairs. Bullets coming in the window chewed up two or three steps, just the height of the window opening. Wood splinters showered Clay as Big Ned shook his head, and cupped his hand around his mouth.

"We'll go out the back window," he said, gesturing behind him with his thumb, and then pointing down. A nod and Clay was gone, slithering backwards to the door at the rear of the house. He crawled over shattered furniture, crockery, horsehair stuffing from an old couch, broken glass, crumbled plaster, shell casings, and blood, but nothing mattered, nothing but getting out, getting out now. He got back to Jake, flat on the floor next to Cooper, who was covered in white dust from all the debris sent flying by the bullets that split the air just two feet over their bodies. Before each thud as a bullet hit the wall, a sharp crack, like a bullwhip, sounded above their heads. Clay touched his helmet to Jake's so he could talk into his ear and be heard.

"Big Ned and Miller are going out the back window. Shorty and Tuck are at the back door, we gotta go now."

Clay tried to ignore Cooper. He was an unsolvable problem. He was dying, and there was nothing to do about it, nothing that wouldn't get at least one other man killed too, and there was no sense in that. Cooper coughed and tried to spit, to clear his mouth of the dust. It hurt, and he spasmed, shrieked, no words this time, only pure terror and agony that came out high pitched and seemed to have no end.

"Go," said Jake, "right behind you. Take my rifle." He pulled out a morphine syrette and jammed it down on Cooper's thigh.

"You can't carry him."

"I have to."

The machine gun stopped. The noise that had been at the center of everything dropped away. It was quiet inside the house, but Jake could still hear the sounds of firing from the other buildings. A section of wall fell away, chewed loose by all the slugs hitting it. As it hit the floor a cloud of dust kicked up, the noise strange in the sudden silence. Even Cooper noticed, or maybe it was the morphine calming him. His leg was still quivering but his eyes focused on them for a second, as if he wanted to tell Clay, yes, he has to, he really has to.

No time to argue. Go. Clay took Jake's rifle and dragged it alongside him. He went out through the kitchen and crawled to the back door. He could see smoke from the burning barn and figures running across a distant field. Big Ned and Miller were hugging the wall out back, putting on gear they had tossed out ahead of them.

"Where's Jake?" said Shorty.

"Coming. What's the plan?"

"Angle left," said Tuck. "Smoke might cover us. Into the woods over there." He pointed to small stand of leafless trees. Not much cover, but something.

"Go," said Clay. "Now."

No one asked a question. Shorty and Tuck sprinted out of the door, Big Ned and Miller following. Clay craned his neck out the doorway, left and right, looking for Germans. Jake! Hurry the fuck up! No time, no time, com'n!

Jake stared at Cooper's stomach, pulling back a hand that covered the wound. Cooper's coat was open and Jake could see the two holes, right below each ribcage. Blood welled up and Jake could feel Cooper's hand tremble as he held it. He sprinkled sulfa powder over the wounds, not even bothering to cut open the clothes. No time, and he didn't want to know how bad it was.

"What—ahh." Cooper grimaced as Jake put a compress bandage on his stomach and wound gauze tape around him, lifting him by the back, twice, to get the tape tight over the bandage. He couldn't tell if it covered both holes, but it had to do.

It had to. No time, no time to explain, he had to go, now. Jake felt his heart beating, thumping and pounding against his chest as if it wanted to get out of here all by itself. His breath came in shallow gasps. Sweat flushed out on his skin and he felt empty inside, everything drained out. Go.

He got up in half crouch and grabbed Cooper by the collar, dragging him out into the kitchen, over the shattered remnants of a cozy living room. Ain't that funny, a living room, Coop? Sorry I can't apologize for this, it must hurt even with the morphine, I didn't dare give you more, shut the fuck up now.

Cooper shrieked and wailed, momma momma momma over and over again as the movement pulled at his torn insides. His arms flailed against Jake as he tried to stop whatever was causing his ungodly pain. In the kitchen, Jake went upright, taking a chance since the Krauts weren't firing. They must be close to the windows now. He turned to lift Cooper under his arm and Cooper screamed louder, his face a twisted frenzy of fear. Jake struggled to move him through the tight space in the kitchen, pulling him like a reluctant child. Cooper grabbed at the edge of the stove, a big cast iron cook stove, putting all his remaining strength into that one grip. Jake pulled at him, trying to free the grip that held them both there. He froze as he heard a clunk clunk from the living room, then a third clunk, as three grenades were tossed in. He slammed his free hand down on Cooper's wrist, breaking it maybe, not caring, holding onto Cooper under his armpit as he leapt out the back door, hitting the snow packed ground hard as explosions blasted out from the house. Shards of glass and wood sprinkled over them, white lace curtains fluttering in the dark smoke billowing out of the doorway and window.

Jake looked up and saw Clay about twenty yards out, down flat in the snow, his M1 aimed to the left, giving them cover. Jake knew there were Krauts a few yards away, and he was going to have to put his back to them. This wasn't going to be easy. He didn't want to do it, but he had to. He couldn't make sense of it, but without thinking about it he knew he had to try and save Cooper. The poor kid was crying for his mother, and all Jake could do was curse him, curse him for having a sweet mother, loving her, loving something Jake could never think of without anger, disgust, shame, and hatred gnawing at him. It wasn't fair. Jake felt as if his cursing added to Cooper's agony, and if he could just get him back he'd be square with him.

Clay signaled Jake to come on, get a move on. On his knees, Jake lifted Cooper by the arms. Cooper had a wide-eyed look like a fish on a hook, struggling against a pain he couldn't understand. His mouth was open, gasping, a wheezing sound coming with each breath. Jake draped him over his shoulders, fireman style. Cooper yelped as his own weight pressed down on his wounds jammed against Jake's shoulder blades.

Momma, momma, momma begged Cooper, as if his momma could stop all this if she only tried. Momma!

Jake knew it wouldn't do any good to tell him to shut up, that the Krauts might hear and follow the sound. They knew what it meant, as he knew what the cries of mutti mutti meant coming from German boys cut down in front of their foxholes. Cooper was somewhere else, maybe in his childhood bed, with his sweet momma spooning some sort of medicine into his mouth, placing her warm hand on his forehead, tucking him in, telling him to say his prayers. Jake knew that feeling too, but Jake also knew it was a lie.

He saw Clay get up and run ahead of them, letting Jake see where he was going, turning and swinging his M1 left and right. Jake had his back to the Krauts, but Clay was his eyes, his protection, his buddy, his brother.

Momma, momma, where'd you go?

Jake pushed off with each step, trying to run as fast as he could with Cooper on his back and a foot of snow at his feet. Cooper's blood on his neck felt thick and sticky, the weight of him compressing his thighs as he lifted each leg, pulling it clear of the snow and then letting it down, crunch, through crusted ice. His lungs heaved as he tried to take bigger gulps of air, trying to feed them, to keep his legs lifting up and down, up and down. He heard himself breathe in and out, gasp and groan, his sounds mingling with Cooper's in a crescendo of agony.

Ow, momma, ow, momma.

Jake heard a shot. His head was down, eyes fixed on the snow, concentrating on each step, trying not to think about the weight, the pain in his lungs and legs, about Cooper, about Ma. M1, must be Clay. He lifted his head, saw Clay get up and sprint to a tree trunk, settle down behind it and fire another shot.

Shit. Krauts at his fucking back. Holler all you want, Coop, might be the last chance you get. Up, down, each leg feeling like it was on fire, his breath coming in fast, deep swallows. The air seemed thin, not enough oxygen to feed his starving lungs.

Momma.

It was a whimper, not a yell or even a cry. Don't you give up on me now you sonuvabitch. You got a real momma, then you hang on, you might see her again. Don't die, and if you do it ain't my fault. It ain't my fault I cursed you, I just couldn't listen no more.

Ohhhh.

It ain't your fault, and it ain't my fault. That's what his big sister Alice said to him when he held the birth certificate up to her. He was going to join the Army at seventeen, not wait around for the draft to get him on his eighteenth birthday. He needed proof of his age, and waited until his folks were out one night to paw through the cardboard box they kept important papers in. He found it, with his name, place of birth listed as Pottsville Hospital, and his birth date. Father's name, unknown. Mother's name, Alice Burnett.

The air broke over his head, the singing crack of a bullet zinging by. He heard Clay fire, four shots, rapid fire. He couldn't look up, couldn't spare any wasted effort. His legs were too heavy to clear the snow, and he slowed as each boot dragged against the thick whiteness. His arms ached from holding Cooper, his chest felt like it was on fire, and his mind worked to clear the memories away, put one foot in front of the other, lift, move forward. Lift, move forward. Momma.

Maybe I should fall down, maybe they won't see me or think I'm dead. Maybe I will. No. Keep going. More shots. What was happening? Who was still alive?

Left leg, lift. Right leg, lift. He felt sweat racing down his backbone. Sweat streaming off his temples and in his mouth, salt. Sweating, crying, bleeding, dying, it all blurred together into a single purpose. Save Cooper so he wouldn't be cursed, so it wouldn't be his fault.

Ain't your fault, Jake. Ain't my fault neither. Don't say nothing. Don't tell nobody. Alice, just thirteen years older than him. Alice, his big sister. His momma. But then who was Ma? Alice's Ma, not his. Grandma to him was more like it. It was two days later Jake realized who his father was. There was a picture of Pa and Ma on their wedding day, he was dressed in a suit, last time he ever wore one, but young Pa had the same face that Jake was growing into. Everyone said so. Same dark hair, eyes, nose. Jake was a little softer around the mouth, maybe, but he could see the man he'd become. And that scared him, more than Pa's switch ever did. His Pa was his father all right. His sister's too, and she was his mother. Made that way by the man he'd grow up to be. God damn it all to hell.

Jake saw snow explode to his right. No strength to weave, zigzag, no strength to do anything but keep going, slow as molasses now, heading for the trees. That must be Clay ahead. Com'n Coop, almost there. He heard a small groan, as if Cooper was saying, about time, too.

He fell. Flat out, face down in the snow. Cooper rolled off him, pitched forward, didn't move. Jake got up on his knees, crawled to Coop, wanting nothing more than to curl up in the snow and sleep, get away from this weight he had to bear, get away from the memories of Alice and Ma and that bastard Pa. No, wait a minute, I'm the bastard, right? Right, Coop? He started to laugh, then grabbed Cooper by the collar and pulled him toward the trees. He could hardly see. He slipped in the snow and fell again as forms appeared around him, and he heard the BAR bang bang bang bang like it was right next to his ear. Big Ned, Coop, Big Ned's here. Maybe he knows, maybe word got out to Michigan that Jake Burnett's Pa fucked his daughter and she bore him into the world and that everything he knew was a lie. Maybe the Germans knew too, and that's why they wouldn't kill him.

Jake gave up. He felt hands pull him into the trees. He heard Clay say something as he carried him along but he couldn't make it out. Miller had him by the other arm. More men were here, the other squads in retreat too. Not everyone though. Not by a long shot. Jake felt his head clear, slowly. Deeper in the woods, behind a ridge lined by pine trees, they stopped. There were maybe twenty of them, should have been thirty or so with the replacements they got yesterday, the ones still alive this morning anyway. Jake saw Shorty and Tuck carrying Cooper, limp in their arms. They set him down. Big Ned and Miller were up on the top of the ridge on lookout. Jake sat by Cooper, holding his head in his hands, trying to get his breathing back to normal. Clay offered him a cigarette but he wagged his hand back and forth, no thanks. He shivered, the sweat freezing on his skin. His clothes were damp and clammy. His teeth started to chatter as his body desperately fought for warmth.

"That was a long way to go to carry a dead man, Jake," said Shorty.

Jake lifted his head from his hands. Cooper was silent. His mouth was open, as if he died calling for his momma. Jake couldn't believe it, didn't want to believe it, and couldn't understand his own reaction either. Cooper was a replacement. Replacements died, that was it. Why get all worked up? He put his hand to Cooper's face, felt the cooling skin, the life gone, no mother's touch bringing it back.

"He was alive, out there," Jake said. "I heard him."

"You tried, Jake," Clay said. "He would've died in the house anyway."

"Why couldn't he hang on? God damn." Jake threw his helmet on the ground, wishing he had the strength to hit something, vent his rage, but the anger died inside him, no fuel left to feed it. The back of the helmet was covered with blood, Cooper's blood from where he had been draped over his shoulders. Coop had been alive, he knew for sure, at least until he fell. Why did he fall? Coop had grunted, he had heard him. Jake leaned forward, lifting Cooper by the shoulder and turning him over. There, right under his left shoulder blade, a bullet hole. Straight on into the heart. Coop had taken a bullet for him. All Jake had wanted to do was save him, to bring this child back to his momma, to keep him from seeing anymore sights like his buddies blown to pieces, to let him feel what Jake never could, never really did, and never would. Feel his mother's embrace, welcoming him home, caring for him.

Tears came to him. He didn't sob or blubber, not that he cared. He was glad it was quiet though, this crying over Cooper's body. He sniffed and rubbed his nose with his sleeve, then brushed it across his eyes. He took Cooper's dog tag, leaving its partner for Graves Registration.

"Is there an officer around?" Jake asked. Tuck laughed and spit, that was the only reaction to that question.

"Non-com?"

"Sergeant Spinelli got it in the barn. He was the last one in the platoon," a guy from First Squad said.

"You hold onto it, Jake," Clay said.

Jake dropped it into his overcoat pocket. He picked up his helmet and wiped the back of it on the snow, leaving a pink smear. Everything was cold, his feet, hands, face, his stomach, all coated in chilled sweat.

"We gotta find the rest of the Company," said Jake. "They should be due south of here." He twisted around, looked at the sun, and scanned the woods surrounding them. Yesterday they had attacked the German line. After the artillery barrage, the Germans pulled back, letting them take their positions without a major fight, including the small farm village the platoon had occupied. Obviously they had wanted it back. Maybe other positions too, so they had to find the rest of their unit before they were cut off and alone.

"That way," Jake said, pointing south. "Let's go."

No one objected to Jake giving an order. No one had a better idea. Jake sent a replacement from Baker's squad ahead to take point. He had Big Ned and Miller bring up the rear, which is where they would have trouble if the Germans followed.

They left Cooper there, and marked the spot on a map. They'd tell Graves Registration, and they'd be by when things calmed down, stacking up frozen bodies like cordwood in the back of their trucks.

Jake felt better walking, warmed a little by the exercise. He put his hand in his pocket, felt the thin stamped metal of the dog tag. Name, number, religion, blood type, everything that identified a man to the army. He could feel his own, pressed against his chest, taped together with electrical tape to keep them from making a sound, a precaution for a warmer season. When would one of them wind up in someone's pocket? He tried to imagine the day when he'd take them off himself, put them in a drawer, forget about them. Think about that drawer. A nice walnut dresser with some small drawers at the top for cufflinks, tie clips, that sort of thing. He'd put them in there, and once in a while take them out, and remember the moment he decided he'd never be going back to that goddamned town.

Momma, momma.

CHAPTER EIGHT

1964

CLAY FLIPPED THROUGH THE PAGES OF THE Meriden Record as Addy unplugged the ceramic coffee percolator and carried it to the kitchen table. She set it down hard on the formica tabletop, as if she'd misjudged the distance, thinking there was space enough to slow it down. Clay winced at the sharp noise as plates, forks and knives jumped and jangled. Without saying a word, Addy cleared the breakfast dishes away, brushed her hands on the apron covering her sea green skirt, and sat down with her husband.

Clay folded the newspaper as he watched Addy settle into her chair. She pushed strands of fallen hair back behind one ear, revealing a large pearl earring. The earrings had been her mother's, a gift from an early admirer, not her father. They were beautiful and perfect, but Clay thought they were nothing compared to the precisely rounded, soft, downy earlobes they sat on. He liked the way she always pushed her brown hair back on one side and not the other, leaving it loose so it hung alongside her face, like Veronica Lake. It made her mysterious, open on one side, offering a treasure to him, white pearl and pink skin. Closed on the other, a curtain of hair shutting her face off from view if she turned away from him, even a little.

Addy looked like a skittish bird settling on a tree branch. Her eyes floated back and forth, to Clay, the coffeepot, and out the kitchen window. Clay knew she wanted to talk. Addy had a way of clearing the decks before talking about something important. He understood she was checking everything, making sure there were no distractions. Coffee on the table, Chris gone to school, dishes in the sink. He waited for her to settle in. As she crossed her legs she fluffed the folds of her skirt, draping it just right across her knees, looking up at him, as if a thought had just occurred to her.

"Clay, how's Chris doing at work?"

"He's doing all right, I guess. He does what he's told. Has a little trouble being on time, though, ever since he started hanging around with that Tony kid."

"He's at the age when a boy doesn't tell his mother much," Addy said, as if she hadn't really listened to his answer, or was disappointed that Clay was so literal in his response. Or maybe that question hadn't been the important one, a way to work up to what it was she really wanted to talk about. As she rested her arm on the table and stared out the window, Clay watched the morning light on her face. It gave her a faint glow, and for a second he wondered if that's what she'd look like in a painting. A portrait of her face lit by the rising sun, with the one earring showing and her light brown hair curled behind the ear and flowing down into the opening of her blouse. She turned to him.

"What are you looking at?" she said.

"You."

She pulled her hair back with both hands this time, lifting and stretching her arms up behind her head as she drew her hair off her neck for just a second and let it fall. Clay watched the fabric of her blouse press against her breasts and doubted he could ever keep his mind off her when she arched her back like that. Did she know what she was doing? Did she move that way unconsciously, her innocence at odds with his desire? Did she know she was keeping him off balance like a boxer threatening with a right hook while aiming a left jab at his jaw? He could've asked, but then he'd only be left wondering if what she'd said was true or not. He also knew that asking might spoil it all, leaving him with an answer but losing the joy of watching her and wondering.

"Okay," said Clay. "The topic is Chris. You're right, he's at that age. Doesn't tell me much either."

"Do you ask him?" said Addy.

"Ask him what?"

"About his friends, what his plans are, what he's feeling," said Addy. "Whenever I ask him I get mumbles and evasions. What does he say to you at work?"

"I don't know; we talk about the job. I did try to talk to him about being on time, doing his homework—"

"I don't mean lecturing him, Clay. I mean talking with him. It's important for a boy to be able to talk with his father."

Clay wanted to slam his fist the table, but he sat quietly. He didn't know how to talk like that, to get his son to open up to him. Addy had no right. Chris had no right to turn surly, to change from a little boy to a secretive stranger. Everyone wanted something from him, something that felt out of reach, impossible. He knew what he was capable of, and what he wasn't. Why couldn't they see that? Why couldn't Mr. Fiorenza just let him be? Why...

Clay took a deep breath and let it go. Okay, calm down. Addy's being a protective mother, it's normal.

"We talked about smoking, too," said Clay, offering another father and son topic, knowing it was a mistake as soon as he said it. They hadn't actually talked, had they?

"You think he's smoking now?" Addy asked. She didn't seem surprised. Clay felt the question was more of a test for him.

"You know how it is," he said. "His friends smoke, so maybe he's trying to fit in. Kind of hard for me to tell him how bad it is, with cases of cigarettes piled up in the storeroom."

"So who are his friends these days, besides Tony?"

Clay tried to envision the other kids who'd been in Tony's car. He couldn't. They were a jumble of laughter, sideburns, and recklessness. If any of them had been Chris' pals when he was younger, they weren't recognizable now. Clay used to know their names, when Chris would have them over for birthday parties and family cookouts. Horseshoes in the backyard, with the kids standing halfway to the stake so they'd have a chance at a ringer. Now that they could make a regulation throw, they were nowhere to be seen.

"You know," Clay said, letting out a sigh, "I can't say. It's Tony this and Tony that. Chris seems to be one of his gang."

"Well, that worries me. Did you know Tony's been suspended from school?"

"For what?"

"Fighting, after school."

"Kid stuff, Addy, don't worry..."

"And carrying a knife, a switchblade. That boy is a real hoodlum, and I don't like Chris spending time with him."

"Jesus. Okay, I'll talk to him. He won't like it."

"He doesn't have to like it, Clay, he needs to hear it from his father. Talk to him at work, he likes being there with you."

"He does?" Clay couldn't keep the disbelief out of his voice. Chris showed up late, sometimes hardly spoke, and when they did try to talk it often led to arguments and misunderstandings. Or worse, silence.

"Of course he does! Yesterday he told me all about cleaning that grease trap for you and how you said he did a great job – in between those Beatles songs playing on the radio, anyway. It was our longest conversation this week."

"Huh!" Clay sat back in his chair and stared out the window. "I'll be damned."

Addy looked at him, one eyebrow raised. She got up, took off her apron, walked over to Clay and sat on his lap. She put her arm around his shoulders and kissed him on the forehead.

Addy leaned into him and Clay held her by the waist. He could feel her ribs, his fingers nestling in the spaces between them. They both looked out the kitchen window, a few houses dotting the slopped land, trees and fields between them. The tops of crosses and monuments in the Polish cemetery stood up above a fold in the landscape, gray sentinels guarding the horizon. Neither of them spoke, and quiet settled in around them. Clay heard the ticking of the clock on the wall, and the faster beating of his heart as he rubbed his right hand against the thin fabric of Addy's blouse. His left hand rested on her thigh, and he tightened his grip, moving his hand up her rounded hip, inhaling her scent, the soft odor of perfume and flesh on her bare neck. Turning his face toward her throat, he kissed her there, moving his lips up to the nape of her neck, pulling the white fabric aside. Oohh, he heard as he felt her quiver. His hand cupped her breast. Mmnnn, and she arched her head back, giving him room to kiss her, to touch her, and this time there was no question about it, no wondering at all.

The bed was a tangle of sheets, pants, lingerie, and her sea green skirt. Addy lay curled up next to Clay, her arm across his sweaty chest, one leg thrown over his as if she were wearing him. He watched her breathe, her chest filling, pressing against his side, her softness against his muscle and bone as she exhaled warm air out over his skin. Her cheek rested against his shoulder, inches from the knot of scar tissue that swirled out from below his collarbone, down the right side of his chest, disappearing between her breasts, shiny tissue marking a trail of pain that ended in the warmth of her flesh.

Clay tried never to touch it, but often found himself lying in bed, or standing in the shower, idly tracing it with his finger, running it up and down the scar, the odd rubbery, numb feeling strange even now. He fought to keep from raising his left hand to it, afraid to awake Addy, afraid of everything.

Clay wasn't shy about it. He didn't think of it as a disfigurement, exactly. It wasn't pretty, but it wasn't as bad as some he'd seen. Guys with big holes in their legs or arms where flesh had been blown away, open wounds that still oozed years later. Or lumps of jagged scar tissue, mounds of it, the result of a rush job in an aid station under artillery fire. No, his was pretty clean, compared. A smooth, curved line from chest to ribcage, front to side. He'd take his shirt off at the beach, no problem. Some guy his age might ask where'd you get that? He'd point, and Clay could tell right away if the guy already knew it was from the war. A vet would ask where, meaning Italy or Okinawa or in The Slot or over Germany in a B-17. Clay would answer, in the Ardennes, and ask where the other guy had been.

Vets knew not to ask how, not to ask for a story. Stories told themselves, sometimes unbidden, playing themselves out like a movie you couldn't get up and walk out on. Maybe over a beer or two in the backyard, the wives inside and the kids off somewhere. But the time and place had to be right, and the guy had to have his bona fides. If he did a lot of bragging and shot his mouth off about what a hero he was, Clay knew he was either an asshole or a liar, probably both. He might have been a rear area supply clerk who stole supplies headed for the front, the kind of guy twenty miles behind the lines, with a regular bed in a real house, who always had the latest and best cold weather gear and hadn't fired his rifle since basic. But if a guy was quiet about it, and sought the company of others who were marked with a scar, walked with a limp, jumped when a car backfired, well, then they might talk, quietly one night, as the fireflies came out, empty beer bottles clinking at their feet, their wives glancing anxiously at each other and out the kitchen window, standing together at the sink stacking dried dishes with a quiet clatter, hoping their men would discover they weren't the only ones who woke screaming in the night.

Clay closed his eyes, counting to six, then opening them. It was a trick, a magic trick that he used to travel in time, or rather, not to travel through time, to the past. Feeling the past come up on him, he'd close his eyes, count to six, and with any luck, here he was, in the present. If he wasn't, he'd do it again. One two three four five six.

If the past came on as a tidal wave, blindsiding him, the counting wouldn't work. But if it crept up on him, like a brushfire moving across a dry, grassy field, it worked just fine. At first it hadn't, but that was because he'd only counted to five. Then he added six, and that did it. If he needed to add more, there were plenty of numbers. Sometimes he'd frighten himself, seeing an old man, counting forever, searching for that magic number. Then the old man would die, his last breath hissing out an unimaginably high number, the really magical one.

Eyes open, Clay brushed Addy's cheek with his hand.

"Gotta go to work, honey," he said.

Addy opened her eyes so quickly Clay wondered if she had been sleeping, or waiting for him to move first.

"Cigarette run today?"

"Yeah. Car's all packed up. Did it last night at the tavern." Clay swung his legs off the bed and started to get up.

"Clay?" Addy said, as she sat up, pulling the sheet to her chest and pinning it back under her arms. Clay turned, swiveling one leg back onto the bed and looking at her. The skin of her chest, just above the white sheet, was shiny with beads of sweat from where she had laid against him. She pulled her hair back behind her left ear, smoothed the sheet against her thighs, and Clay knew she was finally getting around to what she had wanted to talk about.

"What is it?" he said.

"I wish you didn't have to be involved in that numbers business."

"I know, but it's good money, we've talked about this a million times—"

"No, let me start over," Addy said, shaking her head. "I want you to get out of it. The money doesn't matter, what matters is the example you set for Chris."

"Addy, it's not like I'm Al Capone."

"That's not the point. You could get arrested, go to jail. Doesn't that worry you?"

Clay got out of bed and gathered his clothes. "No, and it

shouldn't worry you either. It's not going to happen. Nobody goes to jail for the numbers."

"Chris is old enough to know what's going on, Clay. How do you think he feels, hearing his father is a small time criminal?"

"Where did he hear that?" As Clay closed his belt buckle his hands tightened and his words came out in a growl.

"In the grocery store last week. We stopped on the way home to pick up a few things for dinner. We met Mrs. McBride and Mary. In the check-out line we overhead her telling her daughter not to associate with Chris, since his father was a criminal, if only a small time one. I'm not sure which one she thought was the greater offense."

Clay laughed a bitter snort and sat down on the edge of the bed as Addy drew her knees to her chest. Anger had grabbed him by the throat but the image of Mrs. McBride in the market couldn't sustain it. Her husband ran a tool and die shop over in Milldale, paid the lowest wages around, and was being investigated for attempted bribery of state officials. He shook his head and looked at Addy. She covered her mouth and flicked her fingers at Clay, and he watched her try to maintain her composure.

"Okay," she finally said, gasping out a laugh, "maybe that's not a good example, but you know what I mean."

"What did Chris say?" asked Clay.

"I think it was something along the lines of thank God for that."

Clay smiled at the thought and clasped Addy's hands as they rested on her knees. They sat in silence, and the silence was comforting. Everything outside was demands and unanswered questions. Here, it was just Clay and Addy, and he felt at peace with her, a calmness settling into his bones in her presence. He knew himself well enough to know that she made him a better man than he could ever be on his own. He wondered what he gave her in return, and felt a flush of shame run through his body at the thought that maybe it wasn't very much at all.

"Addy, you know how much we have in the bank, right?"

"Yes," she said. "We have a nice little nest egg there." Addy kept the household checkbook and bankbook from Meriden Trust where Clay made regular deposits from the tavern receipts and his paychecks from Tri-State. After the expenses at the tavern, and money for household bills and spending money, there was still a nice addition to the balance each month.

"We can't risk losing part of that, not now, anyway," he said. "We couldn't afford it." Clay released Addy's hands and busied himself putting on his socks and shoes. He knew what the next question would be, and that his answer would be the same as always.

"How would I know?" Addy said, not even bothering to ask directly. Clay never would answer her questions about how much the numbers brought in and how much the tavern did. It was one deposit, and he refused to tell her how much came from each.

"Let's not start with that," Clay said, trying to keep the anger out of his voice. "I know plenty of guys who don't even tell their wives how much they make. They pay the bills, make the deposits, and give their wives money for the house. Your name is on the bank account, right with mine, you should be happy enough with that."

"All right, all right," Addy said, with a dismissive wave of her hand. "But let's figure out a way to get around the problem. I don't want to be arguing about this ten years from now."

"So what's your idea?" Clay asked, certain she had one.

"Let's use some of that nest egg now. We could add on to the back of the tavern, put a real kitchen in, remodel the bar, and make it a restaurant. I could help, Clay. Chris isn't home that much anymore, he doesn't need me here. We could work together, make Jake's Tavern a real nice family restaurant." Addy was leaning forward, her hands gripping Clay's arm, trying to force her enthusiasm into his body.

"And you don't run numbers out of a nice family restaurant," Clay said.

"No."

He moved his hand over hers and Addy jumped, as if shocked by her own intensity. It all sounded so simple, a grand plan to change their lives for the better. How could he tell her nothing came that easily? Not a restaurant or retirement from the numbers, not a pass from Mr. Fiorenza, not even respect from his son. The only thing he could count on was money in his hand. Wads of cash, greenbacks from the thirsty and the dreamers. Nicotine, alcohol, greed. Guaranteed income. It wasn't that he craved money, wanted it to spend on himself, buy anything fancy, other than a nice car for Addy. He craved security the way he craved time, things he'd felt the shortage of. He wanted life to go on smoothly, one day running into the next, money in the bank, pay off the house, retire, and then keep watching the morning sun over coffee. You needed money to do that, and he'd figured out a way to make plenty. Only now his plan had him by the throat. Addy wanted one thing, and Mr. Fiorenza was going to want another. It occurred to Clay that what he wanted hardly mattered anymore.

"It's complicated, Addy," he said. "Let's talk about it more later, okay?"

Addy nodded her head, holding the sheet up to her chest with one hand and covering her mouth with the other. She looked like she was ready to cry, holding back tears until Clay was out of the room, his footsteps on the stairs echoing in the hall. He got up, shirt in hand, and walked towards the bedroom door. He stopped and turned.

"Really, I'll think about it, and we'll talk later, okay?"

Addy dropped her hand from her face, threw the sheet off and ran to Clay. Silent tears were streaming down her cheeks as she threw her arms around him, pulling him to her tightly, her chin tucked into his neck as she spoke in a whisper.

"Clay, I won't stay with you like this. If you don't leave the numbers and whatever else you're involved in, I'm leaving you. You have to choose."

Addy pushed her face into his neck, her cheeks damp against the warmth of his skin. She pressed her hands into his back, as if she were trying to hold him in place, to remember the feel of his body in her hands. Clay stood frozen, his arms still around her in the confused embrace he gave her when she rose from the bed and ran to him. He heard her words, but their meaning seemed far off, a distant menace that seemed impossible on a sweet morning spent with his wife, in their home, coffee and sex served up together in a steamy brew.

"What?" Clay managed to get out. Addy dropped her hands and took a step back, away from him.

"I've tried to tell you every other way, but you haven't listened. I love you, Clay, but this is not the life I want with you. I will leave you if you don't change it, and I will do it soon."

Clay heard the words, saw Addy standing in front of him, naked and honest, unashamed, beautiful, brutal. He couldn't tell if she was waiting for him to say something. His thoughts were fuzzy, his movements thick. He couldn't figure out what to say, how to acknowledge what he heard. She turned, walked into the bathroom, slammed the door behind her. Lifting his hands to empty air, looking around the room for solace, Clay found none anywhere. He was startled when he came to his reflection in the mirror, holding his shirt in his hand. Compared to Addy's nakedness, his clothing seemed unnatural, dishonorable, a covering for lies and deceptions. He felt that red-hot core of shame inside of him as he cataloged the things he'd kept from Addy, things she'd never guess at, secrets he couldn't even imagine how to reveal. Watching himself, he put on his shirt, buttoned it, tucked it in.

The sound of running water came from the bathroom. Clay imagined Addy checking the water with her toe, swishing it back and forth, watching the steam rise up from the filling tub. The sound of Addy in the bathroom seemed alien and distant, separate now from him, the closed door too great a barrier to overcome. He left the room, shoes in hand, uncertain what to do next other than to sit on the stairs, put them on, leave the house, and go to work.

CHAPTER NINE

2000

CLAY BUTTONED HIS RAINCOAT UP TO THE NECK and glanced out the kitchen window one more time. It was raining, a steady patter of drops, not a heavy rain, but still he didn't like it. Rain wasn't good, it was slippery and slick, hard to walk in and worse to drive through. It turned the world gray and murky, and with each swipe of the windshield washer blade he had to readjust his vision, trying to interpret what he saw through the streaks. But, there was no getting around it. He and Addy had lived their lives around doctors' appointments, and now he had to go it alone. Doctors were the new officers that commanded his time, and he lived under their coercion. The doctors were there for his own good, like the officers who were supposed to take care of their men. They were aloof and snotty in the same way, the sick and elderly something to be handled, processed, tested, manipulated, like G.I.s in basic or on the battlefield. Hurry up and wait. Stand in line. Be on time for your appointment then wait two hours. Fill in these forms. Take off your clothes. Boredom, embarrassment, pain and death were the province of officers and doctors. They were a separate caste, a closed society, always behind the desk or standing over you in uniform, telling you your chances of survival. The petty gods of his life.

It had been two weeks since the funeral, and when Clay thought of Addy, the first thing was, what am I going to do without you? He felt guilty that he thought about himself, and not her. But still, they had been a team, and now he was alone. When he'd think she was the lucky one, the guilt only deepened.

Clay walked out of the kitchen, reaching his hand out to a

counter then to a chair, steadying himself while he navigated the linoleum as if it were a minefield. Traversing the breezeway off the kitchen, he opened the door to the garage. It was dark inside. He patted the wall to the right with the flat of his hand, feeling for the light switch. He rubbed the palm of his hand against the dusty grain of the unpainted sheetrock, sweeping it up and down as he held onto the handrail at the top of the four wide steps leading down to the garage floor. He found the light switch, and two bare bulbs lit up the interior of the garage. Next was the automatic garage door opener, a big red switch now easily visible. Flipping on the mechanism, it whirred as the pulley lifted the door with a series of grinding jerks. Rain splattered into the garage as he carefully held onto the handrail, planting both feet on each step before going down to the next.

The railing was another recent addition. Time was, he'd take these steps by twos, bend down and hoist up the garage door, pushing the weight up above his head like it was an afterthought. Now, he placed a frail, bony hand on bare wood, shuffled his feet on the scuffed steps, and prayed for balance. When did the simple act of starting the car turn into an ordeal, navigating darkness and depths as if he were walking underwater?

He opened the car door. A blue Saturn, two years old, a nice sensible car for an older couple. Roomy, easy to drive. It was the most boring vehicle he had ever been in, but that would probably have been his reaction to any new car. Other models might be fancier, but they were all the same. Plastic instead of chrome, digital readouts instead of dials. He turned the key and it started right up. Of course, the internal computer would make sure of that. No human intervention needed. No more tune-ups in the garage, changing your own sparkplugs or fiddling with the engine. Might affect the programming.

Clay let himself play through his usual list of complaints about modern life as he leaned his head back against the headrest. It gave him something to do while he waited for his breathing to slow down. Everything made him tired lately, and he was popping aspirin like candy for a headache that wouldn't quit. Funny, but the thing he disliked most about new things is that they seemed to come along when he was too old to enjoy them, too set in his ways to make room for them in his world.

So who said life would be fair? The future is here, but the joke's on you, you're too old to enjoy it. Clay twisted his legs out of the car, holding onto the steering wheel with one hand and pushing himself off. He grunted, got halfway up, and lost his balance. His other hand flailed at the door beam, trying to steady himself, but the garage seemed to be falling down around him as he fell back into the car, hitting the side his head on the doorframe. It was a small whack, but he saw stars and the headache thumped inside his skull. He closed his eyes against the pain but it was too much, and he had to open them, afraid the room would spin down around him. But the walls stayed where they should. Steadying himself, he gripped the steering wheel with both hands, pressing his forehead against it. Fear flooded his body as he tried to breathe and relax. Calm down, don't be an old fart about it. Tell it to the chaplain. Whaddy want, egg in your beer?

Closing his eyes again, he laughed, even though it hurt, but the memory seemed to drive the pain down a bit. Who drank egg in their beer anymore? He hadn't seen an egg cracked into a glass of beer since before the war. Although everyone in the Army complained all the time, no one would show any outward sympathy. The usual response was to tell it to the chaplain, he might give a shit. Or, to ask what did you expect, an egg and a beer? The Army might give you one or the other, but to expect both was plain unrealistic. The first time he had heard that was in a line at Fort Leonard Wood in Missouri. Supply clerks were issuing uniforms and Clay ended up with a fatigue shirt too large and boots too small. When he complained, he didn't get the correct sizes, he got, Whaddy want, egg in your beer? Move along.

Clay laughed out loud, oblivious to the pain. It was hilarious. That was his whole problem, in a nutshell. He wanted egg in his beer. Life was quite willing to offer up a nice, white egg now and then, and a cold glass of draft beer whenever he needed it. But no one was cracking an egg into his glass anytime soon. He could see what it would look like, a woman's hand holding the egg, giving it a quick, sharp rap against the edge of the glass, opening it up one-handed and letting the yellow yolk plop into the beer and turn golden as it floated to the bottom, the egg white trailing it down. A gentle bounce as it settled in. He saw the glass raised to his lips, felt the foam tickle his nose as he drank and drank, gulping the beer and letting the egg slide down his throat as easy as can be.

Clay smacked his lips, imagining the taste, and then forced

himself to open his eyes. There was no woman holding a white egg in her hand, no draft beer. He was leaning sideways in the driver's seat of his blue 1998 Saturn, on a rainy Wednesday morning, his legs shaky and his head pounding, and he was about to drive to the hospital. No egg, no beer.

Pulling himself up, Clay sat still for a minute. His left leg was out of the car and his right jammed between the brake and the accelerator. He waited for his breathing to settle down and the pain in his head to recede, conscious of the need to get moving, unable to get his limbs to coordinate with his will. Once it was all smooth motions. Lifting a beer keg and carrying it up the basement steps. Making love. Doing pushups. Diving for cover and coming up shooting.

Stop it, he told himself. It's only a fucking Saturn! He felt a surge of fury rise in his throat, frustration bursting out from the pit of his stomach, and he wanted to yell out to God, scream and damn him, but instead he beat the steering wheel with his fists, two, three times with each hand, hard, thumping it like a punching bag.

I used to dodge bullets, goddamnit! I jumped ditches and dug holes, I threw grenades, I shot people! Jesus H. Fucking Christ! I carried eighty pounds on my goddamn back through the snow, I jumped out of a fucking window two stories up, landed on broken concrete and ran like hell as bullets hit the street all around me. They couldn't fucking kill me then so why the fuck am I like this now?

Clay's hands hurt him as he ran out of words, but the anger pulsed in his head. He didn't think he'd sworn like that in years, maybe decades, and he wondered if he'd yelled all that out loud or if it had all been in his head. Confusion fueling anger, he grabbed his pants by his right knee and lifted his leg, turning out of the car and throwing it onto the concrete floor next to his other foot. He wanted to propel his body forward, make it do all the things it used to do without a thought. More and more he could see himself separate from his body, cursing its uselessness, the fragility of old bones and thin skin his enemy, seeking to destroy him, every day a victory, every fall and each unsteady, shaky moment a battle lost, complete defeat not far down the road.

Clay had killed an old man once. He looked old, in any case, no telling what his real age had been. The Krauts had been dug in front of some small village, when they surprised them with a hidden machine gun that killed three G.I.s right off. The fire held them up, keeping them pinned and wounding two more men until Red called for artillery support. Mortars hit the German position as another platoon worked its way through the woods onto their left flank. Explosions churned the ditch where the Germans fired from and a direct hit took out the machine gun. Between mortar bursts, screams rose up from the ditch and were blown back into silence as the next rounds hit, throwing up red-tinged geysers of smoke and soil. Red called off the mortars as the two platoons blasted the Germans with rifle fire from the side and front, the other platoon firing right down the length of the ditch. It was nearly a full company of Krauts, no shortage of targets. They tried to pull out, but they couldn't take the road into the village since there was no cover, and they'd be picked off. Instead, they took off to their left, over a small, low-lying field. They scrambled up a steep slope of loose, gravely soil trying to make it into the safety of the thick woods. Both platoons were firing at them as the Germans tried to find a foothold, their heavy boots digging into the gravel and long gray coats flapping as they slid back down, the brown, sandy soil, pebbles falling away beneath them. Some turned and fired back. Some raised their hands, but this wasn't a day for prisoners. There had been too many ambushes like this, Krauts opening up on them, then surrendering after they'd been surrounded and G.I.s were dead and dying all around. This was revenge, and as long as there was running, firing, screaming and yelling, it wasn't time for Kamerad, bitte, Kamerad, not yet. So the Germans kept clawing their way up into the woods, dropping their rifles and pushing each other up and into cover. The ones who made it kept going, crawling into the trees, no return fire. It was a turkey shoot. The platoons advanced, firing as they went, taking aim deliberately as they sensed their victory, their power over this mass of scampering sheep. Step forward, fire. Once, twice. Step forward, fire. Germans tumbled down, arms flailing, bodies jumping under the impact of the bullets. Finally they were only yards from the last of them. Clay had to stop to reload, and the slight halt to his pace and shooting broke the methodical killing frenzy. He wiped sweat from his face. Smoke and dust swirled around him as he watched one last German make it almost to the top. Clay was the closest to him, and he saw the German slide down a few feet, then start to work his way up again. The other members of the squad gathered around him and waited. It was like a show.

"Maybe we should take a prisoner," Shorty said.

"Halt!" somebody yelled at the German. Rifles were raised, and other voices called out for him to halt. Clay looked at the men around him, and then he yelled halt too, feeling that somehow it would be wrong to shoot this last man in the back after he had survived this far, knowing what it felt like, that blind rush for cover, all the prayers you ever knew running through your mind, over and over. Heavenly Father... hail Mary, full of grace...now I lay me down to sleep...pray for us sinners now and at the hour of our death. Amen, amen, amen.

But the Kraut didn't halt, he held onto his rifle and used it to push himself up the gravelly slope. He was almost to the top when Clay decided, fuck it, he didn't want to face this guy behind another machine gun at the next village. He should have halted, he had his chance. So Clay raised his M1, aiming square at his back, and squeezed off two shots. Bang bang. Two puffs of dust along the German's spine, a spray of red, and he tumbled down the slope still holding his rifle by the barrel.

It was quiet, except for the clacking of small stones that followed the body down. No one spoke. They all walked over to the base of the slope, checking the pile of bodies for any signs of life. Clay turned over the German and the man's helmet rolled off. His head was shaved close, but Clay could see by the gray stubble on his face he was an old man, too old for the infantry anyway. His mouth hung open, as if he had been gasping for air, winded by this last desperate bid for life. Clay could see his top row of teeth were gone. A really old man, gaunt, with thin, sunken cheeks, probably carrying his dentures in his pocket. The hand that gripped the rifle was blue-veined, bony, swollen knuckles looking huge around the barrel.

It was quiet in the garage. Clay looked into the mirror and saw the old man's face, slack-jawed and surprised. He held up his hands, already bruising dark blue from the hits to the steering wheel. Rubbing them together, Clay felt the thick aching knuckles and could almost see them embracing the gun barrel. It took a second to sink in, for the memory to fade in all its perfect clarity and the confused, murky present to take center stage.

Clay felt the gravel give way.

CHAPTER TEN

1945

UNDER A FULL MOON AND CLEAR SKIES THEY HAD walked most of the night. South, or as southerly as they could, detouring around icy ridges and steering clear of open spaces. You could read a book by that moonlight bouncing off the snow, and twenty dark forms moving across a pure white field would be seen by any Kraut with one eye half open. So Jake kept them in the thick woods, skirting open ground, off ridgelines where they'd be silhouetted against the night sky, moving south, moving to stay warm, moving to not stand still and feel lost and alone. As long as you're moving, you're going somewhere, and if you're going somewhere, you aren't lost, are you? So get a move on.

Sometime after midnight the wind picked up and what had been simply freezing cold became icy frigid bone-chilling cold. The snow glistened and cracked as the top layer frosted over, ice sparkles reflecting little pieces of moonlight like diamonds scattered over their path. Most of the men hung their rifles over their shoulder, warming their hands under their arms. Rustles of frozen cloth stirred up and down the line as they pulled and arranged what protection they had tighter, covering necks and faces, trying to keep the cold from blowing in and freezing the sweat that sheened their skin as they waited. Cold was the enemy now.

Jake stood next to a thick pine tree, shielding himself from the wind, waiting for Tuck to head back. Shorty, with his good eyes and few extra inches of height, had spotted something off to their left, up a small rise where pines lay on the ground, toppled by high winds, or axes, for a clear line of fire, firewood or a display of nature's capriciousness. Shorty had sworn he saw camouflage netting strung up on poles. No one else could make out a thing, but Jake knew Shorty had once spotted a German sentry on a dark night, two hundred yards out, even though the guy was standing still. It took the eyes of an owl to do that, so when Shorty said he saw something, Jake believed him.

Now Jake waited, listening to the sound of Shorty and Tuck making their way up the hill, boots crunching the brittle snow cover with each step. Jake winced, cursing the frozen crust, until he realized the noise was good news. If anyone was up there, they would have been shooting by now and tossing grenades at the noisy approach. So he leaned into the tree, getting as much of it between the wind and his body as he could, warming his hands under his armpits. Another noise rose up behind him, and he realized it was the echo of his own chattering teeth. Men pressed together, trying to gain a bit of warmth from each other, their bodies cooling down as they waited. The staccato clatter of their teeth sounded like castanets as the cold drove itself deep into their bodies, their brains responding, ordering jaws to spasm and run up some heat before everything frosted up.

Jake couldn't stop his own teeth from chattering any more than anyone else could. He felt the cold inside himself, and the fear too. Fear of noise, fear of drawing attention, fear of how the men looked to him, waited for his decisions. Up or down, move or stop, everyone wanting him to decide. Now here they were, closer to death than most of them understood. Jake knew that they didn't have much time left out in the open with this wind. They needed shelter, soon. Leaning his helmet against the tree, he let his cheek rub against the rough bark, the sensation allowing him leave where he was, for a precious moment. Closing his eyes, he left his freezing feet and shivering body behind, holding everything that would ever matter in that hard, cold, sticky pine bark on his cheek. The feeling stunned him. His whole future fell into place. He could see everything. A future as cold and lonely as this night, an agony of life, fear eating at him forever, as it did now. He wondered how scared everyone else was, if anyone felt the way he did. Alone, a freak of nature. Wrong, just plain wrong.

He knew he was cursed, cursed with bad blood, and he thought about the mark of Cain they'd told him about in Sunday school. Pa never went to church, but he always made Jake go, and Alice too. Maybe Pa knew he was damned and church was too good for him. Maybe he thought prayer might do them some good, or maybe he didn't want them around the house on the Lord's day to remind him what kind of sinner he was. Cain was a killer, and his mark was on all men. Some more than others. It ain't fair, it ain't your fault. Well then, whose fault was it? Whose fault will it be, with Pa's mark on me?

Jake heard crying. A whimpering, and he was afraid it was him crying, feeling more like a little boy than he had in years. He took off a glove and rubbed fingers under his eyes. Nothing but pine smell, gritty, sticky, pungent. Pushing his hand back into the glove, he turned and saw Clay with his arm around a G.I., leading him away from the other men. The guy was crying, sobbing, his breath all gone as he heaved in air between gasps and tears. Jake could tell he was a replacement. He was young, barely out of high school, red cheeks and wide wet eyes, coat dirty, but not yet worn at the edges from living in it day after day.

"I'm c-c-cold," he said, looking up at Clay, the effort to speak between sobs breaking his face, knotting his forehead, quivering his lips. Tears froze in tracks alongside his nose as he stopped to look at Jake.

"C-c-can't we s-s-surrender?"

Jake looked away, towards the hill.

"C'mon, boy," Clay said, his arm around his shoulder like a coach at school. "Let's walk a bit, it'll be okay, really. You know your momma don't want her boy giving up first thing. Where you from anyway?"

Jake heard the words and didn't care. Oakland. So what? What was that but a place to hope for, a home, a mother waiting by the fire or on the porch or at the train station, wherever mothers from Oakland waited for their Oakland boys. It had been years since Jake saw that piece of paper, held it up to Alice, figured out who was really who in his life and what that meant he was. But it wasn't until this very moment, leaning against this cold tree, that he understood he really would never go back to the way it was. Bad as the knowing had been, he'd always had it tucked away in the back of his mind that he'd go home a hero, maybe wounded, but nothing bad, and everyone would be waiting, waving little flags down at the train station, and that piece of paper would be long forgotten. Ma would cry and Pa would be proud and maybe smile a bit. But Ma was no one to him now, nothing but a woman too stupid to know what her man was up to, or too scared to stop him. She was no mother, no mercy, nothing. Pa was Pa and that was bad enough right there. Alice, well Alice was another thing. His big sister never again. She probably wouldn't even want him around, reminding her of the shame. Worked both ways, too.

There would be no going home. No one waiting at the station, no flags, no slaps on the back. They could all go to hell. He'd find someplace else to go, someplace safe, where he could keep his secret, where no one knew him, where his past was nobody's business. Jake felt his shoulders shake. Shudders flew through his body. It was the cold, it had to be the cold. Squeezing his eyes tight, he jammed his head against the tree, whispering a prayer to the frigid air, but it didn't stop the shivering or the chattering.

The cold carried Jake back to Pennsylvania, back to the deep winter of 1938, or maybe it was '39, when he and Tommy Owens had gone outside in a blizzard. Biting wind, like this. They were fourteen and foolish, daring each other into acts that were now dazzling in their simplistic stupidity. Bundled up in wool coats, they climbed to the top of Miller's Ridge, where you could look down into the valley and see the twists and turns of the old river, and feel the winds roaring up and slam into the hillside. Then, stripped to the waist, they stood bare-chested to the winds, hooting and hollering their youth and defiance, feeling their oats, daring the world to throw against them what it could. It seemed like it lasted forever, standing there, laughing, the worst winter they could remember harmless against their boldness. Did my teeth chatter? Did I shiver? Maybe, but it didn't matter. There was hot soup and a warm fire waiting for us, our whole lives left to live, and secrets still hidden in desk drawers and cold hearts.

A hand on his shoulder. Jake turned, half jumping, falling back against the tree.

"You okay?" Clay asked, trying to get a fix on Jake's eyes.

"Yeah," said Jake, "good enough."

"There," said Clay, pushing on Jake's shoulder, turning him towards the hill, pointing to Tuck slogging through the snow towards them, grinning.

"Goddamn, that boy's got eyes like a fucking hawk," Tuck said, heaving out frosted air as he tried to catch his breath.

"What?" said Clay.

"Kraut strongpoint up on that hill, what's left of it. Looks like heavy mortars, but they got plastered. Bomb craters all around, lots of empty ammo boxes, they musta pulled out."

"Yeah?" said Clay, waiting for the good news. He glanced at Jake and saw his eyes following the kid from Oakland as he walked back to the knot of men behind them. Jake's tired face had an odd look, hate or some sort of passion. One second he'd been staring blankly at the ground and then Oakland walked by and Jake's eyes widened, his lips showing a snarl as he stared at the kid's face. Clay wondered what was wrong. The thought struck him as funny. What's wrong? Lost, cold, hungry, darkness, Germans, minefields, and I'm worried about the look on Jake's face?

He focused back on Tuck, and realized the fatigue and strain of the fight this morning...no, wait, yesterday morning, and the freezing march through the woods was catching up to him. Tuck's face floated in front of him, and he realized Tuck was talking and he'd better listen.

"...one big dugout with a wood roof, and a bunch of good-sized foxholes, all with log roofs and camouflaged real good, and they're all lined with hay! These Krauts built first class, there's enough room for everyone. C'mon!"

Tuck took off back up the hill. Clay could see he was excited, so it had to be good news, but he was nervous. Kraut dugouts? What if they came back?

"Let's go, guys!" Big Ned said, clapping Clay on the shoulder. "We don't have a lot of choices." Miller followed him up the hill, along with the rest of the men. They hadn't heard everything, but anything was good enough for them. Someone to follow, an end to walking and a place to sleep. It was enough. They all filed by Clay and Jake, who still leaned against the pine tree. He looked almost unconscious, but Clay heard him counting.

"...fourteen, fifteen. You and me, seventeen. There was twenty of us."

"I've been watching for stragglers," Clay said.

"Don't think they straggled," Jake said. "I think they got the same idea Oakland did, 'cept they didn't ask. They went."

"Fuck."

"Yep. Let's get up there and find a spot."

The two men walked side by side up the hill, neither of them saying out loud what they both worried about. That right now, some dumb ass replacement was drinking schnapps with a nice

English-speaking German, probably smoking cigarettes in a warm house somewhere, safe behind the lines. Behind enemy lines. And telling him all about their escape, and how there was still a bunch of them out there, stumbling around in the dark, a bunch of saps, not like him. He was smart, alive, warm, and in his need to explain himself, excuse himself, he'd make them part of his story. And the German would agree, Ja, you are smart, you did the right thing. Then somebody would leave the room and give the signal for a search to start for twenty or so Amis who were too stupid to give up. They'd smoke a few more cigarettes until they got everything out of him they needed, then they'd throw him in a barbed wire cage and bring in the next smart guy, who'd be surprised at how nice the Krauts were and probably end up telling them the same story, about those dumb fucks wandering around out there, trying to get back to their lines. Trying to get home.

The big dugout was impressive. Wood plank roof, covered in dirt with pine boughs and rocks on top. One entrance at the rear, a narrow trench leading to an actual door, a wood frame fit into the cut earth. Inside, ten G.I.s were crammed in, body heat already building up as they lay next to each other on the soft hay. Wood boards were nailed to the supports. It looked like an underground room, but it smelled like a barn that needed mucking out. It was damp and musty, earth and hay soaking up the odors of the former and current occupants and filling the air with a sour smell, maybe cabbage or sweat, it was hard to tell. You couldn't stand up straight, but if you bent over or got down on your knees you could get around. A narrow firing slit with a view out towards the open fields ahead ran the length of the dugout. No one else looked out, but Clay and Jake at the door exchanged glances. A silent fuck passed between them. It was obvious this was a good position, and it was obvious why it had been shelled. And why it might be shelled again, for good measure. It was a hay-lined death trap, and either American 155mm shells or a German heavy weapons platoon would come calling sooner or later.

"Keep it quiet in here," Jake said. "We gotta move out soon as it's light."

He didn't wait for an answer. Head down, he pushed the door open and squeezed out. He watched as the other men split into pairs and went into foxholes. They were as elaborate, a thick roof of pine logs, with a rear trench leading to a hole that was covered by a blanket nailed to the logs. Hay-lined and wood planks inside too. Behind the main dugout was a firing pit that had been covered by camouflage netting strung up on poles and tied off to tree limbs. White fabric was pulled through the netting, moonlight gleaming off it. It was ripped and torn, flapping back and forth with the low winds.

"That's what I saw, Jake," Shorty said. "That fabric, it was moving and all lit up by the moon, and it was too even. I knew it had to be netting, I knew it."

"Nice job, Shorty, you saved our asses," Jake said, looking down into the firing pit to avoid Shorty's eyes. He didn't want him to see the worry on his face as he enjoyed his find. Two large mortars were twisted and blacked, the tubes bent from the explosions. Ammo must've gone off too, there were black gouges in the snow and bits of burned cloth that maybe had been uniforms. The snow was trampled where it wasn't blown away, and wooden crates and other debris were scattered all around them. A blackened helmet with a hole in it, unrolled bandages, all signs of casualties and a quick pull-out.

"Look down here," Clay said, nodding his head down to the ground in front of him. The snow was drifting back over the crater, but where the shell had hit was unmistakable. Right on top of a two-man foxhole. Pine logs were shattered and through the ruined roof were the churned up remains of two Germans. You could tell it was two only by the size of the hole and the fact that three hands were visible. Nothing else was in the right place or attached to anything. Blood had frozen them into a solid mass, clothing, helmets, bones and organs all waiting for the spring thaw. So convenient, dying in a small hole. Fill it in and pound down a marker. Foxhole, grave, it was all the same.

"We can't stay here long," Jake said, moving away, looking for an intact foxhole.

"Why not?" Shorty said, as if his feelings were hurt that his discovery was less than perfect. "We could wait..."

"Jake's right," Clay cut in. "Either the Krauts come back or this place gets hit again and it's us they find in the ground up here. We gotta get a few hours sleep, but then we leave, soon as the sun's up."

"Okay fellas, okay. Shit." Shorty dropped his head and went

off to help Tuck clear out a foxhole. Big Ned and Miller came over to them with something wrapped under their arms.

"We found three overcoats," Big Ned whispered. "Miller did, actually. Not enough to go around, but you could use them as blankets." He handed Jake a rolled up German greatcoat, then went over to Tuck and Shorty and gave them theirs. Miller stood there, a big grin on his face. It was as if Big Ned had tousled his hair after he caught a fly ball on a warm spring day. He'd done good, done good for his buddies, and Clay could see that thought light up his face.

"Thanks, Miller," Clay said, "you don't have a bad pair of eyes yourself."

"Thanks. They're all a little bloody, but your coat's an officer's, Clay."

Clay laughed and turned away as Miller chased after Big Ned, still smiling. It was strange how in the middle of this nightmare, normal thoughts and feelings still stood their ground. Like the odd look on Jake's face, or Miller being so happy at finding three dead men's coats. Little things that shouldn't matter, shouldn't even register in this deep dark cold night. But here they are, as real as if he were back in basic, or back home at a barbeque. Miller wanting to be one of the guys, to prove to them and himself that he was better than the fear that grabbed him and sent his legs running the other day. Jake needing something too, his eyes drifting toward something neither of them could see. Clay had no idea what it was or how Oakland figured in. Maybe Oakland had something Jake wanted, but what could that be?

Clay stood at the trench leading to the hole Jake had crawled into. He looked around, checking to be sure everyone had a spot and that things were quiet. Soft grunts and the rustling of hay, clothing and gear rose up from the ground all around him. Signs of life under the snow, reminding him of late winter back home, when you could feel the plants and roots underground, waking up, getting ready to emerge. The thought was soothing, and it dredged up from the depths of his mind the memory of when he first understood that everything comes back in the spring, nothing really ever died. He had been, what, six years old maybe? He could feel his hand grasping the branch of a bush growing by the front porch, rubbing his fingers against the buds bursting out, understanding that they could grow and bloom and die and come back again. It had seemed wondrous, a silent secret revealed to him alone. Looking back at the two Germans frozen in that hole, he wondered if they'd ever thought about that, and what might creep out of the soil in a few months and further bind them to the earth.

Above ground, it was silent, and Clay looked at the coat in his hands in the full moonlight. The collar was ripped, but the silver stitching was intact. Two sharp angled slashes like lightning bolts. SS.

Fuck.

Inside the hole there wasn't much light. Clay fixed the blanket as tight as he could behind him and reached out his hand. He felt Jake's leg and moved to the opposite side, his head by Jake's feet. The pine logs extended out over the firing slit, blocking most of the moon's light. Clay moved by touch and settled in. With his head propped up against one end of the hole, he stretched out his legs so they were touching the other end, next to Jake's head.

"There's bad news, bad news, and good news," Clay said.

"Save the good news for last."

"Okay. Bad news is that the guy who wore this jacket was SS."

"Jesus fucking Christ," Jake whispered. "And the bad news?"

"We don't have any extra socks. We both left our musette bags back at that house." Clay heard a groan and a half laugh. The groan was real, a pained sound pulled deep from Jake's throat. The laugh died in his mouth, but even so, Jake said what was expected of him.

"Sure glad there's good news."

"The good news," Clay said, "is that there's no more bad news."

They both laughed a bit, the completion of the set up and the punch line relaxing the tension. It was an old joke, an old routine. There never was good news, only an end to the bad. They had said it dozens of times before, maybe more, it was always the same, and they always laughed. But what really gave them comfort was that they'd said it so many times before, and here they were saying it again, which meant that one day they'd be somewhere else, out of this situation, one of them saying sure glad there's good news, in another place, another time. But this bad news was really bad. No fresh socks, and their feet were cold and soaked in sweat. The shoepacs they wore were waterproof, but they kept the moisture in, and after a long cold day and night, their feet were sweaty, damp and freezing. Trenchfoot became a real possibility, and they needed their feet. Trenchfoot out here was death, or a POW camp at best.

"Red was right about pockets," Clay said as he began to unlace his boots. Red never carried a pack. Everything he needed was stuffed in pockets. Shirt pockets, fatigue pants pockets, wool pants pockets, field jacket pockets, overcoat pockets, plenty of pockets. On their legs, arms, chest, everywhere. Red believed in having everything on him, so when he had to haul ass fast he only had to worry about his rifle and his helmet. On your head and in your hand, then run like hell. Extra socks were the most important item of clothing to have, and a lot of guys carried them in a musette bag slung over their shoulders, keeping their pockets bulging with ammo, first aid gear, grenades. Others, like Red, put everything in their pockets. It made it harder to sleep with so many stuffed pockets on all sides, but Clay had to admit, Red had been right. His and Jake's musette bags were on the floor in a back room at the house, and there had been no going back when the shooting started. Krauts were wearing their socks now.

Clay got both boots off and placed them between his legs. He peeled off the damp wool socks and squeezed them, coaxing moisture out as best he could. He could feel Jake moving, doing the same thing. There was only one way to dry socks outdoors in the cold, with no fire. Use your own heat. Clay unbuttoned his coat, his jacket, his shirt, pulled up his wool sweater, and unbuttoned his long johns. He placed the socks on his chest, shivering at the cold damp feel of the wool against his skin. He pulled the sweater down and waited. His feet felt like heavy frozen pieces of meat. They had to dry too, and they were too wet and cold to go back into the boots.

"Ready?" Jake whispered.

"Yeah."

They moved so they lay directly across from each other. Clay felt for Jake's bare feet, pulling them up under his clothes, shuddering at the icy cold feel of them as he buttoned up as best he could and pulled his sweater down tight. His own bare feet went under Jake's clothes, next to his ribs, tucked up as far under his armpits as they could go. He felt Jake shiver as he clamped his arms down as best he could, giving Jake's icy feet all the warmth he had to spare. With no chance of a fire, it was the only way to dry socks and warm feet. Using your own precious warmth to evaporate the dampness in the socks and your buddy's warmth to keep your feet from freezing. What you lost at one end you gained at the other.

Clay spread the German overcoat out over them, covering their legs and the boots they had tucked in between them. By first light the socks would be dry and warm, and their feet would emerge from under each other's clothing feeling like they had been under a down comforter. This was almost good news.

"You okay?" Clay asked. There was a long silence.

"Can't stop thinking about things back home." Clay waited after Jake spoke. He could tell something was bothering him, and Jake didn't usually talk much about his family.

"Funny," Clay said, "I was thinking before about how little things can still eat at a guy, even out here, going through all this shit. You'd think it would just drive everything else out of your mind. But it doesn't."

"You thinking about home too?"

"Yeah," Clay said, after a moment's thought. "I guess I always am one way or the other. Thinking about what was, what coulda been. Just remembering people, can't help it. They drift in and out of my mind all the time. Like visitors."

"Some visitors you're glad to see go," Jake said. Clay could feel Jake's legs quiver as the cold sent his body into another round of shivering.

"What's eatin' at you, Jake?" More shivering, as Clay tried to keep his arms clamped down, giving Jake all the warmth he could. He waited, but Jake didn't answer him. Maybe he was asleep, maybe he just plain couldn't talk about it. Clay let his mind drift, listening for noises outside. If he concentrated he could hear the pine branches rustle in the wind, but nothing else. Good news. For the first time since the Germans attacked the house, he could feel his body relax. He felt it in his thighs, then his stomach. His body seemed to melt into the hay, and even the feel of Jake's cold feet in his armpits didn't bother him. His own feet felt like they were tucked in under the covers, and an image of his mother leaning over his bed flitted through his mind. A visitor. He could feel himself falling asleep, falling, down, down, into a dark safe place, swathed in soft hay. He hoped his mother would visit him as he dreamt. He saw his family in his dreams, enough to keep the memory of their faces fresh in his mind. They'd be sitting at the kitchen table, playing cards or drinking coffee, and he'd look up at his father, suddenly realizing he was supposed to be dead.

But there he was, taking high, low and jack as they played Pitch. The dream always ended as soon as he realized his father, mother, brother were dead. For just a split second, he'd look right into their eyes, and really see them again. If could just stay with the dream a few seconds longer, they might say something important to him, share a secret, tell him it was all right where they were. Or that'd it be all right where he was.

"You asleep, Clay?" Jake's question brought him out of that long fall into sleep.

"Just about," Clay said.

"SS," Jake said. "That really is bad news."

"Yeah," said Clay, struggling to open his eyes. "Probably that's who hit us at the house."

"Yeah, the way they kept coming on. Yeah, probably. Rock and a hard place is what we got here. Could be them or our own artillery waking us up."

"Yeah," said Clay, closing his eyes. "Could be." So instead of falling asleep with images of his family in his dreams like old fading photographs, Clay was left with visions of SS troopers sneaking up the hill, hearing their grunt and snores. Bad news.

"Yeah," said Jake, hoping to keep the conversation going, but he could hear Clay breathing heavy and he knew he was asleep. Sleep should've come easy to Jake, but it didn't. His mind raced between his hometown in Pennsylvania and everywhere else, thinking of where he could go after the war instead of there. Maybe he'd visit Clay in Tennessee, look for a job, settle down there. Let his folks think he died—but they'd know he didn't. No telegram with the War Department's regrets.

The Waffen-SS might take care of that for him. Those bastards worried him, worried any sane man. It wasn't that they were supermen or anything, that was just propaganda. But they were good soldiers, good at what they did. They'd started off on the Eastern Front, most of them, and after a few years fighting Russians, they knew plenty about killing. But so did a lot of Krauts in their regular army.

The problem was that they didn't seem to care much about living. They'd die as indiscriminately as they'd kill, throwing away their lives for a farmhouse or a hilltop or a foxhole. They'd stand, fight and die when any other Kraut or G.I. would pull out and live to fight another day, no shame to it, just common sense. They'd attack over and over again, jumping over the bodies of their comrades to get at what they wanted. You had to kill them all or run away, there was no in-between, no half-measures, no mercy.

Sleeping in ground zeroed in by their own artillery and probably soon to be reclaimed by its former owners, they were between a rock and a hard place, all right. Rock and a hard place, he should feel right at home. It sounded just like Minersville. Like their narrow two-story brick house tucked under the shadow of a mountain of rock.

CHAPTER ELEVEN

1964

CLAY WAITED AT THE LIGHT FOR A LINE OF CARS turning into the Hubbard Park entrance. He felt hung over, as if he'd drunk too much of his cheapest whisky last night. His mind was thick, churning with thoughts of Addy's ultimatum. His head throbbed. Too little sleep, too much thinking, and too many tears jammed up behind his eyes, threatening to drown his face and reveal the emotions he carefully kept stored away, like a folded envelope at the bottom of an old drawer. Most of yesterday had passed in a fog as he went through the motions of work, the shock of what Addy had said wrapping him in a cocoon of disbelief and confusion. He felt like a hundred pounds hung on his back all day long, the fear of losing her bearing down on him until every step was an effort and all he wanted to do was close his eyes and sleep. Fear of the loss, yes, but shame too. The shame of failure, of not being good enough to carry through with even the most basic human behaviors. A wife and family.

He and Addy didn't speak much last night, and this morning they shared the bathroom and kitchen as if they were both trespassers, careful politeness replacing familiarity as they struggled in silence with what had been spoken. Excuse me. Want some coffee? Pardon me. I'll get that. Goodbye.

Sunlight glinted on his windshield as colored leaves drifted off tree branches, fell on his hood and over the road in front of him, dancing across the blacktop like brightly colored insects. He watched as one leaf landed on the hood of his car. Bright yellow and red, its curled edges tip-toed across the hood until the breeze lifted and tossed it into the air. Clay watched it go and felt the sense of loss deepen, reaching down into his gut and take hold, as if it were going to stay with him a long, long time.

Indian summer was making a show on this October day, and plenty of folks were headed into the park for their last chance at a picnic under the bright sun. When the last car crossed his lane, with two women in the front seat and a pack of kids in the back, a boy at the window turned and smiled at Clay. Clay had a blank look on his face, at best, probably a frown. He could feel the grim set of his jaw, his lips pursed tightly against his teeth, drawing down the corners of his mouth. The boy turned his head as the car pulled into the park, watching Clay, the grin gone from his face. Clay wondered if he'd frightened him? Had the kid seen a glimpse of his future in the face of some old guy driving a beat-up station wagon filled with cardboard boxes, passing the park by on a warm fall day?

What would he have thought, back in '47, if he'd seen a face like that as he pulled into the park for the first time, with Frankie Galluzo dragging him along because his girlfriend demanded he find a date for her cousin. Frankie had planned a picnic at Hubbard Park, and convinced Clay to risk a blind date, saying he'd bring cans of Ballantine Ale in a cooler and plenty of bologna sandwiches. His girlfriend Annette had gotten her cousin from Rhode Island a job as a telephone operator at the phone company on Butler Street, and she didn't want to leave her alone on her first Saturday in town.

The first time he saw Addy she was spreading out a blanket under the shade of a maple tree by the pond. He smiled at the memory, Addy grabbing the corners of the blanket and snapping it in the air, letting it float softly down onto the green grass. He could smell the warm air of that day, feel the cold ice as he stuck his arm into the cooler to pull two chilled cans from the bottom. He remembered the dappled sunlight on Addy's face as they started to talk, a conversation that lasted all afternoon. He shook himself, angry at letting the warm memory sneak up on him when it was the last damn thing he needed to think about.

Shifting into first, Clay pulled harder on the stick than he needed to. When he jammed it into second he knew he had to calm down and not take it out on the car. No reason to screw up this relationship too. Taking a deep breath, he eased up on the gas and gently shifted into third as the car crested the hill overlooking the park on his right. Hubbard Park was set just under the mountain, its pond, flowers and paths nestled under the shadow of East Peak and Castle Craig, a stone tower built out of the trap rock that spilled from the mountainside. Way back, the sandstone had originally covered the mountain, but it crumbled with time, age and weather, falling away and mounding up at the base, revealing the harder trap rock at the core of the mountain. Stands of granite like giants overlooked the park, casting their shadows over the lives of picnickers who never gave it a thought between bites of deviled eggs and soggy tuna fish sandwiches.

Clay liked the mountains and their shadows. He and Addy lived under Lamentation Mountain on the other side of town, and he appreciated the twin hills and how they defined the boundaries of their home. They contained him. In the valley between the peaks he could always crane his neck around until he found one, got his bearings, and knew where he was. Once in a while, he'd remember something from the war, a landmark like a hilltop or cliffs along a river that he'd used to find his way. Back then, terrain might lead to death, horror, or safety. Here, it was always the same. Follow this and you'll get home. You'll be safe. He liked looking up at the hard stone that rose up out of the soft sandstone layer, granite slabs that refused to be worn down.

Much as he liked them Clay had a hard time thinking of these long ridges that ended in worn away cliffs as mountains. They might be mountains to some folks, these bottom-land New Englanders, but not to him. He liked them all right, but a mountain was a mountain where he came from, hard crests, coal mines and sharp gaps leaving no doubt that life was lived on a downward slope.

Leaving East Peak in his rear-view mirror, Clay turned on South End Road and drove toward the Silver City Country Club. It was one of the stops he should've made yesterday. After Addy had her say the day went slower and slower for Clay, until he gave up and went back to the Tavern, where he watched customers come and go, nursing a coffee until it was cold and a beer until it was flat. He saw Chris and Brick exchange glances after failing to get him to say more than yes, no or a grunt.

Clay knew he needed time. Time to get used to the idea of life without Addy, because he knew there was a good chance – no, a fair chance – that he wouldn't be able to deliver on what she wanted. He was too good at what he did for them to just say sure,

Clay, we understand, you need to call it quits so your wife'll be happy. Good, that's our top priority.

No, Clay was a cog in a well-oiled machine, a very efficient and productive cog. He hadn't thought about it much, but everything he did to improve his take improved his boss' take even more. He always got the same small percentage, but he had been making Mr. Fiorenza a rich man on nickels and dimes, and now there was no way out.

But there had to be a way. That's what he really needed time for, to figure out exactly what he had to do and when he had to do it. How many times had he done that during the war? A quick huddle under cover and it was Big Ned, lay down a base of fire, we'll swing right, Shorty and Tuck, you go left, give us covering fire from behind those rocks. Or maybe somebody had a better idea, but it was all done in a minute, under fire, pinned down. Under fire and pinned down, that's me all right. But where are my buddies with their M1s?

Well, Clay said, almost out loud, there's bad news, bad news and good news. My wife will leave me if I don't quit the numbers, and Mr. Fiorenza will break my legs if I do. Good news is, there's no more bad news.

There's never good news.

The words echoed in Clay's ears as he turned into the country club parking lot, and he couldn't tell if he had actually spoken them out loud or remembered them from a conversation long ago.

Clay didn't park in the main lot with the Cadillacs, Lincoln Town Cars, and assorted sports cars. Pulling around back of the clubhouse he left his station wagon next to a Chevy Impala. As he was getting out, a pickup truck loaded down with white sand and shovels drove in behind him and braked to a noisy halt as the engine conked several times before turning off. This was Clay's territory, the province of cooks, caddies, and groundskeepers, all those who toiled for small change so the big spenders could have a nice day at the club, and not have to look at the junk heaps the help drove to get there.

Clay grabbed the box with the right mix of brands for the two cigarette machines in the clubhouse. One off the bar, the other in the locker room. No reason for anyone who paid the dues here to have to walk far for a smoke. Clay backed into the double doors at the rear of the building and swung around with the box held in front of him.

"Where the hell have you been?"

Clay stopped short and looked over the cardboard box. A shiny baldhead barely rose above the top. If he hadn't spoken up, Clay would have run right into him.

"Jeez, Dom, you almost gave me a heart attack."

"Don't give me that gee-willikers crap, Brock. You left me holding the bag, the real goddamn thing!"

"You're going to give yourself a heart attack, Dom, never mind me. Things got away from me yesterday, that's all."

"That's all?"

Dominic Telesca backed down the hallway, waving an unlit but well-chewed cigar over his head, at Clay, and everywhere in between. He was about five foot four, a combination of muscle, fat, and nervous anger. He wore a short sleeve white shirt, with the sleeves rolled up an extra inch to show off his biceps. A bartender's apron was tied tightly around his waist, cinched against the fat that was threatening to overwhelm the muscles of his youth. Threads of gray showed in the black hair that edged his head, ear to ear, but no higher.

"Yeah, that's all. You never run late?"

"Noooo," Dom said, drawing out the word as if explaining it to a slow child. "Not when someone is waiting for me with someone else's..." He stopped his backward progress to look down the hallway, then started up again when he saw it was empty. He pushed his face in close to Clay's as he finished the sentence. "...moneeey."

They were next to the cigarette machine. Clay dropped the box at Dom's feet and looked at his face carefully. It was pink and flushed, little beads of perspiration bubbling up at the crown of his head and rolling off, dampening the band of his remaining hairs.

"Dom, what the hell's the matter with you? You don't pull in much here, this isn't a rich man's racket. If it wasn't for the grounds crew and cooks it wouldn't be worth the drive to pick up your numbers."

Both men glanced around as Clay lowered his voice. There was a television on in the bar and the noise carried out into the hallway and covered their words. No one was paying attention to them.

"Fuck the numbers, Brock, this is the real thing I'm talking about. Fiorenza put the pressure on to bring in more dough, so we expanded. Horses, elections, whatever anybody wants to bet on. We had a crew in here Tuesday night from Waterbury, they all put C notes down on the first four games of the Series, can you believe that?"

Dom was grinning and the cigar now clamped between his teeth bobbed up and down as he spoke. Clay could almost see the dollar signs in his eyes.

"So you're a big time bookie now, Dom?"

"God damn right I am," Dom spit back, taking the cigar out of his mouth between two fingers and pointing it at Clay again. "Things are changing, Brock, so don't mess it up for us. I don't like being responsible for eight Gs of Fiorenza's dough."

"Eight?"

"Yeah, eight. Yesterday was Wednesday, right? Golf day for doctors. Once the Series heats up there'll be more, so don't miss no other days. I take it in, you pick it up, give it to Fiorenza, he gives me my cut. Nice and simple, okay?"

"Okay, okay. Nobody told me about this, Dom, I thought this was another nickel dime pickup. Don't blow a fuse."

Clay turned away from Dom and unlocked the back of the cigarette machine. It was nearly empty. Lots of nervous smokers laying big bets.

"Nothing personal," Dom said he walked away. "Come on in for a beer when you're done."

Clay opened a carton of Parliaments and another of Kents, the brands the country club boys preferred. Filtered coffin nails. As if they thought they could hide from death, in their knit trousers and bright shirts, drinking highballs while sucking on their filtered smokes. Who were they kidding?

Clay was steamed, but he knew it wasn't the putters and duffers he was mad at. Goddamn Fiorenza. Raising the stakes and not telling him. And Addy, of all the goddamn times she had to pick to deliver her ultimatum! Why now, right when everything else is falling apart? What the hell was wrong with two months ago, or last year for chrissakes? A year ago I could've walked away, maybe sold the tavern. Who'd want to buy now, in the middle of a gangster turf war?

Clay topped off the rows of the lesser brands, ripping open cartons of Luckies, Kools, and Winstons, each bearing the blue Virginia tax stamp. It was so easy when he started with Tri-State six years ago. Then picking up the numbers receipts, since he was in the bars and shops anyway. Why not pick up a few paper bags full of slips and cash, why not sell them at Jake's Tavern? Swell idea. More cash. Don't worry, nobody pays attention to the numbers. Who said crime didn't pay? Problem was, it did.

Clay finished up in the locker room and headed into the barroom. The bar curved out from the wall on his right, a U-shape slinking back into the far corner where a television was set up. The floor to ceiling windows on his left presented a clear view out over the golf course, the intense green of the manicured grass startling in its perfection. A foursome was putting out on the eighteenth hole, but they had no audience. The dozen or so men in the bar had their backs to the windows, watching gray images swim across the television screen as Dom swiveled the rabbit ear antenna. The picture cleared and as Dom stepped back a roar rose up from the set. Third game of the World Series, first one played at Yankee Stadium. Dom caught Clay's eye and motioned him to the end of the bar away from the television.

Setting down his cardboard box at the far end of the bar, out of sight, Clay sat on the last stool. He felt out of place, a workingman in a roomful of men who didn't have to be at work on a Thursday afternoon. A deliveryman. Dom pulled a small draft and set it down in front of Clay.

"Cards got it tied up in the fifth, one one," Dom said, chewing on his cigar, still unlit. "You a Sox or Yanks fan, Brock?" Dom leaned over the bar, studying Clay as if there might be a hint of his allegiance hidden somewhere in his face. In this part of the state, Boston or New York was a tossup.

Clay took a drink. The beer was cold and crisp, and it washed away the dust that always seemed to cling to the cardboard he carried around all day.

"Neither. Phillies."

"Phillies! Those bums! You gotta be kidding me!" Dom had to take his cigar out of his mouth or he would've dropped it. His eyebrows jumped up his forehead in disbelief.

"That shoulda been them playing the Yanks right now, not St. Louis. Jesus, Mary and Joseph, how can you be a Phillies fan?"

"Wasn't always from around here," Clay said, then lifted the glass again, wishing he hadn't even said that much. Closing his eyes as he swallowed, he could feel his fingers on the radio dial, trying to tune in the Phillies game, the static as clear as if it were yesterday, not twenty years ago.

"Yeah, but geez, the Phillies were all set to clinch the pennant, then a ten game losing streak, how could you stand it?"

Clay shrugged his shoulders. Once a fan, always a fan. If Dom didn't understand loyalty, there was no talking to the guy. Clay had been disappointed, almost angry at the time. The Phillies' September Swoon, the sportscasters called it. Now, it was just another loss to be endured. Maybe it was silly, it was only a game after all, but he had wanted to feel that exhilaration, that joy by association when his team won the pennant. It was nothing compared to his real problems right now, but if his team had made it to the Series, he'd have had something to take his mind off those problems, if only for a minute. The excitement of a win or a good play could block out the pressures squeezing him from all sides, building up in his head, and let a little whoop of joy break through. A Dick Allen home run or maybe even another Jim Bunning perfect game would've let him forget for a few precious seconds, before the numbers, cigarettes, betting and Addy and Mr. Fiorenza and Chris all swarmed back into his mind, each wanting a piece of him.

"Thanks for the beer," Clay said, standing up. He looked at Dom, waiting. He glanced down at his cardboard box.

"Yeah, no problem." Dom looked around the bar. Everyone else was focused on the television. A groan rose up. Bottom of the sixth, and the Yankees left the bases loaded as Tom Tresh hit a pop infield fly. Dom reached under the bar and dropped a paper bag into the box, stuffing it down between half-empty cigarette cartons. Eight thousand in cash. Clay pulled the zipped leather bag he collected the coins from the vending machines in from between a stack of cartons and dropped it on top of the bag.

"See ya," Clay said, wishing he'd never have to again. Dom already had his back to him, heading to his heavy bettors.

Clay walked down the hall to the rear door. The cardboard box was heavier going out than it had been going in, all that loose change sitting on top of the cash. He could feel the pull of it, the desire for easy money overwhelming him. Could he do it? What if it meant he could give up the cigarette route, sit in the Tavern and take big bets on the races, baseball in the summer, football in the fall, basketball in the winter? Greed could work year-round for him. Addy. Addy was a problem. A fleeting thought passed through his mind. Let her leave, then do what the hell you want. Rake in the dough. It startled him in its simplicity and directness.

Let her leave, he wouldn't have to do a thing, just keep on as things are, and it would happen.

No. No, he shook his head, as if trying to clear it. That's not what I want. He wanted it all, but all wasn't in the cards. Addy or lots of money? His wife or paper sacks of worn greenbacks? Holding the box in front of him, he could feel the bag of money near his heart, and hated himself for weighing his family against easy cash.

He hit the lever on the wide delivery door with his box and pushed it open, swinging around to clear it as it closed behind him. He took a step towards his station wagon and saw the pickup truck that had pulled in behind him blocking his car. Shovels stuck out of the white sand piled up in the truck bed. No one was in the cab, but Clay spotted a guy in cherry-red Mustang, backed into a spot at the corner of the small lot. The Mustang was running, and the guy in the driver's seat tapped ash from his cigarette out the window. Clay could see the guy look around, checking to see the coast was clear. Then the guy looked straight at Clay, and laughed. His eyes darted right, and Clay saw who he was looking at.

Leaning against the back of the truck, running his hand through the sand, clutching a fistful and letting it run out between his fingers, was a strangely familiar figure. He wore a black suit, white shirt and pencil-thin black tie. His pointed black leather shoes gleamed, as shiny as his slicked-back dark hair. It was the clothes that confused Clay for a second. A few days ago Clay had seen him in a deliveryman's outfit.

Clay felt his face flush and sweat break out down his back. His stomach felt like it hit the ground and he wasn't sure he could speak without a tremor in his voice. He walked up to the hood of his station wagon and set the cardboard box down on it.

"Liquor on Monday and sand on Thursday, Al?"

"It's nice you remember me, Mr. Brock."

"You got me in a fair amount of trouble last time I saw you. Not hard to remember that." Clay glanced over at the guy in the Mustang. He had gotten out and was leaning against the adjacent car. Al still leaned into the truckbed, playing with the clean white sand.

"Fiorenza must've been pissed, huh?"

He looked over at Clay, smiling, one eyebrow raised in question, as if he were a pal asking about a practical joke.

"Is that what you came here to find out?" Clay asked, crossing his arms out in front of his chest. Al looked up at him, shook the sand from his hands and walked over to stand next to the driver's door of the station wagon. Clay was up on the sidewalk, the cardboard box on the hood, between them, as if it meant nothing at all.

"Why do you think I'm here, Mr. Brock?" Al put his hands in his pockets, rocking back and forth on his heels, very slightly. Clay looked at the other guy again. He was big and beefy, his weight pressing down the car on one side as he leaned against it. He had big ears that stuck straight out from his head.

He looked bored, not jumpy the way you might be if you were about to grab eight thousand smackers. Clay wondered if this was about something else. He had to do everything he could to not draw attention to the cardboard box.

"Lift my smokes and chump change from my first pickup? And at the country club? The numbers are too low class for them, never has been a big stop for me. Doesn't make sense. Maybe if you sent Dumbo over there to my last stop..."

"Richie is very sensitive about his ears, Mr. Brock. I wouldn't say that too loud." Al was smiling, maybe at the thought of telling Richie what Clay had called him. "You're right, I'm not after chump change."

Al took a step towards the box. Clay tensed, and tried not to show it. He felt a line of sweat working its way down his face and his heart racing. He had to hold back from grabbing the box and running like hell. If they didn't know about the cash yet he'd be okay. Al reached into the box and pulled up the leather zipper bag full of change. He shook it, and the silver jingled and jangled inside.

"You work for this?" Al asked, tossing the bag back into the box. "Driving all over, picking up quarters for Fiorenza? Is that what you want?"

"Nobody gives a crap what I want," Clay said, "including you. Now what the hell do you want from me?"

"That's very perceptive, Mr. Brock. And that's why I'm here. I've been studying Fiorenza's operation for a while, and you're a pretty important part of it. You bring in good numbers at your tavern, you're working the cigarette angle, and your pickups are substantial. There's only one problem."

"What's that?"

"He doesn't pay you enough."

"And you would."

"A bigger percentage, yeah," Al said, "and expansion. Bigger territory, more opportunity. Fiorenza's too old to make a move like that. But the DePaoli family isn't. If I don't take over from him, someone else will sooner or later anyway. A matter of time, that's all."

"So you're here to offer me a deal?"

"Yeah. Work with me, Mr. Brock, and it'll be worth it to both of us. Bring over your route to us, and we'll put money into your tavern, make it a real nice place. For you and your lady."

"It's not for sale."

"You think it over, give me a call when you decide. It'd be a partnership, that's all," Al said as he stuffed a piece of paper with a phone number on it into Clay's shirt pocket. Walking back to the truck, he stopped and grabbed one of the shovels that stuck out of the sand. "But remember, this is a one-time offer. Get in on the ground floor..."

He raised the shovel and swung it against the rear window of the station wagon. It clanged against the glass as it shattered. The window held for a second, then disintegrated into a jumble of tiny glass pieces.

"...or end up under the ground."

Al dropped the shovel and snapped his fingers toward Richie. He shuffled over and got into the truck, started it up and drove it forward, enough for Clay to be able to pull out.

"We'll be in touch for your decision," Al said, a smirk lingering on his lips, "if we don't hear from you."

Turning away he walked to the Mustang, Richie following along. As they drove out Clay could see Al gesturing with his thumb towards him, laughing, as Richie leaned forward over the steering wheel, glaring at him. Big ears.

Clay held his stance until they were out of the lot, then dropped to his knees, steadying himself with his hands on the hood of his car, feeling weak and dizzy. Smashing the window had been unexpected, but that's what Al had intended. What would he have done if he knew there was eight thousand bucks in there? The loss of eight thousand, plus the pay-outs, would've hurt Mr. Fiorenza, so much that he'd have to make an example of the dope that lost it. His head swimming uncontrollably he retched, spraying his bumper with a stream of fear, bile and beer.

Leaning on the side of the car, Clay grabbed the box and unlocked the door of the car, stuffing the box in the back seat. His mouth was sour and his throat burned, but he focused on getting out of there and stashing the cash somewhere safe. As he backed up, he could hear the tinkle of glass shards as pieces of the rear window fell to the ground. He drove slowly and deliberately, not wanting to draw attention to himself and then have to answer questions about the shattered window or what he had in the back seat. He turned on the radio, desperate for a distraction. He found the game in time to hear Mantle hit a home run and win it for the Yanks in the bottom of the ninth. He tried to get excited about it, but it wasn't the same. There was no switching allegiance at this point.

Driving down Pratt Street, Clay started to turn onto Mill, forgetting that the road was being repaved. It was a short stretch, but the Town crew had started yesterday, jack hammering up the pavement, blocking off one end of Mill Street. Parking for customers was going to be a problem, not to mention the noise. He took the long way, going around on Cedar Street. He eyed the road crew as he pulled in, slowly coming closer, the constant noise from their generator bad enough without the staccato bursts of the jack hammer. In back of the Tavern, he hosed down the front bumper and rinsed his mouth out from the spigot. Stacking his boxes inside, he checked on Cheryl to make sure she was okay at the bar, then went back into his office and locked the door behind him.

Walking over to his old roll top desk, he moved the chair aside, got down on his hands and knees and stretched his arm out until his fingertips grabbed hold of a groove in the floorboards. Lifting a short section of three floorboards, they came up, held together by a strip of wood nailed across the bottom. He reached in the hole and pulled out a red tin box. Laying it on the desk, he took the paper sack with Dom's eight thousand and put it in the hole, laying the boards carefully back over it. He sat in the chair and laid his hands on the red tin box. Taking a deep breath, letting it out, he opened the box. He pulled out a bundle wrapped in chamois cloth and unwound the cloth, placing the Colt .45 Automatic on his desk. It rested in its shoulder holster, the leather of the strap and holster still supple after twenty years. A two-clip pouch, marked with a round U.S. stamp, lay at the bottom of the tin box. Taking the pistol out of the holster, Clay removed the clip, checked to be sure the chamber was empty and made sure the safety was on. It was the same ritual he followed every year when he took it out and cleaned it, rubbing the leather holster down with mink oil. He never thought he'd need to use it, but couldn't think of anything else to do with it. It was the only thing he'd brought back from the war. Everything else had been stolen while he was in the hospital. Enlisted men weren't supposed to have them, but everyone wanted a sidearm, and although German pistols were easier to get, you were taking a chance if you got captured with one. The Krauts didn't like it when they found G.I.s with their hardware, and you were likely to get beat up or worse if had a Luger or Walther in your pocket.

Pistols weren't actually fired that often, but it was nice to have one. For close in fighting, when there wasn't room to swing your rifle around, a pistol was the thing. But Addy didn't see much use for one around the house, and when Chris started walking she demanded that Clay get rid of it. He told her he gave it away. For the past fourteen years, he had pulled it out from under the floorboards, and every year, he looked forward to it. The smell of the oil, the feel of the blue metal, the soft leather and hard memories.

He didn't know what he was going to do next, but as he took out the gun oil and cleaning rags, he knew that he had to stop letting things happen to him. All his life, others had made him go here or do this. Forced him into things he'd never thought possible. Addy had every right to let him know her conditions. He could meet them or not. It was the way she was, and it was one of the things that had first attracted him to her. Her certainty. She knew the path she wanted to take in life, and at a time when Clay had no direction other than getting from one day to the next, it had appealed to him.

Addy had moved to Meriden to take a job with the phone company. Clay had gotten off the train there because he didn't have the fare to go any farther. Addy had wanted to support herself and get some distance from the rest of her family in Rhode Island. Six other brothers and sisters, her mother and father both mill workers with little left at the end of the day for their brood. There was scant food on the table, birthdays were forgotten, clothes went unmended, and school was not as important as the afternoon jobs the kids held, all their earnings going to their parents to help pay the rent.

It wasn't a life Addy wanted to pass on, so she left the state, got a good job, and decided she'd only ever have one child. That way she could give it all the love, clothes, books and food it needed. She told Clay her plans the first day they met at the picnic. A plan. Addy always had a plan. Now her plan was to get away from the crime Clay had brought into their life. It made sense. She had given him fair notice and a choice.

Mr. Fiorenza and Al, they gave him no choice. It was their way or nothing. He wasn't going to let that happen. Removing the slide he gently oiled the metal, watching the oil settle into the engraved "U.S. Property" letters.

Being in the Army had been the ultimate in control, being told what to wear, what to eat, where to go, who to kill. Oddly enough, it was when they were all together at the front that he had felt the freest of all. He could think about every choice, where to dig a hole, where to place a foot, which way to go, high ground or low ground? No fire, or risk a fire? All life or death decisions, and they were his to make. He couldn't decide to go home, but he could decide how to best stay alive. Stay off the ridgeline, keep out of open fields. Listen. Watch. Fire. Move. Every minute held a decision to be made, if you wanted to stay alive. It was time he started acting like that here. Stop plodding along and assuming everything's going to be okay. The feel of the crosshatched grip made him think that it just might be possible. Stop being the other guy's patsy. He opened and closed his palm around the grip again. Yes, it could work.

Addy wouldn't have to know. I can tell her I'm done, and that's that. I have to plan this out, carefully, so she never knows anything happened. I'll come home one day and tell her it's all over, it was no big deal, no problems.

Clay stared at the automatic, and at his hand wrapped around it. Here, behind locked doors he felt himself at the far end of a long line of space and time separating himself from his wife and son. There was so much they didn't know about him, so much that they'd never know. You couldn't tell anybody who hadn't been there the whole truth. You couldn't even think about it yourself half the time, how could you ever tell them? Even if you could, it would defile them with gore and horror, lathering them with your killing frenzy, opening up a book of death for them to read. He remembered Red writing letters home after guys had been killed. He never knew what hit him, he'd write. Everything was going fine, then out of nowhere...he never knew...it was all over in seconds. What he really meant was you'll never know, thank God, how he screamed and how we couldn't help him and how long he took to die out there and how scared we all were.

Clay's head pounded. He felt the tears pushing against the dam of his eyes. He could never tell them, they should never have to know, and that was right and good. But he knew that it also meant they would never be able to really know who he was, really understand him, his demons and stories and joys and shame. Never.

So much had happened twenty years ago, and so much of that only he knew. He, and this pistol he cradled in his hand. No matter what good and evil it had done, it was his only connection to the past. His past made real by the feel of cold metal, the dull, glistening sheen of the dark barrel giving away nothing, knowing everything.

CHAPTER TWELVE

2000

THE SIREN SWIRLS IN HIS EARS, DIPPING IN AND out, a whining crescendo followed by a chirping whirr that bottoms out and then starts all over again. He's heard the sound before.

Of course he has, who hasn't heard a siren? Coming down the street, whipping by you as you pull to the side of the road. An ambulance appearing in your rearview mirror, the sound coming from nowhere as lights fill your mirror and then disappear, the flashing and noise fading as the ambulance rounds a curve and vanishes. Cars pull back into the road, order and normalcy restored, drivers shaking their heads, poor sunavbitch, hope he's gonna make it. Wonder what's for dinner tonight?

But this sound is different. It doesn't fade away, it just keeps on going, reaching for that high, shrill note and then dropping back, just a bit, letting you think this time it might stop, but it doesn't. Someone's in big trouble. No—wait, it's me. I'm in trouble, I know it.

Something is pressed into his face, and he tries to pull at it, but can't move his arms. They're stuck at his side, immobile. Panic surges through his body, up from his belly and out the top of his head. He can't move! He swivels his head but can't get his arms to move. He feels something pressing down on them, rope or straps tight against his skin. His frail arms, skin wrapped around bone, muscle and flesh worn away under the weight of years, can't move the weight.

Am I tied up? Where am I? Are they taking me off the line? No, no. It was raining. I was in the car. Whose car? Was I driving? Was there an accident?

His eyelids are heavy and they feel thick and coarse as they lay shut over his eyes. He tries to open them, focusing all his energy. Open, open, open. It feels like waking from a deep, sound sleep, when you don't want to get out of bed, or maybe don't have to. What a good idea. Don't even try. Why do I need to open my eyes anyway? What's all the fuss? He can't remember, but know it's important, and he has to struggle against the easy fatigue that could let him drift off if he let it.

Tiny slits let in light as his eyelids part. Somebody in a yellow raincoat is bent over him, fiddling with something, he can't tell what. Water runs off the slick coat and dampens the sheet covering him. The raincoat moves and there's two people standing next to each other. No, that isn't it...everything is doubled up, images stacked onto each other and overlapping. He can see the window to his side. It is dark gray and streaked with rain, and then another, a mirror image, above the first window. There hadn't been windows, and this confuses him. Why is there a window there now, never mind two? He has no idea where he is, where he is going. He closes his eyes, afraid of what else he might see and not understand.

No, there hadn't been a window, he was sure of it. Maybe when they'd opened the doors and slid him in...was there a window on the rear door? Maybe, a half-moon sort of thing, the glass caked over with ice. Hard to tell when your chest is sticky with your own blood and your clothes are cut and ripped half off your body, thick white compress bandages taped down tight. Wait, my arm wrapped tight against my side, more compress bandages stuffed between my arm and ribs. Am I hurt? Was there an explosion? The memory of a white-hot crack plays in his head, a vivid sensation of being lifted up and thrown by the force of a blast, floating in air, suspended in bits of snow, dirt, blood and shrapnel. Then, nothing.

He tries to calm down, but his breathing increases, rapid, shallow breaths. He can't feel any sticky wetness on his skin. Good, he isn't bleeding, or at least not enough to feel. The person inside the ambulance is saying something, to him or maybe to someone else. Yelling. The medic spoke softly, said take it easy buddy, you're halfway home, hang on. Hang on.

Sulfa. The medic sprinkling sulfa on his chest, white powder that he tosses everywhere, like dusting a strawberry cake with confectioners' sugar. He can see the scissors in the medic's hand, shiny and bright against the brown, dirty uniform. One end of a long tattered shoelace tied around the medic's wrist, the other around the scissors. A guy who likes his tools close at hand. He cuts and cuts, through jacket and sweater, shirts and wool underwear, snipping layers of cloth away as he searches for the boundaries of the wound. He can see the medic's face, crystal clear, his eyes widening as he cuts loose the final section, unable to hide his astonishment that this G.I. is still alive. He sees the bags under the medic's eyes, sad sagging pouches above sparse stubble. He's just a kid, and he uses a lot of sulfa.

He feels cold. The damp sheet chills his skin and he wonders if the guy in the yellow raincoat has cut his clothes away. He feels around with his hands, as far as they can reach. He finds fabric and rubs it between thumb and forefinger. It feels like his pants, the trousers he put on this morning...where? Where's his wallet? He can't reach his rear pocket, can't feel the pressure of the leather wallet against his hip. Bastards will probably steal it at the hospital. They steal everything. Who was that guy? Driscoll, maybe, or was it Dawson? That sergeant in the Heavy Weapons Platoon, big gambler, always the first guy to get a card game going or throw the dice. One night, outside Dinant, he won a thousand bucks at craps, biggest pot he had ever seen. He stuffs the dough in all his pockets, so he won't lose it. Next day, a Kraut 88 hits his halftrack. Dawson...yeah that was it, we called him Daws...he's hit bad, shrapnel everywhere, left hand gone. So Daws wakes up in an evac hospital, minus one hand and a thousand smackers. Everything gone but his dogtags. No one knows anything about a thousand bucks, must've gotten thrown out with the uniform when he came in. Yeah, sure.

Feeling a thump, he looks around. He's outside now, when did that happen? He's on a stretcher being wheeled into the hospital, the wheels clattering against concrete. Where was Daws? Last time he saw him he was in a hospital, his torso, face and one arm wrapped in thick bandages. He was yelling at an orderly, calling him a coward and a fucking thief. Seems like he cared more about losing the money than being alive after playing catch with an 88. But then again, a thousand bucks is real money, a fortune. Where is this place anyway?

The room is bright, white, and noisy. All he sees is the ceiling, white tiles with tiny holes. Someone bumps against his stretcher, mumbles an apology, and moves on. The guy in the yellow raincoat is gone, and no one is tending to him. He's in hallway, parked up against a wall, listening to people, doctors, nurses, orderlies, all walking hurriedly by, talking, some laughing, no one paying him any mind. Why am I here, dammit? Where's Addy, who's looking after her? Had he forgotten all about her? Addy. Her name sounds odd in his mind as he says it, as if it carries with it some secret he isn't meant to yet know.

Thinking about Addy, he wonders why he's so worried. She can take care of herself, can't she? I'm the one stuck in this hallway, tied down. Why am I tied down? Where is she? He tries to form the words, ask someone, but nothing comes out. It's as hard to open his mouth and form words as it is to lift his arm from under the straps that hold it in place.

Am I gonna make it? He hears himself ask the question, through gritted teeth and the dull pain thumping against the morphine the medic gave him. Above him, the white ceiling tiles are dark, dingy plaster, cracked and crumbling. He's in a hallway, the stone walls gray and the ceiling high above him, like in a church. Explosions sound outside, but far enough away that no one dives for cover. Moans drift up around him and he tries to look around, pain rocketing up through the drugs whenever he moves. A doctor, a real doctor by his insignia, not a medic, pulls his bandages away. A nurse takes him by the hand and gently pulls his arm away from his bloody side. She's small and slight, the G.I. helmet too large on her head, tipping to one side. She wears thick gloves with the fingers cut off, working with them on. She looks tired, like the medic, bags under sad, weary eyes.

"Course you are, soldier. We're going to take real good care of you. What's your name?"

The doctor pulls the last of the bandages away and drops them to the floor. He peers into the wound, then runs his eyes over the rest of the litters stacked up in the hallway. Another explosion booms outside, close this time, and the doctor flinches.

"What's your name, soldier?" the doctor asks.

"I...it's....I" He can't say it.

"Shock ward," the doctor says to the nurse, after the hesitation. His voice sounds almost firm, a doctor's certainty mixed with fear and resignation.

"Tell us your name, soldier," the nurse says, laying her hand on the doctor's arm without looking at him. The look in her eyes tells him this is very important, and the look in the doctor's eyes says he doesn't much like being held up by a nurse. He understands the shock ward can't be a good place to be sent. "You know your own name, don't you?"

"Yes, ma'am, sure I do. Am I gonna make it?"

"Tell us your goddamn name, that's an order," says the doctor, irritation rising in his rushed, hard tone.

"It's Brock. Clay Brock."

"Prep for surgery," the doctor says, moving off to the next litter.

"You're going to make it now, Clay Brock, don't you worry. You did just fine," she said with a smile that seemed aimed straight at him. She gave him a wink and turned away. Wisps of dark brown hair float out from under the helmet as her voice shifts from soft and soothing to commanding. "Orderly! Prep."

"Mr. Brock? Can you hear me, Mr. Brock?" He looked up, half-opening his eyes against the bright lights and white walls. The nurse was dressed in green pastel scrubs, and held a clipboard in her hands.

"Are you Mr. Brock?" She said this slowly and loudly. He nodded his head, and wished he could speak, tell her how funny it was that her grandma had just asked him the same question a minute ago. She wore green too, but not this bright stuff. Dirty green, covered by a brown sweater with holes worn at the elbow. It felt impossible, and yet so real, so certain.

"Gooood," she said as she made a note on the chart. "Can you say something for me, Mr. Brock?" She spoke in a simple, singsong voice. He wished the other nurse would come back, the one who knew how to work the doctor and who had time for a smile. She'd talked to him as if he were a real man, not a child.

"No? You can't talk, Mr. Brock?" She tilted her head, as if cooing over a baby. Or was she watching him, cataloging his every twitch and response to her?

He fought to send the words flowing out of his mouth. They swirled around in his head. He had so much to say, the story of his life, the story that he had always struggled to keep within himself. Mother, father, war, death, wife, child, work, deception, lies, illness and shame, all these things had been tamped down, folded and refolded on themselves until they laid layered in his gut, secret stacked upon secret, lie upon lie. Now, now that he couldn't speak, they clamored to get out, to unfold before this stranger, to seek the light of day. Was this silence a gift, or a joke?

Hell, why should he even bother to speak? What if he could blurt it all out, right here and right now? Tell this foolish girl the truth, tell the stories as they really happened? Maybe that other nurse could've taken it and stood her ground, but not Miss Sunshine here. She'd either burst into tears or give him an injection, a needle full of silence.

He knew he was getting lost in his thoughts. Something gnawed at the back of his mind, something important. Someone. A distant part of him knew something was very wrong. He had to focus, try to speak. He opened his mouth and tried to speak the name that wouldn't quite come to him.

"Ah...ah..." The words weren't there, not even his own wife's sweet name. Instead, it jammed up in his throat, holding back all the other words he might have spoken in that moment. It was all too much so he wept, eyes clenched shut, leaking tears as he shook his head back and forth, the only motion left to him, the only thing he was capable of controlling in his entire life. Miss Sunshine patted his hand, and walked away.

They moved him. They prodded him, stuck him, pressing cold metal against his white, paper-thin skin. Someone moved his feet and asked him questions he couldn't understand. Then they stuck pins in his feet and asked him more questions. It didn't hurt much, and when he made a face at them they stopped. A woman in pink scrubs held up her finger, asking him to follow it as she moved it left and right. She told him he did fine and then wrote on her clipboard. It took a long time, longer than it should've taken to say he did fine. He could feel them removing his pants, underwear and socks. For a few seconds he was back with the medic, snipping and cutting away at his clothes. He worried about his wallet, then he worried about the .45 automatic he'd brought in. They were sure to steal it. Or maybe court-martial him for having an officer's sidearm. No weapons allowed, the nurse had told him. Everything gets stored away. Good policy, he told her, I should know. But please, take this .45, hide it, I have to have it back, I have to—it belonged to—he couldn't explain it, and finally begged, please, don't let an officer take it or an orderly steal it, it's a souvenir, a real important souvenir. She took it, hiding it under her coat, winking at him as she hurried away, one hand steadying the helmet on her head, the other tucked into her coat, his souvenir held against her breast.

He was being carried along on a conveyor belt, exposed more and more each step of the way, made less a man than a diagnosis, something to be processed until they ran out of tests. Then they covered him with a washed-out snippet of cloth, leaving him alone, his flaccid ass hanging out the open back.

He ended up being hoisted onto another bed. No, these weren't beds, there'd be no sleeping here, and moved into a small room with a large glass window. Cold vinyl and thin foam pressed against his back, head and heels. He was on a narrow gurney, and Miss Sunshine was suddenly there, holding his hand. Where did she come from?

She turned to him, lowering her face so she could speak directly to him, letting him see her lips move, helping him to focus on what she was saying. "It wouldn't be much longer. Just a few more tests." She smiled and patted his hand.

"Ad...." The sound popped out of his mouth, surprising both of them. He tried again, but could only grunt "ah....ah"

"That's okay, Mr. Brock, don't try too hard. Let it happen by itself." She gripped his hand, and he felt the strength in her soft, warm hand.

She let go and stuck her head out the door, speaking to someone on the other side of the large window. It was then he realized he wasn't tied down anymore. He had managed half a word, and they'd untied him. Best news since when? Since what? He still couldn't remember much about the car. Wait. Addy. Addy.

A wave of sadness crashed over him. He could feel it on his body, in it, like at the beach, standing in three feet of water and letting a big rolling wave smack you dead on. It knocked you hard, pulled your feet out from under you, and you felt it. Addy. Her stroke. He hadn't remembered her stroke at all, hadn't remembered she was dead.

Now the realization rushed back, and the memory of her smiling face was gone, an illusion crushed by death. She wouldn't rush to his side. She wouldn't even drag one leg behind her, then pull it along behind her, half a smile bright enough to light his day. It was as if it had all just happened, this realization, this memory, this central truth of his life, her illness, her death. He felt the agony she must have felt every day, every morning as she moved painfully, alone, to prepare herself, until that last morning.

He felt guilty again, as if he had been dreaming about another woman, Addy whole again, Addy alive. He grabbed the edge of the gurney and tried to push himself up. He swung one leg off, then pushed again.

He stood for a second, amazed that he was upright. Both hands were on the gurney, steadying himself. The room began to rock, and it seemed like the wall in front of him tilted up to the left. He gripped the gurney tighter but it didn't help. He started falling, but everything was going in the wrong direction and he couldn't tell where the floor was.

"Mr. Brock!" He felt hands under his armpits, pulling him up. He tried to steady his feet, keep them flat on the floor and balanced. Another larger and stronger set of hands joined Miss Sunshine's and they got him back up, seated on the gurney, his skinny legs bare and dangling over the edge.

"Addy." he managed. "She's gone."

Miss Sunshine nodded.

"Adelaide, is that your wife? Addy, you call her?" She watched his eyes very carefully as she asked him questions. Clay nodded as he looked at her. She had dark hair and very blue eyes that he hadn't noticed before. He felt an odd change ripple through his body, as if a veil of thin gauze had been drawn away, and suddenly he could see and understand things more clearly.

"Yes. Addy."

"Your voice is coming back."

"I tried—"

"Shhh," she said, "don't try too much. It'll come back naturally. I could tell you were trying hard to speak before."

Clay noticed she was holding his hand, cupping it in both of hers. It felt nice.

"I forgot she was gone. Dead. Then it came back."

"I'm so sorry, but it's not unusual." She let go of Clay's hand and gathered up the sheet that had fallen to the floor. She arranged it around Clay's gown, covering his legs and the rest of the skin bared by the flimsy gown.

"It's a little chilly in here," she said, by way of explanation. Clay liked how she covered for his embarrassment, or lack of it, actually.

"Do you remember what happened to you?"

Clay ignored her question, shook his head. How could he explain it?

"I remembered Addy, but I forgot her stroke, and thought she was still alive. It came back to me. It had gone right out of my mind."

"Oh, dear," she said, patting his hand.

"You said Adelaide. Did you know her?" Clay asked, tears creeping out onto his cheeks.

"Yes, I did. She was my patient."

Curiosity crept into his mind, replacing some of the sadness, as he wondered who this young woman was. Did he know her?

"Wait," Clay said. "If you knew Addy, why did you ask me if she was my wife? You knew that already."

"Ah, yes, Mr. Brock," she said. "I did know that. The trick was, did you?" She said it with a satisfied smile, patting his hand again, and Clay knew he had passed some sort of test, passed through something he couldn't yet understand.

"I was pretty confused for a while," Clay said. "Am I going to be okay?" The words echoed in his head, and he felt the great distance from the last time he had asked, am I gonna make it? The answer wasn't quite as important this time as it had been the last. She picked up a chart and read through it, making a quick note, and putting it down before answering him.

"Yes, for now, you are. You've had a transient ischemic attack. Do you know what that is?"

"No idea. You're not a nurse, are you?"

"No. Would you rather have a male doctor, Mr. Brock?"

"No, no. Don't get the wrong idea. It's just that I was thinking, or dreaming, about a nurse from a long time ago. Then I woke up, and there you were. I just assumed—"

"How long ago?"

"Another century," Clay said, his hand moving to his wound without even thinking about it. He rubbed the scar tissue near his neck, then dropped his hand, embarrassed.

"May I?" She didn't wait for an answer, but held down the sheet and lifted his gown to look at the scar on his right side. She moved her fingers along it, pressing it, moving out from it along his ribs. She lowered the gown.

"Not a bad job, but obviously rushed. They dealt with the essentials, but dispensed with the finishing touches. It must have been done under terrible conditions."

"There was a long line behind me, I know that much."

"Korea, or World War Two?"

"1945. Germany, or damn close to it. Who are you, anyway?"

"Emily Krause. I'm Addy's geriatrician. I saw your name when you were brought in. Glad to meet you, Mr. Brock." She stuck out her hand and Clay shook it.

Well I'll be damned. Miss Sunshine sure did have a way about her.

"She never mentioned you."

"I'm new on staff, they brought me a few months ago to consult with Addy's physical therapist. I was so sorry to hear about her. Are you sure you wouldn't like a different doctor?"

"No, you'll do. I like a young person who knows those wars even happened."

"It wasn't hard in my family. My grandfather never came home from the war. He went down with a sub in the Pacific. Grandma still has his picture on the mantle, in his dress blues. I dust it off for her every time I visit."

Clay looked at this young woman. She wasn't quite as young as he first thought. There were a few lines around the eyes, the softness and smoothness of her twenties behind her. There was a lot he had missed, but he wasn't thinking straight, he knew that much. He felt a sudden admiration for her, her steadfastness with her grandmother and the remembrance of her grandfather. Not the least that she voluntarily tended to the ancient and elderly.

"I'm sorry," he said.

"Yeah," she said, slipping for a moment from her professional posture, her eyes drifting as if her thoughts were somewhere else. "Your son is waiting for you, in my office."

"Can I go now? Perhaps you could explain this attack thing to both of us."

"Yes, certainly." The efficient doctor returning, checking his pulse, heart rate, blood pressure, vision, and balance. She gave up looking for something wrong with him, and called an orderly to help Clay get dressed. The orderly wheeled him to her office, knocked on her door, and within a second Chris opened it.

"Dad!" Chris pulled him in the room, and awkwardly hugged him, leaning down over the wheelchair. Clay patted his son on the back, not certain how to respond to the display of emotion. "I'm glad you're okay, you had me worried."

"Here I am," said Clay, at a loss for words but feeling that said everything. Here I am. They can't kill me.

"Chris, please sit," Dr. Krause said. She pulled a chair in front of Clay and Chris so she could face both of them directly.

"Mr. Brock, as I said, you've had a transient ischemic attack. It's called a TIA, or a mini-stroke."

"Is it what like my mother had?" Chris asked, looking at Clay. He thought he could see the fear of the disability flit across his son's face, the terror of the closeness that might require.

"No," Dr. Krause said. "It's nothing like a stroke. It's a temporary blockage of a blood vessel in the brain. It brings on sudden symptoms, like those your father experienced. Vision problems, dizziness, loss of consciousness, temporary amnesia."

"Is he going to be all right?" Chris asked.

"He is all right," Dr. Krause said. "We've done a full set of tests, except for an MRI. I was about to order one when your father came out of it. The symptoms can last as little as ten minutes or as much as 24 hours. None of the other tests showed anything, and he quickly became very lucid. Quite lucid, actually." She smiled at Clay.

"So he can go home?"

"Absolutely," Dr. Krause said. "I'm going to prescribe a blood-thinning medication, to see if we can avoid another one of these events. I'll want to see you in a week, Mr. Brock—"

"Call me Clay, why don't you? Mr. Brock makes me feel old." They laughed at his joke, and Clay felt like he'd won the lottery. He'd thought he was dying, losing everything, and now he was going home in time for dinner. As he watched Dr. Krause smile, he remembered the struggle with his silence, how then he'd wanted nothing more than to tell the world everything. Now he was sitting here, cracking wise, and all those words were safely tucked back in place. For how long?

"All right, Clay, and you can call me Emily."

"Oh no," Clay said. "I call a doctor Doc, no two ways about that."

"So nothing special to look out for tonight?" Chris asked her.

"Your father may be a little tired, that's all," she said as she opened the door. "Will you or someone stay with him?"

"I will," Chris said. To Clay, it sounded like someone volunteering to take point on a patrol, knowing there was no other choice.

Chris pushed the wheelchair in silence, down the corridor to the main lobby. Clay could see the sky out the tall windows, thick white clouds drifting across a blue sky above wet pavement. It had stopped raining.

There had been blue skies before, leaving that other hospital, the first blue skies in days, maybe weeks. No clouds, but white contrails as bombers, fighters and cargo planes dropping supplies streamed overhead. On the stretcher, he had looked up and seen the big four-engine bombers, high in the sky, and trembled with awe and anger. Where were you guys anyway? The nurse walked up to his stretcher, as he was about to be loaded into the ambulance for transport to a General Hospital.

"Take it easy, soldier, you're going to be okay," she said as she re-arranged his blanket. She slipped a medical pouch under his blanket and tucked it in. He felt the hard metal of the .45 wrapped inside.

"It's unloaded," she whispered. "Don't tell who…"

"Don't worry," he said, reaching with his good arm and squeezing her hand. "I know how to keep a secret."

Chapter Thirteen

1945

JAKE KNELT IN THE SNOW, ONE KNEE DOWN AND the other up. The dampness of the wet snow on his knee told him that today wouldn't be as frigid as yesterday, but the air was still filled with cold moisture, a damp, thick, heavy fog settling into the folds of terrain all around them. He held his right hand up, palm forward. Clay stopped beside him. Tuck and Shorty came up quietly, lowering themselves into the snow with care, hands on their gear, holding down the sounds of leather, clothing and metal as they settled in.

Behind them, men flopped down, dropping rifles, groaning, helmets off and rolling in the snow. Turning, Clay glared, raising his finger to his lips, then flattening out his hand in a downward motion. Sound carried in these woods, and he knew Jake had stopped because he'd heard something. He knew by the slight swivel of Jake's head, the slow turning of ears left to right, right to left, searching out who else might have heard all this replacement clatter. Didn't they teach them anything in Basic? Clay doubted the Army had changed a thing since he went through Basic himself. They were probably still teaching them how to set up pup tents for a good night's sleep at the front. Out of sight of the enemy, they had said, in a grove of trees for camouflage. Too bad they never took into account the Krauts setting their artillery fuses to burst in the treetops, sending wooden splinters like daggers showering into G.I.s below. Clay looked at the men behind him as they whispered to each other. Not even enough sense to shut up and set up a perimeter guard. The walking dead.

Jake tried to quiet himself, to let his beating heart settle down so the thumping in his chest and ears would die away, leaving only the sounds of the forest. They had just climbed a ridgeline, and he could feel the fatigue in his thighs and in his lungs as they gasped for oxygen. Gulping air he signaled for Oakland, up ahead on point, to come back. No need to ask twice. Oakland slid down the next ridgeline and ran low, crouching, scurrying over to them. As he neared the bottom of the gully separating the ridges he all but disappeared in the thick fog. Jake saw the top layer of fog swirling as Oakland moved through it, the current creating a tiny gap for the grayness to fill in behind him. Coming up out of the fog as if rising from a dive into a deep lake, he flopped down on his knees next to Jake, hauling in a lungful of air, his eyes on the ground, M1 pointed straight at Jake. With an irritated frown, Jake pushed it away. Tapping Oakland's helmet he waited for the kid to look at him. He pointed at his eyes, then waited some more. The look on Oakland's face was quizzical, uncomprehending. Jake leaned in until his nose was up against the chinstrap hanging off the side of Oakland's helmet.

"Did you see anything?" Jake whispered, desperately wanting to add asshole, but not wanting to expend the effort or the sound.

"No, no. Everything looks the same out there. Fog, trees, snow."

There was enough truth to that. They had spent most of yesterday lost after they'd left the Kraut position where they'd spent the night. Jake was certain they were headed in the right direction today, or at least what once was the right direction. Maybe the Krauts had pushed the line back so far they'd never get home, just wander around in these frozen woods until they ran out of food, ammo, and hope. There were no maps to go by, all those were in the pockets of dead lieutenants and sergeants, caked in blood and frost, under the snow. Nothing but the setting sun to point the way back.

Jake tapped Oakland on the shoulder and jerked his thumb back to the gaggle of replacements behind them. Oakland didn't need that gesture explained. He took off in snap, obviously glad to not be point man anymore. Jake watched Oakland settle in and heard the murmur of his pals asking him what was up. Lifting his finger to his lips, the kid cut them off, turning away from them and watching the trees instead. Nothing like an hour on point for a guy to learn the virtues of silence. Behind Oakland, Big Ned and Miller came up from the rear. Big Ned gave Jake a slight nod and turned away, watching their rear. Miller laid down next to him, his M1 aimed along the trail they had made.

Jake waited some more. Waited for all the sounds of movement to vanish from his mind. Waited for the natural sounds of the snow-laden woods be heard. The pines here were small, interspersed with brush and small trees. Streambeds ran between ridges, and Jake could imagine it in the spring, a mad profusion of running water, rocks covered with green moss, ferns and flowers popping out everywhere. It would be pretty.

He saw a single bird fly out of a pine tree off to their right. A dark, small form, it darted and dove away from them, vanishing in a cover of green pine branches. He looked from where it had flown; letting his eyes travel down the ridgeline ahead of them, off to the right where it tapered down to nothing but a white flatness.

Without moving his eyes, he lay down in the snow and tapped Shorty on his leg. Shorty went prone too, crawling up, his head next to Jake's. Not moving his head, Jake squinted his eyes, trying to focus on what he thought he'd seen. He put two fingers up to his eyes and pointed straight out along his sightline. Shorty looked for about ten seconds, then nodded, motioning Clay into his spot, scuttling back to make room for him. He pointed, then ran his hand back and forth, left and right, indicating a spot ahead about ten degrees wide.

Raising his binoculars, Clay scanned the area ahead. At first all he saw were trees and brush, snow heaped up on boulders. Then he spotted it. Down at the end of two ridgelines, on a flat stretch of forest floor. A road. Muddy, snow-caked ruts showed between the ridges for only ten yards, but it was unmistakable. Clay nodded and handed the binoculars to Jake. Looking through them, he studied the road, and then all around it. Nothing stirred.

Jake raised his eyebrows to Clay as he handed the binoculars back.

Clay tilted his head. Yeah, why not?

Jake looked at Shorty and Tuck. Tuck shrugged and Shorty grinned. What the fuck. Why not?

Jake tapped Shorty and pointed at Big Ned and Miller. Go tell them. Crouching low, Shorty crawled away from the top of the ridge, quick-stepping through the other men, his hand out, palm down, going slowly up and down. Stay put and shut up.

Jake looked back at the road, but he still worried over the

noise he'd heard. What had that sound been? Deeper than a snapping twig. Maybe snow falling from a tree limb, or a deer jumping a log. Or a boot stomping off snow. He strained to listen, sitting quietly letting everything come to him. But he couldn't quiet himself, couldn't turn off the voice in his head, second-guessing everything. The road forced him to think ahead, decide on a course of action, maybe get them back, maybe get them all killed. The fear of failing the men gathered behind him gnawed at his mind, sending up a drumbeat of doubt pounding his head.

The road, the road. Was it a good sign or not? Where would it lead? Was it guarded? By them? By us?

He rubbed his fist against his forehead, trying to drive out the questions and make some sense of things. Everyone was waiting, waiting for a decision that he had to make, a decision that could get them all killed. Or home. Home. Funny how a foxhole in the frozen earth became home when you couldn't get back to it.

Should we stay put? Was it better to stay in the woods?

No. It wasn't. They'd gotten lost yesterday and walked in a big circle, ending up back at their own tracks six hours later. It was too easy to get lost, too easy to fool yourself into thinking you were headed in the right direction when you were going off at an angle, your mistake growing each hour until you made more mistakes trying to correct the first one and you ended up right where you started. Fucked.

Okay, the road. It's gotta lead somewhere, and that somewhere should tell us where we are. We'll have to go slow, point and rear guard close in so they can signal to get off the road at the first sound of vehicles. Or a checkpoint. And if it's our guys, the problem then is how not to get shot when we jump out of the woods and start yelling and screaming. The road.

Jake smiled in spite of himself. Soon as he could, he'd say to Clay, there's bad news, bad news, and good news...bad news is it could be a Kraut road and they'll shoot us. Other bad news is it could be our road, and dogfaces'll shoot us. Good news is there's no one else left to shoot...

What's that?

A noise, a thump from beyond the next ridge. Another bird flew up from the trees in front of them, a large black crow, or maybe a raven. Then another, then five or six more from the trees farther down on their right. Caw, caw, caw, they called, disturbed, as they floated down to another thick stand of pines below the ridge.

Thump, again.

Jake looked around, trying to locate the source of the sound. He caught sight of Shorty, headed back from Big Ned and Miller, as he froze in place. Even the replacements were hushed, looking up into the trees from where they were nestled in a small draw. Shorty moved his head slowly, looking around, his hand flat again, signaling quiet. Miller shifted his rifle towards the sounds. Big Ned kept the BAR on their rear.

Tuck brushed his hand against Clay and Jake as he pointed his finger down towards their right, into the fog-settled gully between the ridges. His hand shook but the finger aimed true. In the fog below them, the top of a helmet broke the surface and floated along, a disembodied steel prow, leaving a wake of gray haze behind it. It was painted white, winter camouflage, and underneath it, shielded by the fog, was a German, not twenty yards from them.

Jake watched the helmet. He could see it turn left and right, then dip down to look at something on the ground. It dipped beneath the fog and vanished, with the sound of another thump. The German had stumbled and fallen. This close, Jake heard the grunt as the guy got up. Walking through the fog and deep snow, it was easy to trip over a hidden log or rock. There could be plenty of them out there, falling over themselves. Jake looked behind the first helmet and saw more white-washed steel following. Two, three, four. If they had crouched, like Oakland, they would have been invisible. But these Krauts were standing up straight, not hiding. The sounds from beyond the ridge meant there were more over there too. A search party, looking for their tracks, hunting them.

Jake lifted his hand slowly and spread out five fingers, then pointed towards the Krauts, and signaled left, the direction they were headed. He felt a hand pat his shoulder, and sensed Clay moving off. Jake and Tuck were up front, Shorty on their right flank baby-sitting the replacements, and Big Ned and Miller holding the rear. They were blind on the left, above the small depression where the rest of the men were huddled together.

Clay cradled his M1 in his arms and crawled, all elbows and knees, pulling himself through the snow as it mounded up in front of him, forcing itself into his mouth and nose. Inching his way around a small pine tree he stopped behind a clump of birch, its thin shoots spread like a fan in front of his face. As the Germans crossed in front of Jake's position, moving up out of the gully, their faces and torsos became visible as the fog fell away behind them. They looked like swimmers emerging from an ocean, draped in wisps of fog and trailing whiteness. Clay could see their faces and expressions clearly, searching the terrain around them with wary, determined, hard eyes. He watched as they came out of the fog, not grouping together, but falling into a four-man diamond, guarding their flanks. Clay saw one of them signal to someone on the next ridge, where he made out other forms flitting through the trees in their white winter camouflage suits. These weren't replacements.

The Kraut who signaled didn't signal in both directions. That was good. It meant this group was the left flank of the patrol. If they were looking for them, they were probably sweeping sections off the road, looking for footprints. If they kept going dead straight, what would they find? Clay tried to remember which way they'd walked in to this point. Had they curved in, so the Krauts would cross their tracks behind them?

It was all a jumble in his head, he couldn't remember. The Kraut closest to him walked right by, about five yards away. Smelling him, that odor of sweat, leather and sausage that always clung to Krauts, Clay wondered what he smelled like to them. Real tobacco, maybe, or coffee? Good thing they'd all run out of smokes yesterday. His stomach grumbled and he prayed it wasn't really as loud as it sounded. The Kraut stopped, shifting his feet and turning his head, as if he were a dog sniffing the air for the scent of cat.

Clay froze, not even wanting to blink. Keeping his gaze on the Kraut, he studied him. Potato masher grenade stuck in his boot. Schmeisser submachine gun hung on a black leather strap over his shoulder. Two four-clip ammo pouches on his belt, along with two more grenades. The hood to his white snow suit was thrown back and open at the neck. He was close enough for Clay to see the SS letters on his collar tab, sharp-edged lightning bolts. Fuck. SS and loaded for bear. He wished he knew how many of them there were. Five here, probably the same at the next ridge. Make that one squad. Two or three more, a full platoon, maybe? Two they could handle. Three, and they were fucked good. Not much ammo left, three or four clips apiece. But everyone had a couple of grenades at least. They hadn't been able to use them from inside the house, but they had gone through most of their ammo.

Yells rose up from the other ridge. The Kraut in front of Clay turned away from him. Clay heard a gasp, a surprised intake of breath behind him. The yelling had spooked one of the replacements. A slight rustling of clothing told him someone was scared, fighting the urge to blot, to drop his rifle and run through the snow, away from everything. It was a powerful urge, and Clay had felt it more than once. Away always seemed like it would be a safe place when your fear got a hold of you. Away was where he'd like to be too, but right now he had a Kraut in front of him who didn't look like he was going away anytime soon.

Hände hoch! Hände hoch! Hands up, in the shrill, excited tones of a soldier who'd be happy to shoot you if you didn't obey him exactly. Clay knew that feeling too, the questions that gnawed at his gut when face to face with the enemy, his hands held high. Is this guy really giving up? Does he have a concealed weapon? A grenade? A knife? Is he going to kill me? Then the thought, why don't I plug him, why am I taking a chance for this fucking Kraut?

Surrendering or taking prisoners was never easy in the first few minutes, right after a fight. Everyone's blood was up, everyone was nervous, twitchy, scared, and still in the tunnel vision of life or death combat. If you surrendered, you offered up your life to your captor, who may not yet have felt the killing frenzy pass. Fear, terror and rage collided in the air as men who couldn't understand each other yelled louder and louder, going desperately beyond language, one pair of hands reaching toward heaven while the other gripped his weapon tighter. These voices sounded all of those things.

The Kraut in front of Clay said something to one of his men and pointed. He took off to see what the fuss was. Then Clay heard a voice in English, an American voice.

"Don't shoot! I give up! Don't shoot!"

Cresting the other ridge, a GI with his hands held high stumbled along in front of a couple of Krauts. His coat was open and his helmet was gone. He looked back at his captors, who were prodding him with their rifles. Every time he did, he'd lose his footing and stumble. Then a poke with a rifle barrel or a swipe with a rifle butt would propel him forward again. If he used his hands to push himself up, it was hände hoch all over again.

"Please don't shoot, I give up, I give up."

Clay risked a look back at the replacements while the Kraut in front of him was turned away. He scanned their faces, taking a quick count. Fuck. One was missing. It was him, this one, begging not to be shot. Clay recognized the face, but didn't know his name. Must've gotten lost, or got himself lost so he could surrender. Maybe he thought the Germans would take him away, far away.

The Kraut in front of Clay took a couple of steps back, to get a better look at the prisoner being brought in. Clay could see him rest his hands on top of the submachine gun that hung by a strap around his shoulders. He looked nonchalant and patient. The prisoner was led straight to him, about twenty feet from where Clay lay hidden. Fuck. This guy's a sergeant or officer. Pretty soon we'll have a dozen of these fuckers within spitting distance.

"Don't shoot, okay? I surrender, okay?" The GI's voice was calmer now. They hadn't shot him, and now they'd brought him to someone in charge. His voice was friendly, as if he were trying to make a deal with them, show them how reasonable he was being. I gave myself up, so don't kill me, okay?

They came up to the Kraut with the Schmeisser and stopped. They were to his left, so Clay could see their faces. The GI was wide-eyed, smiling, a grin of fear to show how harmless he was. Clay heard one of the Krauts call the one in front of him Scharführer, what the SS called their sergeants, as he handed him something Clay couldn't see and nodded his head toward the prisoner. By now there were seven or eight of them grouped around the prisoner and the Kraut sergeant. Clay spotted two more on top of the far ridge.

Two squads. There had to be only two squads. If this sergeant's in charge, then it had to be only two squads. Stands to reason, if there were three or more, he'd be in the middle somewhere, not out at one end of the line. But if there's only two squads, then this makes sense. Bad news twice, two SS squads. Good news, no third squad.

"Where are the others?" The SS sergeant spoke his English slowly, as if he were remembering a distant school lesson.

"I'm all alone here, really, I've been alone since you guys hit us at the village…"

"Langsam. Slow. Talk slow," the sergeant said, with deliberate calmness.

"Okay," the GI said, nodding his head to show he understood.

"Where are the others?"

He shrugged his shoulders. "I'm alone. Since the village. I'm lost. I surrender."

"You have been lost all this time?"

"Yeah, honest, I've been looking for anybody, I'm freezing, hardly had any food..." The sergeant gave a nod of his head and a rifle butt flew up and smashed into the side of the GI's face. He fell to the ground, holding his cheek, cupping blood as it welled up in his hand.

"Do not lie. Tell me, where are the others?"

"No, not lying. I'm all alone."

Clay grimaced, waiting for the next assault to come. Boots whacked the GI in the ribs. He rolled over, curling himself up into a ball to protect himself. Clay thought of a dozen lies that would've sounded better, bought some time, maybe even a hint of mercy. But the GI kept on whimpering, as he was hit, alone, alone, alone.

The sergeant raised a hand, and the kicks stopped.

"So you were all alone?"

"Yeah, honest."

"You were at the village, the village we attacked two days ago?"

"Yeah, first fight I was ever in. I'm new, a replacement. I ran, I didn't even shoot anyone."

The sergeant spoke to the two who had brought the G.I., asking them a question from his tone. The answer came in grim tones.

"You did not have much ammunition left for someone who did not shoot."

"No, I mean yes, I shot but I didn't shoot anyone, didn't hit anyone. I'm a lousy shot."

"Where is your officer?"

"Dead, back at the village."

"Have you seen any other Americans since the village?"

"No, nobody. I saw your patrol and stood up, raised my hands and gave up. Ask your men." He started to get up, still holding his bruised and bleeding cheek.

"Where did you get this?" The sergeant held out a knife, as if he were handing it to the GI. Clay felt his stomach drop. It was an SS dagger, black ebony case with bright silver fittings, with a black and silver handle on the knife.

"Back at the repple depple, in a card game."

"What? Where is that?"

"Sorry, sorry, at the replacement depot. I won it in a card game."

"I think you took it from an SS man you killed."

"No, no, I didn't kill anyone!" Terror rose in his voice. Clay wanted to bang his fist on the ground. Didn't they tell these stupid fuckers anything?

"My men do not like it when you Americans steal from our dead. Tell me where the others are and nothing will happen to you."

"No, please, all I did was play cards with a guy who had the knife. I won the hand, I won, you see?"

Clay admired the replacement's guts. He may have wanted to give up, but he wasn't going to betray them. Clay doubted the poor guy even knew they were listening. He must've taken off earlier in the day and been wandering around, looking for someone to surrender to. Too bad he didn't ditch his souvenir.

"So you gamble for an SS man's dagger. That is even worse. You are not even a soldier."

"I'm sorry, I didn't know, it was only a card game, please."

"All alone then? The last two days, you saw no one?" The sergeant stuck the dagger into his belt. Clay saw the arms continue to move, the shift of the Schmeisser, at the same time he saw the Krauts on either side of the G.I. step back.

"Yes, I was alone, I don't know anything, I just got to the front line."

A burst from the Schmeisser ripped through the air, followed by a gurgling scream as the G.I. flopped on the ground. A single shot ended the sounds.

God damn it. Clay slid down a few inches and rolled on his back, risking that the Germans wouldn't hear it as they focused on the shooting. He pulled a grenade from his pocket and held it up. Jake nodded and did the same. Tuck and Shorty followed suit. Miller kept his eye on their rear as Big Ned sat up, grenade in hand. Oakland too, along with one other replacement. The rest were huddled together, faces buried in the snow, paralyzed with fear.

Clay gripped the safety lever and pulled the pin. He held it up, his hand over the lever, waiting for everyone else. Six other pins were pulled, six hands gripping live grenades, holding the safety lever in place. Opening his hand Clay let the safety lever fly off, starting the fuse burning. He saw the other levers flip off and counted, one, two, and then tossed the grenade towards the Germans. Seven grenades flew through the air, over the embankment they hid behind. Seven explosions cracked the air, sending shrapnel flying through the closely grouped Germans. Even veterans make mistakes. These Germans were good, but even they couldn't keep from bunching up, knowing the G.I. was going to die. No one wanted to miss the show.

Clay heard screams follow the explosions and gunfire all around him. He couldn't tell who was still alive right in front of him but he was more concerned with the two Germans on the next ridge. He felt bullets whip through the air over his head. Trying to ignore them, he sighted in on the German farthest away. Squeezing the trigger slowly he fired, but the German didn't fall. He went right and the other Kraut went left, trying to work their way around to their flanks. Clay followed the one going right, led him a bit, let out a breath, squeezed the trigger, and this time the bastard dropped.

As he reached for a new clip, snow blew up in front of his face and he heard the submachine gun blasting away as if it were next to his eardrum. Was that fucking sergeant still alive? Clay buried his head in the snow and waited for the firing to die down.

Jake saw the bullets hit all around Clay and yelled his name, but it sounded like a whisper among all the screams, curses and gunfire. He emptied his clip over Clay's head, hoping to hit whoever was firing at him. Pulling a grenade out he threw it, unable to see where it landed. As he re-loaded he saw Shorty search his pockets for a clip and come up empty. The grenade came sailing back at them and Shorty dropped his rifle, catching it and flipping it behind them. He dove for the ground as it exploded in the air. Jake rolled around a boulder, getting up in a crouch, trying to see where the fire was coming from, bullets hitting the side of the boulder as he tried to find a spot that gave him cover.

Shorty kicked one of the huddled replacements and grabbed his rifle. His arm was dripping blood but he didn't look badly hurt. Jake saw a white blur above the embankment and squeezed his eyes shut as another bullet ricocheted off the rock inches from him. He leaned left and brought up his M1, seeing the SS sergeant above them, leveling his submachine gun right at him. He squeezed the trigger and nothing happened. The M1 was jammed. He looked into the sergeant's eyes, not ten feet away. His helmet was gone and blood matted the hair on the side of his head. His bloody right leg was shredded but it held him there, above them, grinning, as Jake uselessly pointed the malfunctioning M1 at him. Shorty saw the sergeant too, and fired twice, quickly from the hip, missing both times. The empty clip ejected and the Schmeisser swiveled to aim at Shorty. The sergeant fired a burst that caught Shorty in the chest. As he swiveled his weapon towards Jake, who was slamming the receiver with the heel of his hand, Clay rose up from the snow and swung his M1 by the barrel, hitting the SS sergeant in the chest and sending him falling, a spray of bullets arcing up into the air. He drove the gun butt into his face, forcing him down, praying he wouldn't gain control of the submachine gun for even a second. Faster than he ever thought he could, Clay swung the M1 again and again, smashing the butt against helmet and head until he couldn't tell where one began and the other ended. Then falling into a heap, gasping for air, oblivious to bullets and explosions, he prayed for his lungs and heart to slow down, for the blood to stop pounding in his head, and for the screaming to stop. He couldn't move, couldn't think, or do anything except let his lungs heave and stare down at the red-flecked snow. Seconds, maybe minutes passed. It didn't matter.

The noises lessened and Clay looked up. German bodies littered the ground. Standing with a grunt, he looked back down the embankment. Oakland was gone. The other guy who'd thrown the grenade was dead. He'd stood up to fire his M1 and took a bullet in the face. Miller was looking at Clay, then back down the trail, then at the dead Germans. His eyes couldn't stop darting around, waiting for the next threat to appear. Big Ned let out a sigh, as if he'd been holding his breath the whole time, a long white plume of frosted air blasting out from his mouth.

The other replacements untangled themselves and looked around, as if they'd been awakened from a nap. Skittering away from the faceless dead replacement they moved in a clump, each one trying to put another man between himself and death. They passed Shorty, two empty rifles at his feet, his helmet gone and his chest ripped open, four bullets grouped around his heart. The snow around him had turned crimson as his brown eyes stared up at the gray-clouded sky. Tuck knelt next to him, one hand on his shoulder, the other holding himself up by his M1. He hung his head as the replacements continued to edge away from him, guilt driving them from the reddening whiteness.

Clay felt Jake help him up.

"Shorty's dead," Jake said.

"Yeah," Clay answered, moving away from the dead German. He started to pick up his rifle, but the wooden stock was shattered. Leaving it in the snow he walked over beside Tuck with Jake.

"He saved my life, Tuck," Jake said, kneeling down next to him.

"Yeah," Tuck said, faintly.

Jake didn't know what else to say. It was the best tribute he could give. Saving replacement's lives didn't count, they didn't even lift a finger. But saving a buddy's life, that meant something. Funny thing was, it probably meant the least to Tuck. His life hadn't needed saving, and now his best buddy was dead.

"Yeah," he said again, and touched Shorty's head, running his hand through the unruly hair, as you would to sooth a child.

"Tuck," Jake said quietly. "We gotta move. I'll get his dogtag, then we gotta get out of here, okay?"

"I'll do it, Jake. Give me a minute."

Tuck patted down Shorty's hair some more. Steam rose from the holes in his chest, the warmth leaving his body, drifting out into the cold.

"Okay."

Putting his arm around Tuck, Jake sat with him for a minute, watching as he gently pulled the dogtags out from under Shorty's clothes. He unclipped one, wiped the blood off it, and handed it to Jake. Then he went back to smoothing Shorty's hair as Jake got up and moved off to check the German dead. He prodded and kicked the corpses, making sure none were only wounded and still a threat to them.

Clay handed Jake the dogtags from the two replacements and he dropped all three in his jacket pocket, a dull clink sounding as they mingled with the others.

Jake closed his pocket flap, smoothing it down, feeling the metal tags beneath the fabric, thinking of the next-of-kin names on each. Mothers or wives, all waiting at home, not knowing their names no longer hung next to the warm beating heart of someone who loved them. He got the replacements going and told them to move towards the road. As they shuffled out of the gulley, he saw they had left behind a variety of German belt buckles, knives, watches, and a couple a Walther pistols. They were learning.

Every G.I. wanted souvenirs. You just had to know when to carry them and when to get them to the rear. Hunting souvenirs was a good sign, actually. It meant you thought you had a future, could see ahead to a time when you'd be back home, showing off a Nazi flag or an SS helmet and telling stories. When guys got rid of souvenirs, it was either a sign that capture was likely, or that they'd given up any hope of ever getting home. The first was a smart move, the second almost inevitable.

"Hey, I got one!"

Jake looked up to see Oakland marching a prisoner towards them, an SS trooper, with his hände hoch. He pushed him with the barrel of his M1 towards Jake.

"What the fuck is this?" Big Ned said, advancing toward the Kraut with his BAR raised.

"I saw him trying to flank us, so I went over to those trees to wait for him. Sure enough, he came right along and I captured him." Oakland sounded like a kid who'd come home from school with all As.

"Did you search him?" Big Ned said.

"Best I could, alone. You guys should check him out."

Clay took the German's helmet off and threw it in the snow. "First thing," he said, "is never leave a prisoner's helmet on. It's a big fucking steel pot he could smash your head in with."

Oakland's smile vanished. Clay and Big Ned searched the Kraut, coming out with one hidden grenade and a pistol. Not a German pistol, but an American .45 caliber automatic. Clay took the pistol and opened up the German's coat.

"Look at this bastard," Clay said. "He's wearing a shoulder holster. They shot a G.I. for a lousy knife and this guy's sporting some officer's sidearm."

Big Ned closed in on the German, looking down on him.

"Take it off," he said. The German looked at him with dull, vacant eyes. He knew he was dead. "Take it off!"

Big Ned slammed the German with his fist, sending him to the ground. He pulled at the camouflage smock, ripping it off as he kicked the Kraut in the ribs. He may not have understood

English, but the German knew what he was supposed to do.
He unhooked the leather strap and let it fall to the ground. He
stood, blood flowing from a cut lip, and stared at Big Ned, silent,
unwilling to show the fear eating away inside him.

Miller stood by Big Ned as the replacements gravitated back
towards them, drawn to the drama unfolding just as the dead
all around had been moments before. Not wanting to repeat
the German's mistake, Jake got the replacements moving in
small groups up to the road to stand guard, as best they could.
Watching the last of them head towards the road, he turned to
see Tuck standing near the German.

"Do me a favor, Tuck, head up to the road and watch those
guys?"

"Okay," Tuck said, hesitating. "But if you want someone to
take care of things here, just say the word."

"No, no, I need someone to make sure those guys at the road
are quiet," Jake said, cutting him off.

"Sure, Jake, whatever you say." Tuck looked at the German,
studying him, and then moved away, slowly.

Big Ned and Miller stood back as Jake and Clay approached
Oakland and his prisoner. Oakland had expected to be
congratulated for bringing in a POW. Instead, he felt three hard
stares drilling into his eyes. Miller looked away, pretending to
search the woods, his eyes finally settling on the ground in front
of him.

"So what the fuck are we supposed to do with this sack of
shit?" Big Ned asked to no one in particular.

"Bring him back," said Oakland. "Maybe he's got information
or something."

"You speak English?" Jake asked the prisoner, ignoring
Oakland. He got no response.

"We can't bring him back," Clay said. "Too far to go to risk
bringing a Kraut along. He could yell for help, grab a weapon,
anything."

"We'll shoot him if he does," Oakland said.

"By then it will be too late. We have to take care of this now,"
Jake said.

"He's right," Clay said, explaining to Oakland, and perhaps
himself. "In a fight like this you can't take prisoners. You should've
shot him then and there. It would have been quick and clean."

"I ain't shooting him now," Oakland said. "I don't shoot prisoners."

"You don't know shit from shinola," Big Ned said. "You saw what they did. They could've kept that guy prisoner. It's us behind their lines, remember, asshole?"

Tension crackled the air around the prisoner, who stood calmly in the middle of it, either not understanding, or understanding fully and unwilling to show his fear. Big Ned looked ready to explode, as mad at Oakland as at the prisoner, maybe more.

"Miller," Jake said, "take Oakland up to the road, okay?" It would be better for the veterans to take care of this alone.

Miller looked up from the ground he'd been staring at.

"Go on up," he said to Oakland. "I'm staying."

There was a heavy silence among them, including the German. Looking at him, Jake felt nothing but irritation at Oakland. The kid didn't understand how things had to be done. Killing during a fight was killing fair and square. After a fight too, if a guy was beyond all help and suffering, then it was a fair killing too. But sometimes a minute can make a huge difference, all the difference. Same bullet, same gun, same death. But then it felt like murder. Well, so be it. This SS Kraut couldn't be trusted, he could get them all killed, and Jake was not going to get more of his guys dead before he got them back home. He wanted no more weight in that front pocket. He'd sent Tuck up to the road because losing your buddy was bad enough, no need to let Tuck do this killing and always wonder if had been the right thing. It would've been easy to let Tuck plug the guy, but Jake couldn't play it that way. He looked at Miller and nodded.

"Okay. Oakland, up to the road. The prisoner is my responsibility."

Oakland shrugged, and walked away. The German stood, hands resting on his head, waiting.

"Bring him over here," Jake motioned. Walking over to the body of the dead G.I., he looked back, and saw the first expression of fear break out over the German's face. His eyes widened and Jake could see the sweat on his forehead. Jake watched him looking around, searching the eyes of his captors for something that wasn't there, wasn't theirs to give. Still, he didn't speak as Big Ned and Miller pushed him towards the body of the dead American. Stumbling, the German stood up, still with his hands on top of his head, looking around once again at the G.I.s pointing their weapons at him. His gaze finally lit on the dead G.I., whose blank open eyes answered his unspoken question. Jake thought he saw a rueful, broken grin flash across the German's face. Maybe he thought he'd show these Americans how well he could die. Maybe he didn't believe they'd shoot him. Maybe he didn't give a damn. Slowly he dropped his hands, trying to come to some semblance of attention, looking around one more time. Not at the men, but at the trees and the gray clouds above. Both hands shaking at his side as he closed his eyes, twin clouds of frosted breath flowed from his nostrils.

Clay walked up to Jake and handed him the automatic they'd taken from the German.

"Best do it with this," Clay said. "There's some kinda justice in it."

Jake took the weapon and held Clay's stare. Keeping his hand on the barrel, Clay raised his eyebrow, checking to see if Jake was ready, or wanted him to take over.

Jake shook his head as he gave his M1 to Clay, taking the automatic from him. Pulling off his glove, he checked the safety, feeling the cross-hatched grip cold against his skin. At that second, the German opened his eyes, looking straight at him. Hazel green eyes burned into Jake's. The German's brow knotted, as if he were trying to peer deep inside Jake, trying to understand the man about to kill him, or perhaps wondering if he had the nerve. Jake got caught up in those eyes, the green drawing him in, that same brownish green of his father's. He raised the pistol, his hand trembling. The German was breathing harder now, and his exhales blew up a fog of frost in front of his face. Jake squinted, uncertain of what he was seeing. He was five feet away from the prisoner, but he was sighting down the .45 like it was five hundred. Sweat dripping into his eyes, he blinked as he saw the stern high cheekbones rising above a grim mouth set shut, the collarless white shirt buttoned tight at the neck, green eyes judging him, damning him...

"Jake," Clay said softly.

Jake pulled the trigger. One, twice. The German's legs collapsed under him and he fell backwards, one leg folding awkwardly beneath the other. Jake watched him for a moment, to be sure he was dead. A small swirl of frost drifted out from his open mouth, disappearing as if it were a departing spirit. Jake walked over to him and couldn't help but kick the one leg out from under the other. It looked so uncomfortable.

"Let's go," said Clay, taking the .45 and handing Jake his rifle. Turning, Jake walked away, up to the road, the image of his father's face swimming in his mind. His father taunting him with the sins he'd committed and the promise of sins handed down, father to son, like an ugly family heirloom on a darkened basement shelf.

They stood in the road, Jake, Clay, Big Ned, Miller and Tuck, in a small circle that excluded the replacements. Oakland stood apart from both groups, not a raw replacement or a veteran, but somewhere in between and alone.

"Which way?" asked Clay, as he swiveled his head, trying to find the sun behind the clouds. His eyes narrowed at a faint disc of light and then pointed to their left. "That seems to be northwest."

"Good enough," said Jake. "I'll take point."

"I can take point," said Oakland, loudly, projecting himself into the group.

"You'll get your turn," said Jake. "Make sure no more of your buddies there slip away."

Oakland turned away, muttering, and started pushing the others apart, telling them not to bunch up and to keep their eyes open. Big Ned cranked his head towards the rear, and Jake nodded as Big Ned and Miller dropped back for rear guard. He knew Clay would be right behind him, ready to relay any signal from the point back to the group.

Tuck stood still. While the others moved silently away, gruesome dancers to a practiced tune, Tuck was alone. Jake and Clay exchanged quick glances, and stopped, staying with Tuck.

"You know," Clay said slowly, as if a thought was just dawning on him, "that Oakland kid might be okay if he can manage not to do anything else stupid."

"Least he got up off his ass and did something," Jake agreed. "What do you think, Tuck?"

"I dunno," Tuck said, shrugging.

"Think you could take him on," Jake asked, "until we get back?"

Tuck bit his lip, and twisted his hands around the barrel of his rifle as he leaned on it. "You think it'd be okay?"

"Yeah, Tuck. He needs a hand, and Shorty wouldn't want you all alone out here," Jake said. Tuck thought about it for a minute.

"Okay. Let's see how it goes."

Tuck trudged towards the replacements and fell in next to Oakland. Jake trotted up the road to put some space between them, and settled down into the business of being point man. As he hugged the edge of the road, darting from cover to cover, watching the terrain and listening for man-made sounds, part of his mind drifted as the rest of it focused on the road.

He thought about Shorty, about how he'd gotten that nickname about thirty seconds after showing up with their squad. About how he and Tuck had hit it off right away, like guys he'd known at school, or those older guys you always saw together having their morning coffee at the diner. Jake wasn't the kind to make pals that easily, and remembered how he and Clay had paired up more as a mathematical consequence than anything else. But they had become pals, more than pals, brothers maybe. Suddenly it occurred to Jake that he didn't know how he'd stand it if Clay got killed. Wounded would be bad enough, but if Clay died.... What? What would happen to him? He'd grieve and go on, maybe get himself killed, maybe not. Maybe live through it and go home when it was all over. The possibility of life seemed empty, hopeless as death, the mockery of a promise.

Scuttling across the road to take cover behind a thick pine stump, Jake got a better look around a pile of boulders ahead. If they were headed in the right direction, they'd be coming up on the German rear, facing the Americans in front of them. That was good. As soon as they saw any signs of the German lines, they'd have to get off the road and try and slip through. That would be the hard part. Jake almost laughed out loud. After all this, we still have the hard part to worry about.

He thought again of his father's face floating in front of him. He wanted to tell Clay why he'd hesitated, why his hand shook. But he never could. Could he? No.

Why not? Who was he protecting? After the war was over he'd never see Clay again. How long could that be? Well, they still had the Japs to go, and scuttlebutt was that once Germany caved in, they'd all be shipped to the Pacific for the invasion of Japan. It wasn't fair. No one could survive all that fighting, no one.

He took off, running from tree stump to tree stump along the side of the road. Brushing the snow off the top of one he saw it was fresh cut, sometime this winter. Fuel was probably short, and villagers were cutting the trees along the road for firewood. The clearing allowed him to look back a good length down the road, and he saw Clay's helmet peeking around the side of a tree. Waving, he darted off again, gloved hands gripping his M1 tight, crouching, making himself as small a target as possible, hoping a German wouldn't recognize him and an American would. Of course he knew what he'd do on the front lines if he caught a glance of a crouched figure advancing on his position. Maybe it'd be a replacement and he'd be a lousy shot.

Oakland. Maybe he would be okay. Tuck would definitely help, long as he held it together. He seemed on the edge, but that could be shock, hunger, or exhaustion. As if it made any difference. On the edge was on the edge, no matter how you got there.

Oakland. He'd had a fleeting thought the other night, just before they'd found the empty German position. If Oakland or some other replacement got it, maybe he could switch dog tags somehow. Jake Burnett would be dead. He'd be somebody else. But how could he keep the dog tags a secret? And what would happen when Oakland's mother waited and waited for him to come home and he never showed up? The more he thought about it, the less it made sense, but he liked the idea of his parents getting that telegram. That'd show them.

The road curved to the left up ahead. Good spot for a sentry or an ambush. Stopping, Jake listened, waiting for a shuffle or a cough, any sound or smell that didn't belong. He took small, careful steps, moving quietly, scanning the curve in the road ahead...

He felt hard metal under his boot.

Omigod, omigod, omigod, I'm on a mine! Jesus! Jesus Christ Almighty!

Jake felt the fear melt his skin white, then turn it clammy cold. Urine flowed down his leg as he peed uncontrollably. Sweat broke out on his forehead and he felt his stomach hollow out. Standing as still as he could, he tried to focus, to not move a muscle. His left leg was behind him, his right foot forward where he'd put it down on top of the metal object in the snow. His boot heel wobbled unevenly on the rim of the mine.

Grimacing, he made himself look down at his feet. He could feel his entire body shaking, and wondered if that could set off a mine. The road was rutted, deep frozen cuts from tires and treads filled with snow, some mounds of mud showing above the whiteness, decorated with ice crystals. He found a spot to set his rifle butt into, and held onto it like a cane, steadying himself. With the other hand he signaled, go back, go back, hoping Clay saw him.

He began to see them, round discs set in the snow. Some were nearly uncovered, obvious now that he knew what to look for. With all the mud and unevenness, they hadn't stood out before. He craned his neck left and saw more just behind him. Fuck. Right in the middle. Fuck! It had been bad luck to be thinking about that telegram, real bad luck.

Okay, settle down. It hasn't gone off yet. So it's not a Schu mine. They explode right away and blow off your foot. Made of wood anyway. Not a Bouncing Betty either. Soon as you step on one of those they spring up waist-high and explode a spread of ball bearings, and you're pretty much guaranteed not to be bearing yours after that. Okay, okay, maybe it's an anti-tank mine. I can't set one of those off, can I? Or is it the kind of mine that goes off when you lift up your foot. Oh, Jesus, please help me, please.

"Whaddya got, Jake?" It was Clay, behind him.

"Get the fuck out of here."

"What is it?"

"I don't know. They're behind me too, don't come any closer."

"Hang on."

"Clay?"

"What?"

"Don't come any closer, okay?"

"Don't worry, Jake, I'm being careful."

"No, I—it's not that. I pissed myself."

There was a hesitation, and Jake was afraid Clay would laugh at him. "That's okay, you got a right," Clay said, in a calm, understanding voice. "It's happened to me too."

"Really? Don't tell the other guys, okay?"

Even with panic swirling through his mind, Jake felt ashamed at losing control of his body. Keeping this secret was more important than getting off the mine, crazy as that seemed, even to him.

"Okay."

Silence. Jake listened and heard a scraping sound.

"What are you doing?"

"Clearing the snow off one of these," Clay said. "Using my bayonet."

"Jesus fucking Christ, you're gonna blow us both up!"

"We got to find out what they are," Clay said. "What did they tell us about German mines when we had that briefing? I can't remember."

Jake wanted to say then maybe he shouldn't be fooling with that mine, but he knew Clay was getting him to talk so he'd calm down. He tried to remember, tried to get his mind to think about something else besides the scraping of Clay's bayonet against metal.

"Okay, what are they called, they look like plates?"

"Tellermine," Clay said. "Means plate in German."

"Yeah, that's it. Tellermines. TNT with a pressure fuse. Yeah, didn't they say they took about 500 pounds pressure before going off?"

"That's right. Except for the older models. They took about 150, 175 pounds pressure."

"I forgot about those. Can you see anything yet?"

"Yeah."

"What?"

"You remember what the numbers were?"

"What numbers?" Jake could hear his voice turning shrill.

"There's numbers painted on the top of this one. It says— Ti-M 43—is that the new one or the old one?"

"Jesus, I don't know. If it's a pressure mine, wouldn't it have gone off already if it was the old model?"

"Guess so, yeah. You want to step back?"

"Clay?"

"Yeah?"

"Uh, never mind. Yeah, I'll step back. Back up, okay?"

"All right. When you're ready, step back one step, real slow. And don't trip, no telling what one of those would do if you fell on it."

Jake wanted to speak, to say something, anything that had any meaning, if it might be the last thing he ever said. There was so much, yet nothing came out. He stepped back.

He heard a small crunch as he lifted his boot, the mine settling back in place. Nothing. The pounding in his chest lessened as he steadied himself, lifting his rifle and taking another step backwards, setting his foot down exactly in the footprint he'd left. He wobbled a bit, found his balance, and righted himself, holding his M1 across his chest for balance.

A flicker from within the trees caught his eye and the felt a rush of fear running through him again. What was that? Again, up in the branches, something swift and eerily quiet.

A silent form flew out of the trees and across the road, gliding down, over Jake's head before flapping its giant wings, sending a gust of air to brush his face. A Barn Owl, snowy white underneath, soft light brown feathers covering the wings and body, blending into the forest as it flew between the branches of a barren oak tree, disappearing as swiftly and quietly as it had appeared. Jake was left open-mouthed, gawking at the vanished grace that had passed over him.

"Did you see that?" he managed to whisper.

"What?"

"That owl. He flew right over me."

"Just now?"

Jake looked back and saw Clay about ten feet away. Clear of the minefield, the last one about a yard in front of him, he turned and walked as calmly as he could back to where Clay stood.

"Yeah, just now. I felt the wind from his wings. A Barn Owl, I'm pretty sure."

"Didn't know they had Barn Owls over here," Clay said, looking into the trees.

"It was huge, all white underneath, real quiet."

"That's a Barn Owl all right. I musta been looking down at the road. You okay?"

Jake couldn't answer right away. Remnants of fear still flooded his body, shame following right behind. The inside of his leg felt cold and clammy. Looking back to the oak tree, he wished the owl would come again so Clay could see it, and they could both feel the silent wings beating against air.

"Yeah. I'm okay. We gotta go around, way around. There could be other mines."

"Right," Clay said. "We're probably going to run out of woods soon anyway. Those owls like to be near fields and open ground. We might be coming up on a farm or village."

"It could be ours, you know."

"Why?"

"Look around. The road set with anti-tank mines, under the snow. No other Germans around. Maybe they pulled out, left this here to slow down our tanks. Either way, at least we know there's no heavy stuff in front of us. This is the only road around here. They had to have mined it after their vehicles pulled out."

It made sense to Clay. Getting the others off the road, they looped around the minefield, skirting the road as widely as they could, staying parallel with it as best they could. The sun was low in the sky now, glimmering through a tiny break in the clouds right on the horizon. Jake knew everything was going to be okay. The owl had to be good luck, anything that majestic coming close to you had to be lucky. He watched the sunlight brighten the tree branches and remembered the soft air moving against his cheek. He felt alive.

CHAPTER FOURTEEN

1964

FRIDAY NIGHT WAS THE BUSIEST NIGHT AT JAKE'S
Tavern. It was a winning combination, folks getting off the job
and not having to get up and go to work in the morning. By
six o'clock, the place was packed, and Brick kept busy flipping
burgers as Clay and Cheryl worked the bar and brought food and
drinks to the tables. It was different on Saturday nights, people
drifting in and out, on their way somewhere else or heading
home. Jake's wasn't a Saturday night destination, but it was a
fine Friday night way-station, a place to let the tension of the
week drain away and to settle down for the weekend.

Friday night was a good numbers night too. The more folks
drank, the easier the dollars came. Relaxing into the evening, all
things seemed possible, dreams more achievable, fortunes more
winnable, the numbers luckier. Tonight was a night like that, for
everyone except Clay.

Nothing had gone right all day. The road crew outside was
close to the Tavern, making a racket with all their tools, tearing
up the roadway. There was no parking on Miller Street while
they worked, but at least they'd started to lay asphalt down the
other end, so it wouldn't last long. But that was a mild annoyance
compared to things at home. Addy hadn't even let him finish
when he told her he would be out of the numbers racket soon. All
the things he could've said, should've said, ran through his mind,
perfect in their logic now that it was too late.

"Don't even make a promise to me, Clay. Just do it and tell me
it's over. I can't be bothered with what you promise, I want to
know what's done." With that she'd turned on her heel and walked

out of their bedroom, as certain of what needed to be done as she had been seventeen years ago when Clay stammered out the beginnings of a proposal, stumbling over the words, hesitating and nearly retreating before she grabbed him by the lapels and said yes, of course, yes, I'll marry you. Her determination was one of the things he loved about her. Her ability to see the outcome she wanted and make it happen, whether it was the supervisor's job at the phone company or Clay saying I do, endeared her to him. What he loved was now focused on him full force, a line drawn in the sand.

She hadn't said another word to him the rest of the morning. He'd worked out in the yard, weeding the garden, planting a holly bush in the back yard that he'd picked up at a nursery. When he stopped home after his rounds, she wasn't there. He'd waited an hour, but it was getting late in the afternoon. Damn her, he'd said to himself as he walked out to his car, damn her all to hell.

But he couldn't keep the epithet alive. He didn't want her damned, couldn't even work up a decent rage at her threat to leave. She was right, he knew. He'd brought them to this place, with his ease at lying and covering things up. It had been easy, so easy, except that he hadn't known the hard part would come later, after he was caught up in barbed wire, in the thick of it, taking fire from all sides.

Clay ached for Addy, ached with the loneliness of a man who sees the woman he loves every day, but knows it might be the last. Watching the love drain out of her, replaced by pity. He didn't want to fail, not at this, not now. To save his marriage, his family, he had to get everything right, figure out all the angles, use all the cunning he had to get out of the rackets. Use it all, then drop it like a bag of garbage on the side of the road and don't look back. But first, he had some immediate problems to deal with.

No one had come for the pickup. He had everything from Thursday's run, including the eight thou from Dom, plus today's numbers take. Over twelve thousand bucks, not including tonight's receipts at the Tavern. He'd called Mr. Fiorenza, and left a message, asking when he could expect a visit. Half an hour later, some stooge called and told him to sit tight, they were running a little behind.

Bullshit. Running scared was more like it. He wondered if Al were really that much of a threat to them. Were they scared of him, or had they gone to war, and maybe couldn't spare anyone for a pickup run? Could be. It would be nice if Mr. Fiorenza just took care of that problem, eliminated it for him.

Or would it? That would only mean he was back under Mr. Fiorenza's control. It didn't really solve anything for him, far as Addy was concerned. But, it was his most pressing problem, a hair's breadth ahead of Addy, who was threatening in the home stretch. Compared to Al and Addy, Mr. Fiorenza was a long-term problem. Broken legs and a broken home trumped retirement from the numbers.

What Clay needed was a long-term solution to all three. He kept thinking it through, as he delivered two plates of burgers and pickles to a booth and collected the cash. It was the Town road crew chief and his wife, who apologized for the inconvenience, and said they'd be working through the weekend to finish the street by Monday. That's one small problem solved. Now, back to the other. He had the advantage of surprise. No one would expect him to be anything but a delivery guy, a pickup man, a bartender. Everyone thought they could push him around, a guy past forty who didn't make his living with a gun. But surprise, surprise, he used to.

He took six bottles of Schlitz to a booth crammed full of guys from the AMF Cuno factory who didn't want glasses. Yeah, and the .45 was a surprise too. No one knew he had it. Only Addy, and she thought he'd thrown it away years ago. Maybe he'd have to get rid of it once he used it. He didn't like the idea of throwing it away, like a piece of junk. He could bury it. Grabbing a tray and clearing empties from the tables, he came back with a damp bar rag to clean the spilled beer and crumbs off the lacquered wood. Yeah, maybe wrap it up real nice and bury it someplace, a place he could easily remember, but not connected to him. But that could wait. First things first.

He'd thought about it a lot, and it boiled down to three main questions. Where to do it? How to set it up? And most importantly, could he still do it?

He'd done it often enough. Sometimes at a distance, sometimes close up. Like that old man trying to climb up the gravel slope. Why didn't he stop when they told him to halt? He still wondered about him. Or the sentry he'd killed, grabbing his jaw from behind and clamping it shut so he wouldn't scream as he drove his knife in between shoulder blade and spine. The hazel green eyes of the German he'd killed with the .45 floated in front of him, looking past him to the trees and an unknown future.

He worked the register for a few minutes, totaling up tabs. Hitting the dollar and cent buttons, he worked the crank, made change, and watched the faces pass in front of him. Most were acquaintances, a few friends, some strangers. Most were happy, a few were showing their mean streak after a few drinks, and others straight-faced. Which of them could kill a guy face-to-face? Not the mean ones. They paraded their badness openly, wore it like a badge, not leaving any room for it to fester inside and eat away at them. The smilers, maybe in self-defense. But the ones with the tight lips, neither grim nor glad, they were the ones he'd put his money on. He knew about the cost of keeping secrets, how it blanked out your looks, protecting you from giving anything away.

Bringing dishes back to Brick, he gave him a brief roll of the eyes. Can't believe how busy it is tonight. How much could he actually keep hidden? Sometimes he'd wonder if there was a limit to the secrets a man could keep stored away. Maybe this would be one thing too much, maybe it would show. Or maybe he could pull it off, shake his head when he read the paper, tsk tsk, a shooting, poor guy got killed. Maybe it was better not to say anything. Probably. Why draw attention?

He drew two schooners of Pabst draft and served a couple at the bar. The guy put down a five-spot and Clay didn't take it. He'd learned there was a better chance of a second order if you didn't give change. Change was final. So he moved on, too busy right now to make change, no time for nickels and dimes. What would life be like when he was out of the numbers? Less money for sure, but there was time to be gained, he had to admit. Maybe he could make something more out of the tavern. Fix it up, maybe even get a loan and put in a real kitchen...

"Clay! Telephone," Cheryl said, waving the receiver at the other end of the bar and setting it down. "It's Addy."

Clay glanced at his watch. Ten-thirty. Why was she calling now? He always worked late on Fridays, and she hardly ever called here even when they'd been on better terms...

"Addy?" He felt the tremble in his voice as thoughts of her suitcases packed flew through his mind.

"Chris is in jail."

"What?" He couldn't take in the words, couldn't quite believe what she was saying.

"You heard me. He's down at the station. Your friend Bob called, all apologetic. Said he was sorry, but there was nothing he could do."

"Addy, what's he in—" Glancing around the bar, Clay cupped his hand over the receiver. "For doing what?"

"Stealing a car. Looks like he's getting a head start following in his father's footsteps. You go down there and bring him home, right now!"

Click, and she was gone. Clay listened to the silence on the phone as the buzz of conversation and laughter flowed around him. Cheryl gave him a glance and a slight electric hum came out of the earpiece as he nodded, pretending his wife hadn't just slammed the receiver down on him. He hung up, leaving his hand on the phone for a few seconds, making sure it wasn't shaking.

"I gotta go, Cheryl," he said, walking down the bar.

"What's wrong, honey?" Cheryl yelled to his back as he shut the door to the storeroom behind him. Plenty, he wanted to yell back at her, plenty.

Clay knew the desk sergeant but it didn't make any difference. He still had to sign in and be escorted upstairs as if he were a stranger or a suspect. He'd served the guy a hundred beers, saw him at ball games at Ceppa Field every now and then. Tonight, it was come this way, Mr. Brock, no acknowledgement of any bond at all. He'd strayed past the boundaries, fallen from grace, the father of a troublemaker, more to be pitied than befriended.

The cop's heavy shoes click-clacked down the linoleum hallway, his keys and handcuffs clinking in time as they swayed from his belt. Clay's movements were quiet, his soft shoes made for standing all day silent as he padded alongside the cop. He felt stripped bare, like a POW shorn of his weapons, helmet and gear, more ragamuffin than warrior, being led to the rear by an armed guard. He envied the cop his thick leather belt, snug around his middle, his steel-toed shoes, uniform and badge. It held a man together, let him know who he was. He looked down at his black slacks and white shirt, sleeves rolled up to the elbow, and sniffed, smelling stale beer and grease.

"In here, Mr. Brock," the cop said. He opened door and gestured inside. Clay nodded and forgave him the distance he'd put between them. He knew his place, a barman, deliveryman, lousy father, worse husband.

It was a narrow room, three gray desks in a row against the wall, all strewn with papers, coffee cups and ashtrays. Bob leaned against the middle desk, talking on the phone. He covered the mouthpiece and whispered to Clay to have a seat. Clay stood, waiting for the conversation to finish, too full of nervous energy to sit. There was one other door at the end of the room, a small hand-lettered sign that read CELLBLOCK A taped on it.

He almost laughed. He'd been breaking the law for years, and this was as close as he'd ever come to a jail cell. The laugh choked in his throat. The sins of the father shall be visited upon the son floated through his mind, and he saw the trail of his father's sins and his own leading right here, to this room and beyond the door to Cell Block A.

His son was in jail. Clay thought of his own father, but pushed the thought back down into the darkness of his mind, burying it deep. He had enough of his own sins to worry about. He was a killer, a blood-soaked fraud, a common thief, and here it was Chris who was behind bars. Chris, whose only faults were those of blood and youth, both inescapable, beyond his control. He wanted to cry out, sit down, hold his head in his hands, weep and pray.

He didn't. He stared at a calendar from Pete's Auto Body on South Broad Street. It was still on August, a girl in a yellow polka-dot bikini holding her own against the flow of time. He waited. Bob finally hung up.

"Clay, I'm sorry," he said.

"Me too," Clay answered, sorry for more than he could bear to be. "What'd he do?"

Bob looked at him and blew out his breath, looking very tired. He moved and sat on one of the office chairs by the desk. Rolling it back against the wall he stuck out his legs, planting his big black cop shoes on the floor to hold himself there.

"Stole a car," Bob said, lifting his eyes to meet Brock's.

"What, joyriding? Whose car was it? Can I see him? Get him out of there?" Clay gestured towards the cellblock door, rocking back and forth on the balls of his feet, wanting only to move, to take Chris out of here, to be home with his wife and son. Safe.

"Sit down, Clay," Bob said. "Sit down a minute."

Clay went to the cellblock door. It was locked. "Where is he? Is he hurt?"

"He's fine. Sit down."

Clay shuffled his feet toward the chair at the last desk. He sat, the middle desk separating him from Bob, the cellblock door separating him from Chris, secrets separating him from Addy, time and space separating him from everything else that had once held meaning for him. He hadn't felt this alone in the world since when? Home alive in '45? The fluorescent light above him flickered, then brightened, sending a flash of light against the window. Clay felt his shoulders tighten and he squeezed his eyes shut for a second as more flashes exploded against his eyelids. Opening them, he felt the faint sensation of concussion reverberate against his right side, an echo rumbling down the decades. He rubbed the scar under his shirt, massaging the feeling back down into that dark place where it lived.

He rolled his chair against the wall, as Bob had done, avoiding looking into his face. The phone rang, but Bob didn't move to get it. After four rings it went silent.

"It's serious, isn't it"? Clay asked.

"Yeah, no getting around it. Grand theft."

"But what happened? Did Chris and his pals take one of their parent's cars without asking? I mean, it's not like he's a thief or anything, he's a kid."

"He's a kid, and he hasn't been in trouble before. That will help. But it wasn't a parent's car or a joyride. He boosted a '63 Buick Riviera, for crying out loud!" Clay could hear the frustration in Bob's voice, and the anger at the responsibility of bearing bad news.

"Chris? You mean he was in the car?"

"No, I mean it looks like he stole it, took some pals for a ride to show it off, and got nabbed. I know it's a shock, but there it is."

"Bob, wait a minute. I know Chris has been hard to handle lately, but he's not a bad kid. He's not a car thief, that much I know. Let's talk to him, we'll straighten this thing out in no time." Clay tried to sound upbeat, as if this were all a misunderstanding, a big mistake they'd laugh at later.

"We've talked to him and his buddies. They claim Chris picked them up in the car, bragged that he'd hotwired it. There weren't any keys, and Chris was driving when they got pulled over. Chris said it was the other way around, that they told him they took it for a joyride and were going to get it back by ten o'clock."

"Where—how?" Clay could barely form a sentence. There was something in Bob's reluctant certainty that scared him. This wasn't just a little trouble with the law. He would have been ready for a little trouble. At school, maybe a suspension. A speeding ticket, some drinking, any of the stupid things a kid with too much time on his hands could get into. He would have been ready for that, and angry about it. But this scared him. Sins of the father, after all.

"We picked them up on North Colony Road, coming off the Berlin Turnpike," Bob said, "going about seventy."

"Whose car?" Clay asked, trying to find a fact he could grab onto, make some sense of. He saw Bob shake his head and smile, as if he couldn't quite believe what he was going to say.

"State Senator Grant Flanagan, while he was enjoying the veal scaloppini at Verdolini's, as the guest of the Mayor."

"You mean Chris stole a state senator's car from Verdolini's parking lot?"

"Apparently so." Verdolini's Restaurant on North Avenue was a favorite of local politicians. The absolute worst place to steal a car. The only thing dumber than stealing a car from that lot was to steal the one belonging to a guest of the Mayor.

"Jesus Christ."

"Senator Flanagan was not happy about it. The Mayor was spitting bullets."

"How could Chris be so stupid?"

"Listen, Clay," Bob said, leaning across the desk, lowering his voice. "Some things don't add up."

"Like what?"

"Setting aside the brilliant stupidity of it, things fell into place pretty neatly. We get a call at about 8:30, saying some kids are hotrodding up and down North Colony, laying rubber, stuff like that. We send a patrol car out, and while he's on his way, another call comes in, this time with the license plate. No name, dispatcher wasn't even sure if it was the same person."

"What are you getting at, Bob?" Clay didn't dare let any hope leak into his heart. It was too fine a thread to risk it breaking. He held his breath, waiting for Bob to answer.

"I don't know, it was just awful neat. The Mayor and Flanagan go in for dinner at 7:00, we get a call at 8:30, another at 8:45, and we pick up the kids twenty minutes later. Neat."

"Wait a minute," Clay said, trying to clear his mind of the anguish and confusion flooding his thoughts. "Wait, who was Chris with, which kids? Was one of them Tony?"

"Yeah," said Bob, picking up a sheet of paper. "Two cousins, Italian kids. Vincent Agostino and Anthony DePaoli. Neither have been in real trouble before, but close to it..."

"Say that name again?"

"Agostino or DePaoli?"

DePaoli. Alphonse DePaoli, Mr. Fironeza had said. Al. So who was Tony, his kid brother?

"Yeah, I remember Tony, don't know the other kid. Sorry." Clay stared out the window, not wanting Bob to read his face. It was time to find out, time to see if he could not only keep a secret, but lie flat-out and make it stick.

"Does Chris hang around with these guys much?" Bob asked.

"Tony, all the time. I think he started school in town this year, and Chris has been following him around everywhere. The other kid I don't know. Tony got a new car the other day, they were driving around after work."

"I'll look into that," Bob said, writing something down in his notebook.

"You think they were set up?"

"I don't know," said Bob, shaking his head. "I just wish every auto theft got wrapped up this easy."

"Why take the word of those two against Chris'?" Clay asked. He had his own idea, but he wanted to hear what Bob thought.

"Have to. He was at the wheel, first off. The other two kids had the same story, even admitted they knew it was a stolen car, but they swore Chris picked them up and was at the wheel the whole time."

"And you believe them?"

"Me? I just work for the Chief of Police, who works for the Mayor, who was very happy to inform Grant Flanagan that they'd recovered his Riviera and apprehended the thief. Therefore, they are believed. Like I said, neat."

"Flanagan's pressing charges?" Again, Clay knew the answer.

"Oh yeah, he demanded it. The Mayor suggested he let it slide, probably to keep the bad publicity down, but Senator Flanagan is worried about the corruption of youth by hoodlums and gangs. We heard the whole speech. He wants an example set."

Clay could almost see the wheels turning. Tony moves into town and befriends Chris. Probably Al started watching him then, maybe late summer. Like Mr. Fiorenza said, they'd watch and gather information. Then make their first move, beating up Petey and taking the route. Then the subtle appeal to Clay in the parking lot, followed up by the pay-off. Play ball, or your kid goes to Cheshire. The State Reform School was located south on Route 10 in Cheshire, so everyone scolded their kids by telling them they might end up in Cheshire one day. If you went crazy, then you were going to Middletown, where the insane asylum was. Maybe he'd end up in Middletown, Chris in Cheshire, and Addy who the hell knows where.

He knew how it would play out. If he went over to Al, suddenly Tony and his pal would change their story, confess they had stolen the car, probably say Chris didn't even know it was stolen. If the DePaoli family were really connected, then Grant Flanagan might even decide it was time to show mercy to the younger generation. He could solve Chris' problem, but he'd end up in the middle of a gang war and lose Addy to boot.

"Clay?"

"What? Oh yeah, sorry. Trying to sort things out. Is there anything you can do?"

"I'll look into the new car angle. Maybe it was boosted. You know anything else about Tony DePaoli?"

"I think he's been suspended from school, something about a knife," Clay said, with the ease of someone who's lying by telling part of what he knows, and withholding the rest. A little truth makes the lie go down easy. "Can I ask you a hypothetical question?"

"About what?"

"About what could make this all go away," Clay said.

"You mean some proof that showed Chris didn't steal the car?"

"Maybe," Clay said, shrugging. "Or maybe something else more important, something that trumped a missing car."

"You know something that trumps Grant Theft Auto?" Bob sat up, his eyes boring into Clay's. The policeman's face.

"You haven't said I could ask you a hypothetical question yet."

"Listen, Clay, the department isn't going to get all excited over numbers, hypothetically speaking. Penny-ante stuff."

"I'm not talking penny-ante. Hypothetically."

"Listen, I don't give a crap about the numbers. If a guy in a candy store, or hypothetically, a bar, takes a few slips, then no big deal. No one wants to bother shop owners over a few bucks. The publicity would kill us anyway, there's too many places—so I hear. So forget it, it's noble and all, but forget it."

"Does the name Fiorenza mean anything to you? Guy out of Hartford?" Clay watched for Bob's reaction. Sympathetic exasperation dropped from his expression, and his face went blank. He pulled back on his chair.

"I'm going to tell you once, right now, between friends. If you know anything about a major crime, anything more than jaywalking or betting on the numbers at a Mom and Pop corner store, you let me know right now. Got it?"

"I got it. It was only an idle question."

"Nothing you want to tell me about?" Bob asked.

"No, nothing," Clay said, truthfully, since there was nothing he wanted to tell Bob. He stood up. "Can I see Chris now?"

"Yeah. I'll bring him out, then you sign some papers downstairs. I'll release him into your custody." Bob grabbed a stack of papers from the desk and stood. He faced Clay and waited a few heartbeats before turning away and unlocked the cellblock door. Clay waited for his son.

The two of them left the police station in silence. While Clay signed forms for the desk sergeant, Chris had stood off to the side, eyes glued to the linoleum. He wore his blue Platt High School jacket over a white tee shirt and blue jeans. Clay could see him at the wheel of the car, arm out the window, accelerator floored. James Dean out for a spin.

The walked out past the lights at the entrance and waited to cross the street. Late Friday night traffic was steady, still plenty of places to go and things to do, if you hadn't just been released from jail.

"Well?" Clay said, not looking at Chris.

"Those guys are lying," Chris said, a mutter more than a statement. His eyes were still down, and he wiped his nose with the back of his hand. Clay wondered if he'd been crying. "Really."

"I know," Clay said. "I believe you."

A police car passed them one way, then a white station wagon the other way. Traffic thinned, and then there were no more cars.

They stood side-by-side, toes up on the uneven curb containing the slate sidewalk.

"You do?" Chris' voice shook with emotion. He hadn't expected the sudden agreement.

"Yeah. I believe what you said was true. What I can't believe is why you got into the goddamn car in the first place." As he spoke, Clay's voice went from soft to grim. By the time he got to goddamn, his teeth were gritted hard.

"I dunno," Chris said, with a shrug of his thin shoulders. "It was a boss car. At first—"

"A what car?"

"Boss. It was totally gear. A really nice car, Dad."

"I get it. Now tell me what happened."

"Shouldn't we cross—"

"No," Clay said. "Tell me."

"Okay," said Chris, drawing out the word. He took a breath and began. "At first, Tony said his uncle loaned it to him. He had to get it back by ten, and did I want to drive around until then. I said sure, and I got in."

"Who else was there?"

"Vince, he's Tony's cousin, he lives in New Haven. I seen him a few times before, but I don't know him."

"Vince a little older than Tony?"

"Yeah, he's nineteen. How'd you know?"

"Never mind. Then what happened?"

"I saw he didn't have a key."

"Then you knew it was stolen?"

"Yeah, and I said so. They said they took it from some guy and if they had it back by ten he'd never know. Tony said they'd hot-wired it."

"Why didn't you get out?"

Chris didn't answer. He kicked the curb with his sneaker and looked up and down the street. Clay waited. He felt cold in the cool night air, and rolled his sleeves down. Chris had his jacket open. Clay knew he wouldn't button it up if it were below zero outside

"Why didn't you get out?"

"It was exciting," Chris said, with a note of surprise, as if he hadn't thought of that before. "I didn't want them calling me chicken either, but it was something special, something more exciting than I ever felt."

Clay turned and looked at his son. He knew it was an honest answer. He knew Chris was at the age when excitement overruled good judgment, and when that happened, honesty was about all you could hope for.

"What was jail like?"

"It wasn't exciting," Chris said, looking up and daring a smile at his father. Then he looked back down into the gutter. "I was scared. I was scared when they pulled us over, but when Tony and Vince said I stole the car, I didn't know what was going to happen." Chris' voice caught in his throat, and he took a breath and wiped his nose again. "Am I going to have to go to Cheshire?"

"Don't worry, Chris," Clay said as he put his arm around his son's shoulder and pulled him into his side. "Don't worry, I'll take care of it."

Chris turned his head onto his father's shoulder, burying it in the thin white cotton of his shirt. "I'm sorry, I'm so sorry," he said, and Clay felt the tears soak through the thin material. The street was quiet now, the only sounds the rumble of traffic on Main Street. Clay heard a flutter, a flapping sound, and looked up to see a small shape fly over their heads. One, then another.

"Look," he said to Chris, nudging his head with his shoulder and pointing up. "Bats." Chris rubbed his eyes and looked up.

"Where? Oh yeah, lookit!"

They stood at the curb, necks craned up, watching a parade of bats fly over their heads, silhouetted against the starry sky, swooping under the gable window of an old three-story house across the street.

"Geez," said Chris, "there must be a hundred in there. Think the people who live there know?"

"Probably," said Clay. "Bats always roost in the same place, always come back to it. They don't forget where home is."

They stayed a while longer, and as the flight of bats thinned out, Clay felt hopeful for the first time in a long time. Maybe that would be the difference, if Chris always knew where home was, no matter how far he strayed. Maybe the sins would stop with him.

"Let's go," said Clay, and they stepped off the curb, his hand still on Chris' shoulder.

All the lights in the house were on, and as soon as he pulled into the driveway, Addy was out the front door, her long bathrobe flapping as she ran down the front steps. Chris was barely out of the car before she had a hold of him.

"Chris, are you all right?"

"Mom, I'm sorry—"

"Are you all right?" Addy asked again, her voice rising. Chris looked anxiously around as the neighbor's front porch light flicked on.

"Yeah. I'm fine." Addy stood there, biting her lower lip to keep it from quivering. Clay could see the lines in her face, the reddened eyes, her stress and worry. She reached up and clenched her bathrobe at the neck, as if she'd suddenly felt the late night chill. Her eyes widened, her head shook, and in a flash her other hand came up and slapped Chris on the cheek, the slap as loud as a bullwhip in the empty air.

Chris stood with one hand still on the car door, stunned. He put the other hand to his face, to feel where he'd been slapped. Addy raised her hands to her face, a gasp escaping her lips as she saw the red welt on Chris' cheek. Chris stood silently, waiting for what would come next. Addy looked at Clay, eyes still wide, on the verge of a scream or a sob.

Chris looked to Clay too, shocked at the switch in what he had expected from each parent. Clay nodded his head slightly, towards Addy, guiding Chris with his eyes to his mother. Chris seemed to understand, and as he went towards her, Addy grabbed him in a hug, crying in relief, sadness and joy. Clay put his arm around both of them.

"Let's go in," he said, and guided them up the front steps and inside the house.

Addy and Chris were arm in arm, and for the moment it looked like she wasn't letting go. Clay followed them into the kitchen, smelling the coffee that had been sitting on the stove. Addy's cup was on the table, half full.

"Tell me," she said to Clay as she guided Chris to a chair, her voice quavering.

"I have to do something first," Clay said. "I'll be right back."

"What!" Addy said, the strain in her voice now near the breaking point. "Our son was arrested and you've got something more important to do, at this time of night?"

"It's complicated, I'll explain later. Let Chris tell you what happened. What he tells you, I believe. I'll be right back." He reached into the change jar they kept on the kitchen counter and began digging out nickels and dimes.

"What—what do you need change for?" Addy cried out, screaming as she held her hands to her head. The evening had been strain enough, and Clay knew his odd behavior was too much for her.

"Addy, listen to me," he said, pulling her hands down and holding them in front of him. "Listen to what I'm saying. Chris did something stupid tonight, but not what he got arrested for. He didn't steal a car. I've got to make some phone calls, to try and straighten this thing out. He'll tell you exactly what happened. Right, Chris?" He gave Chris a hard stare and a nod.

"Yeah—yes, everything. Mom, sit down, I'll tell you exactly what happened."

Addy looked at Chris, then back to Clay. Her forehead was wrinkled as she fought down the confusion that was building in her mind. Clay let go of her hands.

"We have a telephone right here, Clay," she said, gesturing with a weak lift of her hand to the wall phone in the kitchen. Clay dropped the change into his pocket. Looking at Chris, slumped in his chair at the kitchen table, and then at Addy, her eyes red, bewilderment etched in the lines on her forehead, he wanted to stay. Drink some coffee, talk, maybe end up laughing a little. It might bring her closer to him. But now was the time. It had to be right now, the timing was perfect.

"Trust me. You both have to trust me." He didn't dare wait to hear what either of them said.

At a phone booth outside a gas station on East Main, Clay dropped dimes into the slot and dialed a number he knew by heart. It picked up on the second ring.

"Yeah."

"Mr. Fiorenza, please."

"He ain't here."

"Tell him it's important, concerning his current difficulties. He'll want to talk to me."

"Who is this?"

"He'll know." Clay heard the phone set down, and the sound of fading footsteps. He put some nickels in and waited.

"Yes?"

"Mr. Fiorenza, do you know who this is?"

"Yes, I believe I do."

"I'm calling from a pay phone," Clay said, by way of explanation.

"Well, I am not speaking on one."

"I understand. I'm calling you to ask a question, on behalf of a friend."

"Yes." Mr. Fiorenza's voice was clear, but disinterested. He was a careful man, one who wouldn't say anything that might incriminate him on a wiretap.

"Well, my friend works for someone, and feels some loyalty to this man. But, he wishes to retire from his business, and does not want to cause any problems for the man he works for."

"That is admirable, and wise."

"Yes. Especially since right now, this man and his business are undergoing certain difficulties. Intense competition. Very aggressive competitors."

"Business is always difficult, as I am sure you know. Now, how can I help your friend?"

"Some advice. If you were in his employers place—"

"But I am not."

"Yes, but you are a businessman. I am looking for a businessman's perspective."

"Ah, in that case, I will try to answer."

"So, if you were in a similar situation, and this person found a way to help you with the competition problem, would you then not feel badly about him retiring from the business. After the difficulties passed, of course."

"Well, help is always welcome, but to what degree?"

"Let's say, for the sake of argument, that this man eliminates the current problem."

"Ah, so he does not simply help his employer, he solves the problem for him. Totally."

"Yes."

"I would award him with a gold watch at his retirement party and wish him well."

"Thank you. I will pass that onto my friend. Your perspective is valuable."

"You are welcome. I wish your friend well." With that, Mr. Fiorenza hung up.

Clay pulled out his wallet, and fished out a folded slip of paper. He dropped a dime in and dialed the number. His finger shook as he aimed at each number on the dial.

"Hello."

"Is Al DePaoli there?"

"Who wants to know?"

"Just tell him it's the call he's been waiting for."

CHAPTER FIFTEEN

2000

SUNLIGHT SLANTED ACROSS THE KITCHEN TABLE, a diagonal shadow cutting off the corner of the tabletop where Clay let his left hand lie. He set down the coffee cup held in his other hand as he heard Addy's footsteps behind him. He leaned back in the chair and turned his head to greet her, the sound of her feet on the floor familiar and comforting.

The room was empty.

He'd dreamed of her too, the same kind of dream he'd had turning the war. Drinking coffee with guys who had been killed, sitting around a table, everyone quiet, until in his dream he remembered they were dead, and the dream ended. He had that dream about Addy, seated at this table. Even while he was awake, the house echoed with her footsteps.

"Morning, Dad."

"Coffee," Clay said, gesturing with his thumb to the aluminum pot on the stove.

"Two to one. Not the worst ratio," Chris said, pouring coffee for himself.

"What?"

"Words."

"Four to three," Clay said.

"Well, you can still do the math. You always had a head for numbers, Dad."

"Is that supposed to be joke?"

"No," Chris said, laughing as he realized what his father meant. "I mean at the Tavern, doing the books and everything."

"Oh, oh yeah." Then he laughed too. "I like numbers. They calm me down. They don't surprise you, they are what they are."

"How do you feel this morning?" Chris asked, watching his father carefully.

"Fine," he said with a shrug. "Like it never happened."

"Really?"

"Scout's honor. Go ahead, go to work, I'll be fine."

"No, I took a couple of personal leave days. Paperwork's done, so I'll stay here for now."

"No need."

"Not for you, maybe. But I'm staying."

"Prepare to be bored."

"Maybe you'll finally tell me about the guys in the photo. You still have it, don't you?"

"Yes. And don't start going through my stuff. I'm not dead yet."

"Listen, Dad. I don't really have much to do besides work, so no one's missing my company. And this attack you had scared me. So let's hang out a couple of days and not make a big deal about it, okay?"

"Fine. I got nowhere else to go."

"Me either. Couple of sad sacks, aren't we?"

"You and me both, you got that right," Clay said, trying to summon up energy he didn't feel. He knew there would be more questions, more subtle interrogations, and he didn't know if he could hold out. He couldn't deny his own son his company, didn't want to, but felt Chris' eyes on him, watching, seeking out a weakness he might well find this time.

Cla-ay, Addy had said, nearly every morning at this table. I'll al-ways want just one more da-ay with you.

Now, Clay was left alone, remembering how they sat, holding hands as the morning sun rose, warming the kitchen and shoving the shadow on the table aside, one more morning of light and quiet joy together.

He didn't want to think about how many mornings like this were left, unsure if he feared there were too few or too many. The spring sun shone brightly outside, coaxing out buds and grasses watered by yesterday's rain. Spring and summer, surely he'd have spring and summer, and then fall, with its rotting crispness hinting at the burden of cold to come. He shivered, feeling that old cold inside him, the frigid air of the last century, the deep cold of the Ardennes, the cold that never really left his bones. Winter. Would he make it through the winter, and sit here again, alone in the spring, the first year of the next thousand years?

The shiver came again, a shiver of sadness that he was down to this, counting out the seasons left to him. Not decades, not years, but seasons. He didn't want to think about it. Looking out the window, he raised his eyes toward Lamentation Mountain, the crumbling rocks and the granite peak. He knew now that everything changed, slowly crumbling over time, nothing staying the same, not even the face of a mountain.

And certainly not him. So little time left, and so much to set straight. There were things Chris wanted to know, but Clay knew what was even more important was that he had to tell him. Tell him before it was too late, too late for the both of them. But could he?

"I'll make breakfast, Dad. What do you want?"

Chris' voice jolted him, bringing him out of the deep thoughts that seemed to carry him away more and more these days. The image of another winter stayed with him, watching Lamentation Mountain coated in ice and snow, covering the sliding shale. His hands felt chilled, and he rubbed them together, but the chill crept deeper, running from his fingertips into his palms and on into his joints. Shivering, the winter of 1945 came to him, as it always did with cold sensations, unbidden, drifting like ice floes through his mind. It played out slowly, a single scene of deep, strange coldness, a single chunk of jagged ice bobbing in thick, gray waters. He found himself speaking, his thoughts bubbling to the surface like the last gasps of a drowning man.

"We found some men once. Frozen."

"What are you talking about? Who?"

"Germans," Clay said, his eyes focused on the mountain. Hardly conscious of speaking, he began to narrate the memory as it unfolded in his mind. "It was the strangest thing."

"Are you all right? Dad?"

He looked at Chris as if he could hardly understand him. What was he asking? Of course he was fine. Now he had to get on with the story, or else it would move too fast and he wouldn't be able to keep up with it. Driven to speak, a force deep inside him wanting nothing more than this tale to be told. With perfect clarity of thought, he understood, after all these years, that he had to be in control, tell the story, not to let it play like a film in his head over and over again.

"Yes, I'm fine. I can't remember where we were. Everyone was there, Red was still with us, so it must have been—aaw, it doesn't matter."

"Dad," Chris said, placing his hand on his father's arm. "Are you talking about the war?" His face knotted up in disbelief, as he had given up waiting to hear him speak of the war long ago.

"Yeah. The frozen Germans. It was cold, Addy, so cold that your teeth chattered all the time, and your whole body shook from deep inside, trying to get some heat built up. We'd been moving toward some village, through heavy pines. Big, thick trees, planted in neat rows, the ground cleared all around them."

"It's Chris, Dad. Mom's gone."

Clay didn't hear him. He could smell the green fir; feel its needles brush against his helmet. He took in a deep breath, and his eyes rested on Chris, seeing his eyes wide, in shock or surprise. Clay couldn't stop, he knew he had to keep going.

"We got stopped in the late afternoon, not even close to the village. Kraut machine guns were everywhere, zeroed in on those open lanes between the pines. It was murder, plain murder. Guys got chopped up trying to go tree to tree, but the snow was two, three feet deep, so you couldn't run fast enough. The orders kept coming all day, push ahead, push ahead. We lost two replacements we'd gotten the day before. The platoon on our left lost half their men in five minutes."

He looked out the window, and in the reflection saw visions of G.I.s laying in the snow, frozen hands clutching nothing as bullets cut through pine branches, showering green needles down over the brown-coated bodies in the white snow. He heard Red holler out an order to dig in, felt the crack of air as a bullet passed by his ear.

"We dug in, but the ground was frozen solid and there were thick roots everywhere. We burrowed into the snow, laid there, three or four guys together, all huddled up. We'd take turns moving into the center, to get warm."

He felt the wind at his back, and could sense the warmth entering his body as Little Ned crawled out from the middle and he took his turn inside.

"We shelled the woods all night. We could hear the explosions and the trees cracking. Tree bursts, we learned that one from the Krauts. We stayed there all night long. First light, we got up, moved out."

"Dad." He ignored Chris. He smelt burning pine.

"We moved slow at first, but there was no firing. It was hazy, smoky from the trees on fire. We couldn't see very well. Then Shorty spotted it. He had the best damn eyes of anyone I ever knew. He signaled and we all dove behind the thickest pine we could find. Once he pointed it out, you could see it plain as day. Kraut machine gun position. You could see the gunner, and three other Krauts, one with binoculars. It was strange. They shoulda had us, shoulda had us dead to rights."

"Why didn't they shoot?" Chris asked, curiosity overwhelming concern.

"We couldn't figure that out. Big Ned fired his BAR, but they didn't move a muscle. We all got up at the same time and walked over to them. That's when we found the G.I.s. We must've drifted over to the next platoon's line of approach. We found ten of them, all around the Kraut position."

One of the G.I. corpses looked straight at him. Propped up behind a tree, he had tried to put a compress bandage on his leg, but it hadn't worked. Blood from his thigh wound had spread beneath him and frozen thick on top of the snow. His eyes were open, staring straight at Clay, as if to ask, how the hell did this happen?

"They were all dead?"

"Frozen stiff as a plank. They'd all been wounded, or killed straight out. The Germans were the strange part. There were eight of them up there. In position, like a picture. One of them was crawling to another guy with a medic's bag in his hand. The other Kraut was flat on his back, holding his belly. Their faces, their skin, it was all white, crystal white, as if they'd been frozen in a second. You could see the expressions on their faces. Fear, pain, grimness, calmness, everything you felt in a fight."

"How?"

"Concussion, we figured. Must've been. A shell burst above them, but the trees were already down. One chance in a million, but there it was. No shrapnel, no wood splinters, not a drop of blood. Concussion from a shell that burst straight on top of them. They all died instantly, in position, and the cold did the rest. That's how cold it was, cold enough to freeze a dead man in place. We left them there. None of us could touch them, not even for souvenirs."

Not even for souvenirs. Everyone wanted souvenirs, until they didn't. Until the very trophy you'd taken turned and took you.

He felt the snow crunching under his feet as he walked away from the frozen Germans, glancing back at them and wondering. Wondering if he'd end up like that, looking like he should be alive, but dead inside.

And then it was gone. The cold, the scene in his mind, the immediate sense of memory, sight, sound and smell that always lingered. He sat and stared out the window, enjoying the absence of visions, enjoying the mountain, still there.

"Dad," Chris said, brushing his fingers against his arm. "Are you done?"

"Yes," he said. "I think I am."

They sat in silence, hands on the table, close to each other, but not touching.

"Do you know," he said, "that's the first time you ever told me anything about the war?"

He had to force his eyes from the mountain to Chris. It was a magical mountain, and he'd finally unearthed its secret. All these years, at the mercy of his own memories, and today, for the first time in five decades, he'd been in control. Speaking the words out loud, containing them within his mouth, letting them out into the air, instead of around and around in his mind, again and again, over and over. It was important that he said these words to Chris, he knew, but it felt like he could've been alone and it would have been the same.

"I'm sorry. I'm sorry about that too. I never knew, never thought—"

"You never thought we could take it. You never thought Mom or me were as tough as you."

Clay felt like he'd been punched in the gut. He tried to speak, but couldn't think of anything to say, except a denial, and he knew that would be wrong. He met his eyes, and saw the determination behind them, the desire burning there, the desire to understand, to pull out the memories, as Addy had pulled him through life, half alive, half whimpering in the snow, crippled by shrapnel and memories.

"Jesus," Clay said, holding his head in his hands, feeling the tears seeping through his fingers. "I don't know what to do. I thought I'd be gone by now, that it would be all over."

Clay remembered Addy telling him to talk to Chris, tell him— he couldn't even repeat Addy's phrase in his mind. Who—no, he couldn't say it. He'd avoided it ever since he'd stuffed it back into the corners of his mind and found the perfect escape. The words terrified him. Who he was. The words fell on him like a wall collapsing, revealing his past behind rotten, moldy sheetrock. Who he was. That depended on who his father was, making him the father that he was. Who he was. The thought circled in his mind like a mosquito driving him crazy on a summer night.

"No, no, I can't," Clay said.

"Can't what, Dad? Are you sure you're all right?"

Clay remembered Addy leaning forward, in the chair where Chris now sat, forcing the words from her uncooperative lips, as if she willed them into coherence. Come out from under tha-at sha-adow. Long enough, long enough.

He remembered what Miller had told him in Clervaux. Sometimes, the right thing to do grabs you and won't let go, and you gotta do it, no matter how much you want to run. He wondered how much longer these distant voices would stay with him.

"Yeah," said Clay, his voice barely a croak. "I'm okay."

They ate breakfast in silence. Chris cleaned up, more time passed. Clay thought about what to do next. Words were not going to be enough. There had to be a better way.

Clay was watching Chris in the driveway, doing his stretches before a run, when he had an idea. If he couldn't tell him, maybe he could show him. They could do it, if Chris were willing. It was time, past time, to be honest with his son, and this might be the only way. Time and age had left them drifting, not close, not estranged, not intimate. Clay had always worried about passing on the sins of the father, and it was time to give it up. His own sins were enough.

How unfair. He hadn't really been worried about Chris, it was his own shame that he was afraid of, and the more alone Chris was, the less chance for Clay's shame to be revealed through him. Maybe he wanted Chris to fail, or maybe his son would've failed at relationships with no help from him at all. He waited, nervous at first, then calm. He watched Chris walk up the driveway, sweaty, his arms on his hips, his mouth drinking in the air.

"I might need a ride," Clay said, as the back door opened.

"Where to, Dad?" Chris asked, walking to the sink and running the tap for cold water.

"Out of state, maybe overnight." Clay said.

"What's up, Dad?"

"There's some sights I'd like to see, things I want to show you. The place I grew up, to start with."

"All the way to Tennessee?"

"Maybe not that far."

"But that's where you grew up, Tennessee," Chris said, his certainty reinforced by the pits and pieces of his past that his father had parted with.

"Listen, it's going to be easier to show you, I can't explain it. It's something to do with those guys in the photograph you're always asking me about. Trust me, Chris, please."

"Okay," Chris said, the promise of actual information about his father's wartime photo overcoming his reluctance. "When do you want to make this trip?"

"Now. Today."

"What? You were in the hospital yesterday, and now you want a road trip?"

"Listen, Chris, let's get into the car and drive. I'll navigate. We'll be back tomorrow night, no problem. It's important."

"Jesus, Dad, why do we have to go all of a sudden? How important can it be?"

Clay spread his hands, unable to conceive of how to start telling his son why this was important. Chris shrugged his shoulders and raised his hands in surrender.

"Okay. Do I have time to shower?"

"That'd be worth the wait," Clay said.

"On the way out we need to stop by the office. There's something I need to pick up. Won't take a minute."

Clay was excited. Scared and nervous too, but at the heart of it, excited. He hadn't felt that way in a long time. He realized Addy would have been excited too. Addy always had a plan for working things out between he and Chris, and this would have pleased her. He ached for her, but he also felt a lightness in his gut, like a tight, twisted cord gone slack. He felt a restful sense of being in the right spot, doing the right thing, at the right time, for the right reasons, knowing the consequences were less important than the act itself.

He finally understood what Miller had said in Clervaux, and thinking about him again, saw the kid looking up at him, calmly explaining it as if it were the most rational thing he ever did.

CHAPTER SIXTEEN

1945

JAKE DREAMED HE WAS HOME, SITTING AT HIS kitchen table, looking out of the small window above the sink, the short white curtains with the red rose pattern his mother had sewn blowing gently in the breeze. She was chopping vegetables at the counter. Seated on either side of him were his father and his sister. His sister's eyes were riveted to the table, his father's to her. Little Ned and Shorty were there too, leaning against the counter, sipping coffee from the green-tinted glass cups that came free in boxes of Quaker Oats. They were dressed in clean, pressed khakis, infantry brass gleaming on their collars. Private First Class stripes were stitched evenly on their sleeves, fore and aft caps folded over their belts. They looked like they were on a forty-eight hour pass, ready to go out and celebrate, paint the town red.

Jake looked down at his hands. His fingernails were black, grimy dirt dug in across his knuckles. His clothes were filthy, the green fatigues greasy and stained. Bringing a hand up to his face, he felt thick stubble scratch against his fingers.

Little Ned and Shorty set down their cups, and gave Jake a smile and a wave. Shorty put his arm around Little Ned as they walked down the back hall, pushed open the screen door, and let it slam behind them. Jake heard them laugh, and wanted to join them, to leap up and chase after them. Wait for me, fellas, wait up!

But he couldn't move. He tried, but for some reason he couldn't get out of the chair. His mother turned away from the counter, a long, sharp, gleaming knife in her hand. Pa turned to look at her, staring, his mouth set in a dour grimace until she turned away and went back to her chopping. Chop. Chop, chop, chop, chop.

Pa turned his stare toward Jake, as if he just noticed his presence.

"You oughta be ashamed of yourself," Pa said, disgust twisting his mouth into a foul sneer as his dark eyes narrowed above high cheekbones. Wind blew the curtains in, flapping and snapping in the breeze, taunting Jake with their delicate red stitching. Shame, shame, they scolded, like nagging fingers tipped with red fingernail polish. Jake looked past them, out the window towards the trees and the rocks rising up beyond the yard to a height that vanished from view. Then he was standing out there, his dirty uniform gone now, replaced by khaki pants and a white tee shirt. The sky turned white, but it was a giant Barn Owl, flying above his head, feathers like cornsilk brushing against his cheek, blessing him, carrying him off, away from here, away to that other place he'd always been looking for, away, away, away.

Explosions cracked through the air, multiple blasts waking Jake, ripping him from the soaring whiteness and sending him bolt upright as if a giant hand had grabbed him and pulled him up.

"What?" Wide eyes darted around as his mind raced to remember where he was, gasping in mouthfuls of air, trying to still the panic rising inside him. Again, the loud blasts tore the air and he instinctively ducked, patting the ground around him for his helmet. He hands felt wool blankets, soft straw. His eyes took in stonewalls, thick horizontal timbers, as he rubbed his face, trying to clear his mind. Holding his hand in front of his eyes, he saw it was the same dirty hand he'd seen in his dream.

As the explosions came a third time, Jake continued staring at his hand, remembering where he was, knowing that the Barn Owl could not pluck him away from here, or save him from his family. Then, without thought or warning, he cried, not attempting to hold back the tears, no scrunching of his facial muscles, no hiding his face in his hands. He cried, Little Ned, Shorty and the owl all out of reach, gone, the purity and whiteness, laughing and flying, gone, gone, gone.

"They're ours, it's okay," he heard Clay saying. "It's okay, those are our 105s, down the road, it's okay."

Clay wasn't talking to him, not directly, anyway. He was working his way down a line of G.I.s opposite him. Big Ned,

Miller, Tucker and Oakland among the rest of their group, all
shocked awake from their beds of straw. Clay had one hand on
Big Ned's shoulder, the other lowering the BAR Big Ned had
grabbed when artillery first went off.

"Coffee's coming, boys. Breakfast in bed," Clay said lightly,
smiling at Big Ned, "nothing but a wake up call."

One more round came from the 105mm battery. Jake flinched,
but recognized the sound. Of course it was their stuff. He shoulda
known, what was wrong with him? Sniffling, he rubbed at his
face. The tears stopped as suddenly as they'd started, the clarity
and reality of the barn, his buddies, and their own artillery
driving the sadness down, tucking it away for now.

Clay walked over, holding two steaming canteen cups in
one hand. When they'd come in last night, Clay had snagged
this single small stall in the barn for them. It smelled of leather
and manure, leavened with the dry odor of last summer's hay.
Everyone else had bunked down along the opposite wall, where
a thick cushion of hay and wool blankets had been piled up for
them.

Last night. Last night, he had seen the Barn Owl again! That
wasn't part of the dream, he knew it had been real. It was the
tail end of dusk, almost dark, only a bit of reflected sunlight left
in the western sky, directly ahead of them. Movement out of the
corner of his eye, white against the darkening green firs, off to
his left, about nine o'clock.

This way, he'd signaled, taking point and trying to stay on the
course he'd seen the owl fly. The Barn Owl, maybe the same he'd
seen earlier, heading back home, to a safe, warm place. He hadn't
explained or told anyone what he'd seen, just trudged through
the snow, trusting the white bird. As the trees thinned, they saw
the field, the barn and house beyond. There was no road, so it
was across the field now, while there was still some twilight, or
else another night in the woods.

Miller volunteered to take point. Jake knew it was important
to him, a step he had to take to feel he fit in among them. Big Ned
tried to take his place, but Jake needed a base of fire in case things
went bad and there were Krauts over there. So it was Miller on
point, as Big Ned set up on a knoll to his left, while Jake and
Clay followed. Oakland and Tuck rode herd on the replacements,
telling them to put their safeties on, shut up and stay low.

They took more care than they needed. The house and barn

were home to a field artillery battery, and they were already a quarter mile behind their own lines. They'd cut through at an angle, melting through the woods off the main road, where the thin defenses were dug in to defend. Miller signaled them to wait, and walked over a crest, disappearing in the direction of the house. He came back minutes later, waving and yelling, a dozen G.I.s clapping him on the back, whooping and hollering. They'd become famous, along this part of the line, anyway. They were the Lost Company, and everyone was on the lookout for them. A few survivors of the attack on the village had filtered back the first day, telling tales of the guys who had held out until driven from the house by grenades, and then kept up covering fire for ten, twenty, maybe thirty other guys to get away. They were famous. And famous rated soft hay, extra blankets, and a sturdy stone barn, roof still intact.

Jake looked up to the rafters, up past the loft, into the darkness where the main beam ran the length of the barn. Was he up there somewhere, huddled in a nest with his mate?

"Jake?" He realized Clay was squatting next to him, holding out a steaming canteen cup for him. "Jake, you okay?"

Taking the cup in both hands, he saw he was shaking, a slight tremor jostling the dark, thick coffee around inside the aluminum cup. It was hot, and he gripped it tight by the thin handle. Clay sat down with a grunt, his back against the wall. The big guns had stopped firing. Except for the rustling and murmuring of the other men as they got up, it was quiet. Jake sipped the hot coffee, giving a sigh of intense pleasure. When was the last time he'd had anything hot to eat or drink? Three, four days? He couldn't remember, couldn't separate the days and the nights from each other. His head felt thick with fatigue, his body tired beyond aching, beyond any pain he'd ever felt.

"I had a dream," he said, in answer to Clay's question. "I was home, sitting at the kitchen table." He didn't mention Little Ned and Shorty. It had to be bad luck to dream about the dead, a sign of things to come. Now he was glad they hadn't invited him along.

Jake felt Clay studying him, feeling the wetness still glistening through the grime on his face. He drank some more coffee.

"Doesn't sound like a bad dream," Clay said, "but I guess that depends on the family. I've known some I wouldn't want to be stuck in the kitchen with."

"Not yours, though," Jake said. "You have good memories, don't you? I mean, even with everything—with them gone."

"Yeah, I do. Sometimes I dream about them, but it hasn't happened in a while. I kinda miss it."

They both drank. It was cold in the barn, not cold like foxhole cold, just plain cold, the coffee losing its steam as Jake felt his body warming inside with the last gulp of the brew.

"I'm not going back there," Jake said. "I don't care if I ever see them again, real or dreaming." He voice was low, almost a whisper, as he stared into the cup, watching the grounds that had settled to the bottom move as he tilted it.

"What happened back there? I don't wanta pry, Jake, but it's plain something's eating you up inside. Bad enough we got all this on our shoulders, never mind trouble back home."

All this. War, death, killing, freezing, sorrow and loss, all this. It was bad, real bad, but Jake knew he'd go through another war just like it if it would erase the shame, the humiliation that marked him.

"It's hard to explain," Jake said. "It's not just trouble, it's worse." Jake felt a lump rise in his throat, as if his body were trying to stop the words from coming out. Or was that the truth, welling up inside him? He gripped the canteen cup in both hands, letting the residual warmth seep into his palms.

"I got a Pa that—well, he's not like most fathers. None that I know of, really, not that I'd want to."

"He beat you? Beat your ma?"

"He gave me a whipping a few times, but that isn't it."

Jake felt dizzy, as if he were walking on a high narrow ridgeline, about to fall off. He couldn't figure what good it would do to tell Clay, but the temptation was strong now that he'd started talking. He sensed a lightness building in his chest, as if saying the truth out loud was some kind of magical incantation, abracadabra, presto, and he'd be okay.

Or maybe not. Maybe Clay would be disgusted, think of it every time he looked at him. Maybe he'd pity him, feel sorry for him, avoid him.

"We've been through a lot, Jake."

Was he reading his mind? He looked at Clay, eye to eye. Pulling up his legs and hugging his knees, he felt the cup, now cold metal in his hands.

"My Pa did something, something real bad. Worst part is, he

didn't seem to care. I think he even enjoyed me knowing it. It gave him power."

"Over you and your sister?"

"She's not my sister, that's the thing," Jake said, his forehead resting on his knees. "She bore me. She's Pa own daughter, and she bore me, you understand?"

There was silence for a full minute. Jake waited for a harsh laugh or a snort of disgust, or maybe for Clay to get up and walk away. Instead, he heard an intake of breath, then a whisper.

"Jesus, that's an evil thing for a man to do, Jake."

"Evil, yeah. And a wife who lets him, she's the same. That's why I can't go back there. I don't want anything to do with them, and if I ever have a family, I don't want them within a hundred miles."

"What about your sister—what about Alice?"

"My G.I. life insurance is signed over to her. If I don't make it, maybe she can get away on her own."

"You're not going to do anything stupid, are you?"

"If I was, I would've done it by now, and avoided all this bullshit."

"Yeah. Jesus."

They sat in silence, staring at the wall opposite them. The others had filtered out to wash up in water heated in the artillery battery's mess tent. The sounds of Jeeps, men and heavy equipment swirled around outside, leaving the inside of the barn quiet, like an old stone church.

"You know I got no kin left, right?" Clay said.

"Nobody?"

"None I know of. So here's what I'm thinking. Let's say we manage to live through this, maybe we both head somewhere else. Someplace where nobody knows us, get some work, live the good life, and forget about everything that went before. Maybe California, what the hell, huh?"

That night in the woods came back to Jake, when he was ready to rip the dogtags off Oakland and go home to California in his place. Had Clay read his mind then too?

"Geez, Clay, it sounds good, but let's not get too excited about this. It's gotta be bad luck. Let's not talk about it anymore."

"Okay, just so you know."

"I know."

"I mean it, Jake. Listen to me," Clay said, leaning in and

whispering, his hand gripping Jake's arm and his voice a low, firm growl. "If I make it outta here, I'm going far from anyplace I've ever seen before. I'm gonna find someone and start a family, put a roof over our heads, bring up our kids right. Not like it happened to me. You can do the same, make things right."

"Someplace no one know us," Jake said, almost a whisper.

"Yeah. Now c'mon," said Clay, getting up and pulling Jake by the hand. "Let's get some chow." A silent agreement passed between them.

Walking out of the barn, Jake saw Big Ned and the others gathered around a Jeep pulled off the side of the snow-packed track that ran between the house and the barn. Big Ned turned and called out to them.

"Hey, guys, it's Red!"

Clay and Jake ran over, pushing through the crowd of replacements who were craning their necks to see what all the fuss was about. They found Red standing next to the Jeep, his arm in a sling, wincing as Big Ned gripped him around the shoulders. Tuck stood next to him, grinning. Miller and Oakland stood behind their buddies, part of the celebration more by association than anything else.

"Jesus, Red, it's good to see you," said Clay. "How you doing?"

"Never mind me, I never thought I'd see you guys again! I been going up and down the line for days looking for you. You know how much trouble you bastards caused me?"

Red grinned when he said it. They'd heard how he'd skipped out of the field hospital, took a Major's Jeep, and went from position to position, telling G.I.s to be on the lookout for the Lost Company. He was the source of that name, and his visits spread the word and rumors like wildfire. They were on a commando mission, they were pinned down by a whole panzer division, all sorts of crazy stuff.

Red's grin lessened as he looked at the men, especially Tuck. "Where's Shorty?"

"He got it yesterday, Red," Jake said.

"Sorry, Tuck," said Red, putting his good arm out and resting his hand on Tuck's shoulder, keeping his eyes on Jake. "How many others?"

Jake reached into his jacket pocket and pulled out the handful of dogtags. Shorty, Cooper, and a bunch of names he never even knew. A handful of lives, a fistful of sorrow and loss. He handed them to Red.

"You guys did good, making it back like you did," Red said, closing his fingers around the metal tags. "I'm proud of you all, proud to have served with you."

The last words came out in a hoarse whisper. Red, looking down at the ground, stuffed his hand into his pocket, leaving it there, clutching the dogtags.

"You goin' home, Red?" Tuck asked, squinting his eyes as he studied Red's face.

"England. They're sending me to a hospital in England to get some work done on my arm. I don't know—aw, Jesus Christ! Listen, I'll probably never see you guys again. I gotta leave right now. We're close fellas, close to the end. Hang in there. Watch out for each other, and the new guys too. I'm sorry, but they won't let me stay, the bone in my arm is all busted up."

"Don't worry, Red. Don't worry about us," Jake said. "You deserve to get the hell out of here. We'll be okay."

"Yeah," Clay said. "Have a nurse give you a sponge bath for us."

They all laughed. It wasn't that funny, but they laughed like it was, buddies laughing together one last time.

"Jesus, Miller, is that you?" Red said, in mock surprise. "You look as bad as these guys now."

Miller stood a little taller, smiling, pride at his inclusion with the veterans showing. "It's me, all right."

"He's not half bad as an ammo carrier either," Big Ned said, his casual comment worth a chest full of medals to Miller.

"I knew you'd do all right, Miller," Red said, reaching out his good arm to shake hands all around. When he was done, he reached back into his pocket and withdrew the dogtags Jake had given him. He nodded his head in the direction of the Jeep's back seat.

"This here's your new platoon leader, Lieutenant Sykes," he said, handing Sykes the dogtags. The new Lieutenant was dressed in an immaculately clean cold-weather parka, the latest issue, too new to have made it beyond the supply dumps and headquarters to the front line. As Red handed them over, the dogtags seemed to take Sykes by surprise. Fumbling, he dropped several on the floor of the Jeep, his thick rabbit-fur leather gloves too bulky to grip them all.

"Pick those up, Private," Sykes said to the driver, handing him the dogtags from his cupped hands. His skin was pink and flushing red as he got out of the Jeep. His face was long and narrow, his mouth a thin-lipped slit underneath an attempted mustache. Taking his carbine and field pack out of the back of the Jeep he turned to Red.

"Thank you, Lieutenant. Anything else you want to say to the men?"

Jake watched Sykes, noting the formality, as if this were a change of command on a peacetime post. And, that he'd said the men, not your men. They'd always be Red's men.

"Nothing else needs to be said," Red answered, looking at each of the veterans, one by one, before he got back into the Jeep.

"One more thing, Sykes," Red said.

"What's that?" Sykes responded quickly, as if he couldn't wait for Red to clear out.

Tapping the driver on the shoulder, Red gestured with his hand towards Sykes.

"These are your responsibility now, like the men."

The driver held out the dogtags in his two hands. Showing a brief frown of irritation, Sykes pulled off both gloves so he could handle them better this time.

"Of course," he said, as if he'd known all along. He took them in one hand, cupping the other hand over them, carefully this time. Red caught Jake's eye, then Clay's. He nodded down towards Sykes' hand, focusing his gaze on the ring he wore.

"Stay low, boys," Red said, as the driver pulled out, spinning his tires in the snow for a second before the Jeep gained traction and sped off. Big Ned and Tuck watched until the Jeep turned and vanished behind a stand of pine, as Jake and Clay exchanged glances and stared at the gold signet ring. West Point, and recent, too. The gold was shiny, the crystal sparkling. Fuck.

"Okay, men. I'm Lieutenant Sykes, and I'm taking over the platoon. I know you've been through an ordeal, and we've arranged for you to have hot showers and a full change of uniform back at Clervaux."

A murmur of satisfaction went through the men, smiles and nods directed towards this new Lieutenant. Clervaux was miles behind the lines. It had been re-taken from the Germans ten days or so before. This guy was taking them in the right direction.

Clay and Jake exchanged glances. This was good news, and they both new there was no such thing.

"How long we going to stay there?" Clay asked. Sykes fixed Clay with the hardest stare he had.

"Military courtesy dictates that any statement to an officer should be either preceded or terminated with the word 'sir'. Is that understood?"

"Yeah, that's easy to understand," Clay said. "Trouble is, it's easy for the Krauts to understand too. We start with Sir and Lieutenant up here, you're liable to draw fire like shit draws flies. Sir."

A ripple of laughter started up and died quickly as everyone noticed Sykes wasn't laughing. He held up his hand.

"Military discipline will be maintained, as appropriate to battlefield conditions. When we close with the enemy, then I expect you will avoid drawing attention to superior officers. Until then, standard forms of address and conduct apply. Understood?"

"We understand, sir," Jake said, stepping in before things got out of hand. "How long we will be in Clervaux, Lieutenant?"

"For the day. Trucks will be here soon. There is a shower unit set up in Clervaux, and fresh changes of field uniform are available. Hot chow, then back here for the night. Tomorrow morning we push off."

"Push off? Jesus, we've been behind Kraut lines for three days," Big Ned said, disbelief and anger in his raised voice. "One hot shower and then back in the line? Sir?"

"We need every man. Now I suggest you get some coffee and food if you haven't already. We leave as soon as the trucks arrive. Dismissed."

Sykes turned on his heel, smart as if he were on a parade ground. Most of the replacements drifted off towards the mess tent. Jake and Clay stood still, Big Ned and Tuck looking to them, Miller and Oakland at their sides.

"Dismissed? Close with the enemy? Who the fuck is this clown?" Big Ned asked.

"He's a card-carrying member of the WPPA," Clay said.

"What's that?" asked Oakland.

"West Point Protective Association," said Jake, kicking a mound of snow at his feet. "Ten to one, he's had a staff job at Division since he came over here. He needs some combat time for his next promotion, so they give him a platoon. If he doesn't get himself killed in this attack, they give him a medal, rotate him back to HQ. He goes home a hero, maybe a captain."

"What about us?" Miller said.

"We didn't go to West Point," Jake said. "All we get is a hot shower."

An hour later, two trucks were lumbering over the frozen, mud-caked ruts that passed for roads in the thickly wooded terrain. In the lead truck, Lieutenant Sykes rode in the passenger seat, a map folded on his knees. In the back of the truck, Jake, Clay, Big Ned, Tuck, Oakland and Miller shared the space with bags of laundry. Wind blew the side flaps against the truck, blowing in a light dusting of snow, covering everything like fine dust.

"This asshole's gonna get us killed, Jake," said Tuck. "I can feel it. We got no sergeants to keep him from doin' anything stupid, so you know he's gonna send us up the middle after the first machine gun he hears."

"They gotta teach 'em about that stuff at West Point, don't they?" asked Oakland.

"Officers look out for other officers, and West Pointers look out for West Pointers," Big Ned said.

"Red's an officer, and he's okay," said Miller, carefully, not wanting to disagree with his partner.

"Battlefield commission, that was," said Big Ned. "He got his bars with a rifle, not in school. Big fucking difference."

"Listen," said Jake, as the truck banged into a deep rut. "Let's just wait and see what happens. Somebody's got to be watching this kid. Maybe the Company commander will run things."

"Yeah, we see captains up front all the time," said Tuck. "Right, Miller?"

"Sure, Tuck, except when all the majors get in the way."

Big Ned looked at Miller blankly, then a wide grin lit up his face.

"All the majors get in the way. That's funny, kid, that's funny!"

They all laughed, again, not because it was that funny, but to disguise the fear and uncertainty. Laughing the loudest, Jake shoved an elbow into Clay's side, nodding for him to laugh too. He had to laugh. It really was funny. After finally deciding the tell Clay about his father, everything was falling into place. He was a dead man. This kid with his warm leather gloves and fur-lined winter parka would be the end of everything. A guy who didn't know shit about being at the front was going to lead them in an attack. A big push. Close with the enemy. He was surprised he hadn't said over the top. It was just about impossible for them to get out of this alive. For an experienced combat leader it took every fiber of being, every brain cell focused on remembering everything he'd ever learned, to bring back most of his men from an attack. The way Jake read him, Sykes was nothing but a pampered rich kid with connections strong enough to get a letter from his congressman to get him into West Point. The kind of guy who felt an HQ job was his due, as was the best cold weather gear for him to wear around the chateau, not for the G.I.s shivering in foxholes.

Maybe that was unfair. Maybe Sykes had asked for a combat assignment. Maybe the attack would be called off. Maybe, maybe, maybe.

As they traveled towards Clervaux, the terrain changed. The low rolling hills became steep, high peaks divided by narrow valleys, the road cutting in alongside a stream at the bottom of the hill. It began to remind Jake of home, the morning sun hidden behind the rocky, tree-lined slopes. Losing any sense of whether they were descending or the hills were rising around them, Jake had a strange feeling of dislocation, of separation from everything and everyone around him, as if he were watching from a distance, outside of his body. The wind had lessened, cut by the high cliffs, but it was colder, the frigid air settling into the shaded valley bottom. Shivering, he watched Tuck smoking, Big Ned sleeping, and Clay sitting with his legs up on a canvas bag of laundry. These men were his entire world. What would happen to them? He realized, with a shock, that he was more worried about them than about what might happen to him.

The truck climbed a narrow road, one switchback after another, until Jake glanced at rooftops when he pulled aside the canvas covering of the truck. Clervaux was tucked between two heavily wooded ridgelines at the bottom of the Clerf River valley. The road descended the ridgeline, houses and churches crowded on either side, the stone buildings lower and lower as they came nearer the valley floor. Some buildings were intact, others crumbled and charred, blackened heaps of rubble. The truck braked to a halt, and Jake could see Sykes turn his map, then point to a side road, up and to the left. The truck lurched forward, grinding gears as it threaded through the tight streets. Between the buildings on this street and those below, Jake saw a narrow stone walkway, large enough for two people to pass each other. More like home all the time, a town shadowed by mountains and even its own buildings, all conspiring to create dark, cold places hidden from the light.

The trucks groaned up the steep grade, as the road narrowed even further, then evened out, ending in a wide courtyard already jammed with two trailer trucks joined together. Tires crunched gravel as they pulled up behind the trailers, parking up against a gray stone building. A walled walkway connected it to a large church, even higher above the street, its sharply sloped slate steeple towering over them like a bayonet advancing on heaven.

Truck doors slammed and boots hit the stones as Jake and the others jumped off the trucks and stretched, groaning from the bumpy ride. The building they were standing in front of had the look of a school, several doors and rows of high windows facing the courtyard. A priest came out of one door, nodded without looking at any of them, and scurried off up the open walkway to the church.

"Friendly guy," Miller said to Big Ned as the men walked over to the walkway. Resting their arms on the wall, they looked out over the town, most of it set below them in what had been a peaceful valley. Streets curved like a witch's mouth set in a permanent grin, rotted, blackened teeth next to healthy, whole incisors, the trajectory of a mortar or tank shell changing the life of a family in a heartbeat.

"Yeah," said Big Ned, lighting a cigarette and blowing smoke into the empty air. "He oughta be overjoyed to see us."

Tuck laughed, the cynical grunt of an infantryman confronted with his handiwork. Jake looked out over the ruined town, wondering at the price of war, and if it was tougher to be a civilian, at the mercy of opposing armies. Or if the worst was being defeated and having someone else liberate you, rather than to go on living, suffering the occupation but being free to hate the occupier with a clean, if quiet, conscience.

The next set of rooftops was below their feet, a narrow alleyway separating them from the buildings facing the next street. Jake watched an old woman walk up the alley, taking the steps one at time. She was wrapped in so many layers of cloth and rags it was impossible to see her face, to make out anything but her bent frame, carrying a basket with what looked like turnips.

He wondered how far she'd walked for that food, and how far she had to go.

"Hey, fellas!"

Jake and the others turned. A sergeant in a wool overcoat and cap pulled down over his ears stood on the steps leading up to the rear of the trailer. With Sykes nowhere to be seen, eyes turn to Jake. He motioned the men over to the trailer, the sergeant chewing on the stub of an unlit cigar.

"Okay, I'll explain the drill," he said, looking and sounding bored. "First thing, you go inside the building to the first room on your right. Leave all weapons, everything from grenades to bazookas, in that room, along with your helmets. The room will be guarded. You gotta leave all weapons in there since we got locals movin' your other gear around, and we don't want any of them gettin' kilt. Unnerstand?"

"Any of those locals girls, Sarge?" asked Miller, with a grin.

"Yeah, all about yer grandma's age. Now shaddup and lissen. Then you go in this here trailer, six at a time. Remove all yer clothes and stuff 'em into a barracks bag. Take one dogtag off and wire it to yer bag so's you can pick it up when yer done. There's canvas bags in there fer your long johns, socks, underwear. All that shit will be replaced at the end. Then you start with the showers, and the next six guys go in. The locals bring yer bags to the end, you take 'em inside, collect yer new underwear, get dressed, get your weapons, get the hell outta here. Any questions?"

"You got hot water in that thing?" Big Ned said, crooking his finger at the trailers.

"There are eight shower stations in this unit," the sergeant said, repeating what he'd explained a thousand times before, closing his eyes as he read from the manual burned into his brain. "You will be handed a washcloth and a bar of soap. You will go through showers startin' at a tepid setting, going up to number four, which is the hottest setting. Then four more gradually cooling down to acclimate you to the outdoor temperature. At the final station you will be given a large towel and a heating unit will blast hot air as you dry off. You will then step out of the trailer, into the building, and proceed as directed." He took a deep breath, glaring at them, daring anyone to ask another question.

"How come we only get new underwear?" Oakland asked.

"On account 'ta the Germans blowing up our fuckin' supply

trucks, that's why. Now shaddup and the first six o' youse guys get in there."

"You gonna shower with us, Sarge?" Miller asked, trying to keep a straight face. He couldn't, and uncertain laughter rippled through the group as they watched the sergeant for a reaction. Descending the steps the sergeant walked over to stand right in front of Miller, rolling his cigar to one side of his mouth.

"How long you been on the line, dogface?"

"Week or so," Miller said, definitely as he could.

"Well, I been up here since first snow, and all I seen these past weeks is nuns and old ladies. Maybe I will shower up with you, sonny!"

Miller looked uncertain for a second, then laughed, then looked uncertain again.

"C'mon," said Big Ned, grabbing him by the collar. "We'll go first."

Jake and Clay followed, the sergeant giving them a wink as he headed back into the building. Tuck and Oakland came behind them, the rest of the men forming into a line. Rifles, web suspenders hung with grenades, ammo pouches, all weapons were stacked along the whitewashed wall of an empty room. Each man left his helmet on top of his pile, then eyeing the bored G.I. guarding the room, they shuffled back out, along the line of men behind them, to the showers.

Inside the trailer, the first compartment held canvas bags hanging on pegs. Coats, sweaters, boots, all their outerwear went into a barracks bag, each of which had a piece of wire strung through the grommets for a dogtag. Jake removed one dogtag, and shuddered at the odd feeling. You were only supposed to be separated from a dogtag when you were dead. He ran the wire through his twice, twisting the ends so it wouldn't fall off. Losing a dogtag had to be bad luck.

The men stripped to their long johns and underwear, the smell from their bodies no longer contained by layers of thick clothing, the odor as foul as rotting road kill. Jake peeled the pea-green long underwear off, the stain where his urine had flowed down his leg dark and matted to his red, irritated skin. They passed around a canvas bag, dropping the gray, formless items of clothing that had been their second skins into it like an offering to the gods of filth. Noses crinkled, eyes squinted, no one could even crack a joke.

A G.I. walked down the narrow hallway on one side of the trailer, wooden gratings on the floor keeping feet above water. Handing each man a bar of soap wrapped in a washcloth, he showed them to the first station.

Jake stood under the water, letting it flow over his head and down his body. It was a strangely familiar, yet alien feeling. Yesterday at this time, he'd been behind the German lines, wondering if he'd be killed or captured. Now, here he was, taking a shower. It didn't make any sense. He stood there, thinking, trying to understand, and he couldn't figure out how to wash himself. He gripped the bar of soap in his hand and willed it to scrub his body, but it stayed put.

"Okay, buddy, move on, more guys are waiting, move on."

They walked on the grating to the next set of showers, where the water was warmer. Jake began to shake, and even though he knew the water was warm, he couldn't stop himself. Closing his eyes, he turned his face up to the water, letting it wash over his eyes, nose and mouth. He heard laughter, whooping and yelling. The guys were enjoying this, a small faraway voice said. Go ahead, enjoy it too. Go ahead. It's okay.

"Keep it moving, fellas, keep it moving, next stop."

They shuffled along the grating, suds and dirty water running off beneath them. The next showers were hot and steamy, and Jake finally felt his muscles relax, his back unknot, as he took a deep breath of warm, moist air. He brought up the bar of soap to his chest and began to move it in a slow, methodical circle. Around and around, a ring of suds appearing and then washed away, appearing again, disappearing. It seemed useless, redundant. But he pressed on, scrubbing his armpits, face, stomach, groin, legs, working at the grim and caked sweat between the folds of his skin.

"Hot stuff coming up boys, step right in."

Hot, hot water. So hot it hurt at first, but hot enough to make the scrubbing easier. More yells from the other guys, but it was like they were a universe away, as if he were walking through a dream and was invisible to everyone. He scrubbed his feet, between his toes, working out clumps of wet lint and dirt and wondering if he'd get this dirty again.

"Cool down boys, move on and cool down."

He'd lost the cloth and soap. He held up his hands in the flowing water, warm now but not as hot. His fingernails were black, but his hands were clean. He looked at them as if they were brand new hands he'd never seen before. The dirt is still under my nails, but my hands are clean, my hands are clean. He massaged his head, getting the water into his scalp and cleansing his thick hair. My hands are clean.

"C'mon buddy, keep up with your pals."

Jake followed Clay, who looked relaxed, happy. Smiling at Jake, he said something, and moved into the next shower. Cooler now, refreshing. Jake felt like a new man. A new man. My hands are clean and I'm a new man. He smiled. Two more stations, and at the last his body was used to the cool water and it felt good, perfect.

"Get your towels, boys, and step into the next room."

With a loud mechanical whirr, a large fan started up and filled the room with heated air. It felt like the hot breath of God. Jake rubbed his head and wrapped the towel around his body. I'm clean, everything washed away, under the grate, down the drain, running under the streets of Clervaux. The voices of the other guys came closer to him, and he didn't feel so far away. He wanted to speak, to join in with them, but he couldn't think of what to say. It had to be the right thing for a new man with clean hands to say, but he couldn't think of a thing.

"Yow! How'd you like that, Jake?" Big Ned's face was red and shiny, his face lit up like a little boy. Jake struggled to speak, his throat hurting from the effort of getting the words out.

"It's like heaven," he said, evenly.

"God-damn right it is," Big Ned said, turning and opening the door of the trailer, heading into the building, wrapped in white. Jake followed, his feet cool on the damp granite stones of the walkway. Inside, they walked along tables stacked with wool long underwear, socks, tee shirts, more underwear, and a variety of U.S. Army shirts, in colors ranging from khaki to dark brown. G.I.s eyeballed them, guessed their sizes, and stacked piles of folded clothing in their arms. Jake looked at the shirts. They were mended in places, and stained with a dull rust color.

At the end of the hall, kids were dragging barracks bags into rooms on the left side. Walking towards them, Jake passed a room where old women knelt over buckets, scrubbing shirts with brushes and dunking them into the sudsy water, pulling them out to view their handiwork. In the next room, four old women sat around a table, stitching up holes in the cleaned shirts. Jake was

reminded of an assembly line, a great factory of death, reusing
worn out parts, wringing every last drop out of them, cleaning
and sewing until they looked like new, unless you noticed the
mended hole you wore over your heart.

"First group in here," a G.I. said, motioning his hand into a
small room. A cross hung above the door. As Jake followed Big
Ned inside, he could see that one wall had been painted with
a portrait of the Madonna. The walls were all whitewashed
clean, except for that outer wall, where Mary held up her hand
in blessing, next to a leaded window on hinges, open to reveal
a view of the building across the alleyway. The room was small,
empty, and cold.

"What kinda joint is this?" asked Tuck.

"Monastery, I bet," said Clay. "This was probably a monk's
cell, looks like a whole row of them along the hall." Dropping
his pile of clothes on the floor he began to open his barracks bag,
first removing his dogtag and putting it back on the chain around
his neck.

Jake looked at Mary, her graceful hand extended, her head
slightly tilted, as if she were inviting him in. Her eyes were set to
look at whoever entered the room, and Jake realized the painter
did that on purpose, to make whoever passed through that door
think of God and heaven.

"Hey, Jake, move aside, huh?" Miller edged around him and
began working open his barracks bag. Jake felt like he were
dreaming, and was surprised that he was actually in anybody's
way. He moved slowly, working his way through the tight room
to his bag, set with the others along the wall. Behind him, he
heard others in the crowded hallway, G.I.s in towels, kids pulling
heavy bags of clothes, soldiers giving directions, laughing, joking,
life flowing through the old building like blood pumping through
veins.

"Goddammit," Miller said, pulling at something in his
barracks bag. "Something's stuck." He gave a hard tug, trying to
disentangle whatever was knotted up in the opening of his bag.
Jake looked, and saw it a fraction of a second too late. A grenade.
Maybe left in a jacket pocket, it didn't really matter, because the
wire run through the grommets of the barracks bag had become
wound around the pin, and as Miller gave a last powerful pull,
the clump of clothing pulled free, and with it the grenade, free
of its pin, rolled onto the floor, the safety level flipped off, its

four second timer counting down under the serene gaze of Mary, mother of Jesus.

One-thousand one.

"GRENADE" yelled Clay, and all eyes riveted on the grenade, slowly spinning on the wooden floorboards. Noises from the hallway flooded in as the warning was heard.

One-thousand two.

"Ohmigod, ohmigod," Miller repeated, diving for the grenade, knocking it toward the wall before getting his hands on it. A young kid, speaking French a mile a minute, came into the room, maybe drawn by the excitement, or to ask a question. Clay dove on top of the boy.

"Throw it, throw it!" Big Ned pointed to the window, stepping to the side, making room for Miller to toss it outside.

One-thousand three.

Miller took two steps to the window. It was small, and he didn't want to chance throwing it. He'd drop it out, it was the only way to go. Big Ned stood to the side of the window, and saw them the same split second Miller did. The whole scene instantly filling his vision. The nun and the children, walking down the narrow alley below them, the nun holding a length of rope, each of the seven toddlers grasping onto it with one tiny hand. Miller gasped at the sight, and clenched his hand tight around the fragmentation grenade, thrusting it out the window, holding the grenade against the outside wall, his cheek planted on the inside wall, next to the Madonna's hand. He felt the grit of the surface on his cheek, the rough cold stone against his knuckles...

One-thousand four.

The explosion threw Miller back into the room, into Big Ned's arms. Screams filled the hall, cries rose up from the alley, and everyone in the room cried for a medic at the top of their lungs.

Big Ned was on the floor, cradling Miller from behind, wrapping one big arm around both his shoulders, wiping the blood from his face with the other. He held the stump of Miller's arm in a vise grip, clamping it to hold down the blood flow and keeping Miller from trying to lift it up.

"There, there, buddy, you're going to be okay," Big Ned murmured in his ear as he cleared the blood from Miller's eyes with the other hand. "Hold on, I've got you, I've got you."

Miller was shaking, his whole body convulsing. Big Ned could hardly hold on, the blood so slippery against bare skin.

"MEDIC!"

Jake went to the window, saw the nun with the children gathered around her, her arms and habit enveloping them as they cried.

"They're okay," he said to Miller, kneeling down and looking straight into his eyes. "Hear me? You saved them, you saved us all."

Miller blinked, his face twitching. "The kids..."

"Yeah, the kids," Jake said. "You saved them, saved us."

Clay moved beside Jake with a belt and tied it around Miller's bicep, pulling it tight. Someone thrust clean tee shirts at them and they wrapped the stump below his elbow, gently padding the broken ends of bone and torn muscle.

"Big Ned?" Miller said, his voice a choked whisper.

"Yeah, I'm right here, kid, I got you, the medics are coming."

"Did I do okay?"

"You did swell, Miller, just fine." Big Ned dipped his head down and rubbed the top of Miller's head with his cheek. "Just fine."

"I had to do it," Miller said, a sudden clarity lighting up his eyes, as if he had to explain himself to all of them. "It was the only thing to do. I had no choice, you understand?"

"Yeah," said Jake, "we understand." He wondered what it would be like to be presented with such an obvious, terrible choice, and if he'd act with Miller's certainty.

"I had to do it, no question in my mind," Miller said, twisting his head to look up at Big Ned.

"That was the bravest fucking thing I ever saw," said Big Ned, as he started to rock slightly, gently, just a few inches back and forth, his bare arm across Miller's chest. Clay placed Miller's wrapped arm on Big Ned's chest. They were all naked now, towels dropped in the tumult, clean bodies dappled in pink sprays of blood, like newborns ripped from the womb.

"Medics are on the way, ambulance will be here in a minute," the sergeant said from the doorway, twisting the unlit cigar in his mouth. Glancing between the Madonna and Miller on the floor, he crossed himself.

"Hold his arm in place," Big Ned said to Jake, as he rose from the floor, in one fluid motion, lifting Miller in his arms.

"You're going home, buddy, you're going home," he said, over and over again as he carried Miller out of the room, down the long hallway, past G.I.s in towels and uniforms, Belgian kids and old ladies. They all made room, clearing a path for the naked giant who whispered gentle comfort into the ear of the boy who knew when to do the right thing.

CHAPTER SEVENTEEN

1964

CLAY COULDN'T HELP GLANCING AT THE floorboards in the back room of the Tavern as he and Chris walked in. The Colt .45 was underneath, oiled and cleaned, a round in the chamber, safety on. Ready for action. Clay had killed before, but it had never been personal. All those Germans were just shooting at the uniform he happened to be in. It had nothing to do with him. Al was a man who wanted to use him, had used his son to get to him, a man who wanted to own him. It ought to be easy. But his palms were wet, his stomach churning, and he'd been up since five this morning, praying for another way out. No answers came, and he was left with the only choice that could set him free and keep Al away from his family. An old automatic, bequeathed to him by ghosts.

"Get started in the kitchen," Clay said. "Get everything up off the counters and clean 'em down good, the cutting board too. I'll mop in there when you're done." He glanced at his watch. Ten o'clock.

"Want me to make the signs first, Dad?"

"Yeah, sure. Use the backs of those posters, and tape 'em in the windows." Clay pointed to thick cardboard promotional posters from Carling Black Label, picturing a smiling waitress carrying a tray of beers. "Hey Mabel – Black Label!"

"They're kinda big, Dad." The posters were about two by four feet, thick enough to stand up leaned against a wall.

"Well, then, they'll be easy to see. One in each window. Closed for cleaning, open at six."

"Oookay," said Chris, in his best tone of teenage disbelief, tossing a stack of books on Clay's desk. Taking two of the posters and a thick marker, he headed up front to work on them. As he opened the door from the back room into the Tavern, jarring noises from the street flooded in. The work crew had their compressor set up next-door, up on the sidewalk. Two jackhammers were working off it, the air-driven metallic sounds driving through the glass and echoing around inside the room.

"I see what you mean," said Chris, raising his voice and turning his head back towards his father. "No one's going to hang around here with that racket."

Clay nodded. It made sense. Folks could walk in, or park up on Pratt Street, but no one in their right mind would sit in here for more than five minutes. So he'd called Brick and Cheryl, gave them the afternoon off, and took Chris along to help him give the place a scrub down. The big signs would keep people from rattling the locked door, he hoped. And obscure the view from the road.

Clay lifted the mop bucket into the sink, poured in soap and ran the water, watching the suds grow, white bubbles climbing to the top of the metal rim. Get through today, he told himself, make sure everything goes as planned, and things will work out. He figured his chances were fifty-fifty. Addy was on the verge of walking out, taking Chris and staying with her parents in Cranston, over in Rhode Island. Clay had stalled her for now, convincing her that moving to another state wouldn't look good when Chris went to trial. He knew she was fed up, nearly done with him, and that Chris' troubles were nothing more than a thin thread holding them together, but likely to break under the strain. Or, the excuse she needed to leave him, removing her son from temptation and herself from her husband. This was his last chance, his chance to salvage everything he held dear.

Wheeling the mop bucket into the bar, he watched Chris fashioning large block letters, filling them in with the dark marker. He looked young, bent over the cardboard, focused on letters, like a child hovering over a coloring book. Even though he was growing, turning tall and lean, Clay could still see the child in him, the smoothness of skin, traces of chubbiness in his cheeks, his tongue licking his lips as he worked to keep the letters even. He had to smile, even with this grim task facing him, thinking of coming home from his cigarette run in the afternoon, finding Addy and Chris coloring, or sitting and pouring over picture books, or in the kitchen surrounded by bowls and the smell of warm cookies fresh from the oven. Chris running to him and jumping into his arms, a look of total contentment and joy on Addy's face as she watched. Everything she didn't have growing up was lavished on Chris, from books and paints to cakes and cookies. Her ultimatum was part of the plan she had envisioned so long ago, a plan that had no place in it for gamblers and gangsters.

This is worth it, he decided. This is worth fighting for, worth taking a life for. Clay could burn in hell, but Chris could never know about any of his transgressions.

He glanced at his watch. Ten twenty.

"Got an appointment, Pop?" Chris smiled, using the term he always did when he kidded with his father. Clay realized it had been a while since he'd heard it.

"No, just checking. I want to make sure you have enough time to finish up here and get to the library." One thing Addy and Clay had agreed upon was that Chris' schedule was now firmly under their control. After breakfast this morning, she'd found Clay transplanting a white azalea from the back border of the house to the front of the garage. She'd said he should've given the job to Chris, that it would do him some good to keep busy, and why didn't he take him to help clean the Tavern? With no reason to argue, he agreed, adding that Chris could head up at noon to the Curtis Memorial Library on East Main, a few blocks away, to do his homework. Chris had wanted to stay with his father and do the homework in the back room, but Clay was firm, saying it would do Chris good to get to know the inside of a library.

"Okay," said Chris, returning to his labors. Clay marveled at how agreeable and pliant Chris had become after he got in trouble. Maybe being punished gave him permission to give up the sullen teen scowl he always wore. A sense of protectiveness overwhelmed him. He wanted to cradle Chris in his arms the way he used to, tell him stories, tell him the world was a safe place. Now, they both knew that was a lie.

He turned away from his son, unwilling to draw attention to himself, fearing his thoughts would be revealed on his face. Things had to look completely normal, logical, everyday. Clay walked into the storeroom and reached for an old can of paint on the shelf, caked with white and rust along the top. He shook it, and pried the top off with a screwdriver. About an inch left on the bottom, plenty for what he needed. Taking a brush and a paint-stained canvas tarp, he brought it all to the kitchen entrance, spread out the tarp on the floor, and began to paint the trim.

"Shouldn't you clean that first?" Chris asked. The molding was marked with grease, stains and even a few phone numbers. His father had always been a stickler for cleaning surfaces before painting, sanding down old glossy paint so the new coats would stick. Chris was surprised to see him breaking his own rules.

"Yeah, but I'm giving this a quick coat so it'll have time to dry. Next time, maybe we'll strip it down to the bare wood and stain it."

"Sure, Dad." Stripping old paint was another of his father's pet projects, and Chris wanted no part of that. Clay knew there'd be no more questions. He finished one coat on the molding, set the paint can down on the tarp, and wiped his hands on an old bar rag.

He watched Chris tape the posters up in the twin windows on either side of the front door, Mabel sideways on the back, ready with her Black Label. They filled up the center of the big windows, blocking out the view of the street. Chris went to work in the kitchen, and Clay moved slowly up front, glancing at his watch. Ten forty-five.

Next Clay moved tables up to the windows, stacking chairs on top of them. The compressor was running not five yards away, the gas engine rumbling. Rolling the mop bucket next to the bar, he dunked the mop head into the sudsy water and slopped it onto the floor, pushing down on the handle, rubbing the floor hard, feeling the muscles in his forearm tense as he moved the mop in circles, wringing it out and moving it over the floorboards, the white suds absorbed into the old, dry wood. Grit and dirt from thousands of shoes caked together between the boards, worn to a gray shine by the scuffing of decades. When had he last mopped the floors? He couldn't remember. A good sweep at night and then another before opening was clean enough, but today was special. Cleaning day.

"Dad? Want me to put the tarp away?" Chris hollered above the sounds of the jackhammers out in the street.

"No. No, leave it, I might do another coat."

Clay rolled the bucket back into the storeroom, dumped out the dirty water and filled it with clean water for the rinse. He opened a full container of bleach and poured some in. He started at the storeroom door, working his way forward.

Eleven-fifteen.

He liked how the floor looked after the wet mop. The diluted bleach gave it a clean, fresh woody smell as the dry floorboards soaked it up. It'd been years since they were this clean. Years too since he'd killed. He remembered the last man he had killed, as if it happened yesterday.

Working the mop, he felt the tightness still gripping his stomach. It was intent, eating at him. He'd been satisfied with the thought that Al was ruining his life, and his family. That was justification enough. But now intent worried him. All the others dead at his hands—well, most anyway—knew what they were in for. Kill or be killed. A few were accidents, terrible, horrible, haunting. But no intent at all. Al was different. Clay had the intent to kill him. Murder. If things went well, Al would walk in alive, unsuspecting, and leave unsuspecting and dead. It was kill or be killed. But Al's type of killing was a lot slower, it might take a life time, destroying a family, a marriage, a man. Okay. The hell with intent.

He was at the windows. The noise was constant, a backdrop to everything he did and thought. Between the stacked chairs and the posters, it was hard to see outside. He walked backwards to the storeroom, swabbing his steps away. Eleven-thirty.

"How's it going, Chris?" Clay stepped on the tarp and looked in the kitchen, avoiding the wet paint. Chris was scrubbing down the refrigerator, wiping off grimy fingerprints.

"Using the ol' elbow grease, Pop," said Chris. "How's it look?"

"Not bad," said Clay, nodding. He'd never seen the frig look whiter. "You getting hungry?"

"Yeah, sure. You want me to cook us some burgers?"

"No sense messing up your clean kitchen. You finish that and I'll give you a buck for lunch at the Liberty Diner. Then straight to the library."

"Okay, thanks. You want me to get you something?"

"No. No listen, Chris. I want you to promise you'll do exactly as you're told. Lunch, then the library. Stay put until I come get you. Understood?"

"Sure."

"You see any of your pals, you keep walking. And don't leave the library."

"Okay, okay, I get it. You sure you don't want me to stay here where you can keep an eye on me?"

"I'm sure. Do your homework, read a book. It'll please your mother to have you spend more time in a library than in the bar." Clay tried to smile, giving Chris a playful punch in the arm. Eleven thirty-five.

By quarter to twelve, Chris was out the door, with five quarters from the till in his pocket for lunch, his father reminding him to leave a good tip for the waitress. Clay caught a glimpse of him walking in front of the Tavern, through a narrow strip of glass at the edge of a poster. He stopped and watched the workers for a minute, then turned and walked towards East Main. Okay, plenty of time. The meeting's set for two. Front entrance is blocked, so Al will have to come around back. The compressor and jackhammers are working out in the street. The tarp is down. He needed to fill the bucket with clean water, and add plenty of bleach. Get the automatic out from under the floorboards. Wait.

Clay leaned against the bar, taking a deep breath, willing himself to go through with his plan. He'd thought of everything, he was sure. Not everyone planning a killing would know about the blood, how much of it there would be. He was ready for that. He held his face in his hands, thinking, thinking—what have I forgotten?

"Praying, Mr. Brock?"

Clay jumped at the sound of the loud voice, loud enough to be heard over the noise from the street. Standing in the open storeroom door, a .38 revolver in his hand, was Al DePaoli, wearing a green sharkskin suit, a nasty smile and thin leather gloves. The second Clay saw him, the noise stopped as someone turned off the compressor. In the silence, Clay heard church bells chiming the hour. Lunch break. Twelve noon.

"You're early," was all Clay could manage as he struggled to keep his emotions under control and think. What should he do? What could he do?

"Yes, Mr. Brock, I am. I make it a practice to arrive early whenever someone makes an appointment to kill me." Al advanced two steps, the revolver leveled at Clay's stomach.

"What? What do you mean?" Clay spread his hands in innocence. "I don't have a gun!"

"Yes," Al laughed, "I can see that. Also, the tarp, the mop, bleach, and those signs in the window, such a nice touch. It's unfortunate they'll all go to waste. And so unfortunate that you decided not to work for me. You would have been very valuable."

"Hey, wait a minute, I called you and told you I'd work for you, if you got Chris out of trouble. You agreed!" Clay tried to work up a righteous indignation, desperate for an idea, or to get within reach of Al. They were both at the bar, about six feet apart, standing like gunslingers in an uneven showdown.

"Yes, and I was pleased. But then this morning I heard about your call to old man Fiorenza. Your offer to eliminate his problem, in exchange for retirement?"

Clay felt like he'd been punched in the gut. Al had an informer. He'd known what was going to happen, and now the tables were turned. He had nothing going for him, no weapon, no noise, no surprise.

"That was to get him off my back, that's all."

"Please Mr. Brock," said Al, waving the revolver back and forth, scolding him for the obvious lie. "So, how were you going to do it? Strangle me? Hit me over the head with a bottle of your cheap liquor?"

Al looked amused, playing with Clay, having some fun with him. Maybe he was curious. Maybe Clay could buy some time, but other than a few more minutes of life, he had no idea what that would get him.

"You know all the angles, you figure it out," Clay said, folding his arms across his chest.

"Okay," said Al, moving around the bar, keeping the pistol trained on Clay. "Let's take a look. Shotgun behind here, maybe? Nope. Handgun in one of these drawers? Nope. Aw, don't tell me!" Al came up with the old wooden billy club Brick kept on a shelf behind the bar. He slammed it once on the bar, the sound of wood against wood cracking like a tree branch.

"Bust my skull open with this, roll me up in a tarp? Is that what you were going to do? Is it?"

"Nah, you're too smart for that. I was going to offer you a drink. A Mickey Finn."

"Now that's more like it, Mr. Brock. Smart, classy. But not smart enough."

"You got me there. Listen, when this is all over, ease up on my kid. There'll be no reason to press charges."

"Oh, no no no," said Al, scolding again as he walked back from around the bar. "There's plenty of reason. Your widow will inherit this place, right? I'm sure she'll agree to my offer in exchange for letting poor Christopher off the hook."

Dying was one thing, but dying while this punk planned to go after his family was too much. Clay lunged at him, not caring if he was shot, wanting to get his hands around Al's throat. Sidestepping, Al slammed the butt of his revolver against Clay's head. Clay felt a sharp pain, saw an explosion of lights, then nothing.

Clay's head was pounding when he woke. The back of his head throbbed and it took a second for him to realize the pounding noise was the compressor outside. Lunch break was over. He opened one eye and saw the blurry outline of Al, sitting cross-legged in a chair, lazily holding the revolver on him.

"Finally," said Al. "I didn't want to hit you that hard, but you made me." He cocked an eyebrow apologetically, as if Clay was a naughty boy.

"Why didn't you finish me off?" Clay said, disgusted with himself and all his plans and schemes. Not only today's botched attempt, but everything, the numbers, everything that had gone before. How did he end up here, on the floor, about to be killed by this punk?

"Now that's the difference between a pro and an amateur, Mr. Brock. You planned to do this thing here, on your own turf. Stupid. You had things set up okay, well prepared, but why do it here? Now that you're awake, we're going to a nice quiet place, nobody's turf, and do this right."

"What if I don't go easy?"

"Either you go easy, or I don't on that pretty wife of yours. Not bad for an old broad."

Clay got to his feet, ready to go after Al again, but by the time he stood up, the barrel of the pistol was pointed at his face. One jackhammer started up outside, then the other. One-fifteen. Time to go. Clay didn't trust Al to keep his word if he went easy, but he damn sure knew he would if he went hard.

"That's real smart, Mr. Brock. Now let's leave nice and easy, out the back. After you." Al stepped to the side, the mock politeness leaving a smirk on his face.

Clay walked toward the storeroom door, thinking about Jake's Tavern, all the hours he'd spent here, trying to understand he'd never be coming back. He thought about the automatic, but he wouldn't have a chance in hell at getting to it. He wondered about the twelve thousand, and if Addy would find it before Mr. Fiorenza did, or Al, for that matter.

Moving into the storeroom, Clay's eye darted towards the floorboard where the .45 lay hidden. He saw the floorboard gone, the empty space below. Catching a movement to his right out of the corner of his eye, he came to a stop one step inside the storeroom.

"Wait a second," he said, raising his arms. "I've got Fiorenza's delivery here, twelve thousand. Maybe we can make a deal."

"Tell me where it is," Al snarled, jabbing the revolver in the small of Clay's back. Clay turned his head to the right, as if to answer Al, and saw the floorboard coming down, the four foot section arcing down over Chris' head, the hard edge smashing into Al's wrist, the sound of wood and bone breaking, a yelp from Al and the clatter of the revolver hitting the floor. Clay turned towards Chris and saw he had the .45 out, set on a stool next to him. Spinning on his heel, he grabbed for the gun with his left hand, standing between his son and Al, a flash of Chris' open-mouthed astonishment frozen in his mind as Al writhed on the floor, holding his broken wrist. He stepped closer, kicked the revolver away from Al, and aimed the .45 at his head. His hand shook, and he forced back the memory of the last time the automatic had been fired.

"Get up," Clay said.

"He broke my fucking wrist!" Al blubbered, tears welling up in his eyes as he held his limp arm in his left hand.

"Chris, are you all right?" Clay couldn't turn away, didn't dare take his eyes off Al.

"Yeah, yeah. Was he going to kill you, Dad, for real?"

"I think so. Chris, listen to me, okay?" Clay held the automatic in both hands, his legs spread apart, putting as much of his body between Chris and Al as he could. He felt Chris' hand on his shoulder.

"Stay behind me, Chris, and listen, okay?"

"Yeah, Dad." Clay could feel his son's breath on his neck, felt his fingers gripping his shoulder. Memories of violence and closeness, carnage, death and friendship flooded through his mind, confusing him. His son had saved his life, rescued him from a certain death, disabling his captor with stealth and cunning. Twenty years ago he'd been with other young men, hardly older, who did the same. But this wasn't what he wanted for his son. He tried to shake off the images and feelings crowding his mind, to focus on Al as he pushed up to a sitting position, back against the wall, his feet folded beneath him and his arm cradled in his lap.

"You have to go to the library, like I said. Just act like nothing's happened, don't tell anyone about this, okay?"

"You're not going to call the cops?" Chris's voice was shrill, the excitement carrying it high and loud.

"Hang around, kid," Al said through gritted teeth. "Watch your old man kill a guy. That's why he wants you out of here. Right, Mr. Brock?"

"Chris, you did great, you saved my neck, but now you have to leave," Clay said, as firmly as he could manage. "Don't listen to him."

"Yeah, Chris, don't listen to me," said Al, sneering at Clay. "Listen to your dad here. Ask him why he's going to kill me, then listen real close."

"Dad, I think we need to call the cops!"

"Yeah, let's get the cops over here. Maybe they could have a look around, see what they find," said Al. "Chris, be a good kid, pick up the phone. I got nothing to hide."

Chris walked from in back of his father, backing up a step as he did so. "Dad?" The question was almost drowned out by the sound of jackhammers, but Clay looked over at his son. How could he ever explain? How could he let Chris see him as a murderer? It would make him his own father, a shameful thing, another generation to be feared. No. He lowered the automatic.

"Call the police, Chris."

"Not so fast," said Al, standing up suddenly, his right arm limp at his side. In his left hand, drawn from a holster around his ankle, was a small .25 automatic. Clay could see the pearl handle between Al's gloved fingers, the shiny nickel plating, and the barrel three feet from Chris' heart. Clay raised the .45, but half-heartedly.

"Put it down or I drill the kid. You decide."

"You pull the trigger and you're a dead man," Clay said, his gun halfway up to Al's chest.

"Leaving you alone to cry over your son's corpse. Like I said, Mr. Brock, you decide." Al smiled, as if he were offering Clay a choice of drinks. Scotch or beer? You decide. Clay looked into his eyes, and saw nothing. Dark pupils floating on milk white. No depth, no emotion, everything on the surface. He knew what he was seeing, but at the same time knew there was no way his son could recognize such evil. If he did what he ought to do, Chris would know, and evil would carry the face of his father.

"If I give you the money, will you leave us alone?"

"If you put that cannon down, and give me the money, I'll walk out of here with you two still breathing," said Al. Clay set the automatic down on the stool, reluctant to release his grip. He didn't believe Al's promise, but he believed his threats.

"Let Chris go, then I'll tell you where the cash is," said Clay.

"No," said Al.

"Pick up the gun, Dad."

"Shut up, kid!"

"He's not going to let us go," said Chris, edging closer to the door.

"Don't shoot, I'll get the money," yelled Clay, "it's right over here." Clay moved to the shelves, pointing to the top shelf, trying to draw Al's interest and aim away from Chris.

"You, kid, away from the door," Al screamed, moving sideways to block Chris from the door, swiveling his automatic between them. He glanced around the room, looking for his revolver. It was on the other side of Clay's desk, too far for him to reach.

"Move over there with your old man," Al yelled, his face contorted in pain and rage, waving the automatic back and forth as he ordered Chris back.

"Okay, okay," Chris said, his hands up in surrender, edging by stacked boxes of cigarettes.

"Brock, move that stool closer to me, now!" Al pointed his gun at Clay and then at the .45. He wanted the more powerful gun, wanted it out of Clay's reach. Clay looked into the empty eyes and saw them calculating, coming to a conclusion, then turning his left hand towards Chris, about to subtract one from the equation.

As Al's gun arm began to move, Chris dropped his raised hands and grasped a box of cigarettes, heaving it at Al, hitting him square in the chest.

Pop pop pop. Al squeezed off three shots as he went down. A bottle on the shelf behind Chris shattered, then pop pop as two rounds went at Clay, breaking more bottles behind him, vodka and glass spilling onto the floor.

"Get down, Chris," Clay yelled as he grabbed the shelf and pulled it down, sending bottles and boxes crashing to the floor.

Al scuttled out of the way, diving for a corner in back of Clay's desk, away from the breaking glass, paint thinner and alcohol, towards the .38.

The falling shelves knocked the stool and sent Clay's .45 automatic flying. Clay yelled for Chris to stay low and get into the barroom, while grabbing a bottle of gin and flinging it as hard as he could at Al's head. Al ducked, and the bottle shattered against the wall behind him. He came up with the .38 in his good hand, a triumphant grin on his face.

"First you, then your kid, then I tear his place apart and look for the money. No one's going to bother me until six o'clock." Al laughed as Clay reached under a box, trying to get to the .45. From behind him, Chris threw another bottle that smashed on the wall next to Al.

"You little bastard," he said, and aimed at Chris. With the automatic in his hand, Clay leapt up to push Chris aside. Al fired once. Immediately there was a whump as the muzzle blast ignited the flammable vapors all around him. Then the paint thinner and alcohol pooled on the floor went up. Penned in by the desk and the fallen shelves, and with only one good arm, Al tried to brush off the flames licking at his feet and crawling over his sharkskin suit. He began to scream, falling over the shelves, rolling on the floor, picking up broken glass and spilled alcohol that sputtered into dancing snakes of fire, winding around his limbs, licking at his face, embracing him.

Al rose to his knees and lifted a burning arm, the .38 aimed at Chris.

Clay fired, twice to the chest. It was easier than killing the German.

Chris stood open-mouthed, shock and fear draining him white. Clay put his hand on his shoulder, and guided him out of the room as the flames crackled and grew, creeping up the walls, gaining a foothold in the old dry wood, the once familiar smell of burning flesh riding on the smoke and hooking itself, deep, in Clay's memory.

CHAPTER EIGHTEEN

2000

CLAY AND CHRIS HAD GOTTEN ON THE ROAD BY noon the day before, after a stop at the Criminal Investigations Bureau on Broad Street. Chris had been ten minutes, then back out into the car with a thick manila envelope. A little work he had to do, he explained. Earlier they had driven down East Main to Noack's for smoked ham, cheese and rye bread. Clay made sandwiches and brewed coffee for the thermos, never trusting that a doughnut shop or diner would make it strong enough to suit his taste.

Their journey had begun with a drive down Main Street, by the War Memorial, then down the hill past City Hall, the library and the old neighborhood of Jake's Tavern. At the bottom of the hill the city began to show its age and decline, the street looking like an old man's grin, grimy gaps showing between decayed structures. The old train station torn down, department stores vanished, movie houses gone, replaced by a new police building and social service offices. Where people used to eat or buy shirts or chat with storekeepers, they now argued with social workers or bailed relatives out of jail. At each block, Clay could recount the disappearance of a favorite stop. A Jewish deli, the bowling alley, the theater where he and Addy used to go to matinees, a favorite luncheonette, the cobbler's shop. All gone or boarded up, replaced by half-empty parking lots, a dollar store, the employment office. The sadness he always felt on this street had overcome Clay again as he looked at the empty sidewalks. So much richness gone, so much of life chipped away until there was nothing left but dull concrete and signposts pointing to the mall and the highway.

They took I-84 and left the city, the mall, and the hanging hills behind them. Heading west, they drove through Waterbury and the twisted highway intersections the locals called the Mixmaster. Traffic thinned and the views broadened over greening hills. They sipped coffee, ate sandwiches and listened to talk radio. Chris hadn't asked any more questions and Clay hadn't offered up any answers. Tomorrow's soon enough he'd told himself. Tomorrow we'll be there, where it all started. Tomorrow.

After crossing the Hudson they'd curved south, picking up Route 209 at the head of the Delaware Water Gap, the roadway threading its way alongside the Delaware River, steep hills casting shadows toward the east. Driving on, following the curve of the Alleghenies, the folds of the mountains slanting southwest drew them on into the past. His past. For Clay it had felt immediately familiar, as if nothing had changed in the last sixty years. Driving past Little Gap, and through larger towns crammed onto bits of flat land along the Lehigh River, his throat had tightened and his pulse raced as the sun settled beyond the western ridges.

Coaldale, the sign said. Welcome to Schuylkill County. That was close enough for Clay, more than enough after a long drive. They had pulled into the next motel as darkness enveloped the valley, snapping a chill into the air, bright lights flicking on in the parking lot. Tomorrow, Clay half whispered like a prayer, tomorrow.

Trouble with putting something off until tomorrow, Clay thought, is that sooner or later it turns into today, and then there you are again. Setting down his coffee cup he gave out a small ahhh of satisfaction. Hot, and as strong as a guy could reasonably expect. The Green Pines Inn had a coffee shop, a small counter and six booths. Thick knotty pine boards on the walls and floor gave the place a warm, relaxed feel, like being on vacation. Clay's eyes flitted around the room, taking in the locals at the counter, solitary guests at two other booths, and finally, his son, walking in from the motel. He carried the manila envelope he had picked up at his office.

"Well?" said Chris.

"How deep?" answered Clay, the long forgotten retort springing out of his mouth before he knew it. That had been one of his father's standard answers when anybody said well? to him in that exasperated tone. Half joke, half obfuscation.

"C'mon, Dad, I've been patient, but it's time to spill the beans. Why are we here?"

"I appreciate it, Chris. You know, it's not easy for me."

"It never seems to be."

"What's that supposed to mean?" Clay asked.

"Nothing's really easy. Not with you, or me. Some people have it easy, but easy was never in the cards for us. I mean, you had Mom, which is great. But you lost your family early on, had to go off to war, then had that mess with the Tavern, not to mention all the trouble I caused you. Not easy."

"And you?" Clay asked.

"That's obvious. Failed marriage, no family of my own. Again, not easy."

"You know," Clay said, "sometimes I feel that's my fault. Like I made some big mistakes bringing you up."

"Like what?" Chris' tone had an edge to it, and he sat back, eyes narrowing.

"I don't know. Maybe kept too tight a rein on you. Worried too much about you, didn't trust you enough."

"Dad, I am who I am. It's not like tuning an engine, for Christ's sake. Do you really think if you'd eased up a bit I would've been a better man? Maybe then you would've had grandkids by now?"

"No, Chris. I didn't mean that. I'm not explaining myself well."

"You're not explaining yourself at all. As usual."

Chris' eyes drilled into Clay's. Clay wanted to look away, change the subject, sip the good coffee, and be left in peace. But there was no peace, only the threads of his past, still pulling at him, drawing him back to the war, to his buddies, and finally to his family. It was overwhelming, too much to explain, how could he? His eyes drifted back to his hands, holding the coffee cup, drawing in its warmth. His entire being seemed to settle into his hands, old hands soaking up what heat they could.

"More coffee?" The waitress stood by the booth, her silent arrival startling Clay.

"Yes, yes please. It's good," Clay said, laying his hands flat on the table. She smiled as she poured for both of them. Clay avoided Chris' stare until she left.

"You're right," he said.

"Damn straight I'm right," Chris answered. "It took a guy

trying to kill you and the Tavern burning down for me to find out what kind of business you were really running. I doubt if you ever would've said a word otherwise."

"I felt awful I got you mixed up in all that."

"That's not the point, Dad. I got in that mess all by myself. I made some dumb choices; I don't blame you for that. But why you did it, that's what you never explained. Just like you never talk about the war. Or your folks. After half a century, Dad, I really have no idea who you are."

Clay was on the brink of getting up and walking out. The more Chris wanted to know, the more the walls pressed in on him, the ghosts of the past gathered and closed in. It was how he'd always reacted, but this trip was not supposed to be that way. He struggled to stay put, to not tell his son to mind his own damn business.

"That's because I tried to protect you," he said.

"I know, you did protect me—"

"No, I'm not talking about Al and Tony. I mean something else." His words caught in his throat, and he saw everything clearly, and saw how wrong he had been. Everything he'd done to cut off his past, protect his son, had brought them here today. His son, a grown man, haunted by the question of who his father was. Just exactly as he was. The sins weren't the same, but the curse of secrets was. What was hidden hadn't protected anyone, it just allowed the secrets to fester and cripple another life. Trying to speak, he couldn't make the words come.

"Okay," Chris said, pulling out his wallet. "This is par for the course. I should've known better than to waste my time."

"What do you mean? I thought you wanted—"

"Listen, Dad, I'm here because you asked me to come. You want this trip down memory lane, fine. I admit I'm curious, but based on how things have always gone, I doubt you'll tell me anything new."

"Maybe you don't care. Maybe I don't care to tell you."

"Maybe you can't," Chris said. He clutched the envelope as if he might throw it at his father. Instead, he grabbed the check, and went to the counter. Clay sat, watching Chris pay, the truth hitting him like a brick. His son might be right. It might be beyond him now to simply tell the truth. He slid out of the booth, slowly straightening his bent body. Sitting in the car for so long yesterday had stiffened him up. He held onto the coat rack, waiting for the dizziness to pass. He took his coat off the hook and put it on slowly, feeling the pain in his shoulders as he pulled each arm back to slip into the flannel-lined coat.

Chris was already out the door and headed to the car. Clay smiled at the waitress, and shuffled toward the door, holding out his hand to steady himself on whatever was close. His joints hurt, his legs ached and a spasm of pain shot through his lower back. Feeling every minute of his age, he sensed something strange, a tingling in his chest. A rush of adrenaline, hypersensitivity, the vigilance of a combat patrol. Behind the lines. Enemy territory. It was only a faint echo of a feeling, the memory of what it was like, but still, it was exciting. Clay tried to pick up his legs, get the soles of his shoes off the floor as he walked, instead of scuffling them along. He stood outside the coffee shop for a moment, heaving in a lungful of the cool, damp air. It smelled of pine and cold running water. Closing his eyes for a second, the odor of the Ardennes crept into his nostrils.

"Let's go," he said, climbing into the passenger seat and buckling up in one smooth motion. No grunts or huffs. It was time, time to tell the truth and cut the ties that bound them both to secrets and fear.

"How far?" asked Chris as he eased the Jeep out into traffic.

"Ten, twelve miles maybe."

"So you know this area real well?"

"Some," Clay said slowly. He turned to look at Chris. "When we get to Minersville, I'll tell you everything."

Chris half turned his face and cocked an eyebrow. "Minersville? Really? You're going to tell me everything?"

"Yep. God help me, I am." Or enough, as least, he thought to himself.

Chapter Nineteen

1945

Stuffing his glove inside his jacket, Clay adjusted the focus on his binoculars, the cold stinging his hand as he slowly scanned the village, across the downward slope of the open fields to his front. Frosted breath obscured his view as he tried to slow his breathing, reduce the visible plume of warmth and direct it downward into the small depression he'd made in the snow. He'd had to crawl about ten yards out from the treeline to see over a hump in the ground, down into the small village nestled in the crook of a basin, overlooked by two ridgelines and a low, rounded hill. Three roads intersected between the ridgeline, two snaking around the hill on the right and the third coming down the narrow valley from the left. Smoke drifted up from chimneys, disappearing into the gray morning haze. It looked peaceful, but somebody, far from here, had decided that was going to change.

Clay could see the tank clearly. Krauts walking casually around it and from one building to another, flapping their arms to keep warm. Turning the binoculars to the right, he focused on a stone farmhouse at the top of the hill. Wooden outbuildings stretched behind it, but the house itself was made of stone blocks, and Clay knew that's where the machine gun would be. Top right window. He could make out the snout of the gun, imagining the gunner swiveling it, covering the wide field of fire in front of him, enjoying a clear view of the open ground that led down to the village. Fuck.

He watched as a German walked from the back of the farmhouse toward the barn, carrying two pails. Breakfast, maybe, which meant more Krauts in the barn. Behind the barn, barbed wire was strung between posts stuck into the recently trampled snow. Fuck.

The tank on the opposite side of the village was pulled back into a side street, covering the wooded ridge that curved around the village and ended abruptly where the road was cut through the narrow passage. Fuck.

Clay pulled his glove back on, his hand raw and numb from the few minutes of exposure. He crawled backwards until he felt Jake's hands grab him, pulling him behind a fir tree. He rolled over and pushed himself up, resting against the thick base of the tree, letting his breath flow freely again, releasing gusts of white frost.

"Well?" said Tuck.

Clay looked at Tuck, not recognizing him for a moment without Shorty looking over his shoulder. Oakland was there instead, kneeling in the snow and leaning on the barrel of his M1. Big Ned squatted nearby, his BAR slung around his neck and resting in his lap. No Little Ned, no Miller, no Shorty, no Red, no Coop, no Marty, no Samuelson. None of the others. They'd come and gone, lived and died, leaving him here now, looking out at a few familiar faces and too many unfamiliar ones, expectant, hoping for good news. The ones who still believed in good news, anyway.

Jake was by his side, but still turned toward the open ground. Clay knew Jake would be patient, listening while keeping his eyes front. Clay saw Sykes coming toward them, from the direction of the Company HQ, on the reverse slope of the ridge. Safe from shellfire. Unlike this position. Two machine gun crews trailed Sykes, carrying their .30 calibers and ammo boxes. They split off, one to each side of the treeline.

"Get ready, men," said Sykes, "any minute now." His voice quavered on the last word, as his eyes darted back and forth, up and down, searching for something to settle on besides snow, trees, gray skies, or the eyes of the men. No one acknowledged him. He had nothing to offer them except wounds, pain and death. It was better to ignore him, unless there was some kind of direct order. Otherwise, he might talk to you, remember you, and pick you out for some asshole stunt that would get you killed. Maybe he'd disappear into his foxhole and stay there, or melt into the rear. It'd been known to happen.

"Maybe twenty Krauts in the village," Clay said, answering Tuck. "Hard to say with them going in and out. Could be less, could be more of them inside."

"What? How do you know that, soldier?" Sykes said. He tried to keep his voice steady and firm, but it came out shaky, his eyes wide, his eyebrows up, fear playing itself out over his face.

"I looked," said Clay. "Have you?"

Either Sykes was taking the advice about not displaying rank at the front, or he was too nervous to remember, but he didn't demand a sir from Clay. "Not yet, I—I was at the briefing. For the attack. The captain said there was less than a platoon in the village. It's very lightly defended."

Turning away from Sykes, Clay looked at the men gathered around him. "Stone farmhouse on the right, heavy MG in the upper floor window. Krauts in the barn behind the house, barbed wire strung behind that." No one said anything. The meaning was clear. No flanking the village from the right. The farmhouse was a strongpoint, covered by the machine gun in front and the Krauts in the barn to the rear. The barbed wire would hold them up long enough to be sitting ducks.

"We can deal with that, men, don't worry about it," said Sykes. "Don't worry about it."

"There's a tank at the other end of town," Clay said.

"A Tiger?" one of the replacements asked. Every fucking tank a replacement saw was a Tiger. Big, heavy killers with a 88mm gun. The word was enough to send whole platoons running. Not every German tank was a Tiger, even though it hardly mattered if you were facing one without a couple of Shermans behind you.

"No. Mark IV. But it's facing that draw where the road comes down on the left. Narrow gap. Too much of a chance of getting bunched up."

"How do you know all this?" asked Sykes again. "You can't see from here. Stop worrying the men, soldier."

"Lieutenant?" said Jake softly, not turning from where he knelt. "You might want to listen."

"I'm not talking to you, soldier, I'm talking to this man. Where'd you get all this about Tiger tanks?"

"It's not a Tiger, and it's one tank," Clay said. "I crawled out about ten yards to see over that rise, down into the village."

Sykes' mouth hung open and he glanced at the men facing Clay, as if he could will them to look at him, to pay attention to what he had to say. His voice came out as a croak, seeming to take note, for the first time, of the binoculars hanging around Clay's neck. "Who ordered you to make a reconnaissance, and where'd you get those binoculars? Only officers are authorized—"

"He shot the officer he got them from, Lieutenant Sykes," Jake said, not so softly this time. "At two hundred yards."

Somebody laughed, a quick snort that vanished on a plume of frost. No one spoke. Jake didn't look at Sykes, keeping his eyes on the part of the village he could see over the rise in the cleared land in front of him. Rooftops, mostly. He saw wooden shutters on an attic window swing open, as if it were a dollhouse, out of reach. He felt the bottom drop out of his stomach, his skin go pale and clammy, as everything went into sharp focus as he eased back, putting the tree between himself and that attic window.

"What rise?" Sykes said, ignoring Jake. Taking a step closer to the tree he craned his head out around it, staring out toward the open window. Jake thought about it, wondered if it wouldn't be for the best, but couldn't do it. Reaching up and grabbing Sykes by his web belt, he pulled him down as the distant crack of a rifle was followed a split second later by the zinging sound of a bullet splitting the air and leaving behind a sprinkle of green needles where Sykes had been standing. Sykes scrambled back further behind the tree.

Clay leaned his head down toward Sykes so their helmets touched. "I said I crawled." Sykes pushed himself away from Clay, and got up on one knee, brushing snow from his clothes, his eyes cast down to the ground.

"So whaddya gonna do, Lieutenant?" said Big Ned, spitting into the snow. "About the machine gun and the tank?"

Sykes looked at him with astonishment. His forehead wrinkled and his mouth parted as if a word had started to come out but got stuck. They all knew he wanted some reaction from them about his near miss, his brush with death. Back home, if you stepped off the curb and a buddy pulled you back from a speeding car, you'd talk about it for a week. Out here, it's nothing special. Getting killed was the big deal. Staying alive was the daily grind.

"A sniper," he said. "He almost got me. They target officers, you know," Sykes said in a petulant voice, as if he'd lost his best aggie on the school playground. He looked at the men, beseeching them, but no one looked back at him.

"Think the captain will call off the attack, sir?" said Tuck. "After you tell him about the tank and all?"

"There's supposed to be no more than a few demoralized Germans down there. That's what Battalion G-2 said. No heavy stuff. He didn't say anything about tanks."

"G-2?" Jake said. "Not some guy named Brooks? Thin moustache?"

"Yes, Lieutenant Brooks."

"Brooks don't know his ass from his elbow," Big Ned said. "He couldn't find a fucking German in a beer hall."

"Show some respect for one of your officers, soldier!" Sykes' voice had that hollow sound, all emptiness inside, with the volume turned way up on the outside.

"Brooks used to be a platoon leader, like you," Clay said. "Sent his men off on a patrol once, but gave them the wrong map coordinates. He stayed behind in his foxhole. They never came back. He got kicked upstairs to Battalion."

"This isn't right, this isn't right at all," Sykes muttered, nervously drumming his fingers on the stock of his carbine. "Not at all. I gotta talk to the captain, he'll know what to do. You men stay put." With that, Sykes pushed off to the rear, crawling on all fours.

"Yeah, like we're going anywhere," Tuck said quietly. "Like down that fucking hill."

"Think we'll ever see him again?" Big Ned said. "Wouldn't be the first officer to evac himself out with trenchfoot or a bad cold."

"They call it pneumonia when an officer gets it, don't you know anything?" Jake said.

"I know I woulda thought twice about pulling that jerk out of the way of a bullet," Big Ned answered.

"I did. The second thought trumped the first."

Silence ended the discussion. The wind picked up and the pines began to whisper as snow swirled around the waiting G.I.s, stinging their faces and driving each man down farther into himself, collars up, scarves wound around necks, chins flattened into chests. It was the same defense against the cold or bullets or shrapnel. Tighten up, be sure everything's laced up good, make yourself as small as possible, blend into the contours of the ground. You believed it too. Believed in your own good fortune, intelligence, quick wittedness, and grace. Until the day came when you saw it was just plain dumb luck that you were still alive, and realized it's got nothing to do with how you ran, or dove for cover, or rubbed your good luck piece. There's simply so much lead flying through the air that it can't be long before you slam into a piece of it.

That's what today felt like to Jake. Too damn much metal in the air, and a lot of ground to cover to boot. Only one machine gun, only one tank, only one sniper. But between them and the couple of dozen other Krauts down there, the air would be thick with it. He felt sick, felt like puking and crying and crapping his pants. His hands shook, and he knew the only reason he wasn't running at that very second was that his legs felt like jelly. This was a bad day, an unlucky day. He didn't feel like a veteran, sorry for the wet-nosed replacements who don't know shit. That had always made him feel invincible, or at the least, let him believe it. They'll get it, but I won't. I'm smart, tough, battle-hardened. Today, feeling the cold bite at his cheeks, watching the gray cloud cover through the pine branches, he felt only sick and scared, certain that the enemy fire wouldn't notice which of the brown forms running through it was a veteran and which a rookie. It terrified him that these could be his last memories, the last thoughts to travel through his brain.

"Jake. Jake!" It was Clay, with Big Ned beside him. They both looked at him with concern. They must have crawled up next to him and said his name several times.

"Yeah, sorry. I was thinking."

"Listen," said Big Ned. "We've been talking. Mostly Clay and me, since we both sorta found it on that Kraut. We want you to have it."

"What? Have what?" Jake said.

Clay held out his hand with the .45 automatic in its shoulder holster. "This. From me and Big Ned, and Tuck."

"Why?"

"Jake, you're our leader," Clay said. "Simple as that. We all know we wouldn't have made it back to our lines without you. You oughta have it."

"Yeah, like you was our officer," Tuck said, from behind Big Ned. "No offense intended."

"None taken." Jake took the automatic from Clay's hand. He knew he could never say no, never turn his back on these guys, the last of the only men he'd ever call brother. He also knew he didn't want to make any more decisions, be responsible for any more lives, not today of all days. But with this gift in his hands, and with Sykes as their lieutenant, he really had no choice. He looked at each of them, square in the eye, even Oakland, hovering on the edge of the group.

"Okay," he said, swallowing the lump that surprised him in his throat. "Okay."

He unbuttoned the top of his overcoat and struggled to get his arms out without taking it off. The guys crowded around him, fastening straps and helping him get his arms back in the sleeves. Jake reached in and pulled the automatic out, then placed it back in. "Good fit. Nice and smooth."

"I cleaned it last night," Big Ned said. "That Kraut didn't take too good care of it."

"I will, I'll take good care of it. Thanks, guys. I'll never forget this. Never."

CHAPTER TWENTY

1964

TAKE A STATEMENT, THAT'S HOW BOB SAID IT. Come down to the station in the morning and we'll take a statement. Routine, he'd said. Now, waiting alone in the windowless room, it didn't feel routine to Clay. Resting his right hand on the table, he noticed it shaking, covered it with his left, and when that didn't still the tremors, rested both on his lap.

One table, two chairs, filing cabinets, fluorescent lights, gray linoleum floor. Clay pushed back on the chair in frustration, the scraping sound loud and harsh as it echoed off the hard surfaces. He walked around the table, once, twice, sat back down and held his head in his hands. He caught a sniff of smoke, and smelled his hands. No, not on the hands. It was inside, still in his nostrils and lungs, maybe burned into his heart.

By the time the fire engines came, the fire had spread throughout the Tavern. With all the road crew equipment out front, they'd had trouble getting close enough, fast enough. Wood floorboards, booths, the bar, plus all the alcohol made the old wooden building a bonfire waiting to burn. The fire hoses had turned flame to steam and smoke, but couldn't wash away the terrible, familiar smell of incinerated flesh. Afternoon had bled into evening, flashing lights illuminating the char and ash that had once been Jake's Tavern. Clay had told Bob his story, and Bob had been considerate. Don't worry about it, come down tomorrow morning and give us your statement. Clay looked at his watch. Forty-five minutes. The doorknob turned. Bob entered, dressed in plainclothes, a white shirt and tie, as if he'd just come from church, except for the shoulder holster and the .38 Police Special revolver.

"Sorry to keep you waiting, Clay. Had to wait for the Fire Marshal's report."

"That's okay," Clay said, trying to sound calm, a little bored, and sympathetic. He felt silly sitting there with his hands on his lap, but he didn't want Bob to see them shake.

"Pretty much corroborated what you said. Fire started in the back room, the guy did have a gun. They did find some slugs in the debris, probably from his .38. Lots of liquor on those shelves. They even found the paint thinner can."

"Yeah, like I said. It all went up."

"Helluva thing," Bob said, sitting back in his chair, staring at Clay. The table between them was empty. No paper or pen.

"You going to take down my statement?" Clay asked.

"Let's talk it through, get everything straight, first. Then the statement will go easier."

"Okay," Clay said, nodding his head, as if his agreement was necessary. He couldn't keep his hands in his lap anymore, so he brought them up and cupped them on the table.

"Tell me about the Colt," Bob said. Clay had already told him last night, but he launched into it again.

"It was a souvenir from the war. You know how it is," Clay said amiably. Bob didn't say he did. "I had it for years, and finally Addy put her foot down, made me get rid of it."

"But you didn't."

"No, I hid it away in the Tavern, and told her I'd thrown it out."

"Chris knew about it?"

"I told you—" Clay caught himself, willed the frustration in his voice to wither away. "Yes, but I didn't know he knew. He must've seen me put it away once. You know kids, he couldn't resist looking. Lucky he didn't shoot somebody."

"So Chris left about what time?"

"It was around quarter to twelve. He was supposed to go get lunch and then do homework at the library. On his way up the street, he sees this guy hanging around the back of the Tavern slip into the back door. So he comes back, hears the guy holding me up, gets the automatic. Thank God he didn't use it. Whacked the guy good with the floorboard though. Knocked his gun out of his hand."

"What happened next?"

"You know, it's all sort of a jumble. He crashed into the shelves, pulled out another gun, a small automatic, from an ankle holster, I think. I grabbed for the Colt, and I think at the same time Chris threw a bottle at him. He must've already been covered in paint thinner. He fired, and everything lit up, like throwing a match into gasoline. He fell, then started to get up—he was already on fire—and aimed the .38 right at Chris. So I shot him."

"Twice."

"Damn right. You know not to trust one shot, Bob, so don't give me that routine. Two to the chest, like they taught us."

"Okay, okay. Then?"

"Then I grabbed Chris and we got out of there."

"You ever see this man before?" Bob said. He hadn't asked that question last night.

"No, not that I remember."

"You have much cash on hand?"

"No, just the usual change in the register we start out with. Friday's receipts were already in the bank."

"Sort of a dumb time to pull a heist, don't you think? Before a bar opens, after a week of road construction out front? Must've affected business, right?"

"Sure it did. That's why I closed, to get the cleaning and painting done."

"So why do you think he tried to stick you up?"

"Like you said. Dumb."

"I didn't say he was dumb. It was a dumb time for a hold up. Armed robbery for register change?"

Clay shrugged, his hands back on his lap. What could he say? The truth?

"Clay," Bob said, leaning in and speaking slowly. "You know that no one gets hot and bothered by the numbers anymore. You hear they're even talking up in Hartford about legalizing it and having a state lottery?"

"Good idea," Clay said.

"So if this has anything to do with the numbers, just tell me."

Clay shrugged again.

"I'd need to know about it. There won't be any charges. About the numbers."

"Yeah," Clay said. "Especially since there wouldn't be any evidence left."

Bob stood, kicking his chair back and slamming his hand,

palm-down, on the table. "Stop fucking around, Clay. We know who it was. I wanted to hear it from you, but instead you give me a line of bullshit!"

"What?" Clay was stunned at the outburst, but it was what he'd been afraid of. If only he'd been smarter. Al had been right. It was foolish to plan to kill him at the Tavern. If it had only been somewhere else—but, then maybe he'd be the dead one. It wasn't so much a question of life or death right now, but of humiliation. The shame of a lie, the humiliation for his family, all of his moral defects laid bare. He couldn't let it all unravel now.

"Al DePaoli, uncle of Tony DePaoli. Remember him from Friday night?"

"Yeah, the kid that got Chris in trouble."

"And now Chris is involved in the uncle's death," Bob said, standing with his arms folded across his chest, every inch a cop, friendship finding no foothold.

"Leave Chris out of this, Bob."

"He's in it. The only question is how far does this go? What did Al DePaoli want from you?"

Clay closed his eyes, trying to figure the angles, how to play it, which way to go. The darkness behind his eyelids vanished and it was stark white, blinding, like a snowfield. Sometimes you couldn't figure the angles, and you just had to keep pushing ahead, no other choice to be made. He could see tracers over the snowfield, luminous white against a gray sky. Smoke. It covered everything, then blew away. He rubbed his eyes.

Chris hadn't done anything wrong, didn't even know about the connection between Al and Tony. He had to bluff, push Bob to see what he really knew.

"How did you know? That it was this Al DePaoli?"

"Got his dental records. It was a match."

"No, I mean how did you know to check his records?"

Bob hesitated. He sat down, folded his hands in front of his face, index fingers up and tapping, as he studied Clay. He seemed to come to a decision. "We've had him under surveillance. He gave us the slip a few times, including yesterday. But we know what car he was driving, and it turned up two blocks from your Tavern."

Clay felt small beads of sweat gather at his temples, beginning to trickle down. The cops had been watching Al. But if they'd ever seen Al with him, surely Bob would've brought that up, thrown it in his face by now. If he could stay one step ahead of the cops, maybe everything would work out.

"So, Clay," said Bob. "What did DePaoli want from you? What did you have that he got killed over?"

"Hell, it was an accident, Bob," said Clay. "It wasn't like I was planning on it, it just happened. Self-defense."

"Never said otherwise," Bob said, cocking his head and looking Clay over. "But fact is, he's dead. In your joint. What was he doing there?"

"Maybe his nephew Tony told him I kept cash around, who knows? If I knew anything more, I'd tell you. I offered you information about Fiorenza, remember? You gave me the cold shoulder on that one, so don't give me a hard time now."

"We have all we need on Fiorenza."

"What?"

"I'm doing you a favor, Clay. We know Fiorenza is the numbers guy around here, but that's not what we were interested in. These guys see the handwriting on the wall, they know the state's going to legalize the numbers pretty soon. So they're looking to expand. Heavy-duty gambling, drugs, extortion. A war was heating up between Fiorenza and DePaoli, and we wanted to stop it, put both of them away. It's part of a big statewide task force. We got enough on Fiorenza, but before we can find out more about DePaoli's operation, he ends up roasted in your storeroom."

"Jesus Christ," Clay muttered. He felt as if he were teetering at the edge of an abyss, having stopped purely by chance before stumbling in. He'd been right in the middle of that war, but too much of a small fry to be noticed. Until Al came calling.

"Like I said, we don't care about a two-bit neighborhood numbers game, but there's a lot of unanswered questions here."

"I told you—"

"Yeah, you told me. You never saw Al DePaoli before he stuck you up for your cash register change. But we've been going over Fiorenza's books, and you know what? There's over ten thousand dollars missing, receipts never picked up. From Meriden."

Clay's mind tumbled with all these facts. Fiorenza kept books? The cops had the books? "Wait. You mean this guy keep records? How'd you find them?"

"Search warrant. Soon as we found out it was DePaoli in that fire, we picked up Fiorenza. No reason to wait and let him consolidate. And they don't call it organized crime for nothing.

He's got a full set of books, no names, but a complete record of receipts by date. There was a notation that "Meriden" had an estimated ten grand that hadn't been picked up yet. So, Clay, let me ask you one more time. What did DePaoli want from you? Bad enough to set up Chris. Bad enough to come gunning for you. Bad enough for you to have a loaded .45 handy?"

Clay looked down at his hands. They weren't shaking. He could see the faint lines of dirt still left under his fingernails. Al was dead. Fiorenza in jail. The Tavern burned to the ground. The twelve thousand, safe as can be. It was like running through a hail of bullets and making it without a scratch. He couldn't believe it, couldn't believe his luck, couldn't take in what had just been handed him. Death and redemption, partners again.

"Couldn't tell you, Bob."

"I have two search warrants, Clay. One for your house, one for the Tavern. I'll give you one more chance. I know there's more you're not telling me."

Clay shook his head. Bob got up and left the room. It would be more than two decades before they spoke again.

There hadn't been time to speak with Addy before the police got to the house. Clay had barely beaten them there, after he'd gotten Chris to a friend's house. Chris had become famous as the teenager who'd saved his father from an armed thief. That the crook died a gruesome death of his own making only added to his newly found status. Clay wasn't sure what the effect of this violent episode would be in the long run, but for now, Chris was enjoying his notoriety.

Addy had put on a good face for Chris, but it was daggers for Clay. He hadn't cared about the search, he only wanted to tell her the good news. But there hadn't been a minute to spare before the police came, two detectives and two uniformed cops, armed with court papers and attitude. He'd tried to explain there was nothing to worry about, but with police cruisers in the driveway and neighbors peering through windows, it hadn't gone well.

They stood in their living room, amidst a mess of cushions, magazines, books and papers carelessly tossed back in place. The police had been almost considerate, but thorough. Everything had been touched, opened, dumped, inspected. Clay watched Addy. She stood with her hand cupped over her mouth, her eyes darting over the belongings in her house that strangers had searched through. She began to shake her head, back and forth, back and forth.

"Addy—"

She stepped to the side, holding up one hand. She took the other from her mouth, seeming to reach deep inside to gain some control. By the look on her face, Clay saw things as she must have. Her home, her marriage, her security ripped apart. All by him. By the secret life he led and the secrets he'd kept from her. From everyone. Hell, he would've kept them from himself if it were possible.

"Addy," he said, softly and slowly. She didn't step away. "It's all over. I—"

He stopped, stunned by the look on her face. Anger had melted away and her eyes were wide with sadness, her eyebrows knotted, mouth agape.

"No, no," he said, holding up his hands as if to stop the words that had already left his mouth. "I don't mean between us, oh my God, no. I mean the numbers, everything. It's all over, done with." He could see relief, embarrassment, anger fly across her face. He held onto that stunned expression, thankful for his clumsy way with words, so glad to have seen her anger betrayed by the sadness there would be for her if they parted. Perhaps enough to prevent it, if he wasn't too late.

"How can I believe you, Clay, after this?" She gestured around the room, the disarray like evidence of his dishonesties.

"Addy, the guy who died in the fire was some sort of mobster. Bob told me when I went down to give my statement," he said, trying to sound like he and Bob were just two pals shooting the breeze. "There's a big statewide task force involved, so they're just checking every possible lead. There's nothing for them to find, believe me." So close. He was so close to everything working. If Addy could just see reason, everything would be perfect.

"Clay," Addy said, putting her palms up to her cheeks, rubbing them, rocking slightly on her heels while looking away from him. "Clay, it's good that you're done with the numbers and whatever else you were mixed up in. But it might be all too late. You've become a stranger to me. When did you turn into a numbers runner? Did it happen overnight? When we met, if someone told me to watch out for that Clay Brock, that someday I'd end up having my house searched by the police after a mobster is burned alive in his bar, I would've told them they were crazy! Now I feel like the crazy one. What kind of life have we been living? Is this the kind of life you planned when we got married? Who are you, anyway?"

Clay stumbled backwards, the shock of her question hitting him physically, a hammer blow to the chest. He felt his face go white, his pulse race, the blood pumping through his veins pounding in his ears. Taking another step back, he dropped to the couch, feeling his own dead weight pull him down. He watched Addy walk over and sit next to him, concern etched on her face. She didn't say anything, but she took his hand and studied him, waiting.

"I always thought that if I could get ahead of things, it would be easier for all of us. Working at the plant, then starting up with the Tavern, it was hard. There was never enough money, especially after you quit the phone company when we had Chris. That's why I took the job doing the cigarette route. Then they told me about the numbers. All I had to do was pick up some envelopes. It was easy money. It helped us get ahead—"

"Clay," Addy said, gripping his hand. "It didn't help us. It hurt. It hurt us because you kept secrets from us. It separated you from us, made you into someone you're not."

She was right, but for reasons she couldn't know. Each sentence was like a shot to the heart, and he felt words form and die in his throat. He wanted to run, but instead he covered his head with his hands, like he used to do, holding onto his helmet while shells thundered into the ground around him. The truth, he was headed for the truth, like that village, it awaited him at the end of a long downward run. Tapping his fingers against his skull, he counted, one two three four five. He opened his eyes and fixed them on Addy. Just keep moving, a voice in the back of his mind told him. This is just the next thing you have to do, keep moving. You can't go back, the past is dead and burned. You can't stay like this. Move, move, move.

He stood rooted to the stop, long after Addy gave up looking into his eyes. He listened to her moving throughout the house, picking things up, cleaning, organizing. Moving ahead.

CHAPTER TWENTY-ONE

2000

THEY SAT SIPPING HOT, STEAMING COFFEE IN A booth by the window at Edith's Diner. It was a twenty-four hour a day place, and it looked serious about just plain food. Two cops sat at the counter, always a good sign.

"Not bad," Clay said, setting down his cup in the saucer. His hand was unsteady, and the cup sat in a small pool of black coffee where he'd spilled it.

"High praise," said Chris. "Are you okay, Dad? You look worn out."

"I am worn out, Chris. Tired, real tired."

"It's been a long week. The hospital, this trip. You oughta be tired."

"That's not really it. You know, I always swore I wouldn't be one of those old folks who complained all the time. Don't think I have been. But if you want to know, I'll tell you what I feel like."

"Yeah, go ahead." Chris took a sip of his coffee, set the cup down, and looked into his father's eyes. "Tell me."

"I feel like somebody threw a ball of string down a big hill, and it's been unraveling for a long time, Clay said, closing his eyes. "I can see it, the center of the ball, ahead of me. The bottom of the hill, too. When it gets there, it's over. No more motion, no more energy, just the end of the string, all played out."

"Life is a piece of string?" Chris raised an eyebrow, then smiled, as if humoring his father.

"No. Life is what you do while the string is unraveling. There's a difference."

"Okay, I can understand that," Chris said.

"No you can't. Wait thirty more years, then it might make sense." Clay felt irritated, first with Chris and then with himself. He wished he could explain himself to his son. But then again, there were things about himself he was still learning. If it took him a lifetime, why expect Chris to understand a story about a piece of string?

"So, this is all about getting here before the string unravels?" Chris said, his tone neutral and open, as if he knew he'd said the wrong thing before.

"I thought so. Now I think it's about getting home."

"You sure you feel okay, Dad?"

"I feel like crap, but I'm still alive, I'm with my son, and we found a good diner. I'll settle for that. I never expected egg in my beer." Clay watched the quizzical look on Chris' face and laughed. Maybe it was good not to explain everything. The waitress brought their plates.

"I haven't heard that since my granddaddy died," she said, in a soft southern accent. She looked to be in her early forties, and had the stocky, settled look of a woman who worked on her feet all day and didn't get to put them up much at home. "Saw him drink one once, and once was enough for me. More coffee, honey?"

"You bet," said Clay. "He live a long life, your granddaddy?"

"Would have, I think, if he didn't lose an eye and an arm in the war," she said. "Your war, I'd guess," nodding at Clay. "Took a lot out of him, my granny used to say. He was in the Merchant Marine. How 'bout you, hon?"

"Army."

"Well, happy you stopped by. I'll go put on a fresh pot, be right back," she said, patting the table as she left. They ate in silence for a few minutes, and she returned with a pot of coffee. Clay looked at her nametag.

"Your name is Cheryl," he said.

"Sure is, honey."

"I used to have a place, a tavern. Waitress there was named Cheryl, too. Haven't thought about her in years. Thanks," Clay said, as she poured a refill. "Wonder where she is now, if she's still alive?"

"Wherever she is, I hope she's off her feet," Cheryl said. "You boys need anything else, you holler."

"Yes, Ma'am," Chris said, nodding.

"Looks like you taught your boy some manners," Cheryl said, giving Clay a wink as she left. He knew compliments were part of the show, what a good waitress did to insure a good tip. But he also knew when they were lines and when they were genuine, and he knew he'd be leaving some extra green when they left.

"Cheryl," Chris said. "We never heard where she ended up after the fire, did we?"

"Nope," said Clay, setting down his fork. "She said something about Florida, but that was it. Brick kept in touch, sent Christmas cards from Vermont every year, but it's been a long time since we last got one."

"You know what I always wondered about?"

"What?" Clay knew, but he wasn't going to be the one to bring it up.

"The money."

"What money?"

Clay had never told Chris about the cash from the numbers bets, but he knew that Chris had access to all the old files on the case, and that he must've let his curiosity take him there.

"Dad, I know about Fiorenza's cash, the betting receipts. The task force estimated that Fiorenza was missing ten to fifteen thousand. He'd been ramping up his operation, taking in more and more."

"What do you think happened to it?"

"I think you know, and I know Bob thought the same thing. But we never talked about it."

"Why ask now?" Clay was curious. He remembered that as Chris grew older, he'd had questions about the things Al DePaoli had said that day, but Clay had evaded them, put him off, something he'd become skilled at. After Chris had joined the force, they'd never spoken about it again.

"I didn't want to take sides. I knew you and Bob had been friends, and that this thing came between you. He helped me out, but never asked me anything about the money, or anything else about that day. So I just kept quiet. And when you two reconciled, there didn't seem to be any point. I didn't want to bring up a sore subject."

"But now you do."

"Bob's gone. It's just you and me now. Fiorenza died in prison. People don't even remember there was a numbers racket anymore. I'm curious."

"Twelve-six," Clay said.

"What?"

"The task force thought it was between ten and fifteen thousand. It was twelve thousand, six hundred and change. They were close."

"Jesus, Dad, that was some money back in '64. What'd you do with it?"

Clay smiled. He felt a gleeful pride in revealing another secret. He'd been so tight-lipped for so many years, and now here he was sharing his secrets as if they were nothing, gumdrops to be shared with children. He almost wished he had more. "I gave two thousand to Cheryl, three to Brick. He'd been with me longer, but they both took numbers bets at the bar. It was only fair, since I'd burned them both out of a job."

"So DePaoli was after the money?"

"Yes, but mostly he was after me. He wanted me to leave Fiorenza and work for him. I wanted out, completely, but I was in the middle of a turf war. There was no way out, until DePaoli went too far. Then the state task force picked up Fiorenza, and all of a sudden the whole numbers game is gone. Anybody left standing knew it wasn't worth starting up again, that the state was going to legalize it sooner or later."

"Where did you keep it, the seven thousand you had left?"

"Remember the white azalea bush by the garage? Half went under it, and half in the hole in the back yard I dug it up from. I did that the morning we cleaned the Tavern, and DePaoli showed up."

"You knew he was coming!" Chris said. "Holy Christ!"

Cheryl walked up to them, about to speak. She looked at their faces, poured coffee for both, and left without a word.

"I was between a rock and a hard place, Chris. Two killers each wanted a piece of me, more than I could give. But the real reason was, your mother would've left me if I didn't quit. So I had to find a way out."

Clay sipped his coffee, glancing up at Chris' face as he did. Remembering the covered windows, tarp on the floor, noise outside in the street. He could see all those memories play across his son's face too. He felt the shock of Al surprising him in the Tavern, the certainty of failure and death staring him in the face. Then, Al dancing in the flames, the shooting and screams like a battleground. He heard Chris talking, and shook off the memories, focusing on what he was saying to him.

"That's why you got me out of there. But he showed up early, right? Got the drop on you?"

"Yes. He was a pro at that kind of thing. I'd done my fighting with a different kind of enemy. If you hadn't snooped around and found that .45—"

"Mom was going to leave you?"

"Yes, she was. She'd given me an ultimatum that very week. I couldn't bear to lose both of you." Clay raised both palms upward, the loss too immense to describe. Chris sat back, studying his father. Clay could see the wrinkles move across his forehead. "I'm sorry, Chris, sorry about it all. If I'd known—"

"You know, Dad, it's funny. That was the day I decided to be a cop. For better or worse, I stuck with that decision. It feels better knowing all that happened because you were protecting your family, trying to keep us together."

"But if I never—"

"However it started isn't important. How it ended is. It ended with all of us together and alive. It could've ended worse. A lot worse." They sat looking at each other, twirling their coffee cups on their saucers.

"One thing, Chris," Clay said, softly, as if he were reluctant to break into the silence that graced them. "Your mother never knew about the money."

"How could she not know?"

"Things were different back then. Husbands didn't always tell their wives how much they made. We had insurance money after the fire, and when we rebuilt, I used the cash along the way, to stretch things. You know how contractors are. A lot was done under the table. By the time we opened Addy's Place, the cash was all gone, but it was the kind of neighborhood restaurant your mother had always wanted. A small bar up front, full kitchen out back, tables with tablecloths and real place settings. She helped out, and we did fine for ourselves."

So fine, that when they sold the business and property years later, they'd made a tidy sum. The name changed, and the restaurant flourished for a while, until the decay of the city reached the neighborhood. It closed one day, and ironically the empty building burned one night. Arson or accident, all that was left was a cleared corner lot.

"This is between us, Dad. As long as we're confessing, I've got something to tell you."

"What could that be?" Clay was worried. Chris didn't have much of a life outside the state police, and he couldn't think what kind of secret he'd have.

"The .45 automatic, remember you tried to get it back?"

"Yeah. They said it was evidence in a major investigation, probably never be released." The Meriden police had taken the weapon from Clay as soon as they arrived on the scene, and it had been turned over to the state task force.

"I have it."

"Why'd they release it to you? How come—"

"Hold on, Dad. I didn't say they released it. I took it, from the evidence locker."

"Son of a bitch!" Clay's mouth dropped open, then changed into a smile. "Son of a bitch." His right hand trembled, and he hid it in his lap.

"I found that thing when I was thirteen. I noticed you once checking that floorboard, and I was curious. I used to take it out and look at it every now and then. I wondered why you kept it hid, what the story was."

"Your mother made me take it out of the house. I told her I threw it away."

"But you couldn't."

"No. Why didn't you ever tell me? Oh, wait a minute. Bob, right?"

"Yeah. I didn't want to take a chance on him finding out I had it. I thought I'd just keep it safe. Then, there never seemed to be a good time to give it to you, to bring it up again. I clean and oil it every now and then, keep it wrapped in a chamois."

"I used to clean it once a year, like clockwork." The odor of gun oil rose in his nostrils, pungent, powerful and evocative. He'd missed the ritual, alone in the storeroom, lifting up the floorboard and feeling the leather holster, knowing that it had been touched by Big Ned and the other guys. Their hands had laid on it, and the hands of their enemies too, and that made it even more sacred, his souvenir, a link to the past. He could still see the German they'd found it on, looking past him, up at the green trees and gray clouds, right before he shot him. What had the German been thinking about in those last moments? Did he face death with no regrets? He thought of that German often, not because he regretted shooting him, but precisely because he didn't. He saw those eyes, lifted up to the skies, while his hand shook even more, hidden at his side, and for the first time realized the German had stood up to dying easier than he had to killing him, and that perhaps that had been some preparation to what had come next.

"You all set, boys?" Cheryl asked, looking at their plates. "I'll get these out of your way. More coffee?" Chris nodded no and Clay covered his cup with his hand. She smiled and left quickly, balancing dishes on her arm. She knew when to leave the customers alone.

"I took good care of it, Dad. You want it back?"

"No. I want you to have it."

"You sure?"

"Yep. That, and everything in the cigar box."

"Really?"

"Yeah, really. Do you know what souvenir means?"

"Sure. Something you bring home from a trip."

"It's from an old French word," he said, as if Chris's answer wasn't worth comment. "It means remembrance. Not a tee shirt or an embroidered pillow. Remembrance."

"Okay," Chris said, unaccustomed to so much information and so many words from his father. He was wary, uncertain what to say, as if the wrong thing might cause him to retreat into single syllables.

"Red, Tuck, Shorty, Big Ned, Little Ned, me, and that other guy," he continued, counting off seven men on his bony fingers.

"That's who's in the photo," Chris said, mentally counting off the faces in his mind, nodding his head in agreement. "But who's the other guy? What's his name? Is he the guy who lived around here? Is he still alive?"

His father didn't answer, his moment of talkativeness slipping away as he stared at his reflection in the window.

Chapter Twenty-Two

1945

An hour passed, then another. The faint glow of the sun behind the clouds moved low across the sky. Daylight was short these days, and what there was of it was half gone. Sykes hadn't returned. A mortar crew set up in a small depression a few yards to their right. The machine gun crews were on either side of them, camouflage netting across their guns, gunners pulled back, lying low. The sniper had fired twice again, killing one G.I. who'd left his head up a second too long. Knowing a shot to the head at that distance meant a telescopic sight, everyone stayed low and deep in the trees.

Big Ned had dragged some branches up to the edge of the treeline and set them between two firs. He had his BAR stuck out between them, his face hidden from the sniper behind dead wood. Jake and Clay were behind one of the trees, Tuck and Oakland huddled behind the other. Big Ned wore a double brace of ammo pouches. No more ammo carriers for him, no new buddies to watch out for, to curse and mourn.

"It's kinda funny," said Clay.

"What is?" said Oakland. Tuck and Jake both had their eyes closed, asleep or maybe dreaming they were somewhere else, far away.

"Well, we can't go forward without orders, not ten miles or ten paces. And we sure as hell can't go back to officer country. They order us to go forward, and we get shot at. If we hightail it out of here, we get court-martialed, then shot."

"So what's funny?" Oakland said.

"I've been fighting for months, through France, Belgium, and wherever the hell this is. It seems like I'm always in the same damn place. This fifty-yard stretch here. If I stay low, dig in real good, then I'm as safe as I can be. Head to the rear, and it's the brass after me. Head the other way, it's the Krauts. This is getting to feel like home to me now. Kinda funny."

"Just not in the way it makes you laugh," said Jake, his eyes still closed.

"Yeah. Not that kind of funny," Clay said, nodding his head.

"Makes you appreciate how good we got it, sitting right here, freezing our asses off and watching out for that sniper," Jake said.

"Hey guys," Tuck said, "it's like the bad news you're always talking about. I got bad news, bad news and good news."

"Okay, spill," Bid Ned said, keeping his eyes peeled through the branches.

"Bad news is if you haul ass outta here, it's a firing squad. The other bad news is, if we hit that village, the Krauts try to kill us. The good news is, we're sitting here freezing our balls off! Right?"

"You nailed it, Tuck," said Clay. "Right on the head."

"They wouldn't really shoot you, would they, for running away?" Oakland said. "I thought they just put you back in the line."

"They did, for a while. But so many guys happened to get separated from their units and got lost trying to find them, they started shooting guys for desertion," Jake said.

"Yeah, since so many of them were looking for their units in Paris," Clay said.

"Some poor slob they shot stumbled into a rear area Canadian outfit and started cooking their chow for them, so I heard," said Big Ned. "I think he's the only one they shot. So far."

"So, how do you guys know, I mean, when to hold on and when to haul ass? If no one gives an order?" Oakland asked. "Back when we got hit in that village, when the Krauts came streaming out of the woods, we didn't have a chance, it was obvious—"

"Did you run right away?" Jake said.

"No, none of us did."

"Did you fire your weapon?"

"Yeah. Well, not at first. I kept my head down. But the other guys did, and I didn't want to seem like a coward, so I did too. Five or six clips, I think."

"You all take off together?"

"Pretty much. Someone yelled we had to get out of there.

Someone else yelled for us to go. I fired off one more clip, and then ran as fast as I could, with everyone else."

"Then you already know the answer," Jake said. "Don't let your buddies down, and don't throw away your life for nothing."

"Everything else is pretty much chickenshit," Big Ned said. "Like Sykes. He's pure chickenshit. Probably sitting warm by a fire, drinking some joe, waiting to be told what to do, while we freeze out here. My old man used to say assholes like him couldn't pour piss out of a boot if the directions were written on the heel."

"He's no Red, that's for sure," Clay said, looking at Jake. "Sykes could fuck things up good if this thing happens today," gesturing toward the village, not taking his eyes off Jake.

"Don't worry about Sykes," Jake said. "I'll make sure he doesn't do anything stupid." Jake didn't want to think about what that meant. He liked his pockets empty. No more stamped-tin reminders of blood type and next of kin, little lives all totted up on a one by two inch piece of metal. "Hey, Oakland," he said, wanting to think of anything else. "What's your name anyway?"

Oakland didn't answer right away. Tuck nudged him, "G'wan, kid, tell 'em."

"Williamson."

"Naw, kid, your first name, tell 'em," Tuck said, squinting his eyes as he tried to keep from laughing.

"Okay. It's Marion," he said, head down, hardly a whisper. Tuck elbowed him again, laughing, until Oakland laughed too. "It's why I didn't mind you calling me Oakland. Don't stop, okay guys? Okay?"

"Okay," said Big Ned, still facing away from them. "Don't worry about it. Marion." That broke everyone up, everyone except Jake, but he laughed anyway, smiling at Oakland, letting him know it was only a joke. Looking at him, he remembered that night in the woods, leaning against the pine tree, thinking about Oakland as he walked by weeping and afraid. Clay had comforted him, asked him where he was from, and the name stuck. But Jake had other thoughts that night, thoughts of another man's identity, coveting his name, wishing him dead so he could take his dogtags. Marion. Jesus.

As it neared mid-day they ate cold K-Rations. Canned cheese, biscuits, candy bars. They waited, rotating deeper into the woods by twos so they could stand up, move their limbs, have a smoke, try to warm up. No fires allowed this close to Krauts. Meanwhile, they watched smoke drifting up from the chimneys in the village. Catching the wind and drifting south, towards them, taunting them with the aroma of a wood fire before it mingled with the low dark clouds.

Jake tried to sleep, maybe he did. Sounds drifted around him, men coughing, teeth chattering, footsteps crunching the snow to the rear. Snatches of dreams flitted between the sounds, visions of his schoolyard mingling with Normandy hedgerows. A sound penetrated the dream, tap, tap, tap, tap, Clay rhythmically drumming the front sight of his M1 against his helmet. Big Ned behind the screen of branches, rustling, snuffling and running his gloved hands across his face. Jake rolled over and moved closer, crawling next to him. Big Ned's shoulders were heaving, his hand pinching at his eyes. Jake put his hand on his shoulder, and felt the vibration as Big Ned silently wept. Jake saw a gasp escape his compressed lips, so only a small, constant breath could escape, sounding like laughter, a hee hee hee to accompany the tap tap tap behind them. Big Ned's eyes were squeezed shut tight, tears leaking from the corners. He shook his head, telling Jake without words that he couldn't stop himself. Jake edged closer, putting his hand on Big Ned's helmet, wishing he could tell him it was okay, they'd be all right. But he knew it was bullshit. They were at the end of it, the long march from summer in France, through autumn and now this hard winter. Too many of them had been lost. They were outnumbered now by the replacements, the Germans, their officers, everyone. It wasn't their war anymore, these frozen battles with strangers. They'd seen every horror the battlefield could churn up, been supplied with nightmares enough for a lifetime, become inured to sudden death and the terrible screams of the wounded. The war had nothing left for them, nothing to teach them, nothing to show them that they hadn't seen in a hundred gaping wounds. Their time was over, their season passed, and Big Ned knew it.

Jake felt Clay hit him on the boot heel, and heard footsteps coming their way. He pressed his helmet against Big Ned's, reaching his hand across those broad shoulders. Big Ned snorted, spit, and nodded. Okay. I'm okay. He rubbed his face with snow and dried it on his sleeve. Okay.

Jake crawled backwards and saw Sykes crouched down by their position. About a dozen replacements drew closer, within earshot. Sykes was panting, his mouth wide open, unable to catch his breath. It hadn't been that long of a run.

"Listen up, listen up," he hissed his words like a steam engine. Exhaling, he took a deep breath, a nervous teacher in front of his first class. "We have to take that village. Now. The captain's sending Third Platoon along that ridge on the left flank. Second Platoon is going on the right flank. We go straight up the middle."

Silence. Three under strength platoons against a village full of Krauts, plus a tank. Down the middle, like a football game back home, the play called in from the bench.

"Artillery?" asked Clay.

"G-2 doesn't think they have any," said Sykes.

"No, I mean ours. We getting a barrage?"

"Oh, oh. Uh, we have mortars. Battalion's sending a Heavy Weapons Platoon. They should be here in fifteen minutes."

"Mortars, against that tank? Who're they kidding?" Big Ned spoke without looking at Sykes.

"Smoke, they're going to fire lots of smoke, it will cover our approach. Smoke, that's the key. All we need to do is advance and keep up suppressing fire. Fire and movement, that's the key."

"We can't do both. There's not enough of us," Clay said. He spoke slowly, his calmness a dam against the chatter coming out of Sykes.

"The machine guns will hit the farmhouse and spray the village. We'll advance in two squads, one laying down fire and the other moving, then firing and covering the other squad. Basic tactics. Understood?"

"That's a helluva plan, Lieutenant, for gettin' us all killed," said Tuck. "You sure the captain came up with that?"

"That's his best judgment, soldier. He talked Battalion into waiting until the Heavy Weapons Platoon got here. But he's got his orders." Sykes let his gaze wander out past the trees, to the gray sky ahead and the tops of the distant roofs. His face was pale. He looked thin and small wrapped in his parka. Without the words spilling out of his mouth, he was nothing, a brittle twig to be snapped in the Ardennes cold. Springing up, he began to walk back and forth, counting the men.

"Everyone accounted for? Where are the sergeants? Don't I have any sergeants? We've got orders, and I've got to carry them out, but I need sergeants. There aren't enough men, not enough, not enough." His forehead wrinkled as if he were trying to work out a difficult algebra problem. "Not enough. Orders. Orders. Sergeants, no sergeants."

Jake watched the faces of the replacements as they listened to Sykes repeating himself, walking among them, counting them over and over. Clay looked at him, and shook his head. Bad news all around. Jake got up and took Sykes by the arm.

"Lieutenant, let's talk."

"Take your hands off me! What do you think you're doing? What's your name?"

Jake ignored the question, tightened his grip and moved Sykes back, away from the replacements. "Listen, Lieutenant Sykes. Are you listening?" Speaking in a low whisper, almost a growl, turning Sykes toward him, he stared into the darting eyes until they calmed down.

"Are you listening to me, Lieutenant?" Jake repeated.

"What do you have to say for yourself?" Sykes said, his upper lip trembling.

"Plenty. But right now, I'm going to tell you how to handle this. Pull yourself together and show some confidence. You look like you're about to piss in your pants, and that's not the best way to lead these men."

"You can't talk to me like this! I'll put you on report, Private."

"Shut up and listen," Jake said, a harsh whisper between gritted teeth. "It's just you and me talking. I'm trying to save your life, and the lives of your men. Put me on report. You think I give a rat's ass about your fucking report?"

Sykes shook his arm loose. "All right. Tell me."

"Forget all that fire and movement crap. The platoon going along that ridge is fucked. They'll never make it. Both the tank and the MG can hit them at the same time."

"We'll have smoke."

"Have you noticed the wind? It's blowing toward us. The smoke won't last, and the Kraut's field of fire will clear up real quick. That's why we can't stop."

"Private, laying down suppressive fire is basic tactics—"

"Yeah, I remember reading that in the infantry manual too. But we don't have time. If we stop in that field, we're sitting ducks. The smoke clears, that Kraut MG and that tank open up on us, and we're fucked. We can't take the time to leapfrog forward like they taught you. The only chance we have is to haul ass down into that village, grenade the houses and kill those bastards before they know what hit them. Before the smoke clears."

"But—"

"Lieutenant, I know they taught you by the book. But the book is only going to get us all killed. I'm telling you, once our mortars and the machine guns open up, we head straight down the hill. No firing, just run. We gotta run like hell."

"But what about the farmhouse and the tank?"

"The tank will be busy with the platoon on the ridge. I'll make sure our guys on the .30 calibers keep hitting that farmhouse window. If they can keep that MG from spraying the field, we got a chance to get in between the buildings and toss grenades."

"The tank, though, what about the tank?"

"Kraut tankers don't like being on narrow town roads with infantry swarming around them any more than our guys. If they see their infantry support pull out, they'll gun their engine and take off. That's how we can do this thing, get in the village, kill Krauts, let the rest run off. Then we sleep in warm houses tonight. What about it, Lieutenant?"

"I don't know," Sykes said. "I don't know. There's no sergeants, no one told me what to do—"

"Well, I been here since before snow fell, and I'm still alive. So I'm telling you what to do. All you got to do is issue the order, like I told you. Get into the village, before the smoke clears. Fast."

Sykes looked at Jake, his eyes alight with fear and his mouth set like a pouting child. Jake knew this wasn't how this fresh second lieutenant imagined his first command. No bugles, no glory, nobody patting him on the back and telling him what a swell guy he was. Instead, some grimy G.I. was telling him he didn't know shit. Jake knew he had to sweeten the pot to make it more appealing.

"The captain likes his officers to show initiative, Lieutenant. You take this village and he'll eat it up. But we gotta be in one piece at the bottom of that hill."

"Okay, okay. But you better be right."

The minutes passed slowly, anxious looks toward the rear for the Heavy Weapons Platoon alternating with glances at wristwatches buried under layers of clothing and gloves. Sykes had given the orders and settled into a restless pacing, tree to tree, counting the men by twos. He whispered to himself, gesturing with his hands as if arguing a point of logic. The wind came up

in spurts, rustling the pine branches, swishing them clean of the
white snow that clung in clumps.

They gathered around Big Ned. Tuck, Oakland, Jake and Clay.
Huddled together for warmth, leaving unspoken that when they
took off downhill, they'd spread out, dispersing the targets for
the German gunners. That this could be the last human contact
they'd feel, the last warmth, however feeble, against the cold. The
last bond holding their young lives together. The last wholeness.
The last love. They tightened belts, checked pockets, leaned into
each other. They passed around smokes, listened to the click of
Clay's Zippo shutting, inhaled the tobacco, checked watches,
waited.

Spread out, Jake told them, but keep each other in sight. Know
where each man is. Try to keep the same distance. Don't lag
behind. Don't listen to Sykes, get to a building and toss grenades.
Spread out, move, watch your buddy. Big Ned, stay between us,
you're the middle man. Make sure the replacements keep moving.
No one stops.

The sound of Jeeps echoed through the woods. Shouts,
commands, frantic words, orders, directions. G.I.s with mortar
tubes, plates, ammo crates, setting up around them. Cigarettes
out. Hands gripping rifles, tensing and relaxing, breath coming
in shallow gulps, as if the air had thinned out.

Shit. Motherfucker. Jesus, Mary and Joseph. Curses and
prayers spit out along the short line, the remnants of two platoons
summoning up courage, banishing fear, going numb with terror,
thinking of home, of nothing, of the hill and the downward slope.

Fumph, fumph, fumph. The strangled sound of mortars firing
was drowned out by the two .30 caliber machine guns, rapid
bursts sending tracer rounds to hunt out the top floor window
of the farmhouse. Jake rose up, watched the smoke rounds burst
in front of the village, saw the puffs of gray dust as machine gun
rounds pecked at the stone farmhouse. He turned to see Sykes,
standing still, face drained white.

"Okay, Lieutenant, just like you said. Let's go," Jake yelled
to be heard. In the hustle of men filtering between the trees no
one noticed that Jake had grabbed Sykes by the sleeve and was
pulling him along.

Smoke blossomed like white roses in bloom. Phosphorous
tracers raced over their heads and met the smoke as it roiled
uphill, the noise of machine gun fire behind and ahead of them

leaving an oddly silent gap where they ran, into the smoke. The incline made it easy to run in the snow, and they picked up speed, spreading out to the sides, trying to keep sight of the men around them in the grayness.

The rapid chainsaw sound of the German machine gun began to assert itself. As the smoke grew, it hid their target from the American gunners. Still, the sound of their own guns firing was reassuring, as they glance quickly at each other, nods of luck and hope. Jake could make out both machine guns, and held his breath as one stopped to reload a belt or clear a jam. Jesus, keep firing, keep firing, keep those fuckers down! He looked to his left, saw Clay, a blur in the air, smoke swirling around him as it blew uphill. Big Ned stood out to his right, his broad shoulders hunched forward, parting the smoke like Moses. Turning, Jake saw Sykes, slowing down, holding out his carbine as if to keep his balance, taking little mincing steps in the trampled snow.

The tank fired, the explosion loud on the left flank, and as the tank's machine gun chattered away as it fired another round of high explosive, then another. The sound of trees cracking followed each explosion, and Jake could feel the men shy away from the sounds, drifting right, beginning to bunch up. Rifle fire rippled out from their front, and he felt hot metal ripping the air above his helmet. He heard a scream, a shout, and a body falling, rolling, still moving fast.

"Take cover!" It was Sykes, shrill terror ripping the sound from his throat. "Take cover!"

"No! Keep moving!" Jake yelled, waving his arm at the forms around him. "Get up, don't stop!" Tuck and Oakland passed him, snow kicking off their heels, and he stepped back up the hill, kicking G.I.s who'd dropped in the snow, searching for Sykes who was still yelling to take cover. There was no cover for them, only snowdrifts and death.

The German machine gun sprayed the field, searching for the attackers in the smoke. Jake heard a short scream, a moan, a soft thud. He found Sykes, digging in the snow with his helmet, half a dozen replacements gathered around him, motionless, deer in the headlights.

"Take cover," Sykes screamed, panic shrilling his voice, "we'll all be killed."

Gunfire crackled in front of them and from all sides. A G.I. tumbled down the hill, blood spraying from his neck like a pinwheel as he went head over heels. Sykes watched the rolling body and his eyes grew wide at what he saw. Not the dead man, or the sprays of blood, but the clear vision of the field and the village ahead. The smoke was vanishing, blowing uphill, over them, leaving them naked.

"You can't stay here. Tell these men to get moving!" The mortar sounds changed. Explosions now. No more smoke. Jesus fucking Christ. "Move!"

"You're right, you're right," Sykes screamed. "I'll get help. I'll go get help."

"Lead these men down the hill, goddamn it," Jake yelled into his face, grabbing his collar. "Now, or we're all dead men!"

"You hold here, I'll go get help. I'll be back. I'll be right back." Sykes shook off Jake's grip, turned and ran, following the blowing smoke, reaching out for it as if it could pull him along. He disappeared into it, his helmet and carbine left behind in the snow.

"Get down the hill," Jake screamed, grabbing two of the replacements who started to get up and follow Sykes. He couldn't let them run away, leaving the others alone at the bottom of the hill. He had to get back to Clay. "Follow me, goddamn it."

He ran in long steps, thundering down the hill, helmet bouncing on his head, gear flapping and pounding him as he forced his body to go as fast as it could. As swiftly as he went, his thoughts still played out slowly, as if he had all the time in the world. Go back, stay put, or move forward. Fucked every which way. I don't want to die a coward, or with strangers. Where's Clay. Where's Clay? I don't want to die alone, where's Clay?

Tears tore at his eyes as he ran through the cold air. He could see the platoon to their left, on the ridge, pulling back. The fire from the tank had chewed them up, leaving blackened craters in the snow speckled with red. He heard explosions, saw the windows blow out of the nearest house, flames following them. Grenades. Somebody made it. The bam bam bam of Big Ned's BAR stood out above it all, steady as a rock.

Jake felt the bullets hitting the ground behind him, heard a gurgling scream, and the screeching of a tank grinding gears. He saw Clay rise up from the corner of the house, aim his M1 up toward the stone farmhouse, and fire off three slow, steady shots. The machine gun stopped. Clay pumped his arm for Jake to hurry, but he was already running as fast as he could. Twenty yards to go, Clay raised his rifle again, fired once, keeping their heads down.

Jake saw the Kraut peer around the side of the house and toss the potato masher.

"Grenade!" he yelled, but he was drowned out by the clanking of the tank coming down the main road. Clay looked at him for a second, a moment, an eternity, eyes locking on Jake's, not understanding. The explosion threw him forward into the snow, at the same time as the tank fired down the street, towards the sound of Big Ned's BAR.

"Clay, Clay!" Jake slid in the snow, coming down next to Clay. "Omigod, I'm sorry, I'm sorry, Clay." He felt as if he'd dropped a delicate crystal and watched it shatter on a cold stone floor. He didn't know what he could have done differently, but he knew Clay had left himself exposed giving him covering fire. Saving his life, losing his own. Grabbing his collar, he dragged Clay away from the alleyway and to the back of the burning building, out of the line of fire from the farmhouse. Clay left a streak of black and red on the snow, smoke curling from the back of his coat. His hands were limp, but his eyes sought out Jake's.

Slumping to the ground, Jake cradled Clay's head in his lap, blood soaking into his thighs. He thought he heard the BAR one more time. Then the tank again. The fire in the building crackled.

"Clay, I'm sorry, hang on, a medic'll get here."

"What's wrong with me? Jake—" His face contorted in a spasm of pain.

"Oh Jesus, I'm sorry," Jake said.

"Nothin' else you could do. I'm ripped open," Clay said, before a scream rose from his throat. Jake saw how his coat was shredded, his side sliced through, ribs showing through blood and burned fabric.

A German heard the scream too, and edged around the building, his camouflage smock and SS runes crystal clear through the smoke and haze. Clay shrieked in agony as Jake looked for his rifle, on the ground at Clay's feet, out of reach. The Kraut worked the bolt of his rifle as Jake's hand reached for the automatic, fumbling with layers of clothes, leaning over Clay to protect him and leveling the pistol at the German, two quick shots to the midsection, watched him stagger and drop to his knees, the rifle still in his hands. Two more and he was down.

Clay's eyes found Jake's. The tank's engine roared, only yards away.

"Go," Clay said through gritted teeth, "go."

Jake looked around. There were only dead men behind him, in a clump where Sykes had left them, and a few who'd followed him. Rifle fire flared up a few buildings down, and the tank's machine gun responded.

"That might be Tuck," Clay said, his eyelids fluttering. "Go."

"Clay, hang on, hang on."

"Leave me, Jake. You're a good friend, the best. Go, find Tuck."

"I can't, I won't leave you," Jake said, his mouth pressed to Clay's ear to be heard over the advancing tank.

Clay groaned, blood seeping from his mouth. His hand grabbed at Jake's, taking the pistol. Jake didn't understand, he thought Clay wanted it to protect himself. He let go, helping Clay to get a grip on it, folding his bloody fingers around the grip.

"It'll be okay," Jake said. "I'll get a medic."

"I don't want to die alone," Clay cried, echoing Jake's own fear. "Help me."

Machine guns, tank fire, yells and screams faded into silence as their eyes locked, Clay's filled with pain, Jake's with sudden understanding. Clay coughed and a spasm of pain wracked his broken body, a red mist spewing from his nostrils and mouth. He lost his grip on the pistol and Jake did help him, holding his trembling hand, guiding it, bringing it back to his temple, watching Clay's face wrench as the pain of breathing became too much, looking once again at the blood in the snow and the terrible wounds, knowing he owed Clay this, pressing his finger on Clay's own wrapped around the trigger.

The sound was louder than anything he'd ever heard.

The burning roof above him collapsed, showering Jake with sparks. He felt the heat at the back of his neck as his hand felt the last bit of warmth in Clay's cheek. He slid him off his lap, cradling his head as he set it on the ground. A crescendo of sounds came from behind him, the burning building crashing in on itself, the tank, rifle fire, yells and curses in German and English rising up in a babble of fury, even louder and more insistent than before.

Still, Jake moved as if in a dream. He knew what to do, how to grant one last wish of Clay's and keep his memory alive. Opening Clay's coat he felt for the metal chain, found it, sticky with blood, and pulled it off. He removed his dogtags and placed them around Clay's head, tucking them into his shirt, pressing them against his skin. He put Clay's around his neck, the thick drying blood sticking to his hands. I'm sorry, Clay, sorry to leave you with my name. It isn't much. But now I'll pass yours on.

He couldn't believe Clay was dead, couldn't believe he was doing this, couldn't believe everything he had known had just come to an end. He felt numb, stunned, alone. Blindly, he groped for his M1, found it. He rose up, stood over Clay for a second, thinking of the dogtags with Jake Burnett stamped into them against Clay's cold chest. A dead man, he turned, heading for the last sounds of battle, an empty vessel, moving forward, never again looking back. Everything was this one moment. Living or dying were both beyond his comprehension, there was only this, his rifle, Clay's dogtags, the fight ahead. He had moved between lives, Jake Burnett left behind, strung around the neck of a dead man, a gift to the woman who bore him, the insurance maybe a way out for her. He was Clay Brock now. He felt detached, cast adrift, free, he couldn't tell.

He crouched behind a low stone wall as the house burned behind him. He swung his rifle up and saw three Germans running down the street, trailing the tank. He aimed at the farthest one, slowly easing back on the trigger, just as Clay would've done. Deliberate, no wasted moves. The rifle kicked against his shoulder and the German dropped. Second shot, easy does it, squeeze, another kick, and the German was down, rolling in the street, writhing in agony.

It all happened in slow motion, and he wondered if he'd discovered some magical power. Was this real? Everything was in crystal clear focus, details in the smoke as sharp as if they were under a microscope. Noise was everywhere but nowhere too. He wasn't sure if he heard nothing or everything all at once.

He'd shot at the furthest Germans so the one closest to him might not notice him right away, might not realize the other two were down. He turned his rifle, and fired off the rest of the clip at him. No more time for subtlety, he wanted the bastard dead and gone. The German fell back, a mist of red bursting out from his chest.

Dropping prone, he scurried away from the tank advancing towards him, toward the sound of rifle fire from the house down the road. Seconds later the stone wall exploded as the tank fired at his last position. Chunks of stone showered him, bouncing off his helmet and back. He wasn't hurt, and he crawled even faster, wondering who he was and where he was headed.

Looking up, he saw rifles firing from the windows of the house across the narrow road. M1s, two of them. Running low across the street, he made for the door, willing his legs to run as fast as they could, to get to the cover of the house. As his feet pounded the road, noises dropped away around him and one sound emerged above the cacophony. A grinding, hydraulic whine told him there was no magic here. He was a soldier in someone else's sights. His name didn't matter, he had run out of luck. The only thing that mattered was the tank swiveling its turret, turning its cannon on the house in front of him. He heard the hydraulics whirr to a halt, and saw the round opening of the barrel, dark and black, a perfect circle, a bull's eye aimed at him. It roared flame, cracked thunder, flashed white, and he was in the air, flying.

He felt the medic working on him. It was night. As his clothes were cut away it felt like tongues of flame licking at his skin, but he was too far away to scream. He thought of Clay, but it was a vague and distant thought, a shadow crossing over his eyes. Sulfa like snow falling. Or was it snow? He saw the frost on the half-moon window, felt the ambulance bounce in the ruts. The medic cut and cut, his scissors tied around his wrist with a shoelace. Compresses soaked red on his chest. Where was he? What had happened?

"What's your name, soldier? Tell us your name."

He hesitated. He didn't know if he could, but something told him he had to speak. If he wanted to live. If he wanted to live this new life, to move forward, never look back. He couldn't remember what to say, he was supposed to tell them—what?

Then he remembered. Clay, in the snow, dying. Remembrance. Redemption.

"Brock—Clay Brock."

CHAPTER TWENTY-THREE

1964

"ADDY, YOU'RE RIGHT. THERE ARE SECRETS, secrets from long ago. I thought they didn't matter. I never wanted to burden you—" He stopped himself. No more lies.

"No, no. I'm ashamed, I'm ashamed to tell you." He lifted his head, looking for a sign that she could take it. All he saw was a stillness in her eyes, a patient waiting. She lifted an eyebrow, as if to say, go on, get it over with, let's see.

"I was afraid I'd lose you if I told you the truth, that you couldn't love anybody like me. You said sometimes you don't who I am. Well, I haven't been straight with you about everything, about my life before we met."

"About the war, Clay?"

"Part of it," he sighed. "Not all of it. It's about my family." He told her about Pennsylvania. About Minersville, and growing up there. About Ma and Pa and his sister Alice.

"I wanted to join the Army at seventeen. I needed proof of my age. Pa kept papers in his study, and he told me never to look through his things. But I needed that birth certificate, so I waited until they were out." Clay sat, wringing his hands like they were soaking wet.

"Were you adopted?" Addy guessed, trying to read Clay's expression.

"No," he laughed. "No, not adopted. I wish I had been." He stared at the wall, studying the curtains that hung around the window. They were gold, newly sewn by Addy to match the colors in the carpet design.

"Well?" she said.

"The name on my birth certificate was Alice's. My sister. She was my mother."

"Oh, Clay, I'm sorry. That's too bad, but it's not the end of the world. If a young girl gets in trouble, it's not unknown for her parents to bring up the child as theirs."

"That's the problem, Addy. It—I was one of theirs. It was Pa. His own daughter."

"Oh my God, Clay! That poor girl! And you—" She lifted her hands, opening them toward him, the gesture saying what she could not as the enormity of it all set in. "And Alice, whatever happened to her?"

"I don't know. I never went back." He shot up from the couch, pacing back and forth, his feet stepping between papers and cushions on the floor.

Addy leaned back and shook her head. "That's why you didn't want to have children," she said, the truth of the matter dawning on her. "You were afraid. That's why you never let up on Chris, always expecting the worst from him!"

"And why I couldn't tell you the truth, I was afraid you wouldn't want to have children with me, wouldn't want to be with me. Addy, Chris is a better son than I deserve. You're a better woman. After Chris came along, it got harder and harder. I'm sorry Addy. I could never tell you. And you have to promise me you'll never tell another soul, ever." She hesitated, drawing in her breath, looking into his eyes.

"I'll leave that up to you, Clay, it's your decision. But didn't you want to know what happened to Alice? Didn't you ever want to go back? Didn't you care?" He could see Addy was still taking his measure, trying to figure out his behavior and what this revelation said about him.

"Wait a minute. I'll be right back." He walked to their bedroom, which was more of a mess than the rest of the house. From an open dresser drawer he pulled out the dogtag on its chain, mixed in with the photo, the battered Zippo lighter, cufflinks and tie clips.

"Okay," he said, back on the couch. "Here's the other part, the part about the war." He took a deep breath, and felt the thin metal he grasped in his hand. He'd never spoken more than a few words about the war to Addy. He realized he didn't know how to do it, how to actually put it into words for someone who didn't know, couldn't know. He looked at the thin metal in his hand, wondering how he could ever do it justice.

"There was a guy, my best friend. My buddy," he said, his voice cracking as tears tried to force their way out. There was no way to tell Addy what that word meant. Now it was something you might say to anyone on the street. Hey buddy, got a light? A foxhole buddy was your partner. Your life. Your warmth. His skin went cold and the memory of Miller bringing him the SS officer's coat swam through his mind, wet socks and cold feet on his torso, the wool coat like a quilt covering them in their hole.

"We were in basic together, shipped over to England together. Went over to France with him and the rest of the guys in our unit. That was in July. It was warm. I remember apples on the trees. By the first week in August, we were in action. It went on until late January, right after the Bulge."

"That's a long time."

"Yeah." He stared at the wall for a while, seeing ghosts instead of curtains. "A long time, especially in winter. He didn't have any family back home, and we got to talking. We talked about everything. There was nothing else to do. Sometimes it was so cold you couldn't sleep." He realized he was making an excuse, worried that Addy would be mad he'd told somebody else before her.

"It must have been horrible," she said. He nodded.

"The only thing that made it bearable was your buddy, and your squad. We depended on each other. To stay alive, and to keep each other sane. We saw so many terrible things, Addy." Did so many things, too.

"It wasn't like the movies at all, was it?"

"No," he said, shaking his head. "No bloodless heroic deaths, no waving the flag. I can't tell you, Addy, how many ways there are to die on the battlefield. It is simply unimaginable."

"But you and your buddies, you knew, you shared all that. You must have been as close as men could be."

He met her eyes, knowing she'd given him an opening. "Yeah. Real close. One night, I told him about my family, about my problem. He was good about it. He's the only other person I ever told."

"And?"

"He and I were going to head out west, maybe to California after the war. He wanted to go somewhere new, and I didn't ever want to go back home. He wanted to start a family and do things right. His folks had died, his brother got it in the Pacific. It was important to him."

"What happened?"

"He was killed. They all were killed, everyone but me," he said, and his face broke, slowly, his chin quivering and lips tensing before sobs gushed from his throat, tears coursed over his face. Anguish burned in his chest. The snow, the tracers, the tank, the explosions, every memory exploded at once in his mind as he gripped the dogtag so hard in his hand that it drew blood. Addy took his hand into both of hers and held it, kissed it, her tears falling into the blood welling in the palm of his hand.

"I'm sorry," he said, not knowing himself if he was apologizing for the truth of what he'd told her, the shame he felt, the blood on his hand, or the tears. Maybe all of that, maybe more, maybe for the truth he knew he'd never tell.

"No, no, no," Addy said, opening his hand. "This is your dogtag, Clay, I've seen it before." She looked confused, as if she'd expected a different story. She didn't understand.

"No, no, it isn't mine. It belongs to Clay Brock." She looked at him as if he were the one confused, shocked by events. He must be wrong, she was thinking, the stress finally caught up with him.

"My name—my name is Jake Burnett." These were the strangest words he'd ever said, after twenty years of not speaking his own name. "Jake Burnett. Clay Brock was my buddy. He died giving me covering fire, saving my life, down in some damn village I don't even know the name of. He died in my arms. God, I miss him."

"Was that when you were wounded?"

"Yes. That same day. Everyone else was killed or wounded, maybe captured, I don't know. We knew every trick in the book, but that day it didn't matter. We ran out of luck. After the Germans pulled out a medic found me and patched me up." He looked down at his hand, the blood welling in the cut. He tried to make it sound like it was easy. There was the truth, and then there was too much of it, after all.

"So you came home as Clay Brock?"

"I did. No one left alive to say different, so I did what Clay wanted. Alice got ten thousand dollars, and I hope to God she used it to start a life for herself somewhere."

"But she thought her son died."

"Lots of mothers got that news. Happened every day. At

least it gave her a chance to get away. Not to have me to worry about any more. About what I meant, reminded her of." He remembered that as the best he'd made of it. A tragedy for Alice, but something of a blessing, perhaps.

"You're a good son, Clay. Or is it Jake?"

"I made Clay a promise to pass on his name, and live a life for him. It's my name now, as much as his."

"Where does this leave us?" Addy said, moving away from him on the couch, giving herself room to move. "I don't know what it all means. What does it have to do with us, now? You've always been Clay to me."

"Maybe everything, maybe nothing," he said. "I know it wasn't right not to tell you, but I thought it was for the best. Then as time passed, it seemed harder and harder to ever bring it up. I was ashamed, Addy. Afraid of what you'd do."

"Do you mean," she said, slowly and deliberately, "like leave you?"

"Yes."

"Well, I was about to, but because of how you shut me out of your life, not because of what happened to you in your life." She stayed on her end of the couch, calm, her hands folded in her lap. He moved to her, took her hand in his, and promised himself that if she stayed, he'd be a different man for her. He knew it was too fragile a promise to even say out loud, to use as a persuasion. He willed her to understand. She squeezed his hand.

"Are you sure you're okay, Addy, having heard all this?"

"Do you mean okay with you?"

"Yes. Now that you know. Know about my family."

Addy thought about it. He could tell she wanted to give the question a proper answer, to let him know how she really felt. Her eyes flitted to some faraway place, as they always did when she was deep in serious thought. "I think that a man who had a friend like yours, who would want to give such a gift to him, has to be a good man at heart. A very good man."

They sat on the couch for a long, long time, a half hour passing as Clay allowed himself to understand that he'd spoken about things he'd never said out loud before. He'd revealed his anguish, his shame and his secrets to Addy. He cast quick glances at her face, wondering what thoughts hurtled through her mind, but he saw nothing but restfulness, maybe even understanding. She looked peaceful, even with the shambles of their belongings around them. He thought of Clay, dead in the snow, and how even with his horrible wounds, he had looked at peace there, the pain gone, never to touch him again. And he thought about the name he'd passed on, with hopefully some of steadfast qualities of his buddy.

Addy got up from the couch, and he froze, afraid he'd read her wrong, that she'd come to some conclusion, couldn't stand to be with him anymore. When she left the room, he wondered if the torment that ate at him all these years would leech out to her, come between them, spreading doubt and fear. He wanted to get up, follow her, but it was easier to sit, waiting, than to run for the truth. He counted, to ten, twenty, almost to one hundred, another of Clay's habits that he'd picked up and kept over the years.

She came into the room with a tray, carrying bandages and ointment to cleanse and bind his wounded hand. She cleaned the cuts, wrapped them in white gauze, winding it around his fingers and tying it off.

"There," she said. "Now we have to let it heal, don't we?"

CHAPTER TWENTY-FOUR

2000

THEY DROVE ALONG ROUTE 209, THROUGH Pottsville, down West Market Street. Down by the Miner's Memorial, a tall statue of a miner holding a lamp and a pickax looking out over a mini-mart parking lot. Paralleling the railroad tracks, the road tucked itself under a high ridge that loomed over them, and Clay felt strangely at home, the steepness all around him a comfort, protection against the outside world, that place he'd been for more than sixty years.

Clay pointed to a side road. "Take this, Township Highway 605." Two and three story narrow houses lined the roadway. Each had a small front porch, some decorated with flower boxes, some brightly painted, others rotting away under the weight of abandoned stoves and discarded furniture.

"Next left, then pull over," Clay said.

As the Jeep turned the corner, Clay closed his eyes. Fear streaked through his body. Fear that he would find the house as it had been, red-trimmed kitchen curtains and all. He saw his father's high cheekbones, the lines in his face, inhaled the smell of his Aqua Velva. Feeling the car pull to the curb and stop, he opened his eyes, and lifting a shaking hand he lowered the window. His fingers wouldn't stop trembling, and he let his hand drop into his lap.

"Oh, God," Clay said. "Oh, my God." He let his head fall back against the headrest, eyes staring ahead, blinking back tears.

"What is it, what's wrong?" Chris asked, leaning over with an anxious look at his father. He put his hand on his shoulder, studying his face. Up close, it shocked him how pale his father was, how loose the skin was along the line of his chin. It was as if he hadn't seen this face of his father's before, never took notice of how age played itself out on his features, reducing hard lines to curves, determination to indecision, smoothness to creases and folds. This close, he couldn't overlay the picture of the man he had known as a youth on his father's face. This was the face of an old, old man. A man whose defenses had finally crumbled, decades of stone falling away like shale from Lamentation Mountain, washed down the slopes by the agony of unwanted tears.

"I don't know, I don't know," Clay said, wiping away the wetness from his cheeks with the flat of his hands. "I didn't expect—I don't know."

Clay felt pressure at his temples, blood pounding through his head. The bottom dropped out of his stomach and he recognized the feeling, the overwhelming certainty that he was going to die. He knew it well. He'd felt it in a foxhole, artillery shells bursting yards away, hot earth cascading over his huddled body as if the devil's own gravedigger were shoveling it on him. He'd felt it with machine gun bullets snapping the air inches above his head, watching other men rise up to run, fear driving them into the path of lead that burst skulls and shattered bone. He felt it now. He wanted to get out, to be anywhere but here, to get someplace safe outside the shadow of these hills. Instead, burying his head in his hands he wept, shaking his head back and forth.

"Dad?" Chris drew his hand back, afraid now of what he was witnessing. A minute passed, and Clay quieted, the weeping reduced to sniffles and gasps.

"I never came home," Clay said, his face still buried in his hands. Sitting up, he rubbed his eyes and nose, and looked at Chris. "I never came home. I thought it was the right way to handle things." He looked out the window, a sense of terrible wonder rising up in his throat. "I never came home," he said, slowly and softly, letting the impact of the words settle in.

"Why?"

Clay spread his hands, feeling helpless to explain. But he had to try. "Chris, there was something wrong with my family. With my father, and my mother too, for that matter." He took a deep breath and blew it out. Chris sat silently, leaning his back against the car door, watching his father. "I had a sister. Alice. One day I found out she was also my mother. But that's not all. It was my own father, he got his daughter pregnant at thirteen, and here I am."

"Jesus, Dad. Jesus Christ."

"Yeah." Clay looked out the window, studying the houses for the first time since they'd parked. It was the same street, but everything was different. Trees gone, new houses, aluminum siding, cars everywhere. He tried to pick out which house had been his. There seemed to be no space left on the small street, homes crammed together with barely enough room for a driveway between them. He gave up, shaking his head at his own foolishness.

"You know what the hell of it is? I've been so ashamed of that for so long, so mad at them for so long, and now that I'm back here, and all I can do is cry like a baby. A baby! I never came home, Chris. I never saw them again. There damn sure wasn't anything pretty about it, but they were my folks, and I never came home to them. Alice was my mother, and I never came back."

As he spoke the words, he knew that wasn't the source of his anguish. Pa. It was Pa, the bastard. He wanted back what he once thought he'd had, until he'd learned the truth. A father. Pa had been strict, but that was the way back then, it didn't really matter. Time would've smoothed over those memories, but instead Pa had left him with jagged glass for a memory, and there was no softening of those edges. Pa had cheated him of a son's right to grow old and remember his own father with fondness. With love.

Clay reached for the car door, and this time his hand was steady. Opening it, he eased himself down slowly. The burst of energy he'd felt earlier was gone, and every step was once again an effort. The ground was soft and wet, the spring damp soaking the earth. Steadying himself with one hand against the car door, he pushed off, down the cracked slate sidewalk, along the street where he'd run and played as a child, remembering the last time he saw it, walking away from the house toward the bus stop out on State Route 209.

Chris walked up beside him, putting his arm through his, and Clay rested his weight on Chris' forearm, thankful for the help. "I'm sorry to have to tell you such a horrible thing, Chris."

"It's no reflection on you, Dad."

"No? I was never sure. Not that I thought I'd ever do anything like that, but I always had to wonder if the bad seed would come out in me some other way."

"Or in me," said Chris, stopping suddenly, tightening his grip on Clay's arm. "You were worried you might pass it on, weren't you? That I might be the bad seed."

Clay made a face, shaking his head, ready to dismiss the idea. He stopped, knowing that Chris' cop sense would detect a false statement if he heard one.

"I only wanted to be sure, sure that it was erased from the family tree. Yes, yes, I worried. I know it sounds so old-fashioned, but I did worry about you, and I worried about myself. I never wanted anyone to know."

"So that's why you never told me the real story after the fire."

"I couldn't tell you anything about that. It would've opened a crack in the dam, and I didn't trust what might happen after that."

"But Mom knew, right? She had to."

Clay pulled away and walked a few steps, crossing a driveway, squinting his eyes to read the house number.

"Dad!" Chris didn't move, his voice sharp, demanding his father's attention. "Tell me Mom knew. You had to have told her, didn't you?"

"That was between her and me. I think this may have been it. My house," he said, pointing. "Number sixty-two."

Chris walked up beside him, and they both studied the house. Two stories, red brick. The bright color of the brick showed it had been sand-blasted recently, blowing off layers of paint. Some of the cement had crumbled, and there were furrows in the brick, an amateur homeowner effort. Crocuses peaked out from along the side of the house where the spring sun warmed the bricks. The front door was painted a glossy black, and a child's tricycle sat on the sidewalk.

"Looks like a young family fixing up the place," Chris said. "Any chance they're related?"

"Not likely," Clay answered, pointing to the mail slot on the porch. "What's that name say?"

"Kandratavich," Chris said slowly.

"Lots of Lithuanians around here. Probably no one left from my family."

"You sure?" Chris said.

"I'm counting on it."

"So you're not from Tennessee, right? Was anyone from your family?"

"Somebody was," Clay said, quietly, a whisper.

They both stood, watching the house. It was silent, no evidence of anyone at home. Noises from the street drifted around them. Doors slamming, a child crying, cars driving by, but where they stood, nothing moved and time passed slowly, as if Clay's visit had shocked the bricks into silence. They told no stories and held their secrets close.

"Let's go back to the car," Clay said, hoping Chris would take his arm again.

"Okay, Dad, whatever you want." Chris took a step, then waited a second, and looped his arm around his father's. As they walked, minding the uneven seams in the sidewalk, they came to a garbage can set out by the road for pickup. Chris took the manila envelope he'd been carrying since Meriden and tapped it against his leg, feeling the stiff cardboard inside, the fingerprint report from the coffee cup he'd sent for analysis. It was unopened, knowledge and certainty sealed inside, courtesy of the state of Connecticut. Before, he had wanted to know everything, to pry secrets out of his old man and confront him. Now, he dropped it into the can, hearing a soft thunk as it hit bottom.

"What was that?" Clay asked.

"Nothing."

Inside the car, Chris started the engine, letting the heater run. Watching his father, he knew it wasn't time yet to leave, and knew also that whatever he would learn about this man, it was best it come from his own lips. They sat without speaking as the heat began to take hold, banishing the damp chill.

"What did you mean you were counting on it?" Chris said. "About your family being gone."

"Well, there were the four of us, no other family around here. And I hope Alice got away."

"Got away?"

Clay sighed. It was too much to explain all at once. "I sent her some money."

"When? I thought you never contacted them. How much?"

Clay smiled as he looked at Chris. He was proud of his son, proud of his work as a detective, but sometimes he seemed to forget he wasn't interrogating a suspect. Or maybe he hadn't.

"Right after the war, no I never did, and ten thousand."

"That was one hell of a lot of money in 1945, Dad. How'd you come up with it?"

"One secret a day, Chris, one secret a day is plenty." He knew this was enough, that it was fact he had shared any secret with his son.

Chris shrugged. "Can't argue with that."

The car warmed up as they sat, the sun finally cresting the hill above, brightening everything around them. A green minivan slowed as it passed them and pulled into the driveway by number sixty-two. A young woman with blond hair got out and slid the rear door open, unbuckling a little girl from her car seat. Her husband, tall and skinny with long dark hair, got out and started lugging groceries up the porch steps. Faint cries of Mommy Mommy came through the glass as they watched the little girl in her mother's arms reach down toward the tricycle.

"Want to say hello?" Chris said.

"No, no need. It's nice to see, though. A new century, new beginnings."

"So, what's it like, being here?" Chris said.

Clay wiped condensation away on his window, and stared out through the streaks. "Feels like something I had to do, but now that it's done, it's just sad. Not awful anymore, just so sad. I'm sorry, Chris, sorry that this ate up so much of me. I'd always worried I'd turn out to be like Pa."

"Dad, you know all those chores I hated that you used to make me do at the Tavern? When you were watching me like a hawk?"

"Yeah."

"No matter how much I bitched, the God's honest truth is I just wanted to be with you."

Clay didn't speak, not right away. He remembered Addy telling him that, decades ago. He couldn't believe it then, just plain couldn't, but he'd never forgotten her words. Now Chris laid it out for him, the simple, beautiful truth. Wiping at the condensation again he rubbed the cool dampness on his fingers across his eyes.

"It's all I wanted too, Chris." It was the absolute truth, and it spread across three generations anchored by Clay, his son to his left and his long dead father haunting the home of his memory on the right. Looking at the newly exposed red brick, like a skin flayed raw, the bright flowers and the yellow tricycle, he finally could know this shiny clean house in the spring sunshine was somebody else's home now. It was a fair trade; overwhelming sadness and the vision of this young family replacing Pa, Alice, deep shame and fluttering red-trimmed curtains.

"Let's go," Clay said. "It'll be good to get home before dark."

"Are we done here?"

"Yep."

Chris did nothing but nod, and pulled away from the curb.

Route 209 took them right to Interstate 81, and after gassing up the Jeep they headed north, riding in silence. Clay lowered his seat a bit, closing his eyes. Exhaustion pressed down on him but he couldn't sleep, only rest and listen to the hum of tires and traffic on the highway. As the miles spun away Clay felt a comfort filling the space between him and his son. There had always been a tension, a tightness in his gut, even at the best of times. But now, he felt lighter than he ever had, as if he'd left a ten-pound iron weight behind on that sidewalk. He had told his secret and it hadn't been a disaster, hadn't blown up in his face, hadn't sent Chris running in disgust. Maybe somehow it would all make sense to Chris, why his old man acted so crazy for all those years.

Still, it might not have sunk in. Maybe tomorrow, Chris would come to realize what it all meant, and look at him differently, masking disgust was politeness. Maybe not. Maybe tomorrow, he'd tell him about the other guy in that picture. Yes, tomorrow, he'd tell Chris all about him.

How many days back then had he wondered how tomorrow would go? He'd made it through so many tomorrows, but it hadn't meant a thing, because there was always another one to get through. They all had made it through more than their share, but that only increased the odds that the next one would be it. You couldn't win. It was bad luck to have stayed alive for so long. It only meant your number was bound to be up. They had known, they had all known that last day. He looked down at the road, a blur under their wheels, the white line at the side of the road dancing closer, then farther away as Chris steered the Jeep. How he took riding in a car for granted, soft seats, heat, even coffee cup holders. Time was, a wood bench in a canvas-covered deuce-and-a-half was the height of luxury. Especially when it was headed away from the front.

On the way back from Clervaux, they'd been headed in the opposite direction, minus Miller, and no one had talked. They'd pulled over for a piss stop, all of them lined up at the edge of the road, watering the ditch. An odd sound rose from the east, a screaming engine in the sky. They looked up, watching a V-1 rocket arc across the sky, bright flame shooting out, stubby squared off wings dark against the light gray sky. He'd thought then, how oddly beautiful war could be, a thing to inspire awe as well as terror. As the sound faded in the west, they buttoned their pants and turned back to the truck, not a word passing between them.

Closer to the front lines, artillery had thundered the air. They were stopped at the edge of a small field, M.P.s telling them that the Germans had the open section of road ahead zeroed in. They hadn't found the OP yet, so it was pedal to the metal or walk through the woods. The driver revved the engine, spun his tires, took off like a bootlegger making for the state line. The sound of a shell ripping through the sky tore at his ears and he wanted to yell incoming...

He woke with a start, his body shuddering, his skin damp with sweat.

"You can take a nap, Dad, I know the route." Chris, keeping his eyes on the road, didn't catch Clay's frantic look as he emerged from the dream.

Jesus Christ, Jesus Christ, calm down. "No, no thanks," Clay said, raising his seat up. "I'm awake." He worked to get his breathing under control, feeling his heart thumping in his chest. He wasn't ready for any more of the past today, there were too many ghosts swirling around him already. It was time for the company of the living. Running his palm over his eyes, he counted to ten, then twenty. It calmed him, as it had so many years before.

"What did you think of Dr. Krause?" he asked Chris, struggling to keep his voice normal, resisting the temptation to keep counting to thirty. "Emily, wasn't it?"

"Dad, don't start with that."

"Just making conversation. Okay, what do you think of the Yankee's pitching this season? Is that better?"

"I thought she was very nice, and I'm even thinking of calling her. And c'mon, Clemens, Cone, Hernandez, Stanton, Pettitte, Rivera, how can they miss?"

They talked about pitching injuries, managers, the designated hitter rule, and about taking in a game when the weather got warmer. They didn't discuss Minersville or the past, just baseball, letting the love they felt seep between the lines, unspoken but as certain as an easy throw to first.

Later, he closed his eyes again, and a breeze blew across his face, turning colder, deep, bone-chilling cold, and he pulled the rough wool scarf tighter around his neck. He saw Red kneeling, two fingers pointing forward, as the rest of them ran fast and low, darting tree to tree with graceful and swift strides, each of them so alive. Big Ned and Little Ned, Shorty and Tuck, followed by all the others, boots kicking up snow, moving out, heading up the line, going forward. The rhythmic noise of leather and gear bouncing on their bodies as they ran was pure music, a melody of canteens and grenades, ammo and knives, strapped like notes across their chests. A column of men moving with a single purpose, nimble and as fleet as angels. He looked for his buddy among them, but all along he had been right there, kneeling in the snow beside him, quiet and calm, that look on his face, that bit of a smile, still playing around his mouth, delight showing at the edges of weariness, as if he'd just gotten a joke that hadn't even been told yet. Ain't we something, buddy?

And then he was gone, off into the cover of the trees. He wanted to go with them, to move with determined purpose, to share their dangers, their fleetness and grace. But the wind died down, and the bitter frost vanished. He opened his eyes to green woods, the white lines of the highway, and the hum of tires on the road. Pretending to sleep, he turned in the seat so his son would not see him weep. There were still secrets to be kept close.

Epilog

2002

CHRIS FOUND DIRECTIONS TO THE GRAVE AT THE Visitor's Center. Section and row number, right at the corner of Bradley and Marshall drives. Spring was farther along here, a rifle shot south of the Mason-Dixon line. Leaf buds popped out from branches, a gauzy yellow and green blurring the trees at the edge of the cemetery. A slight breeze blew pink flowers from a cherry blossom tree and sent them swirling in the air ahead of the two men, the petals shaped like tears.

So many names. They spread before them in rows that fanned out in straight lines like soldiers on parade, the morning sun casting long shadows like dark fingers toward the next row of markers, and the next, and the next. Tourists and mourners, the curious and the reverent, they all passed by, out for a stroll, seeing the sights or searching out a grave. They plodded on, the living on their right, dressed in every color possible, old and young, noisy, excited, awed, flowing in every direction, the vibrancy of life vivid around them. The dead to their left, stark white on green, rows and rows and rows of steady, unyielding reminders. Chris imagined ghosts at the end of each row, whispering to the visitors as they passed each grave.

See my sacrifice, my loss, the span of my life.

1846–1865. 1899–1918. 1763–1784. 1970–1991. 1950–1969. 1925–1944.

He had to look away for a moment, break the spell that the dates cast over him. A blur of faces ran through his mind, young boys under steel helmets, cheeks red from the cold, leather straps cutting into their shoulders, arms around each other, posing for a picture. The worn photo was in his pocket, but he wasn't ready to look into their eyes, to bear witness to his health, his life, all the joys and creation they never beheld.

Emily took his hand, the curve of her pregnant belly graceful as he held her close. His father had seen the beginning, the first blossoming promise of a grandchild. He'd been at their wedding, felt the first quickening of their child, and then, one morning, he was gone, slumped over the kitchen table, a coffee cup shattered on the floor, Lamentation Mountain gray and forlorn in the distance.

Before them was York Drive, and they turned left, halfway there. Along the road they saw a white horse, harnessed to a caisson, a wooden wagon, from which soldiers in their dress blues had removed a flag-draped coffin. An Army burial. Drawing closer, they saw the interment site. No one there except the soldiers, a sergeant standing aside from them, eyes forward, the sun shining on the bright yellow hash marks down his sleeve. Who was being buried today? An old man, perhaps? From a nursing home with no family left? It was too far in to see the name, eight or nine rows in. They stopped to watch as the coffin was lowered into the grave, the ceremony as solemn as if a hundred mourners were gathered. On a small rise, thirty yards off, a line of seven soldiers raised their rifles and fired a volley. Once, twice, a third time, just as Chris had explained to Matthew at Bob's funeral. Gray gunsmoke drifted over the trees as a bugler began the mournful tune, slowly, sadly, each note stretching out over the graves as the coffin settled into the ground. They covered their hearts with their right hands, Chris keeping his left under Emily's elbow. They stood, side by side, until the silence following the last note took hold, and they walked on, the quiet pressing in on them.

They'd buried Clay in the cold of the winter, and Chris thought that was somehow right, from the stories his father had told him, about the war in the winter of 1945. It was only fitting that Clay Brock had been buried in that season.

"It should be over here."

As they turned onto Marshall Drive, Chris felt dizzy from the mesmerizing flow of rows of gravestones, as they seemed to fly by. The rows blurred. He tried to look down each one but the rows changed direction, turning in different angles, going off to the horizon. He'd expected the ground to be flat, but it rolled like waves, each row riding the crest of the next, like wading into a sea of graves. The ground was damp, wet with springtime, the promise of growth and life pushing up through the soil. Life itself, rising up from the ground, wrapping itself around him, pressing his heels into the spongy earth.

"Look!" Emily pointed to the gravestone in back of Chris. He held her hand as so clasped hers under her belly, stepping gingerly on the soft earth.

Jacob Burnett. PFC. U.S. Army. World War II. 1923–1945.

"That's it," Chris said slowly as he knelt down beside the grave.

"Jacob Burnett," he said. "Jake. No wonder he bought the tavern."

Chris fumbled in his pocket, feeling more emotion than he had expected at fulfilling this last request of his father's. He had asked Chris for this favor shortly after their return from Minersville, with no explanation. Chris had agreed, and no matter how often he'd asked why, his father had kept this final secret safe.

With a shaking hand he withdrew the dogtag. He held it for Emily to see, one last time. Clay Brock's dogtag. She brushed her fingers against it and nodded. He pressed it into the ground at the base of the marker, until the notched top lay beneath the finely cut grass, as his father had directed. Patting the ground, he smoothed the grass and thought of a story his father had told him, of Tuck gently smoothing Shorty's hair before they left his body in the woods.

Emily clung to him as they walked to the road. She stumbled once on the uneven ground, and he draped his arm across her shoulder, drawing her close. They stepped from the grass onto the walkway, and neither let go as he began to speak to his unborn child, telling him of his grandfather, who had been a soldier, and of the man who had been his friend. How they had walked across half of Europe together, shared everything, kept each other warm and alive, and cupped their hands around flickering candles beneath the earth. How his grandfather brought home souvenirs, which he had given to him, and which he would in turn pass on, explaining who each man was in the worn photograph. Truly, who they were.

ABOUT THE AUTHOR

James R. Benn is the author of the popular Billy Boyle World War II mystery series. The debut title, *Billy Boyle*, was a Dilys Award nominee and one of Booksense's top five mysteries for 2006. Subsequent titles have received starred reviews in *Publishers Weekly* and *Library Journal*, and two have been tagged as "Killer Books" by the Independent Mystery Booksellers Association.

Benn lives in Hadlyme, Connecticut, with his wife, Deborah Mandel. For more information, visit his website at www.jamesrbenn.com.

OPEN ROAD
INTEGRATED MEDIA

Open Road Integrated Media is a digital publisher and multimedia content company. Open Road creates connections between authors and their audiences by marketing its ebooks through a new proprietary online platform, which uses premium video content and social media.

CPSIA information can be obtained
at www.ICGtesting.com
Printed in the USA
LVOW12s1628240517

535700LV00001B/165/P